Rippercide

Peter Hodgson

PNEUMA SPRINGS PUBLISHING UK

First Published in 2014 by:
Pneuma Springs Publishing

Rippercide
Copyright © 2014 Peter Hodgson
ISBN13: 9781782283454

Peter Hodgson has asserted his right under the Copyright, Designs and Patents Act, 1988, to be identified as Author of this Work

British Library Cataloguing in Publication Data. A catalogue record for this book is available from the British Library.

Pneuma Springs Publishing
A Subsidiary of Pneuma Springs Ltd.
7 Groveherst Road, Dartford Kent, DA1 5JD.
E: admin@pneumasprings.co.uk
W: www.pneumasprings.co.uk

For my friends and colleagues in C&MSD

ONE

Lucy Beckett's anger was swelling as she waited by the road. The cold January rain was bouncing off the pavements and slow-moving traffic. She paced up and down, staying beneath the swaying canopy of a tree.

For a moment she thought *he* had arrived. A vehicle slowed down, then carried on. The next one pulled up. The driver leaned across the passenger seat and wound the window down. 'Hey! Do you want a lift anywhere?'

'Who are you?' she asked, peering through the open window.

'I'm heading for the motorway. I'll drop you off anywhere you like. Get in.'

She stepped back, shaking her head. The man wound up the window and drove off. Lucy was beginning to feel uneasy. She decided to go home if he failed to turn up within the next ten minutes.

Why did I bother doing this? she thought, clasping the white plastic bag with one hand whilst digging the other deeper into her coat pocket for more comfort. The rain was seeping through her clothes. She wiped her eyes with the sleeve of her coat.

There was a break in the traffic. A minute later a car approached, its headlights flashing. She breathed a sigh of relief when it stopped.

'Lucy?'

'About time too,' she said, entering the car, glad to feel the warmth. 'I'm soaked to the skin.' Lucy gave him a long, direct look. He jerked the car into gear, turned full circle and headed in the opposite direction.

'I've got the cassettes and one or two other things,' Lucy said. 'I borrowed them a couple of months back.'

'Well, I expect he'll be wanting to listen to them again. Good of you to bring them, though. He's hoping to speak to you sometime.'

He touched her leg.

'I told him I didn't want to see him again,' she responded. 'I nearly gave him the push a while ago. He hardly goes anywhere, doesn't want to do anything. I can't weigh him up at all.'

Using one hand the driver fumbled for a cigarette and managed to light it.

He stopped the car at a narrow tunnel-bridge, allowing an oncoming vehicle to pass through. Lucy gulped a couple of deep breaths. She wondered where they were going but decided to wait a while before asking.

He slammed his foot on the accelerator and shot a quick glance at her. 'You must be quite bored . . . Are you? . . . Fed up with life, I mean.'

'Not really, no.' *This guy's acting a bit strange,* she thought. She glanced at his scruffy jeans and ruffled T-shirt. He was unshaven and carried a pot belly. Dark hairs ran the length of his arms. His white, soft-looking hands swept round the steering wheel as he swung the car into another road.

There was silence for a few minutes. Lucy was curious. 'Are you married?' she asked.

'Never been married. I've had a few girlfriends but they always seem to move on.'

The car struggled up a hill, its engine sputtering. Rain still pouring. Street lights less frequent.

'I guess I'll never make it. I don't get on with women. Just my bad luck, I suppose. He'll be pretty gutted if you leave him now. How long was it? Three months?' He touched her leg again. This time it was a hard prod. 'I said, how long were you seeing him for?'

'It was a bit longer, actually.'

The car came to a sudden halt. He hurriedly got out and went into The Late Shop. The engine was idling noisily. The hot air blowing on her feet was a comfort. A few minutes passed by. Lucy tossed the bag of music cassettes over her shoulder and heard a sharp noise as it hit the gardening spade on the back seat. She turned to see what had caused the noise. Lucy didn't attach any importance to the spade. She picked up a magazine which was lying there also. *What's this?* she thought, flicking through the pages of a disgusting porn magazine called *Anal Poke.*

'I needed some more cigarettes,' he said, getting into the car. 'Here, take one.' He drove on. Lucy shook her head. 'Take one,' he repeated, his voice loud, almost angry.

'I don't want one, alright?' she said angrily. 'That's a sick magazine you've got in the back.'

'It's one of his,' he said, lighting another cigarette. 'He's got dozens of mags like that, and worse too.'

'Well I didn't notice any porn in his flat.'

One thing she did notice - they were travelling along a deserted country road on the outskirts of town. Street lights and houses were no longer to be seen. Tunnels of white light from the car's headlamps lit up the road ahead. The rain had turned into drizzle.

Her heart was beating faster.

'Where are you taking me? I want to go home.' He ignored her. 'Look, this isn't fair. I asked you a question and you haven't answered me.'

The car picked up speed. She eyed him with suspicion and grabbed his wrist.

'Where are we going?' she asked angrily.

He shook his hand to release her grip. The car swerved. 'Questions and answers. That's all you're interested in, girlie. Just keep quiet. Keep your mouth shut. There's a wood at Plymbey. That's where we're going, if you must know.'

'Okay, take me there if it makes you feel any better.'

He looked at her and grinned. She thought he was deranged. The best thing to do was to go along with it; after all, she had no idea what sort of person he might turn out to be. If she kept calm maybe everything would be all right. *Perhaps it was a harmless prank.* Lucy was looking forward to getting back home to the warmth of the fire and the company of one of her friends. For now, she had to act wisely as they journeyed deeper into black country. The 'filthy' magazine didn't bother her much but she began to wonder what the spade was for.

The car slowed down to a crawl as it passed over a narrow humpback bridge. The Plymbey signpost came into view. Plymbey had a quaint church and woodland. It was a great place to visit in the summer. Lucy had no time for quaint places, day or night, but she would do anything to get out of danger.

'I'll have that fag now if you don't mind,' she said, pressing herself into the seat, trying to relax. 'Come on, then.'

He turned the car into a narrow lane. A solitary street light stood at its entrance, flickering intermittently. The nearby wood was enveloped by an unforgiving darkness.

The car came to a halt.

'I suppose you know what this is all about,' he said, offering her the cigarette. 'I hope you don't mind us coming here.'

She took the cigarette and placed it between her lips. The flame from his lighter created a tiny island of light. His face came closer to hers, his cold blue eyes staring at her as she inhaled deeply, trying not to look scared.

Maybe he'd settle for a quick J Arthur, she thought. That wouldn't be a problem. She had done things in her life that she was not proud of: mucky, sleazy, even filthy things. She was a townie and had done the rounds, but she was scared now.

She could smell the stink of his sweaty armpits as he turned the heater off. The drizzle had stopped. A tree-branch rattled ominously against the bonnet.

'I'm going for a leak,' he said. 'You stay there.'

He got out of the car and tapped its roof as he walked towards the boot. Lucy finished her smoke and unfastened the remaining buttons on her thick coat. Now was the time to get this over with - whatever it was he wanted.

She waited a while, wondering what he was doing.

'What on earth is going on?' she shouted.

There was no sign of him. She reached over to see if the keys were in the ignition.

No keys.

He opened the car boot. She heard a metallic clink, then he came back, a dark shape appearing by the driver's door. Lucy got out of the car and walked briskly towards the road. It was time to leave. Her temper was up, her guard was down. He ran after her - his heart pounding with excitement - and struck her with a large spanner. Lucy slumped onto the muddy ground, her senses numbed with the force of the blow.

'Where were you going? Get up you hussy. Now.'

'Leave me alone, don't hurt me . . . please,' she whimpered.

The moon momentarily peeped from behind a cloud. He looked up at the sky, then smirked at her. She tried to get up, grabbing his legs for support. He delivered a second blow and dragged her closer to the vehicle.

She drifted in and out of consciousness. Her blood, warm against her skin, trickled onto the wet soil. He wrapped his arms around the body, heaving her back onto her feet before releasing her. Kneeling beside the body, he lowered his head and sank his teeth into her cheek. The ecstasy of her suffering was arousing him.

Now she had succumbed to his power, to his will.

The knife.

He opened the driver's door and took the knife from under the seat. The girl was merely an object to him now, waiting to be destroyed. He drove a savage kick into the side of her head and resumed his kneeling position next to the helpless girl. He squeezed her breasts hard, hating her, cursing her. He grasped the knife, ripped her jumper, blouse and bra. He knew what to do next. His hideous plan had been rehearsed in his mind countless times.

The reality of the moment was his to cherish.

I am doing what a thousand men have done before . . . Lightning-steel rips succulent flesh . . . His death-smile reveals red-tainted teeth . . . Succumb to your grave, you harlot.

The silvery moon was shining from a gap in the thick clouds.

Lucy Beckett was dead.

Jack Robson left home at 8.30 a.m. for his usual pre-breakfast walk on a cold, blustery day. Five years had passed since his retirement. He was happy enjoying the quiet life in the village of Plymbey. His wife was at home cooking his usual eggs, bacon and fried bread. The meal would be waiting for Jack when he arrived home.

He passed the picturesque St Anne's Church, trudged down the road for a while before turning into a narrow dead end lane that skirted the edge of a wood.

Something caught his eye.

He bent down awkwardly and picked up a small plastic case containing a music cassette. He looked around to see if anything else had been dropped. There was nothing to see. Even if he had searched the area to his left he would not have noticed the shallow grave that had been dug the previous night.

He stuffed the cassette into his pocket and returned home. Later, Jack played it out of curiosity. His wife said it was 'noisy' music. Neither of them liked it. Just as he reached to switch it off, a male voice sounded through the speakers saying, 'Don't leave me, Lucy . . . Stay with me for ever.'

TWO

Jim Sheridan was thankful that his career was coming to an end. His line of work had often aroused hostility when potential suspects were confronted by him. To them he was just an interfering busybody. Some jobs were interesting; most were boring and tedious. 'I think my husband/wife is having an affair.' He had been through that rigmarole a thousand times before and, more often than not, a client's suspicion was not unfounded. Even Jim Sheridan was unfaithful to his ex-wife. It had taken him some time to realise that he was being followed by one of his own kind. Private detective follows private detective.

He would never forget that.

Sheridan was born in London. His father wrote crime articles for the *East London Advertiser*. As a youngster he always fancied himself as being a bit of a detective. His interest in crime became known to a retired chief inspector who was his dad's closest friend. The ex-chief related many stories to the young lad.

In the early 1960s Sheridan moved to Norwich with his parents and two sisters. By the time he was thirty he was divorced and single. He decided not to get married again.

Blackpool, the town of bright lights, day-trippers and police sirens, welcomed him in 1979. He took on various menial low-paid jobs and then became a taxi driver. After two years of taxi driving he returned to the private enquiry business.

Jim Sheridan was fifty-three years old, lean, and stood just under six feet tall. Dark-brown receding hair topped his benevolent face. He was always smartly dressed and courteous. This man - this gentleman - looked anything but a private detective.

Times were changing fast for this relic of a man. He was old fashioned in many ways, too long in the tooth to cope with the problems of the New Millennium society and too weary to be following adulterers or catching shoplifters. Time moves on relentlessly. There were memories to look back on, but what did the future hold? Fifty-three was not that old. Some kind of income would be better than nothing. Such thoughts pervaded his mind as he walked briskly down Blackpool's Central Drive. The darkness was closing in on a chilly evening. He decided to call in at The Tiger Pizza and order a bite to eat. His favourite deep pan pizza with the extra garlic was prepared and handed to him with a cheery, 'Goodnight, Jim.' He thanked the proprietor and continued the short journey to his office situated around the corner. The office stood on the first floor above a shop that sold miscellaneous items. He stepped into the hall and noticed that the lights had been switched on.

During the day - Monday to Saturday - the front door was usually left open so that anybody passing could see the sign on the wall just inside the hallway: 'Private Enquiries - 1st Floor.' He glanced at the sign, as he had done many times before, and climbed the thirteen steps. The twelfth step made a creaking noise when stood upon. Somehow, this had always been a comfort to him. He reached the top of the stairs and noticed a young woman waiting to see him.

'Ah, Mrs Murray,' Sheridan said. 'The door's not locked. Please go inside.'

The detective's office was clean and plain. An old desk contained a set of drawers at each end. Upon it lay several neatly stacked books. Pens and pencils stood in plastic receptacles next to a telephone, and a mug coloured with blue and red stripes had been left on the table waiting to be washed. A hefty filing cabinet stood in a corner of the room and two small pictures hung on an otherwise bare wall.

Sheridan sat with his back to the window and lit a cigarette. The smoke drifted from his mouth, curling in front of his face. 'You should have waited in here, Mrs Murray. No need to stand on the landing. What brings you back so early? Oh, would you like a cigarette?'

'Yes, thank you.'

Sheridan offered her a light and reached for the ashtray on the windowsill.

'I did what you said. You were right, my husband wasn't seeing anyone else.' She inhaled deeply and blew a cloud across the table. 'He was, as you suggested, dressing in women's clothing. The one thing that bothers me . . .' She looked down at the floor.

'Yes, go on.'

'Well, you see, he has a better wardrobe than I have. I found where he was hiding all his dresses.'

She tightened her lips and raised her eyebrows, displaying her helpless resignation.

'Well now, Mrs Murray, it *could* have been a lot worse. At least you know that your husband is not having an affair. Right?'

'Yes, it could have been worse, but where do I go from here? Anyway, that's not your problem. You did your job. How much do I owe you?'

'Nothing. This one's on the house.'

The detective stood up and held out his 'goodbye' hand. His client rose from the chair and opened her handbag. She pulled out a £20 note, let it flutter onto the desk, and rushed out of the office.

Sheridan stood by the window and watched her heading towards the town centre.

'My last case,' he said. 'Not particularly memorable.'

He removed his jacket, walked across the landing and into the narrow kitchen. He finished his smoke, ate his pizza and returned to his desk. The time had come to start unloading those files from the cabinet.

Memories.

It was the end of an era for the dedicated private investigator. Individual files were marked with appropriate headings: adultery, shoplifting, theft, missing persons, blackmail. Hardly a lifetime's work. Nevertheless, he had made his mark. He began sifting through his case-files containing an assortment of papers and photographs that had accumulated over the years. At 10 p.m. the files were still on the desk. Old memories came flooding back as if it was only yesterday. He was drawn into his own world, taking in every bit of information with renewed interest. Apart from the hum of traffic there was nothing to distract him.

10.30 p.m. The twelfth step creaked. A knock sounded. Sheridan was curious. Before he could answer, the door opened. A woman came in and sat opposite him. She was sturdily built and in her mid-forties. Her short blonde hair was styled to perfection. The gold-rimmed glasses she wore enhanced the colour of her hazel eyes. She was an attractive woman, but her good looks failed to mask the anxiety.

'You don't remember me, do you?' she asked.

Sheridan tried hard to figure out who she was. He placed his elbows on the desk and rested his chin on clenched fists. 'I meet a lot of people in this business, until now. If you've got a job for me, I'm going to have to disappoint you.'

'We were together in 1980. I am Irene Collinson.' She removed the glasses in the hope he would now remember her.

'Irene Collinson. I thought I recognised you from somewhere. I couldn't quite work out where and when.'

'It's been a long time. I must admit, you haven't changed much.'

'I was just about to brew up. Would you like tea?'

'Thank you. No sugar, plenty of milk.'

Sheridan made the drinks, and wondered why she had come to see him.

'You look busy,' she said, on his return from the kitchen.

'Just sorting through this lot. New detective agencies seem to be springing up every day, leaving less work for me. I think it's time to throw the towel in. Anyway, there must be lots to tell me and I've got all the time in the world.'

'I should have contacted you before now,' she began. 'You see, I decided to go back to Skipton to be near my parents. That was in 1980 after we split up. I came back to Blackpool the following year and met somebody else. I was so foolish in those days and now . . . Well, I can't see any logic in what I did.'

Sheridan could not help but notice the sadness in her voice. The vacant look in her eyes told him there was more to come. Obviously, something had happened to cause an ex-girlfriend to visit the office at this hour. He decided to dig a bit deeper. 'Perhaps we should have a chat over at the pub,' he said, looking at his watch.

'No, not the pub. I've come here tonight because there's something you need to know. When I moved to Skipton I found out that I was pregnant. I wasn't really that surprised at the time, knowing what we had been up to . . . It was a girl. Of course she was only a baby when I came back to Blackpool . . .' She turned her head, struggling to continue.

He shifted uncomfortably in his chair. 'Are you saying that the girl is *our* daughter?'

'You can be certain of it. I named her "Elizabeth." When I came back to Blackpool I tried looking for you, but soon gave up. Eventually, I accepted the situation - there was no other choice - and I got on with my life. As I've told you, I met someone else. We parted company after a few years. I wish you and I had stayed together. Things might have worked out for us.'

'I had no idea you were pregnant, Irene. You really should have made more of an effort to find me. A daughter you say?'

'Yes. Anyway, I got talking to this taxi driver and he told me where I could find you. It seems you're quite well known in the area.'

13

'I hope that I'm well known for the right reasons.'

'You have the reputation of being a thorough detective, so I'm told.' She forced a gentle smile and said, 'Tell me, Jim, where were you about a month ago?'

He gave the question some thought. 'I was out of town for a couple of weeks, visiting family and friends in Norwich.'

Irene placed her handbag on the table. She opened it and gave him a sheet of newspaper.

The paper was folded neatly. He opened it, without asking what it was all about, and read the disturbing headline, 'BODY OF GIRL FOUND ON PARK - POLICE HUNT VICIOUS KILLER.'

'Elizabeth was murdered on Aristor Park last month,' she said. 'A dog walker discovered her body under a bush.'

She wiped away the tears. Her eyes followed the detective's tall slim figure as he paced the floor behind her. Finally, he stood by the window and gazed into the street below.

What he had heard sent a shockwave through his mind. It was too much to take in at once. He did not know what to say.

'I am sorry to bring you such terrible news. As you can see, the strain and hurt of it is written all over me . . . I should have kept away from you. I don't know which way to turn.'

'Irene, you did the right thing in coming to me.'

Jim Sheridan remained rooted to the spot. He searched his mind for the right words to say. One long minute passed before he spoke. 'I'm sorry. I can't even begin to tell you how sorry I am.'

Irene replaced the sheet of newspaper in her bag, bravely fighting the urge to break down crying. 'I didn't mention your name to the police. They'll only pester you.'

She finished her tea and prepared to leave. His eyes met hers. She placed a small envelope on the table.

'I'm sorry, Jim, I had to let you know the truth. I hope you understand.'

She got up and opened the office door.

'Wait. If I can help you at all, in any way . . .'

'You're a detective - a private detective, I know - but you might be able to do something to help catch the man who did this.'

She turned and walked briskly out of the office.

Sheridan was both surprised and deeply shocked. He thought about Irene Collinson and the tragic events that had befallen her, and he thought about the daughter he never knew he had until now.

Little did he know that his destiny was about to change.

He wondered if there *was* anything he could do to help. He decided to give it a try. Half an hour later he began tidying the office. He moved the files off the desk and placed the newspaper articles and miscellaneous papers in their respective drawers.

The envelope that Irene had left behind contained her address and phone number. There was a smaller envelope inside. He opened it, took out a 'school' photograph: a picture of a smiling teenage girl wearing a neat blazer, snow-white shirt and coloured tie. She had long auburn hair. Her beautiful cerulean-blue eyes echoed the colour of her father's.

He put the photograph in his pocket, switched off the lights, locked the office door and headed for home.

He stayed awake into the early hours, occasionally glancing at the picture of his daughter. Eventually, it slipped through his fingers.

At last, Jim Sheridan had fallen asleep.

THREE

Sheridan took an early shower and ate a hearty breakfast. The phone rang at 9.30. First call of the day.

'It's Bert. How are you doin'?'

'Not so bad, thanks,' Sheridan replied. 'I'm glad you phoned. You'll be pleased to know I found a copy of that book you wanted, the one by John Whitaker published in 1988.'

'I look forward to reading it, Jim. I'm off work for a couple of days and there are one or two things I'd like to talk about - over a few pints, of course. The Hodgemoor Wood murder has surfaced again. I remember you saying how fascinated you were with that one. What are you doing today?'

Sheridan was hesitant in answering. 'I'm a bit busy at the moment. I'm considering taking on a new case. It all depends on —'

'A new case? I thought you were jacking it in?'

He was careful with his choice of words. 'Well, perhaps this one is going to be a bit of a challenge. It's to do with the murder on Aristor Park. You've read some of the details, I take it?

'There's been no news on that one Jim, not for a few days. I've heard the police are still trying to trace all the joggers who frequent that area, and there's the psychiatric unit close by. They're interested in that too.'

'Hazeldyke, you mean?'

'Yes. They're going to town on this one. It was a brutal assault and from what I can gather the girl —'

'This is the case I may be looking into.'

'You've no chance Jim, not with a murder. I reckon they'll have it solved in a week or two, maybe even in the next few days.'

Sheridan agreed with him and ended the conversation. He did not want to mention his connection with the murdered girl at this stage.

The phone rang again.

'Hello. Jim Sheridan speaking.'

The call came from the young energetic Darren, the owner of the shop below Sheridan's office.

'Jim, there's someone wanting to see you. He says it's important. He's waiting outside your office.'

'Tell him I'm out of town for a few days. Better still, just say I'm tied up with something else for a week or two. He can leave his name and telephone number if he wishes.'

'Fair enough,' came the reply.

Sheridan struggled into his ill-fitting mac. 'I'll probably be inundated with work now,' he muttered to himself. 'Could do with a new coat, too.'

The day was chilly, the sky thick with cloud. He pulled his collar up and set off from his home on Newington Avenue.

On his arrival he made a brew and searched the pages of the national newspaper. No news regarding the recent murder. He picked up the photograph of Elizabeth and stared at it, deep in thought. He knew, only too well, that Irene Collinson's life had been torn apart, shattered and destroyed. He could not experience the loss and sadness himself. Somehow that bothered him. *Perhaps I should pay her a visit*, he thought. He checked the address Irene had given to him and departed. His mind was made up.

Ten minutes later he was driving down Blackpool's North Park Drive which ran along the outskirts of Aristor Park. Irene's house - Number 32 Waldron Avenue - was situated close to the park. He turned into the avenue and parked outside a well-maintained semi-detached house.

He rapped on the front door three times. Irene Collinson answered. Her eyes lit up at the sight of Jim Sheridan.

'Good morning, Irene. Can I come in?'

'Of course,' she replied. She stepped back and opened the door wider. He followed her into a warm room, decorated in soft colours. He saw the flowers and smelled their powerful fragrance. The couple sat opposite each other.

'The flowers are beautiful,' he remarked, looking at the bouquets and condolence cards on the sideboard.

'She was popular, had a lot of friends . . . I didn't expect to see you so soon.'

'I've been thinking about what you said. I know it's going to be difficult, but I'll do all I can to help find the killer. It came as a shock when you told me about Elizabeth. Under the circumstances there wasn't really a lot I could say. You have my deepest sympathy.'

'Thank you,' she said, her voice a whisper.

'No doubt the police have been in touch,' he continued. 'What's the latest news?'

She told him that detectives had questioned relatives and Elizabeth's friends. Irene could not understand why her daughter's family and friends had been quizzed during the course of the enquiry.

'Don't take it the wrong way, Irene. During an investigation like this one all possibilities must be delved into. The police are looking for any lead, however trivial it may seem. They have to trace Elizabeth's last movements and get to know who her friends were. It's possible she may have known the killer.'

'I can't imagine the killer being known to her. Do *you* think she was killed by a psychopath?'

'Possibly. If a member of the family is involved, or if it's a person known to the victim, the murderer is apprehended pretty quickly. Otherwise, it could take months or even years to catch the person responsible. I have to be honest with you, I don't think I can be of much assistance.'

'But you *will* help,' she said, almost demanding.

'I'll do what I can.'

Irene picked up a copy of the Blackpool *Gazette*. 'Have a look at this while I make some tea.'

The front page gave details of the horrific attack on Elizabeth which occurred on Monday 20 March, at about 7 p.m. She had been attacked with a knife and an attempt was made to hide her body beneath a holly shrub. The corpse was discovered at 9 a.m. the following day by a man who was walking his dog. The report stated that Detective Superintendent George Naylor, who was leading the investigation, held the opinion that the murderer could strike again. The attack had taken place on Aristor Park, close to the boating lake and only fifty yards from the busy East Park Drive. The superintendent was appealing for witnesses to come forward - anybody who was in the area between the times of 6.30 and 7.30 on the night in question.

Sheridan was lost in thought until Irene shuffled into the room carrying a tray of drinks.

'Many women joggers stayed away from the park after Elizabeth was murdered,' she said, 'but they're starting to come back again.'

'I don't think the killer would strike again in that area. It would be too risky for him. Is there anything else you can tell me?'

Slowly, and with difficulty, she related what little she knew about the way in which the murder had been committed. Their daughter had been strangled and stabbed several times. She was not raped. Basically, that was all she had been told. Irene gave brief details about their daughter's life.

Elizabeth had studied hard at school, earning several A-grade qualifications, including physics and chemistry. She worked as a dental assistant at a surgery situated close to the town centre. It came as no surprise to Jim Sheridan to learn that she was tidy in her ways and always of smart appearance. As for male acquaintances, she had been on dates with two young men in the last couple of years.

Elizabeth went jogging around the park once a week. The park was a few minutes walk away from Waldron Avenue. Occasionally, she would call for a friend to accompany her. Sadly, on this occasion, Elizabeth had decided to go alone.

Sheridan asked about the specific route she would have taken after leaving the house.

Irene sat upright, eager to give the veteran detective as much information as possible. 'As far as I know she went across Newton Drive, then down Allerdale Avenue which leads to the park. She left home at half past six.'

'H'm. When she reached North Park Drive would she turn right or left?'

'Right, I think. I tried running round the park with her once, about four years ago, but I couldn't manage it. Too many fags, I suppose.'

'Why was she found in the grounds of the park itself, I wonder?' he said, thinking out loud.

'I'm certain she would stay clear of the park,' stated Irene. 'At that time the light would be fading.'

'And she would not willingly enter the park grounds with a stranger; so it stands to reason that she must have been dragged to the spot where she was killed.'

Sheridan considered what might have happened just before the murder took place. Irene listened, and could almost sense the overwhelming fear and terror Elizabeth would have felt as she grappled with the killer.

Sheridan gulped down his tea and stood up. 'I need to see the crime scene for myself. This type of investigation is new to me. If I am to catch this man it might help if I can build up some sort of picture about his method of approach. If I'm going to be a murder detective I need to see the surrounding area. Do you think I'm up to it, Irene? I feel so helpless.'

'Of course you are. You must follow your instinct. Go through the main gates opposite the hospital. You can't miss the flowers.'

She accompanied him to the door. He stopped halfway down the garden path, smiled at her and said he would be in touch. Now, more than anything, Irene Collinson wanted to see justice for *their* daughter.

Inside her house the silence was oppressive, the emptiness almost unbearable. With every knock on the door and ring of the phone her heart momentarily jumped. It was as if Elizabeth was coming home. She was still there in her imagination. Her daughter's voice could be heard now and again, a distant soft tone echoing from the past. These strange episodes had plunged Irene into a state of despair. For a mere second there was hope. It seemed that Elizabeth's presence was real, and when she heard her voice Irene wanted to believe that the dreadful murder on Aristor Park was merely a dream.

It was so hard to accept that she would never see Elizabeth again.

North Park Drive was flanked by detached houses on one side and the Aristor Park Golf Course on the other. A row of cars ran the length of the park. Many of the owners worked at the nearby Blackpool Victoria Hospital. Some were visitors who knew how difficult it was to find a suitable parking space in the hospital grounds.

Sheridan was lucky enough to find a space by the golf course. He found himself walking slowly, each step taking him closer to the murder scene, to the place where his daughter - whom he would have referred to as his 'little girl' had he known her - was savagely killed. He continued along the path by the tall black railings, oblivious to the occasional jogger passing by. The railings formed a barrier between the footpath and the golf course, which was obscured by skeletal bushes and trees. The bushes swayed in the cold wind, adding a sense of sadness to the occasion.

He stopped at the end of the road and glanced to his left as a black well-polished car slowly passed. The driver - a young, dark haired man - looked directly at him. Sheridan had no idea who he was. The car turned left into another road and sped off.

When he reached East Park Drive he saw the double yellow lines along the side of the busy road. The park's main gate stood further ahead. Over to the left, opposite the gate and across the road, was the entrance to Hazeldyke Psychiatric Unit.

From the main gates Sheridan could see the decaying flowers. A short walk, along a gravel footpath, took him to the floral tribute that marked the end of his daughter's life. A holly bush, part of which had been taken away by forensic scientists, stood behind the flowers. It marked the spot where Elizabeth's body was dumped. He stood by the bush, and the sadness erupted.

A few minutes passed by. He walked back to the footpath and surveyed the surroundings. *What can I do? Where do I go from here?* he asked himself, trying to figure out a way forward.

The murderer must have taken a tremendous risk if he had dragged Elizabeth into the wooded area. During the day the branches of the trees would have provided little cover. In the evening it would have been a different matter. He wondered if the murderer had waited for his chosen prey, hidden amongst the shrubs, protected by the fading light.

He noticed the boating lake close by. It was only forty or fifty yards from the holly bush. Could the murderer have washed his hands there and thrown the murder weapon into the cold water?

Sheridan had seen enough.

He made his way back towards the main road and was surprised to see the return of the stylish black car parked at the gate. He could feel the driver's eyes burning into him. A few more paces and he would be able to see his face clearly, but the driver avoided his gaze, started the engine and drove off.

FOUR

Detective Superintendent George Naylor had progressed through the ranks the hard way and had more than thirty years' police experience. Naylor was severe with his subordinates. He expected one hundred percent effort with every case. With a dozen successful murder inquiries under his belt, his confidence in the detection of the Collinson murder was high.

Five feet ten inches of solid muscle had long since metamorphosed into a gelatinous wobble, but the sharpness of his mind was in no way impaired. His pale complexion spoke of the perennial office worker. Naylor could stare you through a brick wall. The troops referred to him as 'Bulldog' - not to his face, unless you were totally mad - owing to the fact that when he lost his temper everyone knew about it.

The superintendent was, however, fair-minded and had a sense of humour. 'You have to have a sense of humour,' he would say. 'Otherwise the days can drag.' He could take a joke as long as it came at the right time.

New recruits instinctively stood to attention at the sound of George Naylor's voice. At the end of the day they knew they could turn to him for help. It wasn't always easy being a policeman. Policing had changed a lot over the years. Police forces in general were criticised. Declining resources had induced the public to regard policemen as being inefficient in their duties.

Nevertheless, his job was to keep law and order. To this end the 55-year-old married police officer, with two daughters of his own, would take up any challenge that fell within the jurisdiction of his expertise. To him staying up all night to read through a mountain of paperwork was just part of the job.

Detective Inspector Derek Oxley was in charge of the day-to-day running of the Serious Crime Unit. He had more time to spare than his overworked superior and was able to keep a clear mind. The inspector had been through a nasty divorce and was now living with a younger woman. No kids, no ties. That's the way he liked it. The 45-year-old DI was a serious kind of bloke who did not mix with other people. He was a loner and not particularly well liked.

Oxley kept a well-trimmed moustache. His black hair was cut to military precision. His words came out in a clipped staccato fashion. Officers admired him for his retentive memory. He could remember names and faces like the hard disc in a computer.

No job was ever too big. Derek Oxley would pursue a criminal to the ends of the Earth if he had to. He was cool, efficient and very thorough. His personal life was a mystery to his colleagues. The boss himself could not even discover that kind of information - not that he would want to. In any case, he had too much respect to ask searching questions. Naylor and Oxley had a good working relationship and an almost uncanny ability to communicate with each other without discourse.

9.30 a.m. Good Friday morning. George Naylor was sitting at his cluttered desk patiently reviewing the information that had come in so far. Before him lay the crime-scene photographs and post-mortem details as written-up by the Home Office forensic pathologist. Detectives had questioned hundreds of people living in the vicinity of the park, including joggers who were stopped during the course of their 'runs' around its perimeter. Had something been missed?

Derek Oxley heard the superintendent calling him. He marched into the office and took a seat. Naylor scribbled a memo then looked up.

'The trail has gone cold. There's no forensic evidence, no murder weapon, no useful information at all. He's got the luck of the devil . . . What's the latest, Derek?'

'Nothing of importance has come in during the last few days,' he replied, straightening his tie. 'Elizabeth's friends have been contacted and interviewed. Our lads are continuing with their enquiries.'

The superintendent handed him a set of familiar photographs. His colleague scrutinised each one. The body had been photographed from many angles. The images were shocking.

At the crime scene the pathologist deduced that the body had been lying in the open for several hours. As the victim had suffered an assault to the anal area it was decided that the liver temperature should be measured as soon as possible. This was carried out at Layton mortuary a couple of miles away, and so the risk of disturbing any trace evidence was minimised. The best estimate of the time when death occurred was between 6.30 and 7.30 on the evening of 20 March. Elizabeth's T-shirt had been left in a raised position. Her shorts had been pulled down, then up again. Intradermal and external bruising indicated that she died as a result of manual strangulation.

There were tiny scratches and abrasions on the body - twenty seven in all - which were due to the body having been dragged and forced under the bush. Elizabeth received thirteen stab wounds in the back.

'I can't believe the murderer was not seen,' Oxley said. 'If only we had a description.'

'What about motive, Derek?'

'With an apparently motiveless crime like this, I think we're looking for a seriously unbalanced individual. That's putting it mildly. It's a sex attack. There's no other explanation for it.'

They walked briskly to the incident room, supported by a team of twelve officers, one of whom had the task of answering the telephone and writing down information which might be helpful to the enquiry. The information was entered into the HOLMES computer system for future reference and possible correlation.

A dry-wipe marker board, fixed to the wall, showed the names of the detectives working on the enquiry and computer codes indicating what leads they were expected to follow up. A large map hung next to it showing the location of the Collinson murder.

'Mrs Collinson told us that her daughter ran round the park in this direction,' Naylor said, pointing with his chubby finger. 'If she left home at 6.30 p.m. we can safely assume she reached the area of the murder site at say, 6.50. So the time frame for the murder is 7 p.m., give or take.'

'By this time she would have been fairly tired and unable to put up much of a struggle,' Oxley suggested. 'It's possible the murderer may have been following her.'

'I'm not so sure, in this instance, that someone would want to be running some distance before carrying out an assault. It would put him at a disadvantage. I think the attack was carried out by an opportunist. Elizabeth Collinson happened to be there at the wrong time. The questions are, of course, where were the killer and his victim situated when the initial contact was made, and did he travel there in a vehicle?'

'It's a tough one, George. If the murderer parked his car on the bend opposite the psychiatric unit he would run the risk of drawing attention to himself, but people *do* park further down East Park Drive where there are no double yellows.'

They returned to the office and discussed the Hazeldyke Psychiatric Unit. The staff manager was questioned two days after the murder. The patients in the wards were kept under close watch, and the ones who were allowed to leave the hospital, for whatever reason, were in no way thought to be dangerous.

Recordings taken from a CCTV camera overlooking the car-park next to Hazeldyke had been carefully examined. The people who were captured on film during the time-frame in question had been eliminated. One witness, however, saw a man running away from the hospital and towards Aristor Park at about 6.45. p.m. He crossed the road opposite the spot where Elizabeth had been accosted. Derek Oxley was of the opinion that this sighting was significant. Unfortunately, the witness was leaving the hospital in her car and only got a brief glimpse. She could not add anything of value other than it was a man who could have been in his forties.

Naylor was rubbing his chin, pacing the room like a restless tiger. 'So, what are we left with?' he said, a hint of despair in his voice. 'A man was seen running towards the park at a crucial time. No description as such. We've got no forensic evidence and nothing that could give us a DNA profile. The psychiatric unit has been checked out, and known sex offenders. We have no reports of any vehicles scouting the area. There hasn't been a similar crime committed in any other county recently. Nothing. We've come up against a brick wall.'

'I say it's a local man. We're going to have to go to the press again, George. We need to make an appeal for people to come forward. Anybody who suspects it could be a brother, a neighbour, a boyfriend or even a husband. Somebody out there should be able to provide us with a lead.'

'I'm inclined to agree. There are no other options left open to us.'

The superintendent opened the office door as a female officer approached, holding out a piece of paper as if she was presenting a certificate.

'This has just come in, sir. A woman who lives on the Charlington estate has phoned the incident room.'

Naylor snatched it from her hand and thanked her.

Oxley decided it was time to leave the office and return to his onerous duties.

'Sit down a minute, Derek. It seems that a woman from the estate has phoned in with a complaint. A couple of her kids, who play on Aristor Park, are scared because a man has been following them. The mother says they are now too frightened to go out, especially as the eldest kid reckons she's seen the man carrying a knife.'

'Charlington estate is about half a mile from the park. I take it that the woman left her name and address?'

'She did, and the man in question lives only a few blocks from her. His name is Ronald Gaffiney. I'm sure I've heard that name before.'

'I remember it well. Gaffiney has a record for indecent exposure. I didn't realise he had changed his address. It's something he should have told us. He's your typical dirty mac brigade.'

George Naylor slumped back into his seat. 'I want him checked out,' he said, his expression serious. 'Anybody who comes under suspicion has to be questioned and eliminated. If they can't be eliminated properly, they remain a suspect. That's it for now.'

The detective inspector got up to leave.

'Derek, whoever committed this crime could be right on top of us. Let's make sure we get him as soon as we can.'

Oxley left the superintendent with his pile of reports and crime scene photographs. He marched down the corridor and into the incident room. The phones were quiet and the general mood was one of despondency. The prospect that a local flasher might be the murderer seemed remote. The inspector knew it would take painstaking detective work to bring the culprit within reach of the law. Deep down inside he had a gut feeling that Gaffiney had nothing to do with the murder. Oxley was hoping for a lead, something he could get his teeth into.

His deepest fears were born of an act of savagery.

The killer might not be brought to justice.

He might even strike again.

FIVE

Two detective constables had visited an address on Charlington Estate - a place well known for its poverty, crime and drugs. They interviewed Ronald Gaffiney at an address there. Gaffiney was a thin dirty-looking wreck of a man who habitually wore a baseball cap. His partner, who was considerably younger, said they were at home all day when Elizabeth Collinson had been murdered. The story ended there. There was no direct evidence to link him to the crime. When Gaffiney was told that he was seen in the park carrying a knife, he denied it saying that the local kids often made up lies to land him into trouble.

Alone in his office he lit a cigarette, leaned back in his chair and studied the newspaper articles that Irene had given to him. One of the headings caught his attention: '£30,000 REWARD. HELP CATCH PARK KILLER.' Part of the report read, 'A local business man, who wishes to remain anonymous, has offered to pay £30,000 to anyone who can provide information that leads to the apprehension and conviction of the killer.'

He knew that a reward would prompt unwarranted response from all kinds of people, sending murder detectives to distant parts of the country to interview people who had visited the resort; after all, Blackpool was a leading tourist attraction. The Pleasure Beach's world-famous Rollercoaster was now top of the bill, attracting 7.2 million visitors in one year - nearly 2 million more than the British Museum. Whoever the murderer was he could have stayed in a lodging house before moving on.

9.30 p.m. He decided to buy fish, chips and curry sauce at Don's Plaice, only a couple of doors down the street. On his way back he noticed a car parked down an alley. It looked familiar - a majestic BMW 3 Series Coupé. It was the kind of car that people like Jim Sheridan could only dream about. The BMW could have been the one he saw at the Aristor Park crime scene. *Could this be a coincidence?* he wondered. *Why would someone want to leave such an expensive car in a backstreet alley?*

Sheridan wondered if he was being followed. Who was the owner of the car and what did he want from him?

A shudder ran through his body. He rushed back to the office and jotted down the registration number before unwrapping his tasty snack.

The telephone sounded.

'Jim Sheridan speaking.'

He took the call standing up. A shop owner was losing money due to a light-fingered assistant. Sheridan agreed to help. He turned and looked down into the street. The telephone slid across the table.

'I see. So, you think the lass might be doing the thieving?'

A middle-aged man came out of the pub opposite.

'If you could wait a day or two . . .' The punter turned left and started running until he was out of sight. '. . . I can bring a small video camera to your shop. They're easy enough to install.'

A younger man suddenly appeared from inside the pub and looked up at the window. Sheridan leaned forward, trying to get a better view. The phone slid closer to the edge of the table. 'Yes, the camera will be hidden. Nobody but you and I will know it's there.'

The man darted across the busy road. His footsteps sounded in the hallway.

'I'm sorry, but I have to go now. Goodbye.'

He caught the telephone as it toppled towards the floor. He quickly re-wrapped his supper and put it in the top right-hand drawer of his desk.

Footsteps sounded louder by the second. The twelfth step did not make its usual noise. Sheridan took a deep breath and stared fixedly at the door in front of him.

Then came the knock.

'Come in.'

The man entered. Smartly dressed. Black jacket and trousers. Dark-blue shirt open at the neck. His hair was short and jet black - almost too black to be natural. He was handsome, mid-thirties, about five feet eight inches tall. He sat down opposite a curious Jim Sheridan.

'H'm, nice smell of curry and chips. Are you going to offer me some?'

Sheridan wasn't amused by his arrogance. 'Before you tell me who you are, and why you've been following me, I ought to warn you that your car is likely to get scratched or even stolen.'

'I'll take that chance . . . and I haven't been following you.'

Sheridan sat upright and folded his arms. 'I'd like to know if it was you I saw at Aristor Park.'

'Yes. Irene Collinson came to see me. I run BB Investigations on Church Street. Collinson wants the murderer caught. She came to us. My name is Carl Lewis.'

He offered his hand. Sheridan reached over and gripped it tightly. 'Obviously, you know who I am. So, you're from BBI private detective agency? I always wanted to know what the BB stands for.'

'Big Brother.' Lewis smiled. 'There's always someone watching you.'

'And don't I know it.'

'Don't take it too hard. Collinson didn't employ my agency to track down this guy. She can't afford it, but she did mention *your* name. I visited this office but you'd gone out. I went to your house. You were just leaving, in that superb little car of yours, so I tailed you for a while.'

Sheridan couldn't quite work out why he had referred to his modest car as 'superb.' He assumed the man had an inflated ego. 'Why did you go to the park then, if Miss Collinson can't afford your fees?'

'You probably know that a reward has been offered for information. When I saw you at the park I assumed you might decide to take up the chase. I thought it would be inappropriate to disturb you when you were standing close to the bush where she was murdered. Private moments like that are special. It wouldn't have been right for me to approach you, would it?'

Sheridan wondered if his apparent sensitivity was genuine.

'Thirty thousand pounds is a lot of money,' Lewis continued, tapping his finger on the desk.

'I know that, but it's not the reason for my involvement in the case. In any event, I don't see that I can be of much use in a murder hunt, which leads me to the inevitable question of why you are here.'

'Murders like this one are difficult to solve. I think the loony will kill again, and I fancy the challenge.'

'I sincerely hope it's the last murder he commits.'

'Maybe. Irene Collinson told me that she was coming to see you. Both you and I want to catch this killer, don't we?'

Sheridan showed a look of disdain. 'Yes, but for different reasons. I suppose thirty grand might buy a reasonable BMW, eh?'

Lewis winced. 'Look, we're both on the case so why not work together, you and me? This case is a big challenge - the biggest ever for me. Who better to work with than an experienced PI like yourself?'

'I've never had a partner.'

'Look, you have the experience that I don't have and I've got the contacts. We've nothing to lose.'

Sheridan leaned forward, elbow on desk, clenched hand supporting his chin. He thought the proposition over. 'You have a point, I suppose.'

'Yeah, course I do. You can't tackle this alone. I believe you're good at what you do. One of my colleagues told me about the missing girl you tracked down some years ago. That one made the headlines.'

'Things have changed a lot since then . . . I'll tell you what Lewis, I don't know anything about you but I'm prepared to think things over regarding this, well, partnership, if that's what you want to call it.'

'That's fine with me.'

The two of them exchanged telephone numbers. Lewis opened the office door. 'This maniac is going to do it again,' he said, with conviction.

'You can't possibly know that.'

'Listen. Whoever he is, he must be *extremely* ill and he's not going to get better is he?' Lewis stepped onto the landing and then popped his head around the door. 'By the way, you've got a noisy step at the top of your stairs. I made sure not to stand on it when I came in. Must get on your nerves. Goodbye.'

Lewis whistled a tune as he descended the stairs, bouncing from step to step.

Sheridan wasn't entirely happy with the proposition. Lewis's offer of help seemed too good to be true. He became curious after learning about his 'contacts,' and was impressed by the fact that he could afford to run an expensive car. If he was that successful, maybe it *was* worth having him as a partner.

He wrote the telephone numbers in his desk diary and lifted his warm supper out of the drawer. He ate it to the radio sound of classical music, which eventually became background noise. His thoughts wandered to the terrible night when his daughter met a psychopath.

And he thought about Carl Lewis's alarming prophecy.

SIX

The hunt for the murderer became national news. Detective Superintendent George Naylor decided to 'go public' in an attempt to revitalise the enquiry. He was offered a ten-minute slot on TV's *Crime Monthly* which, he felt, was just enough time to cover the main areas that were of interest to the investigating team. He was not going to miss an opportunity like this.

The programme's producer agreed to send a small camera unit to Aristor Park, where they filmed two sequences. One of them featured the superintendent at the exact spot where Elizabeth was killed, whilst the other sequence was shot at the busy roadside near to the park's entrance. The interview was to be aired on TV only days afterwards. Blackpool's newspaper, *The Gazette*, primed its readers for the forthcoming programme.

Irene Collinson was at home in the company of her closest friend, waiting anxiously for the programme to start. Less than two miles away, at Newington Avenue, Jim Sheridan was trying to relax. Bert Davies had telephoned to remind him about the 'Park Murder' and its inclusion on *Crime Monthly*.

For some reason Sheridan felt uneasy and agitated. The initial shock of his daughter's death had subsided and now he was experiencing a burning desire to find out *who* had killed her.

At 9 p.m. the crime programme started. Thousands of viewers had their eyes fixed to their TV screens. The familiar theme tune accompanied the introductory images: the flashing police car lights, CCTV footage of a man smashing a shop window and a forensic scientist looking into a microscope. The programme was introduced by Kay Johnson, an attractive woman in her mid-thirties whose charm undoubtedly contributed to the show's success.

The first story described the brutal attack of a disabled boy in Blackpool. This was followed by the Elizabeth Collinson murder.

George Naylor was standing at the park entrance on East Park Drive, opposite the hospital's psychiatric unit. The scene had taken on a new perspective and looked different to the way it was a few months earlier.

Naylor had already considered this. He instructed the cameraman to include the main views: the park, the busy road, the hospital and golf links, so that viewers would have no difficulty in recognising the location.

He began by giving a description of Elizabeth and details of her movements on the evening of Monday, 20 March. He went on to say, 'We believe Elizabeth may have been approached at the roadside here, and dragged down this path to where she was killed. I am asking for people, who drove passed this spot between 6.45 and 7.15 p.m., to come forward.

'It is quite possible that a motorist may have seen something but did not realise the significance of it at the time. We need that person to come forward.'

The interviewer asked if the initial public response had been poor.

'Many members of the public have given us information and we are grateful. Unfortunately, the vital lead that could help to solve this crime is missing. Does anybody remember seeing a man anywhere along this road who was acting suspiciously? What we want is a description of the person who approached her along this road. What does he look like? How old is he? What was he wearing at the time? We need answers.'

The superintendent was asked about the nature of the attack.

'Elizabeth was subjected to a vicious knife assault. The person who did this may or may not live locally. We have no idea at this stage. We believe him to be in the thirty to forty age range.

'He is likely to have been agitated after the attack and would be perceived as behaving in an unnatural way; that is to say, behaving differently to his normal manner. He may have been quiet and appeared to be depressed. There would be something different about him afterwards and we would ask mothers, wives and girlfriends to contact us if they have any suspicions at all.'

George Naylor was prompted to comment on the possibility that the murderer may be married.

'We're not ruling anything out at this stage. Somebody, somewhere knows this man. We need to catch him as soon as possible before he harms or kills someone else. I would also like to ask viewers if they know of anybody who was away from his home or place of work on March 20, when they shouldn't have been. This, of course, *has* to tie in with the abnormal behaviour that I've mentioned.'

The interview ended and the incident room freephone number appeared on the screen.

Sheridan was concerned that the police had so little to go on. He was also amazed to learn that nobody had reported seeing Elizabeth with her killer. He was contemplating his next move when the phone rang.

'Hello, is that you Sheridan?'

'Yes,' he replied, concentrating on the distant, crackly voice.

'Lewis here. Listen, I can't speak for long. There's this guy you might be interested in.'

'What are you talking about, Lewis?'

'I've got an address for you. If you're interested all you have to do is go there and wait for him. If you see him, just tail him.'

Sheridan was taken by surprise, and intrigue. Lewis relayed details concerning a man named Mick Taylor who lived in a flat at Number 15 Law Street, close to the town centre.

'From where have you got the info about Taylor?'

He waited. No reply. Familiar noises sounded in the background. Lewis must have been travelling by car.

'Why don't you inform the police if you've got something on this guy?'

'It's up to us to handle it our way. This man is a tasty character, known to be nasty to women. He once threatened a girl with a knife. She never pressed charges. He's been bothering one or two women of late. He could be our man. Taylor is a stocky guy with black hair. He drives a silver-grey Metro. He walks a bit like John Wayne used to, so I believe. You can't miss him. He'll probably be out and about tonight. Go check it out, Sheridan.'

'Hello! Lewis, are you there?'

Silence. The dead tone kicked in. He wondered why the line had been closed so abruptly.

'Left in the dark,' he said wearily. 'Just my luck.'

He climbed the stairs, entered the bedroom, removed his round-the-house clothes and dressed himself more appropriately. Five minutes later he was standing by his own Metro parked at the front of his home.

Destination - town centre.

Parking was notoriously difficult in the area surrounding Law Street. It was Sheridan's lucky night. He reversed into the only available space. The silver-grey Metro stood on the forecourt of Number 15. It was gratifying to know that Lewis's information was accurate. But who was this Mick Taylor who had been seemingly plucked out of the air?

The vigil began.

Watching and waiting was all part of the job. You had to have patience - a lot of it - and you had to be prepared for that itchy bum rash to start eating away at your resolve. He was well aware that his 'watch' could be the first of many. Taylor might not make an appearance. He could have left the flat earlier in the evening.

Sheridan was situated in front of the Abberly Hotel. He kept a nonchalant air to avoid attracting attention. An hour passed. The boredom started to kick in. He shoved a cassette into the player, one which featured his favourite songs from the country field of music. Several songs later the door to Number 15 opened. It was almost midnight. The man who entered the street was stocky. His hair was black, his gait similar to that of 'Western' hero, John Wayne. Taylor walked down the street and disappeared behind a line of vehicles.

Sheridan carefully tailed him on foot, maintaining a safe distance between himself and the suspect. Taylor finally reached a pub called Silver's Bar situated on Blackpool's breezy Promenade. The bar, situated below ground level, was well known for serving after hours drinks.

The suspect waited at the pub's entrance, unaware that the man across the Promenade was watching him. Ten minutes later the action started. Taylor followed a couple who came out of the bar: a middle-aged man and a girl who looked to be in her twenties. The situation quickly deteriorated into what was obviously a domestic argument. Taylor floored the man with a heavy punch to the jaw, then set off in pursuit of the girl. Sheridan came to the rescue and helped the injured man to his feet. *Enough is enough*, he thought. It was time to go home.

When he reached Law Street he caught sight of Taylor again, and witnessed his foul language towards the girl who had out-run him.

'Not that way,' he bellowed. 'Come back 'ere.'

The young woman displayed the 'V' sign at Taylor and continued along the road towards a car-park.

Sheridan's first impression was correct. What he was witnessing was merely a fracas between a man and his girlfriend. He waited for one minute, hoping there would be no further violence, then a shrill scream rang out.

Taylor was dragging her into the parking area.

Sheridan experienced a dull tingling sensation in the pit of his stomach. He ran for all he was worth, the energy rapidly draining from his legs. He reached them in time to witness another altercation.

The brute slapped her across the face and forced her onto the ground. A thin trickle of blood was visible on the side of her mouth. Taylor tried to haul her into a standing position. Sheridan grabbed him from behind and slammed his body against a car. Its lights flashed, the alarm sounded. This sudden impulse was totally alien to Sheridan's character. He abhorred violence of any kind but felt compelled to protect the wretched girl from further harm.

'What's going on here?' Sheridan growled, dreading the prospect of a punch-up. He gripped Taylor's collar and pushed him harder against the vehicle.

'What's it to you, old man? Get your hands off me or you're dead.'

Sheridan held firm. The girl shot up and grasped a handful of Sheridan's hair.

'Leave him alone, mister,' she screamed, tugging furiously. 'It's nowt to do with you.'

The owner of the car, who had witnessed the assault from a nearby hotel, came to offer assistance. His arrival placated the situation. Sheridan released his grip and received a hefty right hook to his chin. He slithered helplessly to the ground as the girl pointed at him and laughed.

Taylor took her by the hand and they departed, leaving behind the bewildered car owner and an dishevelled private detective who had gone down in round one.

The man helped Sheridan onto his feet, and, true to form, he apologised for causing the alarm to go off.

'Not to worry,' the man replied. 'I'll call the police.'

'It's all right. I thought the girl was in trouble, that's all.'

'They're probably drunk,' he added, brushing dirt off the detective's coat sleeve. 'I've seen that sort of thing happen before. Are you sure you're okay?'

Sheridan nodded, thanked the stranger for his offer of help and departed.

The flat above Number 15 became occupied once more. The arguing continued, audible from the street below.

I'm too old to be getting knocked about by burly street ruffians, Sheridan mused. *I should stick to the more mundane cases. Come back all you cheating husbands and wives - all is forgiven. Better still, why not just retire altogether as previously planned?*

He drove away wondering why Lewis hadn't done the job. After all, he was younger and fitter, and much more capable of taking a blow to the chin.

At least Sheridan had a good enough excuse to hit the old Jack Daniel's Tennessee Whiskey.

And he did.

Only a couple of glasses. No more.

It never worked out that way.

The cursed drink problem was looming on the horizon.

SEVEN

The side streets branching off Blackpool's Seaforth Road resembled the alleys of a foggy Victorian London. The noise from the slow traffic smothered the rumble of the Irish Sea, its waves toppling as they succumbed to the Promenade's robust walls, foaming on their retreat. The austere red-bricked houses faded from view, resembling figments of the imagination rather than part of the austere construction of the town's dwellings. Taxi drivers left their engines ticking over whilst waiting to take customers into the town centre where they could enjoy further drinks, music and dance. Groups of boisterous men and women were keen to make the most of their Friday night out.

The weekend had begun.

Raucous laughter and chanting from the lager merchants rang out. There was bound to be a fight or two as the night progressed, and you would be sure to come across a couple of discarded half-eaten Chinese takeaways and splatters of vomit along the way.

At 10 p.m. the music of local band Hot Fever thundered from the stage of The Elms public house, renowned for its heavy music, underage drinkers and pot smokers. The band's second set was in full swing. Its four members lapped up the attention and adulation from the crowd during their performance of an original song called 'Smash Me Out' which featured a heavy bass line that never left the key of E. Despite the bad weather conditions the usual patrons had turned up to revel in the atmosphere.

Angela Ross and Karen Lawson were standing at the farthest point from the stage.

Both girls were in their twenties and had known each other for a number of years. Every Friday night they met at The Elms to enjoy the music, the conversation and the alcohol. The girls - a friendly, lively couple - were not averse to going off to nightclubs with men who were looking for companionship or a 'good time'.

Karen was tall and slim. Her dyed blonde hair, showing black at the roots, always looked greasy. As usual, her long shapely legs were on show. Her tight black skirt was riding high, and her favourite high-heeled shoes made her look a lot taller. She liked to be noticed.

Angela was several inches shorter. She had medium-length brown hair, cut in a fringe. Her cheap jacket was open, exposing her low-cut pink vest which struggled to contain her pendulous breasts. She had large green eyes and a stunning smile. The two girls attracted male admirers wherever they went.

It was a typically hectic night for the bar staff. After waiting for nearly ten minutes, Karen managed to get served. She edged her way through the crowd, carrying two bottles of Bacardi Breezer. Angela was waiting for her.

'You'd better make it four bottles next time,' Angela shouted when her friend appeared, 'or we'll be stuck here all night.'

Angela took the bottle and downed nearly half its contents in one swig. Karen watched her. 'Take it easy you, or you'll end up being carried home.'

Angela smiled. 'Don't worry,' she bellowed. 'I won't have too much. We can have a few more drinks at The Unicorn a bit later.'

'Oh, not there again. Do we have to?'

'You always say that, Karen.'

Angela winked at her friend. Karen shook her head with an air of disapproval, but she was all for it.

The band finished playing and the musicians dispersed amongst the crowd. The jukebox kicked in. Angela finished her drink and slammed the empty bottle on a table. She adjusted her pink vest which had slipped down an inch or two exposing more bare flesh. Karen had a similar problem with her skirt. It seemed to get shorter whenever she moved, causing her to stretch it down a bit. Perhaps these actions - the pulling up and pulling down - were subconscious rituals sending out signals meant to attract members of the opposite sex.

One man was already eyeing them up, leering at Karen's long legs, feasting his eyes on Angela's captivating assets. He took note of the Barcardi Breezers they were happily swilling down.

Maybe I should buy them a few more drinks, he thought.

Five minutes later he approached them, carrying two bottles. 'Here you are ladies,' he said cheerfully. 'Cop for these.'

'Are those for us, then?' asked Karen, showing a look of faked surprise.

'That's right.'

Karen snatched the bottles without thanking him, and began to laugh and joke with Angela. He stayed with them, trying to think of something to say whilst the girls drank avidly.

'How tall are you, then?' he asked, looking up at Karen.

'Taller than you, obviously,' came the reply.

He gently edged his way in between them. Bad move. Angela immediately walked away and made conversation with an acquaintance. Karen became annoyed and irritable. He closed in on her and said, 'I was going to tell your friend . . . I'm a fan of this, uh, sort of music.'

'Really?' Karen said sarcastically, her patience running thin. 'You haven't told us *your* name yet.'

'Tony.'

'I'll tell you what, Tony, why don't you buy us another couple of drinks before the band come on again, eh?'

'Certainly. No problem. That friend of yours is something else. I really like her.'

'She's more than you can handle,' Karen said. She swallowed the rest of her drink and held an empty bottle in front of him. He beckoned with his hand, indicating he wanted to tell her something. She reluctantly lowered her head and listened to his words, struggling to make sense of what he was saying. He then left her and made for the crowded bar.

Karen caught sight of a friend. 'Martin. How are you doin'?' she said.

'Fine thanks. I can't stay long. Anyway, I see that you've already got company. Who is he?'

'Don't know. He's a funny one. He talked about Angie and said something about a dolly-house parlour maid. I can't imagine what he meant by it.'

'Sounds weird. Must go. See you around.'

Martin melted into the crowd. Ten minutes later Tony came back with the drinks. Karen gave a weary sigh of resignation. The band started playing their last set. Angela came back and noticed that angry look on her friend's face. It was time to drink up, time to move on. Tony watched them drain their glasses. He wanted them to stay longer but they waved goodbye and left for the next port of call.

Now his heart was really pounding.

The swirling fog was thicker now. Street lamps and illuminated shop windows were shining dimly. Karen unfastened her handbag and fumbled for her lipstick and small mirror.

'Come on, Karen,' said Angela impatiently. 'You look fine. Let's go before that stiff comes out. We don't want him trailing us, especially in all this fog.'

'Right you are, Angie. So, it's off to Blackpool's premier pub, the lousy Unicorn . . . And here we are, ladies and gentlemen. We've got our Jamie who is gonna sing "Uptown Girl." Thank you, Jamie. Who do we have here? It's our Margaret. She's gonna sing, "Feel Like a Woman" . . .'

Angela laughed heartily and they made their way through the damp mist, relieved to leave The Elms, and the man who was so irritating.

The smoke-filled pub was packed solid with locals and weekend visitors. Two young attractive girls - Babs and Tina - were hosting the karaoke. Young Jamie had already sung the popular Billy Joel number, in the wrong key, as always, and was suitably rewarded with lukewarm applause. Tina called out the name of the next 'Star'. Fred, who was pushing sixty, totally destroyed 'You'll Never Walk Alone.' The McGregor PA system struggled to accommodate his high-pitched voice.

The audience consisted of a mixture of athletic youngsters and painfully paralytic geriatrics. Everyone was having a great time. Women were supping Slambas as if they had gone out of fashion, and the steadfast male drinkers happily let their stomachs bathe in chilled Boddingtons, served with a smile. It was 10.35 p.m. when Angela and Karen bought their drinks. The excitable crowd rocked to the sound of 'Red River Rock,' giving Babs and Tina the opportunity to take a well-earned break. Five minutes later Angela took the stage. She sang the opening lines of 'Jolene,' an appropriate number for her. Applause sounded and the locals cheered, especially the older men who drivelled at the sight of her opulent figure. Every week the same punters sang the same songs. Nobody ever got bored with it.

Angela finished the song and passed the microphone to the next participant. After several songs Karen told Angie she was going home.

'All right, love. See you whenever.'

Karen didn't fancy going to a nightclub, and her mate had supped far too much already. *Better call it a day,* she thought. She waved goodbye and went in search of a taxi. By now they were all smothered by the relentless fog rolling in from the sea. The light from the pub's external wall lamps failed to penetrate the enveloping mist. Karen didn't see the solitary figure standing close by - the stranger waiting for *the* moment to arrive . . . and it was his lucky night. She was alone. The moment was getting closer. The opportunity for him to satisfy his sexual urges - in a way that normal human beings would find absolutely horrifying - would soon be his.

Karen found a taxi. She was safe. Soon after, Angela staggered into the street accompanied by two male friends.

'Look at this lot,' one of the men said, referring to the weather.

'It won't take *me* long to get home,' said Angela, slurring her words.

Her companions asked if she wanted to join them for further drinks at a late bar. She declined. They disappeared into the fog. She tried in vain to fasten her imitation leather jacket but her senses were too dull. Even connecting the zip proved to be too hard of a task.

She turned left into Hailey Road where she lived. The Unicorn stood between Hailey and Selbourne Road. A covered passage ran along the back of the pub: a narrow alley, in effect, joining the two roads.

Angela reached the entrance to the passageway and felt a hand touch her shoulder.

The stranger walked by and turned to face her. There was no option but to stand her ground. He stared at her breasts and smiled.

'Where are you going?' he asked, lowering his head as a man passed by, coughing and sputtering.

'I'm . . . I'm off home.'

She tried to pass him but he blocked her way. If she had been sober, Angela Ross would probably have slapped his face and told him where to go, but she was tired and - being under the influence of drink - found it difficult to deal with the confrontation. She was vulnerable now. He came closer, grinning. His passionless eyes were running up and down her body.

Home was about sixty yards away. That knowledge was a comfort to her. Occasional bouts of laughter, shouting and conversation could be heard coming from the direction of the main road, but Angela felt isolated in the thick fog.

'It's getting late,' he said, touching her shoulder. 'I'll walk along with you for a while. Better to be safe than sorry, eh?'

There was nothing else she could do but act accordingly. They moved on, slowly. *Not far to go*, she thought.

Suddenly, without warning, he covered her mouth with his hand and dragged her into the gloom of the narrow passage. She was numb with fear and stifling disbelief. Halfway down the passage he forced her against the cold wall, keeping one hand tightly in position over her mouth.

'Now, listen to me,' he said, breathing heavily. 'I've got a knife. I'll use it if you make a sound. Do you understand me?'

She was too terrified to answer. If it was sex he wanted she would obey his instructions. She would do anything to stay alive. He spoke again, more softly this time.

'I'm going to take my hand away now. If you scream, *if* you scream, or make a noise, I'll kill you.' He gradually reduced the pressure of his hand. She did not scream, nor did she speak a word.

She was gasping for air, her chest heaving.

He tastes her filthy sweating body, allowing rivers of blood to trickle onto his eager tongue.

He removed a strip of black tape from the inside of his jacket and pressed it firmly over her mouth. He reached for his knife. Her thin vest came apart with one swift downward cut of the razor-edged weapon.

Her bare flesh lay before him, tempting him. He squeezed her breast as hard as he could. She closed her eyes tightly, squeezing out her final tears. She thought her time was up, but he thrust the knife inside his coat pocket.

Hope flashed through her mind. Maybe he would only sexually abuse her or rape her. That would be better than death.

He pulled a pair of pliers from his trouser pocket and held them in front of her eyes. Her fear excited him.

Naked breasts. Whitechapel damsels in distress.

The fetid vapour drifts away from the gaping wound . . . He slashes the helpless harlot again and again.

The hope faded.

Her futile scream, muffled by the tape, was her last cry for help. As if in a nightmare she expected to wake up.

The assault was about to begin.

EIGHT

The previous night's fog had completely evaporated, giving way to the first of many light showers. Another cloudy day. The stallholders along Seaforth Road were busy preparing their rickety tables and canopies for another day's trading. But times had changed.

In the 1960s the pavements were jammed solid with holidaymakers spilling onto the roadway. Families from all over Britain visited the most successful seaside resort to see the famous Tower and enjoy the Golden Mile with its piers and box-like arcades. In 1975 the opening of the M55 motorway link into Blackpool gave rise to an increase in the number of day visitors, including younger single-sex parties that were attracted to the new licensed premises in the town centre.

Ernie Mitchell's DIY stall was one of many along the Seaforth Road, standing a mere thirty yards from The Unicorn public house. Mitchell reached for a plastic box containing an assortment of household tools. He felt a hand tugging vigorously at his coat and turned to face a man in his early twenties, panting and visibly shaken.

'What's the matter, young fellow?'

'There's a body in the passage behind the pub. There's blood all over the place. She needs help.'

'What pub are you talking about? That one there do you mean - the Unicorn?'

'Yes.'

Ernie Mitchell's wife, who was helping to prepare the stall, was shocked to hear of the discovery.

'You'd better go with him,' she urged. 'I'll stay here.'

The covered passage was four feet wide and seventeen feet long. Mitchell's pace became slower when he approached the opening. A woman's body was clearly visible, lying on its front about halfway down the passage and next to a recess in the wall. Spatters of blood adorned the wall opposite the recess and a large quantity had spilled out from beneath the body and onto her hands. Nearby, lay her handbag and a black shoe which had fallen off during the struggle.

Mitchell knelt beside the body. The unnerving stillness of the body and the alarming facial features told him that she was beyond help.

The young man crept into the passage.

'Don't come any closer,' said Mitchell, motioning him to stay back. 'I'm going to contact the police.'

George Naylor took one last look at himself in the long mirror, making those minor adjustments to his appearance. During the past few months he had slept for only six hours each night and, occasionally, had worked a seven-day week.

Don't worry. You're doing a fine job. Keep your nose to the grindstone. Don't rush. Take it easy.

It wasn't always that easy.

He was still taking the tablets for high blood pressure. His wife, Dorothy, kept a close watch on him most of the time. The intensity of the Collinson murder enquiry had put a tremendous strain on the investigating team and was beginning to affect the Naylor's home life. She did everything in her power to make life easier for him - and he knew it. Other incidents had stalled the superintendent's efforts to solve the murder of Elizabeth Collinson.

Dorothy Naylor came down the stairs and took her husband's jacket off the wall hook. 'You look respectable, my dear,' she said, showing a look of admiration. 'Here's your coat. Let me know at what time you want tea - if you get the chance.'

'I'll let you know,' he said.

She accompanied him to the driveway and heard the phone. 'I'd better see who that is,' she said, dashing off into the house. A few moments later she reappeared. 'It's Derek Oxley. He wants to speak to you right away.'

Inspector Oxley rarely called his boss at home - only in matters of urgency. The conversation was finished in seconds.

'We've got another problem,' he said grimly. 'The body of a woman has been found near to one of those streets branching off Seaforth Road. She's been viciously attacked.'

'This is terrible. Well don't start rushing about everywhere trying to do it all yourself.'

'I'll try my best not to. Talk to you later.'

Naylor got into his car and drove off.

9.30 a.m. Naylor arrived at the scene of the attack. The blue-and-white police tape was in position.

Inspector Oxley was the first person to speak to the superintendent.

'The police surgeon is examining the body right now. He arrived here a couple of minutes ago,' he said, gently pushing his way through the mass of curious onlookers standing by the entrance to the alley.

'It's confined in there,' remarked Naylor. 'Not much space for our boys to move about in.'

Oxley was concerned about preserving the scene.

'Look at this lot, George. It's turning into a circus.'

The inspector summoned a couple of uniformed officers and instructed them to keep the public as far back as possible. Naylor surveyed the immediate surroundings.

The covered passage afforded access to Selbourne Road. At its exit a back alley ran to the right, separating the backyards of the two roads: Selbourne and Hailey. Oxley described the layout of the area surrounding the crime scene, whereupon his superior gave orders for both roads and the back alley to be sealed off.

'Do it right away, Derek,' he added, looking around furtively.

Oxley carried out his task in a quick and efficient manner. Meanwhile, more police vehicles arrived. The commotion attracted much public attention. It was becoming busier by the minute and, being a Saturday, the number of shoppers was increasing.

The police surgeon, Dr Charles Scott, was a local GP with over twenty years' experience. He was a rotund small man whose black-rimmed spectacles looked too big for his face. He approached the superintendent who was eagerly awaiting the outcome of his preliminary findings.

'She's been dead at least several hours,' he said, glancing at his watch. 'I would say that she was killed in the early hours, possibly midnight.'

'Cause of death?' asked Naylor.

'Well now, undoubtedly a knife attack. There are numerous stab wounds to the chest and abdomen. She's probably bled to death. I would put her age around the mid-twenties. Her handbag is lying next to her. That's all I can tell you. Her injuries are appalling. She's been through a terrifying ordeal. You see, some of the wounds are suggestive. There's evidence of a physical assault and a struggle, more so than with the Collinson murder.'

Naylor pressed the doctor for his views on the two attacks.

'If you're asking me, are they related? I don't know. Put it this way - if it's a different killer who is operating in the same way then you've got two psychopaths roaming the streets. This crime is just as pointless as the first.'

The doctor gave a courteous little bow and went his way.

By now the morbid onlookers had been dispersed and the traffic along Seaforth Road was moving more steadily. The scene of crime officers and the police photographer had arrived and were awaiting instructions from their senior investigating officer, George Naylor.

A fine drizzle began to fall. Inspector Oxley pulled up the collar of his long black coat, thankful that the murder scene was under shelter, preserving trace evidence. The police cordon was in place.

Naylor stared at the lifeless body. He heard the inspector's voice but his words didn't register.

'Sorry, Derek, what did you say?'

'The Home Office pathologist is on his way.'

'Good. Sooner he arrives, the better. I want the search team to start looking for the murder weapon. I want an incident vehicle down here, and get the names and addresses of all visitors who are staying in the area.'

'We'll have to move quickly on this, George. There's a few pubs close by including this one here. I'm going to arrange for the landlord to be questioned. Someone's bound to have seen something.'

Naylor was in agreement. 'Every conventional line of enquiry will have to be pursued. We can't afford to miss anything. Once we know her identity we can focus the investigation.'

'It shouldn't be too difficult . . . *if* she's local.'

Hailey Road was busier than ever. Hotel guests and lodging-house tenants were curious to learn what had happened.

Sandra Ross was one of them.

Her husband was still asleep so she decided to join the spectators. Sandra was forty-four years old and looked considerably older. Her long hair was dyed black, her eyes heavily marked with mascara giving her a witch-like appearance. She watched the police activity with interest knowing that a serious incident had occurred. She caught snippets of conversation. Certain words sent a shudder through her: blood, knife attack, girl's body. Her latent fears were intensifying as news of the gruesome discovery filtered through the onlookers.

Sandra's heart sank.

She staggered back, hand covering her mouth. *Angela hasn't come home,* she thought. *She should have rung by now. She must have got drunk and gone off with some bloke. She's not been killed. Not our Angie. It can't be her.*

But she didn't know the truth. She wanted to believe her daughter was alive and well. She could not bring herself to believe anything else. She *had* to know. Sandra Ross was not prepared to wait for answers. She approached a WPC and naively asked if anybody knew the identity of the girl, adding that her daughter had not returned home.

'It's far too early to say,' she replied. 'You say that your daughter hasn't returned home?'

'That's right, miss,' the mother humbly replied. 'She usually rings to tell me what she's doing. There's been no sign of her.'

She made a note of her name and address. Sandra gently tugged at her sleeve and asked, 'Can I have a quick look then, just to put my mind at rest? She was wearing a pink top.'

Sandra's composure was disintegrating by the second. The officer placed a friendly hand on her shoulder.

'I'm afraid we can't let you do that. Look, you go on home and leave the rest to us. I'll let the superintendent know that you're worried about your daughter.'

The officer passed the information to Superintendent Naylor. She asked him if the girl *was* wearing a pink top.

The answer was affirmative.

The village of Plymbey lay on the outskirts of Sedgeburn, just fourteen miles away from Blackpool. Jack and Avril Robson decided to drive the couple of miles into Sedgeburn's town centre to do some shopping. They passed the medieval stocks outside St Anne's Church, and continued through the winding roads of the scenic countryside. The wood was visible to the right - the seemingly innocent wood which attracted visitors in the summer time.

In the future this delightful location would become well known, but not for its beauty and serenity.

A gruesome secret was waiting to be discovered.

The body of Lucy Beckett was slowly decaying in its damp grave.

NINE

The Home Office pathologist, Dr Christian Purslow, performed his initial examination *in situ*. He was one of Britain's foremost pathologists. 'Death is my life,' was one of his sayings. The forensic work had been his 'life' for over thirty years. Although in his fifties, Purslow's brown hair was only just starting to turn grey. His rectangular glasses, mahogany-coloured tie and waistcoat gave him an air of unspoken dignity which became more apparent whenever he checked the time on his gold pocket watch.

By midday his preliminary examination was completed and the body was taken to the mortuary at Layton.

Later that afternoon the dense clouds had turned black. Large raindrops came down, heralding the beginning of a blustery spell of wet weather.

The post-mortem room was cold and austere. Channels ran the length of the floor. They transported water - used for rinsing post-mortem tables and trolleys - into a drain situated at the far end of the room. The room was specially designed for ease of cleaning: perfunctory, Victorian in appearance.

Dr Purslow removed his surgical gloves and made notes in preparation for his final report. George Naylor's face tightened when he saw the naked mutilated body. Then his eyes wandered to her clothing and personal belongings, sealed in plastic bags ready for forensic examination.

The pathologist waited a short while, then spoke softly. 'George, we meet again - unfortunately.'

The superintendent took a deep breath and turned away from the corpse. 'I'm afraid so. I see you haven't started the internal examination yet. Just as well. It's bad enough looking at the external wounds. I can't remember ever having seen anything like this, Christian.'

'I agree. I *can* tell you that this girl has been cut more extensively than the first victim.'

'Are you suggesting the two murders were committed by the same hand?'

'Undoubtedly so.'

Two women killed by the same man. George Naylor was, in a sense, relieved to learn that this latest atrocity was not an unrelated homicide.

'How can you be sure the two murders are linked?'

'The killer has, in both instances, inserted a sharp instrument inside the rectum - probably a knife. Are you going to release this information, or is it still restricted?'

'I shall inform Inspector Oxley about the anal assault, but nobody else. I want you to keep it a secret.'

'You can count on me. Now, I have estimated the time of death as being between 11.30 p.m. and midnight. That's the closest I can get it. I suspect this unfortunate girl died from internal bleeding. She's certainly been made to suffer.'

'In what way?'

'She was gagged with some kind of masking tape. There's evidence of adhesive round the mouth and cheeks.' Purslow pointed at the chest wounds. 'As you can see, she was stabbed in the breasts - fourteen times. She was in a standing position when this happened. A sharp knife was used.'

'In your opinion, what was the length of the blade?'

'I would say about five inches. Now, look at these marks.'

Purslow raised one of the victim's hands. A straight knife wound was clearly visible running across the palm.

'I see what you mean,' said Naylor. 'She tried to defend herself by grabbing the knife.'

'Correct. There is also damage to the nipples. In fact, her right nipple has almost been torn off.'

'How? Do you mean bitten off?'

'No, I don't think he used his teeth. I'm not sure how it was done, but I will take a closer look at those injuries.'

He described the other injuries. Bruising to the face indicated that she was forced against the wall whilst the chest assault was carried out. The abdominal area had also been targeted. Several slashes, ranging from five to seven inches in length, had been made to the abdomen, each cut running in a direction from the ribs toward the groin.

The superintendent had seen enough.

Dr Purslow covered the body and glanced at his notes. 'There are no strangulation marks on this girl, whereas the first victim *was* strangled. That is unusual, is it not?'

'It *is* unusual. A murderer usually keeps to the same method of attack, and Elizabeth Collinson was attacked from behind. In this instance, the victim has been attacked from the front.'

'Indeed. The state of a killer's mind is one of life's most intricate problems. I shall rest for a short while. There's much work to be done.'

'I'd like to know your opinion on the killer's state of mind. Was it a frenzied attack?'

Purslow carefully considered the question. 'With regard to the chest wounds, yes, it was frenzied. The cuts to the abdomen are not quite the same. There was more deliberation, in the sense that he took his time. This, to my way of thinking, would indicate planning on his behalf - someone who is in control.'

'Frenzied and controlled? That's a contradiction. How can it be explained?'

'You need to speak to a criminal psychologist for the answer to that. It does seem strange, but there's something else I find odd about this attack. You don't mind my theorising do you, George? I find this murder particularly interesting.'

'Not at all. Please, carry on.'

'I was thinking about the crime location. At the entrance to that covered alley you have the pub to the left, the terraced houses to the right. Now, at that time of the night - bearing in mind the number of people who were roaming the streets - the murderer could easily have been seen or even caught red-handed *if* somebody decided to use that alley. Also, if the girl had screamed the occupants of the house might have been alerted.'

'I take your point about the alley. Unfortunately, the girl was probably too drunk to scream out and, no doubt, scared out of her wits. Did you know there was thick fog in Blackpool last night, giving the killer a tremendous advantage?'

'No, I didn't. That explains it then. It explains how he committed his deed with impunity.'

Purslow became thoughtful and said, 'You know, George, the narrow alley, the fog and those terrible mutilations are reminiscent of the Jack the Ripper murders in Victorian London.'

'Christian, please don't mention that name. If the press latch onto the idea of another Ripper they'll have a field day.'

'Indeed. The press will print anything in order to sell newspapers . . . By the way, I haven't got round to determining the presence or absence of sperm. I'll let you know the outcome in due course.'

'You do what's necessary, Christian,' Naylor said, making his way toward the exit. 'I appreciate your help.'

'That's what I'm here for.'

As soon as the superintendent left the building he was greeted by a distant rumble of thunder. Black ominous clouds told of an imminent downpour. In the area surrounding Seaforth Road, scene of crime officers were working faster so as to preserve any trace evidence that might be destroyed or washed away by rainfall.

The incident room phone lines were busy as a result of the superintendent's appeal on television. With more leads to follow up, the hunt for the killer had intensified. Many names were put forward as possible suspects, including Ronald Gaffiney.

7 p.m. The superintendent arrived at his office carrying a cup of coffee and a packet of sandwiches. He phoned his wife to say he would be late home.

Derek Oxley, feeling energetic as ever, was eager to learn what the post-mortem had revealed. He tapped on the office door and walked in.

'Take a seat, Derek,' said Naylor amiably. Oxley was no fool. He could tell by the tone of his superior's voice that something was wrong. Naylor was perspiring and looked paler than usual. He enlightened the inspector with details of the post-mortem examination.

'Anal assault, you say? It looks like we're dealing with the same man,' Oxley suggested.

'The pathologist is certain about that; but remember, Derek, not a word to anybody. It might turn out to be important.'

'I understand.'

'So, what's the latest?'

'The murder weapon has not turned up.'

The superintendent sipped the lousy coffee. 'I thought as much. This one's a little bit too clever to give us an important clue like that.' Naylor was staring into his cup.

Oxley was curious. 'What's the matter?'

'This coffee tastes like gnat's urine.'

'You're right. It never gets any better, does it? I'll get somebody to make you a proper drink.'

'Don't bother, but thanks all the same . . .Well, we can't afford to dwell too much on the downside of things. Who was this woman who said her daughter was missing?'

'Sandra Ross. She lives on Hailey Road with her husband. They have a 28-year-old daughter called Angela. There's no sign of her and she hasn't contacted her parents. Angela Ross was wearing a pink top when she went out last night - the same as the murdered girl.'

'As soon as the pathologist has finished his examination get all the details you can about Ross's daughter. Then we can look into it further. We shouldn't jump to conclusions.' The rain was beating harder against the office window. 'Lousy weather,' Naylor said. 'Forensic are having a bad time down there with all this rain. They may have to continue their search tomorrow. The murder weapon could be anywhere in Blackpool. Chances are, the killer's taken it with him. With a bit of luck something might turn up on the victim's clothes.'

'If I could make a suggestion, George.'

'Go ahead.'

'I think we should check Gaffiney again. I'm sending a couple of DCs to his address to find out where he was last night.'

'You do that, Derek. I'm going to talk to the press soon, and I must inform the Chief Constable of the latest developments.'

The inspector immersed himself in the routine of the incident room. The computer analysts and indexers hardly ever left their seats. The waste paper bins had spilled over with empty plastic coffee cups. Oxley was impressed by the diligence of his officers.

An hour later a crime analyst handed him a typed sheet which contained details of a possible sighting. An elderly lady named Jean Glover had driven by Aristor Park on the night of the murder. She had spotted a man talking to a girl matching the description of Elizabeth Collinson.

Oxley shook his head. 'She should have told us about this straight away,' he said, showing frustration. 'How old is this lady?'

'The officer who took the call thinks she could be in her seventies.'

'Seventies? It's a wonder she can drive at all at that age. Let's hope she can tell us something useful.'

'You'd be surprised, sir. Old women can be extremely perceptive.'

TEN

The man in the ground-floor shop was busy sifting through a pile of long-playing records that littered the floor. He looked up and saw the weary look on Sheridan's face. 'Keeping busy, Jim?' he asked.

'Luckily, yes. You know, Darren, whenever I think about quitting the enquiry business somebody always seems to come along and ask for help.'

And so up the stairs he climbed. The twelfth step creaked for the millionth time. He shuffled into his stuffy office, opened the window and switched the radio on.

3 p.m. A tired Jim Sheridan put his feet on the table, sipped a cool drink and enjoyed a luxurious long-awaited cigarette.

The radio music faded, giving way to the news. The reader's voice carried a sense of urgency: 'Good afternoon. I'm Clive Goodwin and this is Wave Reports. A second murder enquiry is underway following the discovery of a woman's body in Blackpool. The woman, who has been identified as Angela Ross, was found on Saturday morning in a passage close to Hailey Road. She had been stabbed repeatedly. The police are linking this latest attack with the murder of Elizabeth Collinson on Aristor Park over two months ago . . .'

Another murder, and it seemed that the police were no nearer to catching the maniac responsible. How old was he? Did he drive a car? What did he look like?

The detective, who worked in a small room above a 'cheap' second-hand shop, was just as far away from knowing the answers as Superintendent George Naylor. *Time to speak to Lewis. Time for decisions,* he thought. Sheridan reflected on his next move.

Detective Constable Steve Rivers was haunted by bad habits. Rivers was thirty-eight years old and slightly overweight for his height. Everyone in the force knew or had heard of DC Steve Rivers. The women, especially, knew about his reputation. He was a bum pincher, a boob ogler, a sex maniac - everything that a detective constable should not be. Rivers was always popular with the female staff down at headquarters; not so popular with his superiors. Oxley detested him, couldn't even stand the sound of his voice. George Naylor - whom Rivers always referred to as 'Bulldog' - would not have permitted him to join the force had it been down to him.

Palmer, his partner, was fairly new to the job. He was eight years younger and his career might have held promise. He could not have been saddled with a worse tutor, which was a pity. Although punctual and trustworthy, Palmer was naive at times and shy to the point of giving the impression of timidness. Rivers loved to capitalise on his vulnerability. He found him easy to control and belittle.

The two men were supposed to be busy doing the rounds, questioning witnesses and suspects in the Collinson–Ross enquiries. They were sitting opposite each other in a quiet dirty pub on the Charlington estate.

DC Rick Palmer sipped his beer nervously.

'Rick, get it down your neck. What's the matter with you?'

Rivers gulped his second pint and debated whether or not to buy a third.

'I'm not one for drinking on duty, you know that. What would you do if George Naylor came in here? Answer me that.'

'Old Bulldog? He wouldn't come to such a hovel. It's too lower class for the likes of him.'

'You don't like him much do you, Steve?'

'Not really. He's pretty good at his job though. Trouble with him is, he's too rigid in his approach to things. Look at me, for example, nice and relaxed but as sharp as a pin.'

Palmers's mouth fell open in disbelief.

'There's no detective as good as me,' Rivers continued. 'Nowhere near as good.'

'So, what do you reckon to this bloke we've just interviewed, this Gaffney fellow?'

'Gaffiney's his name, you idiot . . . He's got nothing at all to do with these murders.'

Rivers belched. Palmer winced.

'What makes you say that, Steve? Go on, how do you know that?'

'Because he bats for the other side.'

'What?'

'Come on Rick, don't act so stupid. You know what I'm on about. He don't fancy women. No, not the likes of him. And that's why he ain't the killer. Women just don't interest him at all, so why should he risk his neck by killing a woman?'

'You can't be a hundred per cent certain he's gay. You don't know for sure.'

Palmer took a tiny sip of beer and gingerly placed the glass on the table.

'You're drinking that like it's poison . . . Gaffiney's definitely that way inclined. He's not the psychopath we are searching for.'

'Why all this fuss about him, then?'

'The reason is simple. It's not young girls he watches on the park, it's young lads; and because people have complained about him, he needs looking into. He has to be eliminated, see?'

'I understand what you're saying, but he's still a suspect. He has no alibi.'

'He doesn't need an alibi. Believe me, Rick, he's not the murderer. I'm absolutely certain about that. Take Dennis Nilsen as an example. He murdered homosexuals and he was gay himself. Now, if it were men that were being stabbed and ripped apart here in Blackpool I would regard Gaffiney as a possible suspect and I would know how to make him talk, believe me.'

'You would force a confession out of him? What I mean is, you would make him confess to something he hadn't done?'

'Eh, who's bothered? Come on, drink up. We've got a witness to go and interview.'

Rivers finished his drink in a matter of seconds. Palmer struggled with his. He raised the glass higher and swallowed the remainder of the liquid nectar.

'That's it, Ricky, my lad. Drink it all up, there's a good boy.'

Palmer slammed the empty glass onto the table. 'You're a sarcastic git, aren't you?'

Jean Glover's house was situated in one of the more respectable and quieter parts of the resort. She was in her late sixties and lived alone. When the door bell sounded she peered through the curtains to see who it was. A moment later she opened the door. Her cat, Dobie, ran into the garden.

'Oh, he's a lively one,' she said. 'Always runs out when he gets the chance. And what can I do for you two gentlemen?'

Rivers explained the reason for their visit. Mrs Glover welcomed them into her home. She insisted on preparing tea and biscuits.

The two detectives waited in the front room on a two-seater settee which was barely large enough to accommodate them. A few minutes later, the old lady came into the room and lowered the tray onto a small coffee table.

'Allow me,' Palmer said, taking the tray from her bony hands.

'Thank you, my dear. I am sorry, but I don't keep anything stronger.'

'That's quite all right,' Rivers said with a restrained smile.

'If I did, I would be drinking it myself. You shouldn't drink on duty, you know. It's naughty.'

Palmer was surprised. Old Mrs Glover must have had an excellent sense of smell. She poured the tea into delicate patterned cups.

DC Palmer reminded her of the date when the first murder had occurred. He politely asked her how she could be so sure that her sighting was on the date in question.

'I remember the date because I had been to see my friend, Pat. She's not been too well, you know. I visit her most Mondays. I remember that particular night because she gave me some fresh chicken for Dobie. He loves chicken, so he does.'

Rivers took over the conversation. 'You telephoned the incident room about a man who, you say, was talking to the murdered girl. How do you know it was her?'

'I told the officer what she was wearing. She had those distinctive yellow shorts, and her hair was lovely and long.'

'What time would this have been?' asked Palmer.

'It was gone seven o'clock. It could have been ten past. The girl was knelt down, rubbing her ankle. This man, whoever he was, was probably helping her.'

Palmer asked about the location of the sighting. According to the old lady it was only a few yards from the park entrance. He asked her to describe the man.

'He was smartly dressed and wore a tie. He was tall and thin. His hair was dark and combed back. He was in his forties or early fifties.'

'Can you be certain?' Rivers asked. 'You seem to have noticed quite a lot.'

'Oh yes, I'm quite certain. You see, I drive slowly and I always keep my eyes open to see what's going on. You never know what you might see.'

'You should have informed us earlier,' commented Rivers. He took a sip of his tea and said, 'And that's it? Nothing else?'

'No. I am so sorry for not telling you before now. You see, I don't watch much television, and I only occasionally buy a newspaper.'

They thanked her for the information. Palmer gulped a mouthful of tea. Rivers left his. They followed the old woman to the front door. She opened it, allowing Dobie to wander inside. He hissed as Rivers bent down to stroke him.

'Oh dear,' said Mrs Glover, holding her hand close to her mouth. 'He doesn't seem to like you.'

'Goodbye then,' said Rick Palmer with a grin on his face. 'And once again, thank you.'

Mrs Glover gently picked the cat up and cradled him in her arms. He licked at her face. 'Call any time,' she said, moving her head back to avoid Dobie's hairy tongue. 'You're always welcome.'

She waved goodbye and closed the door.

'Looks like you've cracked it there, Ricky,' joked Rivers.

'Oh, really? I thought she was more your type.'

Rivers laughed. 'An amiable lady. Seems reliable enough. She was right about the yellow shorts.'

'What about the sighting of the man? That description could apply to thousands of men living in Blackpool.'

'It fits one man I know about - Jimmy Sheridan.'

'Never heard of him. Who is he?'

'Private detective. Collinson was his daughter, but he kept quiet about it.'

'I don't buy that. A private eye murders his own daughter? Come on.'

'We don't know that for certain. He fits the description and he's going to get a visit from us. Here are the keys. You can drive this time.'

'Detectives, private or otherwise, don't commit murder. You're barking up the wrong tree. We're just going to make fools of ourselves.'

'Rick, don't talk rubbish. It can't do any harm to have a sniff round. Now then, drive up this road to the lights, turn left and stop at the Mini Market. I'm out of ciggies.'

ELEVEN

Sheridan was sitting opposite Irene in the living room of her home. She knew nothing about the fatal attack on Angela Ross until he gave her a newspaper opened at the relevant page.

'I don't believe it,' she gasped. 'Another girl dead. Why is this happening?'

She felt like crying, but somehow managed to stop herself. Sheridan sensed her emotion.

'Irene, how are you coping?'

'I don't think I'll ever get over losing Elizabeth but life has to go on, doesn't it? I feel so sorry for that girl's parents. I know what they're going through . . . Are there no suspects? I mean, it could be some crazed drug addict couldn't it?'

'It's impossible to say. I remember when I was a kid living in Fulham. The body of a little girl was discovered by the banks of the River Thames close to where we lived. She was strangled and sexually assaulted. Georgina Cook was her name. She was only ten. If I remember rightly, her father was the main suspect for quite some time. In the end the police eliminated him.

'They interviewed thousands of men. People in the area thought a local man, living alone, was responsible. He was a bit eccentric and wore black-rimmed glasses with thick lenses which made him look pervy. The kids loved him, though. He always found time to play with them and he was kind. But at the end of the day it was his love for the kids that got him arrested.'

'Was he arrested and charged?'

'As far as I can remember he was taken in for questioning. They had to release him in the end. There was no evidence against him whatsoever. It turned out to be a caretaker who killed her. He worked at the same school that the little girl attended. He was the quiet type, wouldn't hurt a fly, so they thought. He was married too. People just couldn't believe it was him who'd done it. So you see, Irene, people who don't fit into society, for whatever reason, aren't always the ones we should be quick to condemn.'

'So, it could be anybody: a bank clerk, a shopkeeper, a mechanic, a fairground worker . . .'

'You're right, of course. Anything is possible.'

Irene went to the kitchen and prepared a couple of cool drinks. Sheridan scanned the room and noticed a photograph of Elizabeth on the fireplace. For the first time he recognised certain features which were similar to his own - a sad reminder of part of his life that was missing. Her death was so utterly pointless.

Irene's voice broke the silence. 'Jim, come into the back garden for a while. It's too hot in here.'

He followed her outside and they sat opposite each other on white plastic chairs. Sheridan sipped cold pineapple juice. His eyes ran down her body as she lit a cigarette. He noticed she had lost considerable weight since their first meeting several weeks earlier. To Jim Sheridan she was still an attractive woman.

'Have you made any progress?' she asked.

'I hate to say it, but I haven't had any success. It's so different to my usual line of work.'

'I should have known better than to involve you in a murder hunt. Perhaps you should give it up as a bad job.'

'You want me to catch the killer. That's what you want, isn't it?'

'You are one man working alone and you don't have the authority or resources that the police have. What are you going to do?'

'I don't honestly know. My enquiries were useless. Even with the help of Carl Lewis there doesn't seem to be a way forward.'

'Carl Lewis?'

'Yes. The man from BB Investigations. We're supposed to be working together on this.'

'That's not the impression he gave me. He said a murder case was beyond his scope and that it was pointless to consider it.'

Sheridan frowned. 'Really? When he came to me he said you couldn't afford to employ him because it would be too costly.'

Irene looked up at the sky, then lowered her gaze. 'I'm not without money. So what's his game?'

'He thinks we can work together as a team, that's all. He *did* mention the reward.'

'He's not interested in catching Elizabeth's murderer. He just wants the money. He's a spiv, an entrepreneur, a crooked salesman.'

'I don't know what this man's motives are,' he continued. 'I've been around for a long time and he knows it. He probably believes we can catch this killer. He said the murderer would strike again and he wasn't wrong.'

'Come on, Jim, anyone could have made a prediction like that. Don't be taken in by him. You might regret it.'

Sheridan finished his drink. After ten minutes of casual conversation he decided to return to his office.

Irene showed him to the front door and left him for a moment. On her return she showed him an earring. 'I asked the police to let me have it back. Elizabeth was wearing it on the night she died. It's yours to keep.'

'What happened to its partner?'

'The other has gone missing. More likely than not the killer took it with him.'

'Did *they* tell you that?'

'No. She was wearing the pair on the night she was killed. I told them she only wore the one.'

'Thanks, Irene. Well, I'll love you and leave you. Look after yourself. Call me any time if you need me.'

Irene Collinson could feel a deepening emotional attachment to Sheridan, and was yearning to see more of him. He drove away, turning things over in his mind. The missing earring was an important clue regarding the killer's state of mind. He recalled having read about murderers who took personal items belonging to their victims as trophies so they could be incorporated into their fantasies at a later stage. Such items gave them a feeling of accomplishment.

He shuddered at the thought.

The taking of items of clothing or jewellery from a victim was an idiosyncrasy associated with serial killers.

Sheridan opened the window, threw his jacket over the client's chair and put the earring on his desk. Apart from the photograph of Elizabeth, it was the only memento he had.

He thought about his next move and considered calling Carl Lewis. There again, why should he? Lewis hadn't telephoned him for some time and it was difficult to determine whether or not he was really interested in solving the case.

He slumped into his chair, picked up the earring and held it in front of his eyes. Tiny points of light were blinking as he slowly rotated it. It was impossible to imagine holding such a dainty article and feeling the thrill of excitement that a murderer feels as he mentally re-enacts his crime.

Somebody, somewhere, was doing just that.

He held it tightly and shut his eyes, trying to picture his daughter when she was alive. He became oblivious to the noise from outside, until the office door crashed open.

He looked up, startled.

'Please forgive us. We knocked, but there was no answer,' said DC Palmer.

DC Steve Rivers explained who they were. Sheridan arranged a couple of chairs for them. The sudden intrusion caused a feeling of tension in his stomach.

'We're making enquiries into the deaths of Elizabeth Collinson and Angela Ross,' Rivers began.

Sheridan was never quick to judge people, but there was something unpleasant about Rivers' manner. He could sense trouble. 'I see. How can I help you?' he asked, in a pleasant manner.

'What sort of relationship, if any, did you have with Elizabeth Collinson?'

Rivers wasn't pulling punches.

'I believe you already know the answer to that.'

'Just answer the questions Mr Sheridan, please,' Palmer said, as if acting the part of a referee.

Rivers gave his partner a dirty look. Palmer decided to keep his mouth shut.

'I did not become acquainted with Elizabeth Collinson.'

Sheridan decided to say as little as possible. Rivers continued questioning.

'Where were you on the evening of March 20th?'

'I was in Norwich,' came the quick reply.

'You seem to have a good memory,' said Rivers. 'What were you doing?'

'Visiting family and friends,' Sheridan replied, emotionally hurt.

'Well now, Mr Sheridan, we'll have to check your story to see if it ties up. I believe you once spent some time with the girl's mother . . . Well?'

'That's correct.'

'But you didn't tell the police that it was your daughter who had been murdered. Seems odd to me.'

'Look here, I never met her. Why on Earth should I want to kill her? And who told you she was my daughter?'

'We're checking the report of a sighting of a smartly-dressed, middle-aged man who was seen talking to Collinson shortly before she was murdered. That could have been you.'

'It wasn't me,' Sheridan said calmly. 'And you haven't answered *my* question.'

'Don't get cocky with me,' Rivers said, leaning forward. 'We're here to ask the questions. You just be a good lad and answer them. Okay?'

'Well what about Irene Collinson's previous relationships? Have you checked those too?'

Rivers smiled. 'You don't listen, do you? Don't try to tell me my job or I'll make life difficult for you. Now, you wouldn't like to lose your little detective job, would you? I'm sure you wouldn't want to be driven out of this festering hovel.'

Harsh words. Rivers offensive attitude was most unprofessional. Sheridan became increasingly annoyed but managed to keep his subjective feelings hidden. At Palmer's request he wrote down the names and telephone numbers of the people he had visited in Norwich.

The detective constables were ready to leave. Rivers reached for the earring which was lying on the desk.

'Where did you get this from?' he asked, looking perplexed.

Sheridan sighed and explained that Irene had given it to him as a memento.

'A memento, eh?.'

Rivers tossed it onto the desk. The answer seemed reasonable enough. Nevertheless, he would check to see if he was lying.

Without saying a word the two men left the office.

Sheridan was left feeling dazed by his encounter with the detectives. He was vulnerable now, and the hurt of Rivers' ridiculous suggestion that he could be the murderer would stay with him for a long time.

He opened the drawer and placed the earring in an empty matchbox. Perhaps it was a good thing that the police knew he was Elizabeth's father, but how they had come by that information was still a mystery.

The fact that he was a potential suspect fuelled him with determination.

He had nothing to hide, nothing to lose.

He picked up the telephone and called the local newspaper.

The hunt was on.

TWELVE

The Blackpool incident room was buzzing with activity. Much to his satisfaction, Naylor now had the help of an extra twenty officers, and the public were responding to the appeals. The information coming in was analysed and entered into the system.

The two men, who had accompanied Angela Ross when she left The Unicorn, made themselves known to police officers. They were extremely helpful but were unable to say if anyone was loitering near the public house. The murderer had, so it seemed, taken advantage of the dense fog.

The superintendent removed his jacket and opened the office window. He took several deep breaths in a vain attempt to revitalise his jaded body and troubled mind. He was disappointed with the investigation so far. The killer was lucky or clever; perhaps a combination of the two.

Naylor couldn't stop the thoughts and images. He knew that the monster inside the man was ugly to the point of being pure evil, yet the appearance of the man himself might be totally innocuous. He might be charming, good-looking, intelligent, helpful. He was the man next door. He might be somebody's husband. He was somebody's son. *Somebody's son. What kind of a life could instill such violence in a person?*

George Naylor could only imagine the impact of the heartache and feeling of loss experienced by the victims' parents, friends and relatives. He had watched his own daughters grow into adults. He was always there to help and advise them. Now, he was a proud grandparent.

The callous knock-on effect of the murderer's aspirations had severed the bloodlines that might have provided the same pride and happiness for Irene Collinson and the Ross family. He thought about a mother and father who might have held their tiny baby and cried with joy. A newborn child to be loved and cherished. Another human being to make his way in the world, only to be engulfed in violent thoughts and grotesque daydreams ultimately leading to murder as a way of gaining self-worth and contentment.

There were so many unanswered questions. He needed results. Despondency was setting in, and frustration for allowing the case to get under his skin.

Naylor's resolve was beginning to crumble.

Dr Christian Purslow's examination revealed no semen in or on the body of Angela Ross. Forensic scientists arrived at the same conclusion after examining the girl's clothing and personal effects. Naylor was irritated by the lack of clues. DNA evidence was a powerful tool in the conviction of a murderer; without it the police would need compelling physical evidence, such as fingerprints or fibres, in order to convince a jury.

Murder squad detectives were searching for a mentally deranged person. Unfortunately, the killer was in control. He would not show any outward signs of his condition. Dr Purslow intimated as much in his conversations with the superintendent. The murderer, he said, was boiling with revenge and violence. He hated women with a passion, as was evinced in the deep cuts, frenzied stabbing and the use of pliers. This deduction came about after a close examination of Angela Ross's nipples. Other marks on the body - not immediately apparent to the pathologist - were thought to be bite marks, situated on the breasts and face. The indentations were indistinct and could not be used for comparison purposes by a forensic odontologist in the event of a suspect being arrested.

The killer was forensically aware.

What was the driving force behind his desire to murder? What was the trigger? George Naylor was troubled particularly by this man's methods, his awareness and brutality. The man they were hunting was an extremely violent offender who was planning his moves, and was being driven by uncontrollable hideous desires.

The superintendent tried to shut out the voice in the back of his mind that kept saying, 'Who's next?'

The office door swung open. Derek Oxley walked in and said, 'George, one of our uniformed lads has found an important witness: an elderly man who lives on Box Street, close to the murder scene.'

Naylor felt a surge of excitement.

'His name is Edward Kearney,' Oxley continued. 'Reckons he saw Angela Ross shortly before she was murdered.'

'Any details?'

'Very few, I'm afraid. Kearney was a little worse for drink at the time of the interview. The officer who spoke to him said he was incoherent at times.'

'Derek, this could be important. Go to the address yourself and speak to this Edward Kearney. Take your time and get everything you can out of him. Report back to me straight away. I want to know the outcome.'

Oxley left immediately. Naylor hoped for a description of the murderer. It was something, at least, he could use to his advantage.

Old grey-haired Kearney offered the inspector a chair in his small gloomy living room. Although in his seventies he had sobered up enough to be able to offer a satisfactory account of what he had seen. Oxley explained who he was and the reason for his visit. The old man sat down and coughed heavily.

'I've already told the police what I know,' he said, his voice croaky.

'I appreciate that, Mr Kearney. We need to go over the details again.'

'I'll do what I can for you.'

'Thanks. Now then, I want you to think back to the Friday night when the murder occurred. You left The Unicorn at eleven p.m. Is that correct?'

'I think it was after eleven.' Kearney pondered whilst scratching the white straggly hairs on his chest.

'Think very carefully. This is important. Was it *after* eleven?'

'I usually leave the pub at about eleven o'clock, sometimes a bit later, by five or ten minutes.'

'Are you sure?'

'Let's put it this way, inspector, it was *definitely* between eleven and quarter past. I can't say exactly when I left the pub.'

'And what did you see?'

Kearney cleared his throat. 'It was really foggy, but I do remember seeing Angela talking to a man. I got close and almost bumped into them.'

'Did you see her face?'

The old man admitted that he only saw her from behind. He was certain it was Angela, owing to her build and the clothes she was wearing.

'What can you tell me about the man?'

'I only saw him for a second or two. He put his head down, you know, like he didn't want me to see his face. He wants locking up forever, he does.

Nice girl, Angela. She used to get me baccy and fags sometimes. Grand lass. You will catch him, won't you?'

Oxley had no intention of pushing Kearney for quick answers. He wanted to assess the witness in order to judge the validity of the information.

'We're trying our best. You can help us to catch him. Do you remember anything at all about this man? Please think carefully. Try to remember.'

'I'm sure he had dark hair . . . He was wearing a dark jacket.'

Oxley jotted down the details. 'Age? Height?'

'Difficult to say his age. About thirty, maybe. He was a little shorter than me.'

'And how tall are you?'

'I'm five foot nine. I used to be taller in my younger days.'

Dark hair. About thirty. Medium height. It was coming together. A basic description was better than none at all.

'Did he say anything? Did you hear him speak?'

'No.'

'Did anyone pass you *after* you carried on?'

'I'm sure nobody passed me, inspector.'

'If you thought it was Angela, why didn't you speak to her?'

Kearney coughed heavily again, trying to release the thick catarrh from his windpipe. 'Don't know, really. I was feeling a bit tired and wanted to get home. I didn't think she was in any kind of trouble.'

'You *definitely* saw Angela in The Unicorn?'

'Yes. She was with her friend, the tall girl. I can't remember her name. There were plenty of blokes in the pub, you know. This fellow who killed Angela might have been one of them.'

Kearney had helped all he could. The inspector thanked him. He was glad to get out of the house, away from the overwhelming stink of stale tobacco smoke.

George Naylor was busy, as usual, working his way through a pile of reports. As soon as Oxley appeared he waved him into the office.

'Did you get much, Derek?' he asked.

Oxley told him what Kearney had seen. Naylor seemed disappointed. 'How much credence can we allow him? He's old and he was probably drunk when he came out of the pub. How reliable is he?'

'He seemed to know what he was talking about. Let's face it George, we've nothing else to go on. I know what you're thinking. The description he gave could apply to half the men in Blackpool.'

'That description could fit half the men in this police station. If only we could be more specific about the age. Kearney reckons he was around thirty. That means he could be mid-twenties to mid-thirties. If we trawl the system for men in that age range - men with a history of violence - we'll be looking at thousands of potential suspects.'

'Let's concentrate on Blackpool first. The murders occurred here. There's a fair chance he's on our own doorstep.'

'I agree with what you're saying, Derek. There are many leads to follow up and names are being put forward by the score. Even a school headmaster has been reported to us. Let's keep at it. We'll catch him. It's only a matter of time. Has anything come in on Karen Lawson?'

'Not yet. Her husband has been questioned. He doesn't know where she is, and doesn't seem bothered either. It's no wonder they're getting divorced.'

'She could hold vital information. When did she go missing?'

'She was last seen with Angela Ross on Friday night. Nobody has seen her since then. If they have, they aren't telling us.'

'What a carry on. Another thorn in the arse of this investigation.'

'The local radio station and newspaper could help us on that one, George. What do you think?'

'Give it another day or two. If she doesn't turn up we'll *have* to find her, whatever it takes.'

THIRTEEN

BB Investigations was situated on Church Street near the town centre, and above Topline Insurance Services.

Carl Lewis was sitting in his favourite position next to the open blinds, speaking into the telephone whilst gazing at the street below. Rebecca Watts didn't always see eye to eye with Lewis, but she was a valuable asset to the business and had four years' investigative experience under her belt. Lewis could trust her, and had learned how to handle her moods. After four years of working together he still fancied her like mad.

Rebecca Watts was thirty and divorced. She lived with her mother and 8-year-old son in Bispham, an area in the northern part of Blackpool. She was five feet six inches tall - the archetypal blue-eyed blonde with long hair resting on powerful shoulders. She was a 'keep fit' girl who enjoyed walking and weight training when she had the time. A two-year karate course provided the finishing touch, making her a woman with a sting in her tail.

Rebecca Watts' main priority was to provide for her son, Johnny. Her mother often looked after him when work took Becky out of town. She was lucky to have a mum like that.

Lewis and Becky were alone in the office. The other two guys, who worked for BBI, were out on business. At last, after a twenty-minute conversation, Lewis replaced the phone.

'Back to the showers again,' he said. 'A month in sunny Spain wouldn't do any harm. Just imagine it, Becky - the sun, the booze, the food, the nightlife.'

She rotated on her chair and smiled. 'And who would run this place while you were away?'

'The other two. Who else?'

'Oh. Not me, then? I thought I'd be first choice.'

'You are coming with me. You'd love it. Promise.'

Becky flashed an even bigger smile. 'Oh, that would be great; just you, me and little Johnny. And *you* can pay for all of it. All right then, it's a deal.'

'No little Johnny. Just the two of us.'

'Yeah, yeah, sure.'

'Ah, well, it was worth a try.'

Lewis glanced at his watch, confirming what his stomach was telling him. 'Becky, go and get us something to eat.'

She threw her pen onto the desk. 'Carl, you're worse than a pig. What do you want this time?'

'Fish 'n' chips with curry sauce. Here's the money. Get yourself something to eat as well.'

'I'm not hungry. By the way, you owe me money from last week, remember? I bought two lots of fish and chips, and there was the Jack Simmons Special.'

Lewis looked puzzled. 'Jack Simmons?'

'Yes, Carl. Don't tell me you've forgot. Steak pudding, chips and peas with a fish on top. That's a Jack Simmons Special according to you.'

'Oh, yeah, I remember now. Get me a JSS, then.'

When Becky returned she threw a copy of *The Gazette* onto his desk. Lewis's attention was absorbed by the newspaper article. 'Have you seen this picture of Sheridan on the front page? . . . Just listen to this.'

'I'm listening.'

'The headline reads, "Detective Hunts Daughter's Killer." It goes on about private detective Jim Sheridan, who has vowed to find the man who murdered his daughter. It then goes on to give details of Elizabeth Collinson and her mother, Irene. Well, I never. He's gone and done it. He's gone public.'

'Why shouldn't he?'

'Hang on a minute.' Lewis ran his eyes down the columns.

'What's the matter?'

'The report doesn't mention *my* name.'

Becky laughed. 'Why should it mention your name?'

'Don't you remember what I told you? Sheridan and I are working together. We're a team now.' He pointed to a paragraph near the bottom of the page. 'The reward has gone up. It now stands at fifty thousands pounds, thanks to the local tabloid throwing in an extra twenty grand. Wow!'

Becky went over to him and sat on the edge of the desk. 'Two private investigators on the trail of a vicious psycho, and a clever one at that. What chance do you think *you* have of catching him?'

Lewis got up and gave her a friendly tap on the head. He wandered into the kitchen. 'I'll let you know . . . when I've got the answer.' He returned with his meal and attacked it with ferocious determination. 'You know, Sheridan has made a smart move—'

'Carl, don't talk with your mouth full.'

'Okay, sorry. It's like I was saying. Sheridan is a smart guy. He'll get loads of leads to follow up. He needs my help more than ever now.'

Lewis finished the rest of his meal, crushed the wrappings into a ball and pitched them toward a small bin in the corner of the room. 'Good shot,' he said, triumphantly raising both arms in the air.

Becky pulled a face and asked him if he was going to visit Sheridan.

'You ring him. See if he's at the office. If he is, tell him I'd like to come and see him straight away if it's okay to do so.'

She rang the number and listened. 'He's not there.'

'Try again. Let it ring longer this time.'

Eventually, she got through. 'Sheridan said it's all right for you to go and see him.'

'Thanks, Becky. I don't know when I'll be back. You hold the fort while I'm gone,' he said, donning his leather jacket.

'By the way, the man in the van who was seen talking to Elizabeth Collinson . . .'

'What about him?'

'He works on the market, selling fruit and veg. He's a nice guy, from what I can gather.'

'Oh, really? So, if he's a nice guy he can't be the killer.'

Becky folded her arms and gave him a look of consternation. 'I didn't say that. Look, you asked me to check it out and I got results. Whether he's your killer or not is immaterial to me. He's probably one of dozens of men who knew Elizabeth Collinson. It's just my opinion. That's all.'

'Well, thanks for letting me know. I value your opinion. Honestly.'

'I should think so, too. You'd better be on your way.'

Creak, creak, creak . . .

'What on Earth's going on?' Sheridan said. He opened the door to his office. Lewis was standing at the top of the stairs, pressing his foot repeatedly on the twelfth step.

'Lewis!'

'Nothing to worry about. I'm just trying to stop this step from creaking.'

'I'd rather you leave it alone, actually.'

Lewis removed his foot and became serious. 'I'm sorry. I've come to see if you fancy visiting the Ross murder scene.'

'Well, I . . .'

'Come on, Sheridan. We've nothing to lose. Let's have a look round. We're partners now, aren't we?'

He considered. 'Very well. Let's go.'

Sheridan followed him to his car and admired it before getting in.

'What do you think of this for a car?' Lewis asked proudly.

'It's nice. Posh, you might say. I hope you don't mind me asking, but how can you afford it? After all, you're only a PI like myself.'

'Inheritance. I'm no big shakes as a detective. Never seen or heard of a rich private detective.'

He fired the engine. The motor powered ahead, the inertia forcing their bodies against the seats. Lewis stopped at the traffic lights. 'I read the article in the paper about you and your daughter. You must be serious about catching this monster. That was a clever move, Sheridan.'

'I probably wouldn't have gone public. The thing is, I've had a visit from SCU.'

The lights changed. Lewis pressed the accelerator. Inertia kicked in.

'I wish you wouldn't do that.'

'Sorry . . . You were saying, about SCU?'

'Two detective constables came to my office. They questioned me about my relationship with my daughter, the implication being that I might be involved with the murders.'

'Well, just tell me if you are and I'll collect the reward.'

'I think that's in rather poor taste, Lewis. If you're serious about catching a murderer you are going to have to change your way of thinking. I can do this alone you know.'

'I'm sorry I said that.'

'They ought to be more tactful. The question is: How did they know I was the father? Have you told anybody?'

'No. Your ex-girlfriend might have said something. The police will have questioned her...Not far to go now, Sheridan.'

71

Lewis pulled into a side-street off Seaforth Road. The two men crossed Seaforth and headed towards Hailey Road. Sheridan fastened his jacket and turned his face away from the snappy seafront winds. Lewis's black mop of hair was momentarily whipped into a frenzy, his hairline finally resting above his eyes.

They quickly surveyed the area before entering Hailey Road. Five days had elapsed since the discovery of Angela's mutilated body. The concentrated police activity was at an end. The presence of flowers at the entrance to the passage was evidence enough that something tragic had occurred there. Sheridan stooped and read several heartbreaking, sentimental verses and last farewells from those who were acquainted with the murdered girl. He remarked on how similar the passage was to a lobby: the ones which separated houses built in the late 1800s. The two men walked cautiously down the passage and stopped halfway. The victim's bloodstains were etched into the stone flag - a grim reminder of the shocking last moments of the poor girl's life.

Lewis spoke into a tiny cassette recorder indicating the date, time and location. 'What's that for?'

'It's a microcassette recorder. I use it for my investigations. It saves taking notes, and it comes in handy for taping interviews and stuff.' He released the 'pause' button and resumed his summary. His partner continued down the alley and out into the open. To his right was the wide back alley separating the two roads: Selbourne and Hailey.

Lewis joined him. 'You know, it must have been pitch black when he committed the murder. How could he have seen what he was doing?'

Sheridan pointed to the street lamp situated at the end of the passage.

'But the fog, Sheridan. It was foggy that night, wasn't it? Do you think he had a torch or something?'

'Don't know. Anything's possible, I suppose. Perhaps there was just enough light for him to see what he was doing. Have you noticed anything significant about that passage?'

Lewis looked down the passage and shrugged his shoulders. His partner pointed upwards and said, 'Look what's above it.'

Part of the terraced house, standing beside the passage, continued over and above it.

'I see what you're getting at. Someone might have heard something.'

'It's a possibility. I think you should start your enquiries there and find out what you can.'

'It's a secluded spot,' Lewis observed. 'The killer might possess knowledge of the area. He could be local.'

'Maybe. Angela Ross was on her way home. The killer could have been stalking her. What do you think, Lewis?'

'Yeah, sure he could. There's a chance he was drinking at the same pub. He decides to follow her because she leaves the pub on her own. It shouldn't be difficult to trace her last movements. What's our next move, then?'

'Talk to people. You concentrate your efforts around here for a while. I'm going to visit the pubs, starting with this one. Call me if anything important turns up.'

Lewis spoke into his recorder. The man from BBI visited the house next to the murder scene. Jim Sheridan ordered a pint of bitter at The Unicorn, where he introduced himself to the burly landlord. He said he was investigating the deaths of Angela Ross and his daughter, Elizabeth Collinson. The landlord remembered seeing Angela drinking there on that fateful night; after all, she was a regular, and who could forget her - the girl with the opulent figure, the girl with the stunning smile?

The killer could have been here, Sheridan thought. *He might even have occupied the same chair that I'm sitting in.* He sipped chilled beer and eyed the punters. The landlord started collecting the empty glasses. After a while he turned to Sheridan and said, 'Try The Elms.'

'Sorry, what was that?'

'The Elms. It's down the road toward the traffic lights, left-hand side. Angela went there most Fridays, so I'm told. You might try there.'

'Thanks, I will. Oh, by the way, did you see her leave here on Friday night?'

'Yes, as a matter of fact I did. She was one of the last to leave.'

'Did you notice anyone follow her out?'

'No, can't say I did.'

'Was anyone acting strange that night?

'Acting strange? You must be kidding. Half o' them that comes in here are complete idiots. I tell you, if Frankenstein came in here on a Friday night he'd look normal.'

'Thanks for your time.'

Nothing to go on as yet, he thought. *At least people are willing to talk.*

Next stop: The Elms. Sheridan ordered half of bitter and introduced himself to the landlord. He referred to Angela and Karen as the 'happy-go-lucky girls.' He couldn't remember having seen them on the Friday in question.

Sheridan made a call to his companion. Lewis was making progress. The family who lived next to the covered passage heard nothing unusual on the night of the murder. He had also visited Angela Ross's parents and managed to obtain a description of Angela and Karen. But where was Karen? Nobody knew.

The Elms' Saturday evening trade slowly filtered in. Sheridan stayed for a couple of hours and spoke to many of the punters, including a man named Martin Shaw. Sheridan was in luck. Shaw had spoken to Karen on the night in question. The detective was eager to find her.

'Do you to know where Karen might be? With a friend, perhaps?'

The young man shook his head. 'Sorry, no idea at all.'

'Did she seem to be in good spirits when you saw her?'

'Yes, everything seemed normal. I only spoke to her for a minute or two. I think Angela had gone to the bar.'

Sheridan asked if he had spoken to Angela that night.

'No, I didn't. I noticed this guy sitting next to Karen. He left her for a while, and I went up and said hello. She said this guy was a creep. Apparently, he'd been chatting them up all night.'

'What did he look like?'

'Well, I'd put him in his thirties. Black hair. Nothing unusual about him.'

'Anything else?'

'No. Like I say, I only spoke to Karen for a few seconds. I wish I could tell you more.'

'You've been most helpful. Can I get you a drink?'

'No thanks.' Shaw shook the detective's hand and said, 'Good luck with your investigation.'

Carl Lewis was resting in his town centre apartment waiting for his partner to call him. Sheridan phoned to say he was waiting for him outside The Elms. He ended the call and lit a cigarette. Martin Shaw came out of the pub.

'Mr Sheridan, it's me again. I've just remembered something Karen told me.'

'Go on, I'm interested.'

'This guy said something to Angela about a dolly-house parlour maid.'

'A dolly-house parlour maid? Are you certain?'

'I'm fairly certain that's what she told me. It doesn't mean anything to me. I thought it might be worth mentioning.'

Sheridan thanked him. *Strange expression. Sounds Victorian,* he thought, and wondered if there might be a sexual connotation. Maybe it was a meaningless expression. Separately, 'doll's house' and 'parlour maid' conjured up simple yet totally different images. Was there a connection?

When Lewis arrived he told him what Shaw had said. The strange expression meant nothing to him.

Later that evening Sheridan spoke to his friend, Bert Davies, who was an avid reader of true crime stories and Victorian mysteries. He was mystified and intrigued by the expression, 'dolly-house parlour maid.'

In time, he would discover a possible solution to the riddle.

It wasn't a meaningless remark at all, but something far more sinister.

FOURTEEN

Naylor was ploughing into his egg, chips and peas. His appetite was, as always, keen. In contrast, Oxley was eating nervously as if testing each morsel for any sign of poison.

Steve Rivers and Palmer were seated a few tables away from their superiors. Palmer picked at his salad. Rivers made chip butties smothered in red sauce. 'Look at old Bulldog go at it, Rick. You'd think it was his last meal.'

'Steve, keep your voice down will you? Let's keep focused on the job.'

The superintendent chewed his last mouthful and patted his stomach. He was pleasantly exhausted with repletion. 'I enjoyed that,' he said. 'How's yours, Derek?'

'Not so bad, for a change.'

Naylor seemed cheerful enough, but Oxley knew something was amiss. He waited a few minutes then asked what was bothering him.

'I was thinking about the Collinson murder.'

'What about it?'

'We're not getting the right response from the public. Remember Jean Glover?'

'The old lady who says she saw a man talking to Liz Collinson shortly before she was murdered?' Oxley asked.

'Yes. Dozens of other sightings have been reported. They don't tally. From the account given by Glover, it looks like the girl may have twisted her ankle or pulled a muscle. His information could be vital to the enquiry. It just adds to the frustration, doesn't it?'

'And we all know how notoriously unreliable eyewitness accounts are.'

'If the smartly-dressed man *is* a real person, do you think he killed her, Derek?'

'No idea. For what it's worth, I don't believe a man of that age would engage in such a murder.'

Oxley was bating Naylor.

'I know what you're hinting at.'

'Yes you do, George. We've been down the same road before.'

'It's what they call offender profiling. Charlatans and amateur sleuths. Profilers are only armchair detectives. Besides, we've got outside help now.'

'How do you mean, outside help?'

'You've read about Sheridan, the PI?' Naylor was purposely flippant.

'Come on, you can't be serious.'

'I'm not. Anyway Sheridan's been questioned. Obviously, we like to know everything. Irene Collinson was evasive when questioned about *who* the father was, as well you know. It's a mystery no longer.'

'So what?'

'Don't you think we've got enough busybodies poking around already? We don't need profiles.'

'George, we need all the help we can get. It's a big world out there.'

'It *is* a big world. Trouble is, our world is different to that of the man in the street. Our kind only converse with each other. We don't communicate enough with the outside world. We learn things about ourselves and repeat our own myths.'

'So, it's time to change.'

'I prefer things the way they are. We've got private investigators thinking they can catch this murderer and, to make matters worse, we bring in some profiler who comes along and says, "Ah yes, the culprit is probably mid-to-late twenties, lives alone, out of work, picks his nose and wasn't breast fed." He can't help what he does because he was sexually abused as a kid.'

'Perhaps he does need help. Maybe we need it, too.' Oxley was not going to give up on this one.

'Nobody is going to tell us our job.'

'Nobody will, George. A profile could help us to narrow the search.'

Naylor stood up sharply. Oxley followed him out of the canteen. Rivers was listening as they passed him, trying to pick up the conversation.

'What's all that about, Steve?'

'Don't know, Rick. Something seems to have upset the old bulldog.'

The two officers were out of earshot. Oxley was determined to have his say. 'Let's give it a try - please.'

'Listen to me. We can solve this on our own.'

'But how long will that take? We're talking Blackpool here. We're talking about the gay capital of Britain with its millions of tourists; we're talking weekend visitors, scum-bags, hordes of lads looking for a quick jump outside some poky nightclub, and the suspect list is increasing by the minute.'

'It's going to look great in the newspapers!' Naylor shouted. 'Blackpool's SCU bring in Cracker to help solve the case. That's like saying we can't do our job properly, we are failing.'

Naylor walked on, his anger engulfing him.

'The newspapers don't need to know about it,' Oxley said, catching up to him.

The officers squared up to each other like two boxers before a fight.

'If we didn't tell the newspapers what we were doing and they found out, they would lose confidence. The journalists would take us to the cleaners.'

'George, you're being paranoid. It's not the attitude and you know it.'

A WPC approached and waited her turn to speak.

'I'm not in the mood to discuss this, Derek. We've got a murderer roaming the streets who is either lucky, or very clever, and you are prepared to let somebody come in and balls it up. It's not good enough.'

'Excuse me, sir.' The WPC raised her hand slightly, as if addressing a school teacher.

'Wait a minute,' snapped Oxley. 'It might turn out that we're not as clever as we think we are. You'd rather listen to Christian Purslow's views. He's a pathologist, for goodness' sake.'

'Enough for now. We'll talk about this later.' He turned to face the WPC.

'Sorry to interrupt, sir. There's a woman waiting to see you. She specifically asked for you.'

'What's it about?'

'She wouldn't say much. Her name is Karen Lawson.'

A sense of relief and excitement came over the two men. They looked into each others eyes. Oxley gave a double nod: an apologetic gesture that Naylor understood. Their contrary perspectives on offender profiling melted away . . . for the time being.

Naylor instructed the police officer to bring the girl to his office. He wanted Oxley to be present.

Karen Lawson was wearing a lightweight zip-up jacket, pale-blue pedal-pushers and trainers. She sat down opposite George Naylor, removed her tinted sunglasses. Naylor was moved by the sadness in here bloodshot eyes.

The inspector was seated to her left, pen and notebook to hand. He made the usual introductions. Karen said she had information that might prove useful.

'It must be a terrible shock,' Naylor said. 'Would you like a cup of tea?'

'Yeah, wouldn't mind one.'

The inspector left the office and asked for some tea to be brought in. On his return Karen began her story.

She had lived in the South Shore part of Blackpool for several years. It was quickly ascertained that she had indeed gone home after spending the evening with Angela Ross. Following a blazing row with her husband she had packed a few necessary items and left to join her sister in Manchester.

Naylor started his line of questioning.

'Do you often have rows with your husband?'

'Yeah, all the time.'

'Your husband was definitely at the house when you got home?'

'Yes, he was.'

'What time was it when you arrived home?'

'About ten past eleven. I went home in a taxi.'

Naylor asked if Angela had any boyfriends. Karen became fidgety and irritable.

'No regular boyfriends. Not for a long time.'

'Was she sleeping with anybody?'

'Whenever she got the chance, yeah.'

'Who was the last person she slept with?'

'Look, I didn't come here to answer questions about her sex life. If you're asking me if she slept around, then yes, she did.'

'Mrs Lawson, we appreciate you coming here to speak to us,' Oxley came in, 'but we're not trying to paint a bad picture regarding your friend's . . .'

'Shagging around?' Karen said. She smiled, then the sadness came back.

'I wouldn't have put it quite like that,' Oxley murmured.

A gentle knock sounded on the door. Karen's tea had arrived. The superintendent asked if she knew of anyone who wanted to harm Angela. 'Not to that extent,' she answered. 'She had rows with people, but that was Angela. Nobody hated her. I can't think of anybody who would have wanted to hurt her.'

'Was she into drugs?' Naylor asked.

'No. Look, I want to get to the point of why I've come here. There's a man I think you need to know about.'

This was *the* moment - the chance for a forbidden peek into the life of a deranged killer. Naylor decided to ease off with the personal questions. It was time to learn the reason for her visit.

'Is police tea usually as good as this?' Karen asked, feeling more relaxed.

'Not usually,' Oxley replied. 'Would you like another one?'

She shook her head.

'Well now, Mrs Lawson,' Naylor said, formally, 'you've answered our questions, and it can't have been easy for you. We are grateful. Now, tell me about this man. Do you know him?'

'Never seen him before. Me and Angie would meet up at The Elms, usually on Friday nights. This bloke came up talking to us and was acting a bit weird and started to annoy us. He wouldn't go away, you see, couldn't take a hint. We just wanted him to knob off.'

Naylor was not overly impressed. Oxley shared the same sentiment as his boss. Why did this particular man stand out from the others? He put the question to Karen.

'We had lots of men wanting to go out with us. I mean, most of them are just out for a quick jump or a blow job. He bought us a few drinks and told me he fancied Angela. He kept staring at her all the time. There was something strange about this one.'

'Was he there all night?' asked Naylor.

'Dunno. It was so busy we wouldn't have noticed him.'

Oxley was starting to believe that there might be something in her story. Naylor remained sceptical, but asked her to describe the man. Karen pictured him in her mind. She described him as late thirties, wearing a dark jacket and blue jeans. His hair was fairly long and black. He wore a moustache.

Oxley made notes and asked the colour of the man's eyes.

'They were blue.'

'And you're sure about the moustache?'

'Yes, inspector. He told me he came to the pub because he liked the music. Oh, and he said his name was Tony.'

Naylor took over the interview.

'Did he look dangerous or appear to be menacing in any way at all?'

'I wouldn't say dangerous. He had shifty eyes.'

'What about his height and build?'

'I reckon about five feet nine, average build.'

'Any distinguishing features: moles, scars, tattoos, unusual teeth?'

'Nothing like that; not that I could see.'

'Any particular accent?'

'Normal. What I mean is, like ours. I'm quite good with accents because I work in a chippy. You get used to talking to people who are on holiday. You've got a bit of Scottish in your accent.'

'I was brought up in Glasgow,' Naylor said meekly.

'Anyway, it sounded like he was from round here.'

Naylor asked if she could remember anything else.

'Nothing. This guy was a weirdo. That's the best way I can describe him.'

'Have you seen him before?'

'Never. He just turned up out of the blue.'

'Did you or Angela see him at The Unicorn later that evening?'

'No. If Angie saw him she would have mentioned it.'

'What time did you leave The Unicorn?'

'About eleven o' clock, but Angie stayed behind.'

'I see. Do you think you could help us to create an image of the man's face?'

'I'm sure I can,' she replied eagerly. 'Do you think he's the murderer?'

'Let's just say he's somebody we would like to speak to if only to eliminate him from the enquiry.'

Oxley got up and opened the door. She followed him into the incident room. Naylor stayed at his desk and wondered if the man who called himself Tony could be the killer.

'It looks like we're in business, George,' Oxley said, breezing into Naylor's office. 'She's helping to create the e-fit right now. Good thing she came along.'

'Indeed . . . I know you like to be as objective as possible, Derek, but what are your feelings about this man?'

'It could be significant. That's my opinion, for what it's worth.'

Dorothy Naylor rolled from one side of the bed to the other. Her right hand fell onto the bed sheet. The space next to her was unoccupied. She got out of bed, crept down the staircase and quietly entered the study.

'George, what are you doing up at this time?'

'I couldn't sleep. I'm better off down here doing some work.'

'You shouldn't be working so late.' Dorothy pulled up a chair and sat next to him. 'I think you need a break,' she said, placing her hand on his shoulder.

'I couldn't take a break, not even if I wanted to.'

'This case is getting under your skin, isn't it? Be honest.'

'I have to stop this murderer. I must stop him.'

'How is Derek Oxley coping with the enquiry?'

'Derek plods on, doesn't let anything bother him. I hate to say this, but I nearly lost my temper with him today.'

'What was it about?'

'He wants me to bring in one of these offender profilers, or whatever they call themselves these days. I don't go along with that sort of thing.'

'I know you like to do things your way, George. You've said it many times before, but suppose you wanted a profiler to help; how would you go about getting one?'

'I'd have to contact the National Crime Faculty.'

'And what kind of murderer are you dealing with?'

'He's a sex murderer. Why do you ask?'

'Are you an expert in sex murder, George?'

'Of course not. I like to think I'm an expert in catching criminals.'

'There you are then. You do your job and let the experts do theirs.'

'How do you mean?'

She walked over to the door and placed her hand near to the light switch. 'I think you should contact this National Crime Faculty, and do it soon. That's my advice. Come on back to bed now.'

She switched the light off. He followed her into the hall.

'You really think I should?'

'Yes, my dear, you should.'

'All right, I'm not going to argue with you. Let's see if they can help us catch this maniac.'

FIFTEEN

The sight of Blackpool's famous Tower was taken for granted by many of the town's residents. It was, thankfully, a major attraction to millions of holidaymakers. Its pulling power began on 14 May 1894. This huge replica of the Eiffel Tower could hardly fail to mesmerise the kids with its Adventure Playground, Circus and Aquarium, all housed within the belly of its foundations. It was made from 2,586 tons of mainly steel and took two years and six months to build. The original entrance fee was six 'old' pence.

Jim Sheridan gazed towards the top of the 518 feet construction. *Such a fantastic sight*, he thought. The weather had been unpredictable, and the blustery winds were bearable due to intermittent sunny spells. The high-sided buildings created a constant breeze which helped to sustain the mid-air suspension of the world's smallest kite, on sale for £3 each.

Sheridan stepped into a doorway and attempted to light a cigarette. He succeeded after the fourth flick of his lighter. He thought he had done well when he felt the weight of his shopping bag which contained bread, tea, milk, notebooks, folders and G-2 Pilot pens. But of course the detective was used to snacks consisting of steak puddings, pizzas, fish and chips. He couldn't buy a week's worth of food if he tried. His stock of stationery was the preparation for a busy week ahead. Since his photograph had been printed in the local newspaper the office phone had rung incessantly, sometimes late in the evening.

Sheridan finished his cigarette and carried on down Hey Street, guided by his subconscious mind. It seemed as if the world was empty, devoid of sound, devoid of human beings.

The letter was bothering him. Posted by hand at his Chapel Street office, and written anonymously. He was uncertain of its authenticity. Its contents were disturbing.

Still deep in thought, he turned left towards the Hounds Hill Centre.

'Out shopping, Jim?' Irene Collinson seemed to appear from nowhere. Her hazel eyes - minus the glasses - were as clear as spring water and looked less troubled than before.

'Irene, what a pleasant surprise. How are you?'

'Not too bad, thank you. I've started getting out and about again.'

'That's good. Do you fancy a bite to eat?'

'A tea would be nice,' she replied. They found a cafe. Sheridan ordered two teas and a sandwich, then sat down opposite Irene.

'I thought you might have called to see me,' she said.

'What makes you say that?'

'Two detectives came to see me a few days ago. They questioned me about Elizabeth's earring. I told them I gave it to you.'

'I'm not surprised they interviewed you. Was one of them called, "Rivers?"'

'I think so. Surely, they don't believe you're involved.'

'It's their job to ensure that all the suspects are checked.'

'It must have been awful being questioned by them. I have to say, I didn't think you'd want to appear in the local newspaper.'

'Why shouldn't I? It could work in my favour.'

She gave a look of disapproval. Sheridan became wary of her. She asked him why he was not embarrassed to admit to having a child he did not know about.

'These things happen, Irene. It could have been different, but it wasn't. And why should it matter any more? I want to catch this murderer.'

She raised her eyebrows and asked if he had seen Carl Lewis.

'I thought you might ask about him. We visited the place where Angela Ross was murdered.'

'What was it like?'

'You mean, the murder scene itself?'

'Yes.'

'It's a sort of covered passage. It's not far from where she lived.'

'He got lucky then. There aren't many places like that where a man can take a girl and murder her.'

Sheridan took a bite of his roast beef sandwich. Irene could sense something was wrong, and asked what was bothering him.

'You could be right in saying he's lucky. Desperate too,' he answered.

'He'll trip himself up, sooner or later. They've printed a picture of the suspect in the newspaper.'

'He could be a holidaymaker, or somebody passing through town.'

Irene offered him a cigarette.

'No thanks, not now. I've got to get back to the office soon. I need to speak to Lewis.'

'Look, Jim, about this Carl Lewis . . .'

'What about him?'

'Get rid of him.'

'I can't do that.'

'The reward has gone up. He's only interested in the money. He thinks two heads are better than one.'

'There are easier ways of making money. Do you think Lewis doesn't know how hard it is to catch a lone murderer? Come on Irene, get real.'

'He's a kid compared to you. You're good enough on your own. And remember, I did ask *you* to find our daughter's killer.'

'You didn't ask me directly; and don't forget, you were the one who went to BB Investigations before coming to me.'

'I'm aware of that, but I didn't know what Lewis was like. He wanted too much money and . . .'

'And what?'

'Well, I said you were the father. I also told him I would go elsewhere if I had to.'

'I thought as much. I should have been the first to know about Elizabeth, not some outsider!'

'Keep your voice down, Jim. You know what this means, don't you?'

'It means he told the police about you and me.'

'That's right. I wouldn't be at all surprised if Lewis is investigating you.'

'I can't believe that.'

'Can't you? I bet he's following you right now. You could be a prime suspect.'

Sheridan shook his head. 'Even if that were true, those detectives would have checked my alibi. I was in Norwich when Elizabeth was killed. Let's not get into all of this, Irene.'

'If you know what's good for you, you'll keep Lewis at arms length. He's dangerous and deceitful.'

They finished their teas and sandwiches and sat on a bench outside the cafe. Irene moved closer to him, feeling happy to be near him once again.

A small crowd gathered around the blind guitar soloist. His faithful guide dog was lying on a blanket, its head close to the open guitar case which served as a receptacle for anybody who chose to make a donation. The guitarist played the last chord of a Shadows number, paused for a few seconds, then strummed the chord of the next tune. He played on, beautifully, with depth and feeling.

Sheridan turned to speak to her. His words were crushed by the sight of tears running down her face.

'Irene, what's the matter?'

'He's playing Elizabeth's favourite tune,' she replied, lowering her head; 'the theme music from *Titanic* . . . I'll be all right in a minute.'

He handed her a couple of tissues. Sadness momentarily erupted in his heart. He swallowed deeply, determined to maintain his composure throughout the touching rendition.

At last, it was over.

'I'm sorry about that, Jim.'

'No need to apologise.'

'There was a time when she played that song over and over. I swear I can sometimes hear it playing in her bedroom.'

'It's a beautiful song,' he murmured.

Irene wiped the tears from her eyes. 'I'll be on my way. I've kept you long enough.'

'Don't go yet. I want to ask your opinion about something.'

'Go ahead, I'm all ears,' she said, composing herself.

He recounted details about Angela Ross, Karen Lawson and what she had told Martin Shaw.

'Apparently, Karen Lawson was accosted by this stranger who took a fancy to her friend. This is what Shaw told me.'

'And this is the man who's picture is in the paper: the police artist's impression?'

'Yes. The stranger said his name was Tony, and he said something to Angela Ross about a dolly-house parlour maid.'

'You think it could be important, Jim?'

'I'm not sure. Does it mean anything to you?'

'Dolly-house parlour maid,' she repeated. 'I Don't know. "Parlour maid" could be some reference to outfits that parlour maids used to wear.'

'Yes, I suppose it could. What about "dolly-house?"'

'He might have said "doll's house," but it doesn't make any sense. It's meaningless drivel.'

'Perhaps. If you come up with any ideas, share them with me.'

The couple stood up and faced each other.

'I will. Please keep in touch, Jim. Take care.' Irene wanted to kiss him, but felt the moment wasn't right. Sheridan promised to keep in touch. He waved goodbye as she mingled with the crowd, and had forgotten to show her the letter.

Sheridan joined the onlookers in front of the guitarist. He played another well-known tune. He dropped a £2 coin into the open case and stroked the Labrador's head.

Time to get back to the office.

He walked slowly, thinking about Irene, wondering if she wanted him back again. Understandable, under the circumstances; but he knew what the outcome would be. As time moved on she would become more possessive. She could be persistent, even clever. She was like that when he dated her all those years ago. He felt sorry for her, but would do anything to help ease her pain. He couldn't afford to allow himself to get too close.

Why did Irene want to destroy his relationship with Lewis? Did she really believe him to be deceitful? Or, was Irene trying to push him into 'going it alone' by instilling mistrust and uncertainty in the hope that he would give up the investigation and come to her?

Sheridan ended up in the King Edward V11 public house where he ordered a double whisky and a pint of bitter. He tried to forget about Irene Collinson, Carl Lewis, the investigation, the murders . . . and the letter. It didn't take long for the alcohol to take effect. He wondered what he would be doing with his spare time if he was in retirement. Detective work was the only thing he knew, and the challenge was out there waiting for him - perhaps the last challenge he would ever have.

Jack Robson was sitting comfortably in the living room of his home in Plymbey, a few miles from Sedgeburn. He turned to the next page of the *Lancashire Evening Post*. A picture of 25-year-old Lucy Beckett caught his eye. The caption above it read, 'Where is Lucy?'

The article stated that detectives had recently travelled to Blackpool to question acquaintances of the missing girl. Previous lines of enquiry had proved negative. Friends and relatives were in fear for her safety.

Jack Robson held the key to solving the mystery of her disappearance. The cassette, which he found on that damp morning in January, was sitting on a shelf next to him - the cassette with the 'noisy' music on it and the haunting voice uttering the words, 'Don't leave me, Lucy . . . Stay with me forever.'

SIXTEEN

For a moment he didn't know where he was. A movement from above the skylight startled him as he looked up from his dilapidated camp bed. The herring gulls had gathered along the roof top. Their piercing *kyow-yow-yow* cry was better than any alarm clock. It was 6.45 a.m. *What a fool I am,* he thought. He looked around the tiny attic room and noticed the empty bottle of Benmuir Scotch Whisky lying on its side. He knew what it was all about. A couple of drinks always helps when you've got problems. Why not? Forget your worries. His worries were still there, accompanied by a monumental headache and a feeling of failure. It wasn't the first time. Was there ever going to be a last time?

Sheridan used to have a drink problem. It was something he learned to live with. In the end he managed to control it. A pint of beer every now and again. No harm done. An occasional tipple of whisky. No problem.

He got dressed, slowly climbed down the narrow stairs and went into the kitchen. He splashed his face in cold water. He reached for the cabinet on the kitchen wall, found what he wanted. *Two headache tablets and plenty of water. That should do the trick.* Then he cooked two eggs, bacon, sausage and prepared strong coffee. He ate breakfast in the office and listened to the radio for a few hours. There was no update on the murders.

10.30 a.m. Sheridan was walking on the beach. The sea air finished off the headache, taking him beyond the death-warmed-up stage. White cotton wool clouds were gently sailing through the sky. A fresh wind blew from the Irish Sea, carrying the innocent jingle of the donkeys' bells. The revered donkeys were trotting tirelessly and obediently, carrying excited children for £1 a ride.

The beach was almost deserted. Times had changed. He could remember visiting Blackpool on the train, accompanied by his parents and sisters. It was a great feeling when the Tower came into view, looming on the horizon. He could even remember the Punch and Judy shows. His sisters watched them, laughing and shouting at the comical puppets whilst mum and dad searched for a spot to place their deck chairs.

Old times. Good times. Times to remember.

In the 1960s you could hardly see the Sands for deckchairs. The cheeky era of 'Kiss Me Quick' hats and penny slot-machines - look through the viewfinder at the naughty ladies - had gone forever. Thankfully, the donkeys and Golden Mile fortune tellers were doing the rounds. They were reminders of the old Blackpool that Sheridan, like millions of other people, had not forgotten.

He embraced the cool breeze and tried to forget his problems - easy when you're drunk, almost impossible when sober. The reality of the harsh world returned like a recurring nightmare.

The trip to Norwich was bothering him.

He could not remember exactly what he was doing at the time when Elizabeth was murdered. Perhaps his alibi *was* weak, after all.

Sheridan kicked the stone steps to remove the sticky sand and began the journey back to his office on Chapel Street. When he arrived Darren told him he had a visitor.

The man was sitting in the client's chair, facing the window. Broad shoulders, black hair. The face was familiar.

'You don't know me, do ya?'

'Oh, but I do. How could I forget the man with the right hook?' Sheridan replied, sinking into his chair.

Sheridan opened the right-hand top drawer and saw that nothing was missing. He shook the matchbox and heard the rattle of his daughter's earring.

'What brings you here, Mr Taylor?'

'I'm tired of these detectives bothering me and questioning me about these murders. I want it stopped.'

'There's nothing I can do about it.'

Taylor got up and showed a clenched fist.

'Just a minute . . .' Sheridan stood up and raised his open hands, hoping to pacify the brute. 'You start any fistycuffs and I'll have you for assault. Be sensible.'

Slowly, the unwelcome guest lowered himself into the chair.

'Now then, why have you come to me? You know I can't do anything to influence the police.'

'Maybe so, but you've been watching me.'

'That's not true. I'm a private investigator, just an everyday private investigator going about my business.'

'Going about what business?'

'My work doesn't involve you, Mr Taylor. Now that you're here, would you mind telling me what you do for a living?'

'I'm not a killer, if that's what you think. I'm a thief.'

'That's nice.'

'The Pigs already know about me, so it's no use telling on me. Got it?'

'Don't intend to. When was the last time the police visited you?'

'About a week ago.'

'What did they ask you?'

'Hey, come on. What is this?'

'I'm interested. Did they ask you about your whereabouts on the nights of the murders?'

'They did.'

'Were you arrested?'

'No. I can prove where I was when these girls were wasted.'

Wasted. Nasty American term. Sheridan hated it. 'You have nothing to worry about. You've been kept under surveillance. They're checking you out, making sure you don't get up to any mischief.'

'Sounds about right. As long as it's nothing to do with you.' Taylor stood up sharply, knocking the chair over.

'Tell me something before you go. Do you know of anyone who would be capable of committing these crimes?'

'If I knew the answer to that I wouldn't be telling the likes of you. This killer's worth a lot of money. I read the papers too, you know. Don't come bothering me, Mr Private Eye. I don't like you, and I know where to come looking for you.'

He would never see Taylor again.

Sheridan then listened to a call on his new answer machine. Bert Davies had left a message, saying he was looking forward to a visit from him. No doubt he would want to know why he hadn't mentioned Elizabeth Collinson before now. Sheridan would have some explaining to do. Right now, other things were playing on his mind. The letter. Probably a hoax just like the hoax messages being left on his phone.

It was a pity nobody saw the person who posted the letter. *Might be someone local,* Sheridan thought. *Someone trying to throw me off the scent, for whatever reason.*

Sheridan rubbed his eyes and stared at the wall, admiring his own version of an incident room display showing maps and photographs of crime scene locations. His photos were taken from the newspapers and included the recent e-fit of the man wanted for questioning in the Ross enquiry. The crime scenes were marked with circles drawn on a map of Blackpool. The map was secured with long strips of Sellotape. Occasionally, it fell down. He was still trying to figure a way of sticking it firmly onto the wall.

6 p.m. Darren knocked and entered the office. 'I'm off home. Will I see you tomorrow, Jim?'

'I don't know what I'm doing tomorrow.'

Darren gave a quick wave. Halfway down the stairs he shouted, 'Don't forget to lock up.'

The slamming of the front door echoed throughout the building as the phone started ringing. Sheridan answered and listened as Lewis told him about a new suspect. A man, matching the description of the e-fit, was known to have slept with Angela Ross. Apparently, the suspect owned a van and carried a selection of tools. There was a possibility that the killer used tools to torture his victim.

Lewis's knowledge about the 'new' suspect, coupled with his previous concerns about Mick Taylor, could only mean one thing - he had access to 'inside' information.

He rang Irene, and was careful not to mention the drink problem otherwise she might nag him to death. She seemed fine and asked if there had been any developments.

'Nothing at the moment, Irene.'

She droned an about Lewis and the reward.

'Irene, we went through this yesterday. You're wrong about him, believe me.'

But she didn't believe him.

'I wanted to ask you about this dolly-house parlour thing,' he said, changing the subject. 'Have you thought about it?'

'As a matter of fact, I have. There's a shop in Coventry called Dolly House. They sell a wide variety of dolls.'

'Dolls? That doesn't sound promising.'

'Well, try this one. There's a string of shops up and down the country called Parlour Maid. They specialise in sex toys and lingerie.'

'That *is* interesting. Anything else?'

'Yes. Dolly's House happens to be the most famous brothel in Houston.'

'That sounds promising. How did you find out?'

'Oh, I got some of it from a friend, some off the Internet.'

'Well done. It's beginning to make sense when you think of it in the context of girls in sexy outfits working in brothels.'

'I suppose it does.'

'It doesn't make the e-fit man a killer.'

'Maybe not, but it's a start. At least you've made some progress. Are you going to see it through to the end?'

'It's hard to say. Life's full of surprises . . . I must love you and leave you.'

'One more thing, Jim, before you go. A friend has asked me to join her at the Bloombury Club. They do Line Dancing. Do you fancy coming along?'

'I'll think about it.'

Sheridan brought the conversation to a close. Irene was beginning to pick up the pieces of her life. He was pleased for her, and thankful for the info on the enigmatic dolly-house parlour maid. He wondered about its meaning and if any inference could be made about the mind of the person who said it - if indeed that was what he said.

It's true meaning would soon be revealed to him.

Jim Sheridan would be one step closer to understanding the mind of the murderer.

At 3 a.m. the following morning he woke up from a fitful sleep. The rain was pounding the windows of his home on Newington Avenue. He threw off the bedclothes and fumbled for his cigarettes and lighter. A few steps took him to the window. He peered incredulously into the street below. The tumultuous torrents were drilling relentlessly against the roofs of the parked vehicles. The road was a gushing river. He lit his cigarette and drew heavily on it, watching the water flow down his garden path.

He went downstairs, prepared a cup of hot chocolate and settled in his living room. He switched the table lamp on, sat down and listened to rain.

Then came the images: the beautiful face of his daughter; the flowers and the heartbreaking messages that accompanied them; Irene's hazel eyes burning into him, almost beckoning; Carl Lewis waiting in his car at the park's entrance . . . and the dingy attic above his office where he fell asleep from alcohol intoxication.

He wondered why he had got himself involved in a murder hunt. He needed to succeed in a big way, but in truth he was struggling with his own emotions, and doubting his ability to cope with the investigation.

The telephone rang.

'Jim Sheridan,' he barked.

'You got the letter?' The voice was deep and croaky.

'Yes. Who is this?'

'It doesn't matter who I am.'

'Look here, it's very late. I can do without this.'

'You understand the meaning of the letter?'

'I'm not sure I do.'

'Listen, there's more to come . . . I'll call you again.'

'What is it you want to tell me?'

'I know who the killer is. He's not too far away. Not far at all.'

'I don't believe you. You must know there's a reward waiting to be collected, so why not tell the police?'

'I don't need that kind of reward, Mr Sheridan. I'm not, let's just say, I'm not eligible. See you soon.'

'Wait. Hello! . . . Hello! . . .'

The caller hung up.

Sheridan dialled 1471.

The number was withheld.

SEVENTEEN

Jim Sheridan drove into town early next morning. His destination was BBI, on Church Street. He parked his Metro next to Lewis's BMW and gazed up at the office above Topline Insurance Services.

The time had come to share his concern about the letter, and consolidate the partnership.

Sheridan knocked on the office door and walked in. Lewis was sitting at his usual spot by the window.

'Come in, Sheridan,' he said. 'You look tired. Sit down and have a rest.'

'I didn't sleep so well.'

'I had the same problem. Terrific rain last night, wasn't it?'

Sheridan was about to answer, then noticed Rebecca Watts coming out of the kitchen. He was struck by her long blonde hair and athletic figure.

'Becky, this is Jim Sheridan.'

Sheridan offered his hand. Becky gripped it tightly.

'Rebecca Watts,' she said.

'Pleased to meet you, Mrs Watts.'

'Miss Watts, actually.'

The handshake lingered a little longer than Sheridan expected.

'A cup of coffee for Mr Sheridan, there's a good girl. Do you take sugar?'

'Just one, thank you.'

Sheridan took a seat opposite Lewis. 'I thought there would be a lot more people working here,' he said, looking around.

'It's a small unit. We're a bit quiet at the moment, luckily enough. How's your side of the investigation going?'

'Nothing promising. I'd like you to have a look at this.'

He passed the letter to Lewis who read it quietly: '"Need to speak to you urgently about Elizabeth murder. Mercenary killer involved. Can't reveal name yet. Soon, I hope. Man with blood on his hands seen running. I hate this evil bastard who rips and stabs the girls. He loves to hear them scream. He wants to do so much to them. He hurts them so much. He wanted Lizzie so much and now she's dead. He is sharpening his knife ready for another kill. Wait for my call."' Lewis shook his head. 'This is a hoax. You're not taking it seriously, are you?'

'I've given it careful consideration. But suppose it is genuine.'

'If it was genuine the writer would call the incident room here in Blackpool.'

'He could be scared. Maybe he doesn't want to involve the police.'

Lewis shrugged. 'Did you check the postmark?'

'It was delivered by hand to my office. Nobody saw who posted it.'

Becky returned with the drink. 'Coffee with one sugar,' she said, smiling.

'I've had a phone call too,' Sheridan continued. 'Early this morning. The caller mentioned the letter.'

'He actually rang you at home? What did he sound like?'

'Deep voice. Certainly not a young man. He said he knows who the killer is. He also said he was not eligible for the reward.'

'Anything else?'

'He just said, "See you soon," and put the phone down.'

'What's all this about, if you don't mind me asking?' Becky asked.

'I'm sure Sheridan would value your opinion, Becky.'

Sheridan handed the letter to her. She read it carefully, her expression changing from serene to one of disgust.

'I don't like the tone of that,' she said, her voice almost a whisper.

'What's *your* opinion, Miss Watts?'

'The letter talks about a mercenary killer. That means someone's getting paid to do the killing or . . .'

'Go on, Becky,' Lewis prompted.

' . . . or it's a soldier - a professional killer gone bad. It could be somebody who's been kicked out of the forces.'

'Yeah, could be,' Lewis said, raising his finger. 'That would explain his stealth and ability to remain unseen. This letter is hard to interpret. If it's genuine, what is he trying to tell us?'

'It's somebody who has met the killer,' Becky suggested. 'The letter-writer has seen the e-fit in the newspapers and thinks he knows who it is.'

'The e-fit could merely be a visitor to Blackpool, Miss Watts.'

'Good point,' she said. 'Getting back to the letter, it says, "Man with blood on his hands seen running." How does this guy know that? Not unless *he* is the one who saw the killer running from the murder scene.'

'That would be the logical interpretation,' said Sheridan.

'Why, then, is the letter-writer not eligible?'

'Becky, this isn't your case, remember. Me and Sheridan are working on this one.'

'I'm only trying to help. You don't mind me helping, do you Mr Sheridan?'

'Always open to suggestions, Miss Watts.'

'In my opinion it's a hoax. It's got to be. He's a nutter and that's all there is to it. Why don't you show it to the police?'

'Not yet, Lewis. There's nothing much they could do, and even if there was it would be given low priority, especially as it involves a private detective - and one who has been interviewed as a potential suspect.'

'They think you could be the killer?'

'I'm afraid it looks that way, Miss Watts. Two detectives came to my office and questioned me about the murder of my own daughter.'

'That's ridiculous,' Becky said indignantly.

'You're a private detective trying to solve the murders of your daughter and Angela Ross,' Lewis added, on his way to the kitchen.

'I know that. I can understand being questioned as a matter of routine. It was the way in which they went about it.'

'How do you mean, the *way* they went about it?' asked Becky.

'One of them was particularly nasty and arrogant. I resented the way they carried out the interview. It's bad enough when somebody is murdered, but to be spoken to in such a way . . .'

'Have you heard anything from them since?' she asked.

Sheridan shook his head. 'The trouble is, I can't remember exactly what I was doing when Elizabeth was murdered.'

'I wouldn't worry too much about it, Mr Sheridan. Nobody can remember everything they were doing at any particular time.' Becky swivelled on her chair and looked towards the kitchen. 'Carl, don't forget my cuppa.'

'I'll be right there,' came the reply.

Sheridan thought about what Irene had said concerning the man from Big Brother. The time had come to question Lewis about the origins of his investigative leads.

'Here's your cuppa, Becky. Your turn next time.'

'I *always* make the tea,' she said. 'Thanks a lot.'

'So, what's the next move?' asked Lewis.

'I'm going to wait for him to call me again.'

'And if he does call, you're going to go along with what he says?'

'That's right. Hoax or no hoax, I intend to find out who is behind all of this. What would *you* do?'

'I'd tell him to bugger off.'

Becky snorted.

'That's not my style. I have to know for sure whether or not it is a hoax, and besides, I can do without people calling me in the middle of the night.'

'You know best,' Lewis said, folding his arms. 'Suppose you get hurt?'

'Why should I get hurt?'

'You're taking a risk. He could be dangerous.'

'I'll take that chance.'

'I want to be there on the day.'

'That's thoughtful of you, Lewis. I'll keep in touch.'

'I'd like to know the outcome too,' said Becky.

'I thought you weren't interested in these murders?' Lewis snapped.

Her eyes shifted from one man to the other. The telephone rang. She turned her back towards them and took the call.

Sheridan stood up and looked down at Lewis. 'By the way, you mentioned a suspect: the man with the van and the tools.'

'What about him?'

'I'd like to know where you got the information from.'

'Always keep my ear to the ground. It's amazing what you can pick up from local gossip.'

'I see. Any luck, so far?'

'Nothing yet. I'll find out as much as I can about him.'

'Very good. Did you discover anything regarding the dolly-house parlour maid?'

'To be honest, I forgot all about it.' He waited until Becky ended her telephone conversation, then addressed her. 'Dolly-house parlour maid. Does that expression mean anything to you?'

'Not a thing,' she answered, throwing a glance at Sheridan.

'Thanks, anyway. Keep in touch, Lewis. Goodbye Miss Watts.'

Sheridan made his way to the door.

'Let me know if you hear from this mysterious caller again,' Lewis said. 'You don't have to face this alone.'

Sheridan pursed his lips and closed the door behind him.

Lewis drank the remainder of Sheridan's coffee and began tapping away at the computer keys. His attractive colleague moved closer to him and peered over his shoulder. He turned to face her.

'What is it?' he asked.

'Local gossip. That sounds interesting. Who told you about this man with the van? And what's the connection with tools?'

'You're being inquisitive.'

'I like to know what's going on.'

'Well, people talk about things, especially in pubs.'

'You don't drink much in pubs though, do you?'

'What's all this about?'

'It seems odd that you can suddenly come up with details about a possible suspect.'

Becky returned to her desk and fell into silence.

Why the questions? Lewis thought. *That's not like her.*

Becky accepted what he told her.

She knew he was astute enough to be able to latch onto new leads, but he had not told all that he knew.

EIGHTEEN

Sheridan had made discreet inquiries into the movements of three men whose names and addresses had been given to him by members of the public who believed they knew who the killer might be. They could not understand why, after calling the Blackpool incident room, their suspicions had not been given any credence. He assured them they were wrong. Police suspects were prioritised, as a matter of course. By now, their list of potential killers ran into the thousands. Sheridan was able to follow his leads immediately. They were the only ones he had. His detective work, however, was only peripheral. He had no way of finding out if any of them had previous convictions, other than by making discreet enquiries. The job of trying to ascertain their movements on the nights of the murders had also proved difficult. Carl Lewis's strategies were, more or less, the same. Both men were beginning to realise the inherent difficulty in obtaining pertinent information regarding their suspects.

Sheridan scored out the three names and wondered what to do next. He stood up and looked out of the window. The pub opposite seemed to be beckoning him. He fought the temptation.

Ten minutes later, his friend Davies walked into the office.

Davies was the same age as Sheridan, but looked ten years older. He was friendly, cheerful, and the kind of bloke who was always willing to give a helping hand. The arms of his glasses almost disappeared amongst the vestiges of what was once a full head of thick wavy hair. Most of it had disappeared in his twenties, leaving a bald smooth dome which shone whenever the light caught it. His protruding belly had evolved from years of taxi driving, with practically no exercise to keep the excess weight at bay. Owing to his shortness - five feet six inches - his work associates dubbed him, The Little Big Man.

'You scoundrel, Sheridan,' he barked, shutting the door behind him. 'You never told me, did you?'

His friend laughed and shook his head. 'Take a seat, Bert. What's bothering you?'

'You might have offered me a couple of chairs,' he replied jokingly.

'How's business?'

'Not doing too badly, I suppose. To get to the point, Jim - I didn't know you had a daughter.'

'Neither did I. Not until Irene Collinson came and told me. I was surprised . . . and shocked.'

'So was I. Me and the wife were upset. You have our sympathy. You know, I can still remember Irene Collinson. She was an attractive woman. That was some years ago. How come you're involved with this lot?'

'She thought I might be able to help.'

'Every credit for trying. The police ain't come up with much. If anybody can, it's you.'

'I wish I shared your optimism.'

'I thought it was a bit strange when you mentioned the Aristor Park murder. I thought to myself, Jim Sheridan on the trail of a murderer. That's not his bag at all. Then I learn about this daughter of yours.'

'I *was* going to tell you.'

'Not to worry. Have you discovered anything worthwhile?'

'Nothing, really.'

Sheridan put his friend in the picture. He explained his partnership with Carl Lewis, and his unfortunate encounter with Mick Taylor. Davies slid deeper into the chair, resting his chubby hands on his protuberant belly as he listened to his friend recount details of the Ross murder scene.

'There you have it; most of the story so far.'

'And how's this Lewis character doing? Is he any good?'

'He seems keen enough. He's managed to come up with a few suspects of his own, I'm happy to say.'

'So, what's it all about? Irene turns down BB Investigations because they're too expensive, and before you know it Lewis comes here knocking on your door offering to help you. What's his game?'

'Good question. Irene believes he's got an ulterior motive.'

'What's your view?'

'I think he's genuine. Maybe he wants the experience. Maybe he fancies the reward; well, half of it. It's not the kind of investigation private investigators take on, and yet I have a certain feeling about Lewis. You never know, but he might just come up with the ace card.'

'It sounds like you have faith in him. Perhaps he wants to be a hero.' Davies altered his position in the chair and took a folded sheet of paper from his trouser pocket. 'I've got something here for you, concerning your dolly-house parlour maid.'

'Oh, that! It's sorted. I spoke to Irene about it. Apparently, Dolly's House is a well-known brothel somewhere in Houston. Parlour Maid is the name given to a string of shops specialising in lingerie and things connected with sex, like, uh . . .'

'Dildos and things?'

'Yes, I suppose so.'

'This may interest you.' He threw the sheet onto the desk: a photocopy of an article from a True Crime magazine. Sheridan read the heading, 'Parlour's Dolly House - Murder of Patricia Burke.'

'Where did you get this from?'

'A friend from down South. He's an avid collector of crime books and magazines. We got talking about the murders up here. I told him about you and the parlour maid stuff. Bells started to ring. It took him hours to find the article. What you have there is a photocopy. The print is a bit murky, but it's readable.'

'I'm grateful, Bert. Tell your friend I appreciate his time and effort. Yours too.'

'No probs. On the subject of crime mysteries, you said you had a book for me.'

'I certainly have.' Sheridan lifted the book from the bottom drawer and handed it to him.

Davies held it in both hands as if it was an antique. 'Excellent, excellent. *Perfect Murder*. I've been trying to get a copy of this for years. How much do I owe you?'

'Nothing. It's a gift.'

Davies stood up and stretched his arms.

'Can't you stay a while longer?'

'I'd like to, Jim. I've gotta get back to my taxi or the people at the office will wonder what's going on.'

'Busy at the moment?'

'At the moment, yes. Sometimes busy, sometimes slack. You know what it's like. I get chance to read when it's slack. This book will come in handy during the day. Nightfall is a different matter. It's always busy at night. More young girls are hiring cabs now. They're not taking any chances. Nope, no chances at all. I'm making more money than ever before.'

'I'm glad to hear it. By the way, how's the wife?'

'She's fine. I must be on my way. See you soon. And thanks again for the book.'

'You're welcome.'

Davies made his exit. Sheridan made a brew, went back to his desk and read the photocopied article, 'Parlour's Dolly-House - Murder of Patricia Burke':

In the district of Finsbury in 1971, 54-year-old ex-stripper, Celia Parlour, purchased a large property which she used as a brothel. She produced a booklet listing the names of her girls and the prices of the services on offer. Parlour referred to them as her 'dollies' and, subsequently, the brothel became known as 'Parlour's Dolly House.' She only employed women with ample attributes in the belief that the majority of clients would find such women to be more desirable. The services included massage (plus extras), straight and kinky sex. Acts involving bondage and flagellation were available at extra cost.

25-year-old Patricia Burke was a favourite of the clientele. She regularly serviced a man who used the alias, John Edwards. Edwards' real name was Leonard Bertram Haines, a 53-year-old bank manager who lived with his wife on the outskirts of Epping Forest.

Haines was a sexual sadist who gained pleasure from inflicting pain on others. His sadistic sex acts were mild to begin with, becoming increasingly severe as time went on. He enjoyed caning sessions with his sex partner, striking her bottom and masturbating between strokes. He offered large sums of money to Burke - which she accepted - in return for prolonged periods of sadistic sexual abuse. Eventually, the pain became too intense and Haines was told to back off. The bribes continued. Burke complained to Parlour regarding his persistent requests to inflict pain. He was told to stay away from the establishment or suffer the consequences.

Two months later, Haines - by now desperate to fulfil his bizarre urges - followed Patricia Burke back to her flat in Bermondsey. After several unsuccessful attempts, he managed to talk his way in. He persuaded her to accept him as a private client by offering money on a regular basis. She was in debt and needed money for her alcohol addiction. His demands escalated to a new and dangerous level. Their last session took place in January 1972, and culminated in the girl's death. Patricia Burke died from internal bleeding after Haines thrust a wooden implement inside her rectum.

Detectives discovered that Burke had worked as a prostitute, and the trail led them to the brothel in Finsbury. Parlour, who was reluctant to divulge any information about the brothel and its inhabitants, finally agreed to co-operate by helping a police artist create the features of the man who had shown particular interest in the murdered girl.

Haines's neighbour, Ronald Maitland, eventually gave detectives their lucky break. After seeing the artist's impression in newspapers he contacted the police. He told detectives that he remembered seeing images relating to sadism and bondage in magazines kept in Haines's garage. Bertram Haines was identified by Celia Parlour. After lengthy questioning he confessed to the abuse and murder of Patricia Burke. He was sentenced to life imprisonment.

Sheridan could hardly believe what he had just read. The contents of the article gave 'dolly-house parlour maid' a whole new meaning. An icy tremble skipped over the surface of his skin. He was left in no doubt regarding the behaviour of the man who called himself Tony - the man who ogled Angela's ample attributes; the man who harboured sadistic, violent fantasies; the man who strangled his daughter and stabbed her repeatedly.

A strange remark made to a girl in a pub, and an obscure article from a crime magazine, had opened the door to the mind and motive of the man responsible for the murders.

The killer had left his first clue.

Night became early morning. The mystery caller came back to haunt him. Sheridan woke up startled, his pounding heart drowning out a familiar sound. He listened carefully, hoping that the sound was coming from next door. The ringing continued inexorably until Sheridan answered the call.

'Who is this?'

'I hate this bastard who rips and cuts the girls.'

The caller was quoting the letter. Either he was a crank, or the murderer himself. Sheridan had to know. He kept calm and tried to elicit as much information as possible.

'I'm getting tired with this. Tell me who you are and what it is you want.'

'It's not what *I* want . . . You want to catch this man.'

'You say you know who this person is. Just tell me his name.'

'It's not that easy, Mr Sheridan.'

'In that case you're playing games with me. You don't know anything.'

'I don't play games. I have to be careful what I say and do, otherwise I might get hurt . . . or killed. You want to find this madman, don't you?'

'Who do you mean? Are you talking about yourself?' Sheridan asked calmly, listening for any background noise.

'You're asking too much of me. Meet me this Thursday and I'll tell you what I know. Agree?'

'Yes. Where and when?'

'Car-park next to Hobbs Superstore. 11.30 p.m. I'll be watching. Come alone, or I won't turn up.'

'Hobbs? Did you say, Hobbs?'

'You got it. Hobbs, on Vincent Road.'

'Hello . . . Hello.'

The caller hung up. The tone of the conversation was decidedly antagonistic.

Sheridan could sense danger, but his mind was made up.

NINETEEN

Derek Oxley kept in close contact with his team of officers. Always helpful, always willing to give encouragement and offer advice while maintaining an officious manner that was typical of him. 'Keep going. If he's in the system we'll find him in the end,' was an oft-said remark from a hopeful inspector. But something was amiss with Naylor. For a start, he'd taken to wearing a striped shirt and dotted tie. Oxley didn't care much for dotted ties, and didn't take kindly to Naylor's untidy appearance.

Oxley was told to go to Naylor's office. A question had already formed in his mind.

'Yes, George, what is it?'

'Si'down, si'down.'

'What's with the shirt and tie, George?' Straight out with it.

'Shirt and tie? What's wrong with the shirt and tie?'

'Well, don't you think . . .' Oxley was hesitant, didn't fancy an argument right now.

'Out with it, Derek.'

'The match isn't a good one, George. Not good at all.'

Naylor shot up, pulled a large mirror from inside the filing cabinet and positioned it to his left, then his right, admiring himself with a satisfied look. Oxley was unaware of the mirror's existence.

'What's up with this shirt and tie?'

'Oh, nothing. If you like it, that's all that matters.'

'This is the distinguished look, the type of thing that Purslow and Scott would wear.'

Naylor's eyes were fixed on the incident room. Fellow officers had clocked the shirt and tie also, as well as the vain display with the mirror. They continued working in an attempt to allay the superintendent's apparent indignation.

'What's the matter with that lot?' Naylor said, sinking into his chair, knocking a pile of folders onto the floor. Oxley reached for the folders and handed them back.

'Thanks, Derek. Sorry about the mess. Things are getting a bit hectic round here.'

'It's to be expected with a case like this.'

'I'm sinking under a mass of paperwork.'

'You're working too hard . . . What was it you wanted to see me about?'

'The recent suspect, the one Rivers and Palmer brought in for questioning. What happened to him?'

'I was going to mention it. He's been released. Cast iron alibi for the Ross murder. As a matter of interest, he was a perfect match for the e-fit.'

'Oh, the e-fit,' Naylor said disparagingly.

'Karen Lawson is convinced he killed her friend.'

'Rubbish. How can you put any faith in a girl like that?'

'Come on, George, it's the best lead we've got and you know it. I see you took my advice on the use of a profiler. He's due to arrive shortly.'

'Yes, he might be able to provide that lucky break. I'm confident he will. You're right, of course, those kind are extremely clever at their jobs, better than we are even.' His sarcasm was obvious. Oxley did not rise to the bait. The services of a profiler was a powerful tool to his way of thinking. An insight into the motive and mind of the murderer, coming from a person well versed in his field of study, could open new avenues of approach for a murder squad already overwhelmed with thousands of leads to follow up.

Naylor was staring into space. Oxley marched off into the incident room. The level of noise suddenly dropped.

'Is he okay, sir?' someone asked.

'I'm sure he is,' Oxley replied, embarrassed.

'He looks like a comedian in that shirt and tie. And where's he nicked that mirror from?' A wave of subdued laughter rippled throughout the room.

Oxley's mouth twitched. 'Get on with your work,' he snapped. 'If he finds out you are talking about him he'll have your guts for garters.'

1.30 p.m. The profiler arrived. Forensic psychiatrist, Dr Andrew Simmons, worked at Longheath Special Hospital near Manchester. His job was to treat people who had serious mental disorders, including the country's most violent criminals. He had worked as an advisor on offender profiling for the

Association of Chief Police Officers' Crime Committee, and earned the prestige that came with being one of Britain's foremost authorities on the psychology of the criminal mind - in particular the mind of the serial killer.

Simmons was fifty years old. His grey hair stood in contrast to his dark eyebrows. He spoke in soft tones. During discourse his mild manner often lessened the impact of his analysis and deductions arising from crime-scene evaluation. It would be easy for investigating officers to miss an important point. Simmons liked to be precise when answering questions. If he wasn't sure of the answer he would say so. Though his track record was excellent he would be the first person to admit that he was not infallible.

Oxley proudly escorted him to Naylor's office which was now neat and tidy.

'This is Dr Andrew Simmons,' Oxley said, in a tone reminiscent of a butler announcing a royal guest. Naylor stood up and introduced himself. Both men shook hands.

'Please, take a seat. Would you like tea, or coffee?'

So far, so good.

'None, thank you. I've already had a bite to eat and drink.'

'Well then, I'm sure the inspector has given a brief overview of the case. It's the first time we've asked for an offender profiler to be brought in and, to be truthful, it wasn't my idea.'

'There's a first time for everything.' Simmons waited for some kind of a reply. Naylor kept quiet. Oxley was worried that his boss might say the wrong thing.

'Obviously, I need to know a lot more before I can come up with the characteristics of the man you're looking for,' Simmons said.

'We'll provide as much information as you need,' Oxley added. 'How accurate do you think the profile will be?'

'The accuracy depends on a number of factors. Putting aside the obvious ones, such as crime-scene evaluation and the victims' injuries, there's something I refer to as the mind-factor.'

'Do all murderers possess it?'

'It's an evaluation of the criminal's mind. Let me explain. Some criminal types, particularly that elusive breed known as serial killers, are becoming more adept at what they do.'

'In what way?' Naylor asked.

'Well, some killers have the ability to step outside what they have done. They look at the crime as if they are another person. When they commit another one they try to make it more difficult to translate.'

'In order to stay one step ahead?' asked Oxley.

'You could say that. If you are looking for a murderer who tries to avoid leaving obvious clues, then you are dealing with a sophisticated mind. They are the most difficult to catch.'

Oxley leaned forward. 'Do some murderers never get caught then, because of this mind-factor thing?'

'There are those who escape the net for long periods. Some are never brought to justice. You've heard of Ted Bundy? His mind-factor was very high, but he got caught in the end. Usually, these killers are trapped by the power of forensic science, coupled with diligent detective work.'

'If our man has the capability of laying down false clues then your profile could be wrong from the outset. So what's the point?' A challenging question from Naylor.

'First of all, let me say this: some folk tend to regard us as fortune tellers, making assumptions based on supposition and guesswork. It's not like that at all. Profiling highlights characteristics of the offender, enabling one to prioritise certain lines of enquiry. What you end up with is a psychological portrait. My profiles are never wrong. Oh, yes, there may be some discrepancies; there are bound to be. I'll tell you everything you need to know about the man you are looking for.'

'How can you be so sure?' asked Naylor.

'My expertise has been called upon in no less than ninety-three murder investigations. Eighty of those ended with success.'

'And the remaining thirteen?'

'My profiles were ignored, superintendent. In my opinion it took them longer to detect the crimes. People suffered as a result.'

Naylor frowned. Simmons could sense his scepticism. It was obvious that he harboured doubts about profiling, but Simmons had a job to do. He was not going to be deterred because of one man's lack of faith.

'I need to know as much as possible about the victims, their injuries, when and how they were killed. I'll ask the necessary questions as we go along.'

'Is that all right with you, George?' asked Oxley.

Naylor sighed and gave the doctor a folder containing the crime-scene photographs. 'We'll cover as much as possible here, and then you can see the murder locations. I take it you'll need to visit them?'

'Yes, superintendent,' Simmons replied, opening the folder. The photos were horrific. The forensic psychiatrist had seen it all before. He appeared to be unmoved. Like Purslow, he managed to suppress any feelings of emotion that might be stirred up: emotions that might affect his judgment. He replaced the photos inside the folder.

Naylor appeared disinterested, said nothing. Simmons was beginning to feel uncomfortable and had a feeling that his presence was not welcome.

Oxley spoke before the silence became embarrassing. 'Right. We'd better make a start. Victim Number One: Elizabeth Collinson . . .'

The detective inspector began with all the known facts about the victims' lives, where and when they were murdered, and the appalling injuries that were inflicted upon them. Dr Simmons asked questions as they went along, occasionally jotting down a quick note and referring to the post-mortem reports and crime-scene photographs. Naylor added little to the conversation. He stressed that the anal injuries were to be kept a secret. Simmons understood why this was so.

DCs Rivers and Palmer were in the incident room, reviewing their next assignment. Their heads turned towards the office as Simmons and the Oxley came out. Naylor was following behind as they headed for the wall map.

Rivers had heard on the grapevine that an offender profiler was to be brought in. Palmer casually sauntered off to the far end of the room, leaving his friend to eavesdrop on the conversation.

Oxley placed his finger on the map. 'The first victim was murdered at this spot. It's not that far away. We are situated here.'

'I see.' Simmons ran his finger along his left eyebrow. 'And this occurred about four months ago?'

'At around 7 p.m., give or take. It was going dark.'

'H'm. She was jogging by this busy main road - East Park Drive. The location of this murder is interesting . . . She was *definitely* wearing tight-fitting top and yellow shorts, inspector?'

'That is correct.'

Naylor didn't realise the significance of the top and yellow shorts. In any case, he was quite happy for his inspector to answer all the questions.

Rivers' ears were burning. It was obvious to him that the academic-looking man was the forensic psychiatrist called in at the request of a senior officer to help solve an extremely difficult case.

Oxley indicated the location of the second murder.

'And this one occurred in May, a couple of months later,' Simmons said to himself.

'Angela Ross. She was the one discovered in the covered passage on a foggy night,' Oxley explained.

Simmons was beginning to see a pattern. 'And she was displaying an abundance of flesh?'

The inspector nodded. He knew what he was getting at. Simmons asked if it was convenient to be taken to the crime locations. Oxley offered his services. He asked how long the profile would take to complete.

'I'm extremely busy as, no doubt, you are. I'll try to have it done in a couple of weeks.'

'Too long,' Naylor snapped. 'We need results as soon as possible.'

Simmons pursed his lips. 'I understand. Well, I suppose I can make an exception in this case. I'll see what I can do.'

Exit Naylor. Oxley apologised for his boss's tactless behaviour and explained that the pressure of the case was wearing everybody down. Thankfully, Simmons took it well.

Rivers had picked up every word.

Inspector Oxley collected the necessary reports and crime-scene photographs, and led Dr Simmons to the underground car-park. Once inside Oxley's car, Simmons cleared his throat and said, 'I understand the superintendent's dilemma. I've seen several senior officers crumble with the pressure of a problematic case.'

'It's no wonder,' Oxley said. 'This town is teeming with potential victims. It's a popular resort - hen parties and all the rest of it. Girls come from all over the place to strut their stuff.'

'Am I correct in saying the superintendent is not altogether in accordance with the application of offender profiling?'

'He doesn't like to be beaten.'

'I'm right in what I say, aren't I?'

'Yes. He is convinced we can catch him by using traditional methods. It's always been that way with him.'

'And what do you believe?'

'It's possible, but it could take a lot longer. I was the one who suggested bringing in a profiler. I think he's worried about public perception: Blackpool's SCU bring in Cracker.'

Simmons gave a perfunctory laugh. 'Cracker does fine. Unfortunately, it's not that simple in the real world.'

'That I can well believe. By the way, we don't want any publicity with this business about the anal assaults. George wants it kept secret.'

'I understand. Your secret is safe with me.'

Oxley fired the ignition. 'Is the murderer gay? Is that why he targets the anus?'

Simmons considered the question. 'You're not looking for a homosexual. I think I know something about this man's motivation. I'll tell you more in a couple of days when I've studied all the details.'

'Will he kill again?'

'I think he will, inspector. I think he will.'

TWENTY

Sheridan was sitting in his car at Hobbs Superstore. The nip flask resting in his pocket hardly contained enough whisky to calm the nerves of his stomach. At 11.20 p.m. he took a swig, and wondered if his night caller would turn up

A man, sitting in a vehicle not far from Hobbs, was watching and waiting.

Bert Davies was patrolling the area and spotted the stranger. He made a call on the 2-way radio which he had borrowed especially for the occasion.

'How's it going, Jim?'

'Fine. Nobody's turned up. Anything to report?'

'There's a man sat in a car near Hobbs.'

'What does he look like?'

'Don't know. I'll drive by and get a closer look. I'll call you back.'

Sheridan saw the taxi turning into the street opposite. The radio bleeped.

'He's up to something. Gave me a funny look when I drove by. He looks to be about fifty.'

Davies made his way back to Vincent Road and stopped at a point where he could observe the entrance to Hobbs.

11.35. A group of noisy teenagers lingered at the entrance to the Superstore. Sheridan checked his watch. The teenagers left after five minutes. He called Davies again. 'Anything happening, Bert?'

'Nothing. Stay cool.'

'I'll *try* to stay cool. We'll give it another ten minutes. If he hasn't arrived by then, I'm calling it a day.'

'Fair enough . . . Jim, somebody's crossing the road. Can you see him?'

'I see him, coming straight this way.'

'It could be somebody taking a short cut on his way home.'

'It's possible. I'm keeping the radio open.'

The street lights afforded a view of a man in a long dark coat and wearing a trilby. The man looked behind, and to his left and right. Seconds later he was standing next to Sheridan's car.

The moment of truth had arrived.

Sheridan wound the window down and asked who he was.

'It doesn't matter.'

The croaky deep voice was immediately recognisable.

'Are you Sheridan, the private detective?'

'I am. I believe there's something you want to tell me.'

Davies could hear every word.

'We need to talk. I've got something for you.'

Sheridan was straining to see his face. 'It's safe to talk. Get in the car.'

'I'm not getting in with you. Look here, I've a photo to show you . . . and a name you might be interested in.'

Sheridan got out and confronted him. Davies heard a sharp noise followed by a commotion. He pushed the accelerator to the floor and sped into the car-park. Another car raced into the parking area and pulled up sharply. The driver jumped out and went to Sheridan's aid. Davies, seething with anger, heaved himself out of his vehicle and saw Sheridan staring at the broken radio and baseball bat lying on the ground.

'I'm all right, Bert,' he said, rubbing his face.

'And who on earth are you?' Davies asked, squaring up to the younger man. 'You nearly caused an accident.'

'It's okay. He's Carl Lewis,' Sheridan explained. 'The man who tried to attack me ran off.'

'Who is he?' Davies asked.

'I don't know.'

'He won't be far,' Lewis said, scanning the area. 'You two wait here.'

He picked up the bat and ran off toward the car-park exit.

Sheridan's attacker didn't get far. Becky Watts' well-aimed kick had put an end to his escape, bringing him crashing to the ground.

'You okay, Becky?' Lewis asked.

'Just fine,' she replied, pressing her foot harder into the man's chest.

'Take your foot off me, woman. You're hurting me.'

Becky shone a torch into his squirming face. Lewis bent down for a closer look. 'You'd better tell us who you are,' he snarled.

'You're coppers, aren't you?'

'Never mind who we are,' he replied. 'Get up.'

Becky lifted her foot off his chest. The man struggled to his feet and spat on the ground. He was at least sixty years old. His rough features spoke of a troubled life.

'I didn't expect to find you here, Miss Watts,' Sheridan said, joining the trio.

'It was Carl's idea, Mr Sheridan. You're lucky you didn't have your brain caved in.'

Sheridan took a hard look at his attacker and knocked his hat off his head.

'Look, I'm sorry about this, honest. I don't want no trouble. This bloke in a pub paid me money to clobber you. Don't ask me why. I just carry out orders.'

'He hasn't done *you* any harm,' Becky said, raising her leg. 'Maybe I should kick you in the balls again; and maybe we should take you down the nick.'

'Leave it out, Becky,' Lewis said, gesturing with his hand.

The man nervously looked around. Sheridan was still studying his face, and the answer came in an instant. He pointed a finger at his face and said, 'I know you, don't I? Of course I do. I've seen your face before. A face from the past. Meet Mr Kenny Dawson. He stole an old lady's life savings some years ago. I remember her name - Lydia Thornton.'

'What a bastard,' Davies added, hand on hip.

'The police had a good idea who had taken the money but their man left the area suddenly and became elusive. That's when I was hired to find you. Remember, Dawson?'

'Now look 'ere, that was ages ago,' Dawson countered.

A group of teenagers gathered round, wanting to know what was going on. Lewis motioned them to go away, but to no avail.

'Clear off before I deck the lot of you!' Becky shouted, venom in her voice.

'But you haven't forgotten, have you?' Sheridan continued. 'You've been calling me in the middle of the night. You are the man who wrote the letter about the mercenary killer. You've been taunting me with bogus information about a killer who murders innocent girls.'

'And if I'm not mistaken, he's not been long out of prison,' Davies suggested.

'Right you are, Bert.'

'The motive is revenge,' Lewis added. 'This has nothing to do with helping us catch a murderer. You've been wasting our time, Dawson. What are you going to do with him, Sheridan?'

'Well now, at least we know who the caller is. I think we should let him go.'

'You can't just let him go,' Becky insisted.

'No point in prolonging this,' Sheridan said. 'You just go home, Kenny. I never want to see you again.'

'Now listen to me,' Becky said, stepping forward. 'You make one more call to Mr Sheridan and I'll personally rip your testicles off. You crawl back into that cesspit from where you came and stay there.'

All eyes were on Dawson, and he knew he had bitten off more than he could chew. 'I'll go now. You won't hear from me again,' he said, defeated.

'What about the damage to the radio?' Davies asked. 'I borrowed them specially for the occasion. They cost a hundred quid.'

Dawson threw his hands into the air. 'No trouble, no trouble.' He took a wallet from his coat and counted £200 in tenners. Becky snatched the money from his hand. He picked up his trilby and marched away.

'That's too much,' Sheridan said.

'Is it buggery,' Davies responded indignantly. 'Think of the trouble he's caused.'

Becky gave the money to Sheridan and departed without saying a word.

'She'll follow Dawson and find out where he's staying,' Lewis explained.

'Smart move,' said Sheridan, handing £100 to his friend. He offered the remaining money to Lewis. He refused.

'Get yourself a drink, Sheridan. You deserve it. And let me know if you plan anything else. We don't want to be left out next time.'

'I understand. What about this recent lead of yours? You said Angela Ross was seeing a man who drives a van. Any luck?'

'I'm visiting Karen Lawson, tomorrow. She might be able to help. See you around.'

Lewis waved and got into his car.

'What a night it's been, Jim,' Davies said. 'Good job that Becky was waiting in the wings. I wouldn't like to get on the wrong side of her.'

'She's dynamite, Bert. Come on, let's go.'

The two friends went their separate ways.

Sheridan drank whisky at home, his mind filled with the night's events. He could hardly believe an old case had come back to haunt him. Even now he felt on edge, hoping the phone wouldn't ring again, at least for a few days.

Dawson never rang again. He had been taught a lesson and came dangerously close to receiving a second helping of Becky Watts' testicular remedy.

What a marvellous show, Sheridan thought. *Lewis and Watts working as a team, preventing a further attack on me, not to mention the timely capture of the spiteful, odious ex-con.*

Irene was wrong about Lewis.

Sheridan had a friend, somebody who was on his side.

She was young and pretty. Physically frail from too much drink, she staggered out of Blackpool's premier nightclub. She ignored the row of taxis, having decided to walk back to the hotel. She only had a couple of quid left and a ten-minute walk seemed a good idea.

Down the noisy Promenade she went, young men leering at her, shouting sexist comments and whistling. Many of them had just purchased hot dogs and greasy fish and chips. The smell mingled with the sea air.

She ignored the attention. All she wanted was her comfy bed. Nothing else mattered.

Tight black dress.

Opulent figure.

Succulent flesh, beckoning . . .

His hidden obscene passion was burning like hell, his grotesque fantasy nearly a reality.

Lunar night.

The silvery moon was back again.

Blood flowing, hot and sticky.

Echoes of sweet agony . . . Obey me . . . Die for me.

Tattered dress, ripped apart . . . ripping, tearing, ripping.

Sharp blade, sharp as a razor . . . Searing pain and ecstasy of unspeakable torment.

The agony of death . . . Ripping flesh . . . Eyes wide open . . . Damsel in terror.
Stab, rip . . . again and again.

The knife.

'Taxi?'

She shook her head. 'I'm walking. Haven't got much money left.'

'It doesn't matter.'

He waved her to come closer. She bent down, resting her arms on the open window. He leaned towards her, his cold blue eyes ogling her breasts; but she was too drunk to notice.

'How much do you want?'

'Where to?' he asked.

'Don't know the name of the place,' she said, her eyes blinking slowly. 'Down to those lights and left, I think. How much?'

'I'll take you for nothing. Come on, get in.'

She pulled the door open. Her bag fell to the ground. She bent forward and reached for it, exposing more flesh. His blood was racing, his mind frantic with anticipation. He checked the rear-view mirror. Cold blue eyes staring back at him, his black hairline in stark contrast to his smooth white forehead.

A police car pulled up a few yards ahead, blue lights flashing.

She was almost inside the car. He pushed her out of the car, swearing at her as she staggered backwards.

'Eh! What you doin'?' She was too drunk to comprehend what was happening. He slammed the door shut and looked behind, trying to edge his car into the passing traffic. A taxi slowed down allowing him to pull out and drive off.

Blue lights still flashing. He kept checking the mirror until the police vehicle was out of sight, and now his frustration was boiling anger. *Another failure*, he thought. *Good job they didn't question me.*

He turned the music louder. 'Bird Doggin'' was a great song. He sang along with the record. 'Got to find some sweet little thing to love . . . Bird doggin'. Well I know I just can't last another night . . . I've got to get some love somehow . . . I'm bird doggin,' yeah I'm bird doggin''

His eyes were shooting along the Prom.

Harlots. Filth.

Teasing. Laughing. Provocative.

He sang louder and louder. The singing ended in a scream of torment.

The lucky bird had beaten him tonight. The next bird was going to pay.

He thought about the knife and the next victim, and he thought about good old 'Jack' and how he wanted to be like him.

The next one was going to suffer.

The next bird is going to be ripped, he thought.

Better luck next time.

'I'll be back,' he cried.

And he laughed insanely.

'I'll be back . . . Jack is coming for you.'

TWENTY-ONE

The Monster of Düsseldorf, Jack the Ripper, the Boston Strangler, the Vampire of Sacramento, the Son of Sam, the Zodiac Killer, the Yorkshire Ripper . . .

Dr Andrew Simmons knew them all. He had dreamed their dreams and entered into their minds to witness the irresistible fantasies that made them commit crimes the world would never forget.

'You know, these murders remind me of a man who was operating in Germany in the late 1920s,' Dr Simmons said. 'Peter Kürten became known as the Monster of Düsseldorf.'

Oxley thought for a second. 'I don't think I've heard of him.'

'There's quite a lot of literature about Kürten.'

'I'm interested. What do you know about him?'

'He came from a large family. There were thirteen kids in total.'

'The father was cruel?'

'To the wife and kids, yes. The father couldn't perform sex normally; there had to be violence involved.'

'Did the kids see the violence?'

'Peter Kürten certainly did. His father used to beat the mother severely before having brutal sex with her. He would often inflict pain by subjecting her to anal intercourse.'

'What did he do to the kids?'

'The evidence suggests that the kids suffered terrible beatings. Peter Kürten was the one who became affected. He saw his mother being beaten and raped. He saw his own sister being raped by the father.'

'And because of all this, he turned to murder?'

'Yes. It had a severe effect on his mental development. Kürten committed his first murder when he was thirty. He continued killing for sixteen months. He strangled his victims. Others were bludgeoned to death. Some were strangled and bludgeoned. He killed men, women and children.'

'Was he married?'

'Incredibly, yes. Apparently, his marriage was normal - if any marriage can be referred to as *normal*. And there didn't seem to be anything unusual about the sexual relationship, in the sense that he found her to be desirable.'

'Strange man.'

'He was. You see, inspector, the sight of suffering and blood were his sexual stimulants. Kürten tortured animals when he was young. He hung a cat by its front legs, beat it almost to death, and set fire to it. The cat's suffering caused him to ejaculate many times.'

'That's sick.'

'This man was the worst kind. He had sex with a sheep, and ejaculated only when he stabbed it with a knife. He also cut off a swan's head and ejaculated at the sight of the blood spurting from the stump.'

'He must have been a sadist.'

'More than that. He was a vampire. He drank the blood of some of his victims. He was everything rolled into one: arsonist, paedophile, rapist, sadist and murderer.'

'He must have been demonised.'

'You might say that. Peter Kürten was, in fact, charming, well groomed. Outwardly, he looked and behaved in a normal way, but the man inside was a perverted sadist.'

'What did he do with the bodies?'

'Many were killed in the woods near to where he lived.'

'Did he take away any body parts?'

'No, he took items of clothing. Your killer took Angela Ross's bracelet, which will become part of his fantasy.'

'What about the anal assaults? What does that mean?'

'I'll speak more about that later. The vagina and anus of some of Kürten's victims were injured, indicating a sexual motive.'

'If I met the man we are searching for would there be any signs that would indicate mental instability?'

'Not initially. If he walked into this canteen with a group of people you would be unable to pick him out by appearance or talking to him on a superficial level.'

'So, he fits in, appears to be normal in everyday situations?'

'In everyday situations - yes. But when you say "fits in," the answer is no. There's going to be something odd about the man you are seeking. He spends much time alone. He's hopelessly trapped in his own world . . .' Simmons paused, staring into space.

Oxley was curious. 'Tell me something, doctor - do you hate this man?'

'I wouldn't say that. We hate what he does, what he has become. Believe it or not, some serial killers are actually quite likeable.'

Simmons asked for more details about the stranger who spoke to Angela Ross and Karen Lawson on the night of the murder. Oxley went on to say that the person in question had not come forward to eliminate himself.

'That's a pity. Am I correct in surmising that the e-fit created much local interest?'

'Yes. We received hundreds of calls from people saying they recognised the man in the e-fit. They've all been eliminated. Personally, I believe the reconstruction depicts the face of the killer.'

'Keep an open mind. Don't allow your intuition to take over your objective judgment.'

'Well, I'm inclined to agree. There was some talk about Collinson's father being involved with the murder. Apparently, he didn't even know he had a daughter, not until his ex told him the shocking news.'

'How old is he?'

'Fifties, I believe. He's a private detective making his own enquiries.'

'Interesting. It certainly doesn't look as if he's involved in any way.'

'Maybe not. In any case it appears that he was out of town when the girl was killed.'

'One suspect less to deal with.' Simmons looked at his watch. 'I need to go over these notes before I deliver my profile.'

Oxley stood up and straightened his jacket. 'I'll leave you to it. See you shortly.'

Chief Superintendent Matthew Greenwood escorted Dr Simmons into the packed room. He introduced him to the troops and gave a brief overview of his work. Senior Officers Naylor and Oxley, seated at the front of the assembly, were only too aware that their close working relationship was being eroded by a difference of opinion.

Simmons began to talk about the history of profiling, saying that much scepticism existed regarding the role of the forensic psychiatrist in criminal investigation. He assured the Blackpool murder squad that his offender profile, if used judiciously, would help them to focus on the most likely suspects.

His 'portrait' of the killer was concise, offering details such as probable age, marital status, level of intelligence and family background. He explained, as best he could, the psychology of the killer's mind, the meaning behind the crimes and the cause for such abnormal, deranged behaviour. At the close of his speech he invited questions from the audience.

'All this guesswork could be wrong. How are we supposed to know if it's correct or not?' A direct question from Rivers.

'It's not guesswork, as you put it. We do, of course, make assumptions: assumptions based on our knowledge of how the criminal mind works. We identify characteristics of the offender.'

'Is the killer a local man?' A question from a detective sergeant. Naylor and Oxley were interested in that one.

Simmons carefully considered before giving his answer. 'There are probably people from around the country who know Blackpool as well as their own towns; so he could be a visitor.'

'You're saying, you don't know?' Naylor said flippantly.

'Frankly, yes, that's what I'm saying . . . Any more questions?'

No reply. No raised hands. 'I thank you for your time, ladies and gentlemen. It's been a challenge for me in that I was given a short time in which to create this profile. I wish you luck with your investigation.'

Simmons would not have mentioned the word 'luck' under normal circumstances. He felt that his time had been wasted. He collected his papers together. Discussions erupted immediately. The inspector went to join Simmons who was waiting in the corridor.

Naylor stayed behind and addressed the enquiry team. 'I don't want any publicity about this. No publicity. Do you hear? Dr Simmons' visit is our business. Let's keep it out of the press.'

Simmons took a folder from inside his briefcase. 'Here's your profile,' he said, with a look of dismay.

'Thank you. I'll put it to good use,' Oxley returned, almost standing to attention. 'I appreciate what you've done.'

Simmons brushed an eyebrow with his right forefinger. 'I know. I'm not so sure your superintendent shares the same sentiment.'

The inspector gave a wry smile. 'You're off back to Manchester, I take it?'

'Yes. I've got a mountain of work waiting for me. You know, I've been working fifteen hours a day over the last three months.'

'I know what it's like, believe me. By the way, can you tell me about the killer's mind-factor?'

'On a scale of one to ten, I would say the murderer is a seven.'

'Quite high.'

'Yes, he's fairly clever, but not clever enough. He'll cause problems. Sooner or later he will make a mistake. This man has a strong sexual drive that can only be satiated by the use of violence. It's a lethal combination. Don't be pushed into ignoring the profile.'

'I won't . . . I was wondering about the anal assault. Why is he attacking that area of the body?'

'It has nothing to do with sex. It is part of his fantasy, in the sense that he is defiling and degrading their bodies. It's an act of violation. These women are no more than trash to him.'

Degradation and violation. Oxley shuddered at the thought. His insight into the killer's mind was becoming clearer.

'You have no idea at all where he might live?'

'I'm not even going to hazard a guess. If it's Blackpool he is likely to live or work close to the first murder scene. Don't eliminate suspects because they live further afield.'

'Point taken.'

'It's a difficult case indeed, inspector,' Simmons said. 'I hasten to add that it is not unsolvable . . . Goodbye.'

Oxley watched Simmons' car ascend the ramp. He would never see the eminent forensic psychiatrist again. He rushed back to his office and read Simmons' condensed report:

Unknown Subject: male. Age - early to mid-thirties. Likely to be fairly strong.

Lives alone or with single parent. Will watch and stalk females in their twenties and thirties.

Victim type: scantily-dressed females. They will attract killer's attention.

Collinson victim - frenzied stabbing after strangulation. This was an opportunist killing with no signs of pre-planning. Likely to possess own transport. No trophies taken. Disorganised offender.

Ross victim - no strangulation. Use of pliers to torture victim indicates planning. This deduction is confirmed because tape was used to gag victim. Knife used also. These three items - knife, tape and pliers - constitute 'murder kit.' Bracelet taken as trophy. Organised offender.

The two murders are linked owing to anal injuries sustained in both cases. These injuries are acts of violation, meant to degrade the victim.

Mixed organised/disorganised characteristics is not unusual in itself.

The offender is forensically aware, hence, no weapon found. Will try to mislead the investigation; for example, by pulling up the shorts of the first victim.

Offender is in touch with reality and appears 'normal.' Likely to have had previous unsuccessful, short-lived relationships with women.

Offender is categorised as a 'lust' serial killer. He gains pleasure from the kill. There is a disturbing element of sexual sadism in his psychological makeup. (Torturing of the Ross victim.) Nipple and breast mutilation being the indicators. Post-mortem mutilation, i.e. the ripping of the abdomen, suggests a deep mental disturbance that indicates a hatred for women, particularly younger females.

The killer has fantasies involving brutalising, torturing and mutilating women.

He is likely to be involved with a trade, e.g. car repairs, electrician, handyman. He will be derogatory towards women, but can sustain the ability to appear charming and helpful.

He is likely to possess magazines, e.g. crime magazines, bondage, pornography, sexual sadism, torture. If he possesses videos they will depict scenes of torture and sadism. A 'snuff' movie, featuring the torture and murder of a woman, would be a powerful stimulant for his sexual fantasies. He has now progressed to the 'real thing' and is almost certain to continue until he is caught.

Access to the Internet would provide another source of stimulants, i.e. punishment, bondage websites etc.

Oxley read the profile for a second time, his enthusiasm for solving the case bubbling inside him. The profile stimulated new ideas for refocusing the investigation. He headed for Naylor's office and breezed in without knocking. Naylor was standing by the window.

'What's the matter, George?'

'How do you mean?'

'Dr Simmons has returned to Manchester without any thanks from you.'

'I was the one who brought him in, Derek. It's what you wanted. You got what you wanted.'

'That's right. The profile offers a valuable insight into the mind of a killer. We're going to catch him. We've got to catch him.' Oxley threw the folder onto the desk. 'At least have a look at it, will you?'

The superintendent stared ahead. 'I might just do that, sometime in the future.'

'You fool. You don't give a toss about the profile.'

Naylor shook his head in despair. He remained placid, allowing Oxley the opportunity to play out his tantrum. But it was all over. Oxley slammed the door on his way out. He went home, tired and dejected.

Lucy Beckett's disappearance had been registered with the National Missing Persons Bureau at New Scotland Yard. Her body remained at its original burial site, slowly decaying beneath woodland soil in the village of Plymbey, on the outskirts of Sedgeburn. Plymbey was only a forty-minute drive from the Blackpool incident room.

Every Blackpool copper knew the face.

Naylor and Oxley passed the poster everyday as they entered headquarters.

TWENTY-TWO

Jim Sheridan carried two mugs of coffee into the office and gave one to his partner. Lewis had phoned to say he would be there in ten minutes. He was as good as his word.

'I suppose you came to discuss last night's events. What a disaster.'

'No doubt about it, Sheridan. Tell me again: Who was the little guy with the bald head?'

'Bert Davies. He drives taxis for a living. I've known him for a number of years.'

'A good friend, but he's not a detective like you and me. I asked you to tell me if there were any new developments.'

'I'm sorry, I should have told you what my intentions were.'

'Not a wise move, Sheridan. You could have been hurt. Worst still, you could be dead now.'

'I know. I'm thankful for what you and Miss Watts did for me. You both handled it very well.'

Lewis swallowed a mouthful of coffee, then laughed. 'Yeah, she knows how to handle herself does our Becky.'

'Indeed.' Sheridan lit a cigarette and looked at the newspaper articles on the wall. 'What do you make of the e-fit?'

'Don't know. Could be anybody. It could be me even, or a weekend visitor like you suggested.'

'There is always that possibility. What did you learn from Karen Lawson?'

Lewis produced his little cassette recorder. 'I taped most of the conversation. Do you want to hear it?'

'Just give me the details.'

'Well, she went on about this guy called Tony, the one who spoke to her and Angela Ross on the night of the murder.'

'What did she say about him?'

'She thinks he killed Angela. She told the police as much when they interviewed her. Two senior officers, Naylor and Oxley, asked her lots of questions.'

'Do they think this Tony might be involved?'

'She doesn't know. She must have appeared credible otherwise they wouldn't have printed the e-fit.'

'What else did she say?'

'I was going to tell you about the man with the van and the tools. I discovered that he once slept with Angela Ross. He was a generous bloke, so it seems. I even paid him a visit.'

'Go on.'

'He resembles the e-fit all right, but he's not the killer.'

'How do you know?'

'Well, I know for a fact that he wasn't in town when the murders were committed. And he's got an artificial leg.'

Sheridan raised his eyebrows. 'What the devil was she doing with a man like that?'

'Takes all kinds, doesn't it? Lawson told me that her friend was a bit loose. She put it about quite a lot.'

'I understand what you're saying.'

'I got the impression that Lawson's a bit loose, too. I think she was eyeing me up.'

'For goodness' sake Lewis, what's it all coming to?'

'She took one look at my BMW and said she'd like to have a ride in it. I told her I didn't think the seat would go far enough back.'

'That's a horrible thing to say, Lewis. Did it not occur to you that she's lost a close friend?'

'I was trying to be funny. I was referring to her long legs, Sheridan. She must be six feet tall.'

'So, you reckon she's got loose morals?'

'Definitely. She's a tart and so was Angela Ross.'

'Do you think they were into prostitution?'

Lewis shook his head. 'There's nothing to suggest they were into that sort of thing. I can tell you something else, too. Angela Ross was wearing a bracelet on the night she died. The killer took it with him.'

Interesting, Sheridan thought. The murderer was taking items of jewellery as trophies, and one of his daughter's earrings had been taken away.

'He's taking mementos from his victims,' Lewis continued, leaning forward. 'Serial killers take objects belonging to their victims.'

'Some of them do, yes. I've seen documentaries about it; but the man we're looking for isn't a serial killer.'

'How come?'

'There has to be three for it to be a serial killer, so I believe. This maniac has killed two up to now; and my daughter was one of them.'

'I know. That's why I came to you - to offer my help.'

'If you're so interested in catching this fellow why didn't you offer your services to Irene Collinson? I can't work it out, because now you're doing all this for nothing.'

'I'm not just in it for the money, you know. I have enough of my own. What I can't work out is why she didn't come to you in the first place?'

'She wanted to tell me about Elizabeth, really. I had no idea she was pregnant when we split up. After she told me about the murder she suggested that I might be able to help.'

'What you are saying makes sense. I can understand the girl's mother wanting to see you.'

'Can you? Are you really capable of that sort of reasoning?'

'My reasoning was good enough to stop me from approaching you when you visited the murder scene on Aristor Park. Remember? You started walking towards me and I drove off.'

'I remember. Fair enough, Lewis. You deserve more credit than I've given you.'

'It's all right. No bother.'

Sheridan shifted uncomfortably in his chair. 'Why are you working with me on this case? What's in it for you?'

'The experience of working with someone else. It's a challenge and the chance to learn more about the job from an experienced PI, and maybe we'll catch ourselves a serial killer.'

'You think he'll strike again?'

'Hope not. One thing I do know - I'm running short of ideas. It's not the easiest case I've worked on.'

Sheridan showed him the Patricia Burke article. 'Bert Davies managed to get that. Read it and tell me what you think.'

He read it quickly, mouthing the words as he went through it. His mouth tightened as he looked at the e-fit.

'What are you thinking?'

'I can't believe it. This is too good to be true. Parlour's Dolly House,' he mused. 'A sadistic psycho goes too far and ends up turning to murder.'

'So, Karen Lawson's recollection of a dolly-house parlour maid was due to faulty memory. Is that a reasonable assumption, Lewis?'

'Yeah. This guy in the pub is talking to Lawson. He tells her how much he fancies her friend and says something like, "She's the type who would have been great working at Parlour's Dolly House."'

'That's probably something like what he said.'

'But could it be a coincidence?'

'Think about it, Lewis. Only somebody who had read the Patricia Burke article could have said something like that. Agree?'

'Maybe. We need to know if Angela Ross received injuries like that. I mean, did she have something stuck inside her . . . rectum?'

'Only the police can answer that. There was no mention of anal interference with the murder of Elizabeth.'

'Even if there wasn't, it doesn't rule out the e-fit man. I think you have a point, Sheridan. Let's just suppose the e-fit *is* the killer.'

'Go on.'

'We know what he looks like: black hair, moustache. And we also know he's into things like sexual sadism, maybe BDSM.'

'What's that?' Sheridan asked.

'Bondage, domination and sado-masochism. There's loads of mags on that kind of stuff. The world's full of pervs.'

'Interesting observation. Our next line of investigation could involve talking to prostitutes, find out if they know someone who fits the bill.'

'Let's do it then. I'll check the mags to see if there are any women out there offering sadistic sex. You can check the massage places. You look as though you need a good massage . . . By the way, Becky sends her regards.'

'It's appreciated. Tell her the late phone calls have stopped.'

'Yeah. No more mercenary killers to worry about. See you around.'

Exit Lewis. Sheridan went to the window and watched his partner dodge the traffic along Chapel Street. *Good old Lewis*, he thought. *At least the man from BBI is willing to try anything.*

Sheridan picked up a past edition of the local paper. He soon found what he was looking for. He read the names in the columns: Tanya, attractive escort, discreet; Bianca, super blonde, call any time; Toni, new attractive escort, discretion assured. Paula, gorgeous brunette . . .

He dialled the first number and got a recorded message. The 'super blonde' answered his second call. He gave brief details of his investigation before asking the all-important question. She said she couldn't help. So that was that. A few more calls elicited the same response. The girls were not prepared to pass on any information about their clients. 'Miss Whiplash' was more helpful. She had serviced a regular who enjoyed both receiving and inflicting pain. He was a local man in his late fifties.

Sheridan thanked her and dialled the last number. A girl with a Liverpool accent answered. He explained the situation. She thought he was connected with the police and told him to get stuffed. Dead end.

He pushed the telephone to the middle of the table. Lewis had forgotten to take his microcassette recorder. Sheridan didn't bother listening to the Lawson interview. He pushed the coffee cup away and reached for the bottom drawer where the whisky was kept. It was becoming a regular thing.

The habit was getting worse.

Later in the day he called to see Irene and told her that his investigation was not going too well. He also said that his partner was a valuable asset. She advised him to quit the case and suggested he went back to routine, less demanding jobs. But he was as committed to the case as Naylor and Oxley.

Irene believed the case would be solved by the police. She changed the subject and asked him to join her for a night at the Country Line Dancing Club. Sheridan wasn't bothered about any kind of recreation but said he would let her know. His feelings for her were running high, though she didn't know it. The job came first. Everything else had to wait. His short stay ended with the familiar, 'I'll love you and leave you.'

Lewis's town centre apartment stood above Henrietta's Unisex Hair Salon on Bank Street, a couple of minutes drive from BB Investigations. Nice and easy for Lewis. No need to get up early.

Sheridan thought he would pay him a visit and return the cassette recorder. He slowed the car down when the salon came into view. Two men were talking to each other. Lewis was easily recognisable. The other man looked familiar. Sheridan threw a glance as he drove by. Fortunately, neither of them noticed him. The other man was gesturing with his hands and looked towards the road.

Jim Sheridan had not forgotten the face of DC Steve Rivers.

TWENTY-THREE

The door swung open and cracked into the wall. Everyone in the incident room was expecting trouble. The superintendent, pale as ever from lack of sleep, was standing in the doorway clutching the latest newspaper edition. He looked like a cowboy who had come to take on the fastest gun. Oxley knew what was coming. A recent newspaper article ran the heading, 'Park Murder - Police Chiefs bring in Top Profiler.'

All staff stopped working, including the civilian helpers. Rivers was busy looking over the details of his next assignment. Palmer tugged his sleeve. His partner grinned and stubbed a half-smoked cigarette in the ashtray.

Naylor strolled up and down the centre aisle, waving the newspaper in the air. 'What was it I said? What did I tell you *not to do* after Simmons gave his talk in the conference room? You!' He pointed at a female officer.

'I don't know what you mean, sir,' she replied, blushing.

'You do read the papers, I take it? . . . Well?'

'Yes.'

'My instructions were clear,' he raged. 'No publicity! . . . Derek, do you know who is responsible for this?'

'I've no idea.'

'It's not you, then, *Inspector* Oxley?'

'I resent that, George,' Oxley replied with a stern look.

Naylor threw glances in various directions. 'Does anybody have any idea at all?'

'What does it matter, *Superintendent*?' Oxley asked, trying to remind him of his position.

'It matters to me,' he hissed, furiously tearing the paper into shreds. He picked up the larger pieces and re-tore them like a man possessed. The female officer giggled uncontrollably.

Let's see what Bulldog does now, Rivers thought.

'You think this is funny, lady? I'm the one who runs this place - I'm in charge. I say what goes. I tell you what to do and what not to do. My authority is being undermined by some incompetent fool who won't obey orders. When I find out who it is, I'll—' An expression of pain came over his face.

Oxley went to his aid. 'You all right?' he asked quietly.

No reply. Both officers looked towards the door as Chief Superintendent Matthew Greenwood marched in with a face like thunder.

Palmer gave Rivers a serious look. Rivers couldn't care less. He winked at one of his colleagues and waggled his tongue at her.

Greenwood had been listening from the corridor.

'George, Derek - to my office, now.' They sauntered off like a couple of naughty school kids, Greenwood following behind them.

Discussion erupted, not so much about the press report, but Naylor's astounding tantrum.

'Good lad, Greenwood,' Rivers sounded.

'Don't push your luck, Steve,' Rick Palmer warned. 'If Naylor finds out you're behind this you won't see your feet for dust.'

Greenwood's office smelled of furniture polish. His uncluttered desk shone like it was brand new. Walking on the plush carpet was like walking on air. His books and periodicals were arranged in precise groups in a huge wall cabinet, its glass doors polished with loving care. He was every bit as neat as his office: meticulous dress, wavy blond hair combed to perfection. His chubby smooth face spoke of the good life.

His subordinates remained standing. Greenwood motioned them to sit down and cleared his throat. 'This is one of the biggest manhunts we've ever encountered. We need objectivity.' His voice was smooth, his manner calm. 'It has come to my attention that there's, shall we say, a certain friction developing between you two.'

'Look, Matthew, how can I run an investigation with traitors in the camp?'

'Traitors in the camp, George?'

'Yes. I briefed the troops about this so-called profile and now the press has got hold of it.'

'It shows we're doing our job properly. The profile is nothing to be ashamed of,' Oxley said.

'It is,' Naylor countered. 'It's tantamount to defeat. We're saying the job is too big for us.'

Greenwood frowned. 'You two are the best officers for this job. You work well together. What's the problem?'

'Difference of opinion, sir. George isn't into profiling. He's wary about public opinion.'

'Too right I am. Look here, Derek, I'm not going to let this become a major media event.'

Greenwood leaned forward. 'Newspapers and television are a necessary means of communication in any murder enquiry, and you're forgetting one thing - I'm in charge. I have the final say.'

Naylor clapped his hands together. 'No, Matthew, you're not in charge of this investigation. Your mind is set on too many other minor things.'

Greenwood's eyes grew bigger in disbelief. Naylor got up. Oxley was stunned.

'Sit down, George. Please sit down. Under the circumstances I'm prepared to ignore your offensive attitude which is due, in part, to your tiredness. You're exhausted.'

'Nonsense.'

'This investigation is getting the better of you,' Greenwood added, pointing with his expensive Waterman fountain pen.

'You need a rest,' Oxley added. 'The chief superintendent knows about your late hours. If you carry on like this, you'll end up—'

'End up what?' Naylor challenged, standing up again.

'Having a breakdown, if you're not careful.' Oxley sprang to his feet, ready for a face-to-face confrontation.

'You're on *his* side, aren't you?' Naylor growled.

'There's no sides to it, George. The inspector has a point.'

'Oh, has he? I bet it was you who told those reporters, Derek - you.'

'That's enough.' Greenwood stood up and raised a hand in an attempt to prevent a slanging match between the two men. Naylor rushed towards the door.

'Come here, Superintendent Naylor,' Greenwood commanded.

'You are losers, the pair of you,' Naylor said, slamming the door behind him, leaving an intolerable silence that lasted several seconds.

'This could be the end for George. Is it, sir? Is it the end?'

'No, Oxley. Not yet.'

'What are we going to do?'

'Give him time to cool off. I'll talk to him tomorrow. I've never seen him behave like this before, and I can't understand why it has happened. Nevertheless, we have to find this killer, and find him soon before he takes another life.'

Sheridan was strolling around the office, stopping occasionally for a swig from the bottle and a glance at the e-fit. He couldn't get that face out of his mind. *He's the murderer,* he thought. *That's got to be him. Black hair, in his thirties, moustache. It has to be our man.*

At 6.15 p.m. he heard footsteps ascending the stairs, then the familiar creak of the twelfth step. Lewis stormed in and fell into the chair, breathing heavily. 'Sorry I'm late. I could have come in the car but it's too busy. I decided to have a jog. It might help to keep me in shape.'

'You look exhausted, man. What have you come to tell me?'

'I've made a few enquiries, a couple of phone calls here and there. Nobody's talking. Client confidentiality, or whatever they call it these days.'

'I know exactly what you mean. I had the same trouble myself.'

Lewis paused for a few deep breaths. 'I've got to tell you this one,' he said, laughing.

'Sounds interesting. Go on.'

'Well, I came across this advert in a magazine called *Extreme.*'

'Did you purchase a copy?'

'You must be kidding. There's more than a hundred mags dealing with every kind of perversion imaginable. It would cost a fortune to buy them all.'

'I'm surprised there are so many.'

'Believe me, there are. Anyway, this advert came under the heading, "Miss Rhino Sadism," so I wrote the number down and gave it a try.'

'You were intrigued?'

'Yeah. I had to know what it was all about. I ring the number, see, and this woman thinks I'm a punter. I ask her what she does, and she sells her own excrement.'

Sheridan closed his eyes for a few seconds, a smile falling from his face. 'I don't believe I'm hearing this.'

'Nor could I. Anyway, I says, what am I supposed to do with it, apart from flushing it down the toilet? She replies, "You're supposed to smell it, you idiot, like the others do."'

'Seriously?'

'*Seriously.* I mean, this woman's selling stools for twenty pounds and there are sickos out there willing to pay for it.'

'Disgusting.'

'Truly. Imagine sending that through the post,' Lewis squealed. 'What's happening with your side of things?'

'I've made numerous phone calls. No luck there. I might try the shop window ads, maybe a couple of massage parlours. I have to say, I don't think it will take us anywhere useful.'

'Why not?'

'Whoever he is, he's gone beyond that stage.'

'Maybe, but he might have used prostitutes in the past.'

'Even if that was the case, we don't know where he's from. It could be anywhere in the country.'

'Yeah, true enough. We'll stick to what we've got here in Blackpool. What do you say, Sheridan? We're not giving up yet, are we?'

'Not yet.' Sheridan opened the drawer. His partner's microcassette recorder was lying beside the matchbox containing his daughter's earring. 'Here's your recorder. You forgot to take it with you.'

'Thanks. I couldn't remember where I'd left it.'

Sheridan thought the time was right to clear the air. He popped the question. 'What's going on between you and DC Rivers?'

'How do you mean?'

'I've suspected, for quite a while, that you were receiving information from someone. I thought I'd drop the recorder off at your place. I changed my mind when I saw you talking to Rivers.'

'I've known Rivers for a while. He tells me things, now and again.'

'Like the man with the tools and the van? And people like Mick Taylor?'

'Yeah, that's right. No harm done.'

'Are you telling me he simply gives you information, at the risk of jeopardising a major police enquiry?'

'Not quite.' Lewis shifted uncomfortably in his chair.

'You'd better tell me what the script is. I won't be taken for a fool.'

'Okay. I pay him for the information, and that's all there is to it. You see, the police don't always follow up every single lead. They don't interview all suspects because they don't have the manpower. I buy bits of info. It's no big deal.'

'I bet Rivers' superiors wouldn't see it that way.'

'Maybe not.'

'There's no "maybe" about it. You should have done the right thing and told me what was going on.'

'Look, nobody but me and him know about it - not even Becky. You've nothing to worry about.'

'I disagree. It's not professional and you know it.' Sheridan's indignation was beginning to show.

'It had to be kept secret. Anyway, I can buy more info which might help with our investigation. What do you think?'

'That's up to you. It's obvious why Rivers came here to question me. It was a degrading experience, I can tell you.'

'How was I to know he'd come here?'

'You told him about me, didn't you?'

'I only mentioned it in passing. He knows we're working together and thinks it's a smart move.'

'Does he, now? I know what he does think: he suspects me of being the murderer. I resent that. I'm beginning to wonder whether *you* thought I was the killer.'

Lewis's mouth fell open. Sheridan looked hard at him, waiting for an answer.

'I wish you hadn't said that, because it's not true. If I thought it was you, I wouldn't involve the police. There's a big reward. Remember?'

'You don't need the money.'

'No, I don't. Doesn't mean to say I wouldn't take it if it was handed on a plate. Listen, I'm sorry I lied to you. I knew it would blow over in time. Like I say, I don't want people knowing about me and Rivers.' He displayed open hands as if to say, 'And that's all there is to it.'

'Very well.' Sheridan got up and faced the window. 'I accept you had good intentions, but you should have thought it through first.'

'We're still together?'

Sheridan turned and offered his hand. His partner looked up and reciprocated.

Lewis pushed the small cassette recorder into his pocket and rose from his chair. He spoke about the task ahead. There was no trace of despondency, only a willingness to do the job to the best of his ability.

Sheridan admired him for that.

Becky was alone in the office. She shook her head and cursed when the phone rang. It had been a long day.

Sheridan told her that Lewis had just left. He wanted to see her at his office on Chapel Street. Becky agreed to go there. Ten minutes later she was sitting opposite him wondering what it was all about.

He told her about the Lewis-Rivers relationship and asked if she was aware of it.

'I don't even know this Steve Rivers.'

'He was the nasty one who came here questioning me about my daughter's death. Lewis told him I was the father.'

'What a stupid thing to do. I didn't think he'd pay a police officer for information. That's Carl for you - always close to the edge. He'll never change.'

'I don't think you should mention this.'

'He's a big lad now. It will do him good to get a dressing-down, especially from me.'

'Please, let's keep it quiet. At least for a short while.'

'Fine, Mr Sheridan. Whatever you say.'

'Thanks. There's something else. I want you to do me a favour.'

Becky couldn't decline. She was attracted to him in a way that she could not understand. 'Then ask me. I might just do it.'

'Are you busy in the evenings?'

A faint smile passed her lips. She thought he was going to ask her to dinner or something. 'Usually, yes. I can always make the time though.'

'I want you to watch Rivers.'

'What for?' she asked, disappointment showing.

'Find out what he does, where he goes.'

'Is this really necessary?'

'It is. I have a feeling, a hunch. There's something about him I don't like.'

'You're supposed to be looking for this killer. Why don't you follow him?'

'He knows me. You stand a better chance.'

'All right, I will. But only for a couple of nights. If nothing happens, I'm pulling out.'

'I'm grateful. I'll pay for your trouble, as long as I can afford it.'

'I don't want anything for it. I'd like to know what you expect to get from this.'

'Perhaps something will turn up,' he said. He wrote down his home telephone number and a description of Rivers. She stuffed it into her back pocket and got up from the chair.

'I won't easily forget the day he came to this office,' he reflected.

Becky gave him a lingering look before leaving.

The elderly couple had been watching him for over an hour. The man was pacing up and down the passage where Angela Ross died.

At 10.30 p.m. they called the police.

The patrol car arrived ten minutes later. A young officer got out and casually strolled to the passage entrance where he heard the man muttering to himself. He shone a torch in his face and asked what he was doing.

'Don't you recognise me? Don't you know who I am?' the man said, scowling.

'You've been loitering here for quite some time,' the officer replied. He closed his eyes momentarily as the man's identity became crystal clear.

TWENTY-FOUR

'Take a seat, Oxley,' Greenwood said, rotating his fountain pen with finger and thumb of both hands. 'I left a note on George's desk as I haven't been able to speak to him. It's ten-o-clock and he's not in his office.'

'I don't know where he is, sir.'

'Has he left any message at all, with anyone?'

'Not to my knowledge.'

'I see. I haven't had the opportunity to have that chat with him. It is clear that this investigation is taking its toll.'

'He will not rest, not until we solve this case. I wonder if we ever will. This one seems to know what he's up against.'

'Failure is one thing we can't afford. The massive reward has, I'm sure, given rise to a large number of spurious leads. Too many people are eager to get the money, eh?'

'I quite agree. With your permission, sir, I'd like to step up surveillance. The holiday season is approaching which means more visitors and a greater opportunity for the murderer to strike.'

'A difficult problem. You know what it's like in town at the weekends.'

'Do I?'

'How many incidents do we respond to? How often do we encounter drunken brawlers and disputatious courting couples?'

'Just for a month or two, please.'

'Can't be done, Oxley. Sorry. You can get our press officer to remind the newspapers that we still have a problem in this town. We must warn the visitors.'

'Very well. I'll do what I can.'

'What's the latest regarding the suspect list?'

'I've arranged a meeting for this afternoon. I haven't had chance to collate all the information.'

'Carry on then, inspector. Keep up the good work and keep me informed of any new developments. Remember, the Assistant Chief Constable is watching us closely. We must keep him happy . . . and the public too.'

Oxley returned to the incident room. HOLMES officers were hard at it, searching the system for criminal types that might be considered worthy of inclusion in the Simmons profile. Known sex offenders were looked at again, and men who had records for violence against women. Specially trained officers were monitoring excessive users of sado-masochistic websites. Names were beginning to surface. Oxley began the task of prioritising them. It seemed to be a job that would take forever. An hour later Palmer's voice interrupted his concentration.

'Sorry, Palmer. What did you say?'

'One of our patrol officers responded to a call last night. A man was hanging around the Ross murder scene for ages. It was the superintendent.'

'George Naylor?'

'Yes, sir.'

'What did he have to say?'

'Nothing much. He didn't explain why he was there or what he was doing. He seemed to be in a bad mood so the officer left him to it. There was nothing else he could do.'

Oxley's suspicions were confirmed.

Naylor was sinking fast, and somebody was pushing him under.

A re-examination of the entire suspect list was in progress. After two days of intense scrutiny an interesting suspect emerged. Jean Carr was one of the intelligence officers assessing the vast number of messages contained in the police files. 'You'll find this interesting,' she said, handing Oxley the two printouts.

He read the relevant details: 'Dean Cooney, thirty years old and living at Number 2, Wilkes Parade . . . Previous conviction for attempted rape . . . Served eight years of his sentence . . . String of minor offences against women including stalking and public masturbation . . . Threatened a woman with an SAS-style knife and bit her arm . . .'

'He carries a valid driver's license,' she added.

Oxley read the other sheet with greater interest: 'Teresa Moore, thirty-five years old and of the same address, called the incident room to say that Cooney returned to his flat on the evening of the Collinson murder. Moore went to see him to borrow some milk. She said he had blood on his shirt and appeared to be agitated.' The inspector could hardly believe what he was reading. 'Why hasn't this been acted on before now?'

'I couldn't tell you. It was one of those actions that ended up at the back of the queue. You know what it's like, sir.'

'I certainly do.'

'And this is the clincher . . .'

'More to come?'

'Yes. Teresa Moore phoned again two weeks later. She told the officer that Cooney had kept all the newspaper reports on the Collinson murder. He also said he'd been on the park on the night of the murder, and he wanted to show her where the body was found.'

Oxley couldn't help the feeling of elation. It sounded too good to be true.

'Good work, Carr. Where's Wilkes Parade?'

'Not that far away. Wilkes Parade has a lot of bedsits, so I'm told.'

'I see. Thank you.'

Carr went about her business. Oxley wondered what Dean Cooney looked like. He would find out soon enough.

Oxley struggled to keep his subjective feelings from boiling over. Cooney seemed so promising. The more he thought about it, the more convinced he became of Cooney's involvement. This man *had* to be their Number One suspect.

Greenwood saw it as an important breakthrough and gave the thumbs-up for a surveillance operation to be set in motion. An hour later Oxley caught sight of Naylor shuffling through the incident room.

'Working late again, George?' he asked nonchalantly.

Naylor didn't answer. Oxley followed him.

'Shut the door,' Naylor said, unzipping his beige jacket and pulling up his baggy, brown corduroy pants. It was the first time he had turned up for work dressed in casuals.

'The chief super wants to see you as soon as possible,' Oxley said. 'He thinks you need a break. I'm inclined to agree.'

'Greenwood can wait. We've business to attend to.'

'I think you should see him right away.'

'Let's not be official, Derek. I'll wait until he comes down here to see me. How does that sound?'

'If that's how you feel. What's the matter, George? You can tell me.'

'There's nothing to tell.'

'Look at yourself, George. Look at the things you've been doing of late. Surely—'

'Don't start mothering me, Derek.'

'For goodness' sake, listen to yourself.' An argument was looming. It was the last thing Oxley wanted at a time like this. 'And before you say anything else you can listen to me for a change. You're not the only one who wants to catch this maniac and you're not the only one who works late hours, so pull your self together, get a grip of yourself.'

Naylor bowed his head. 'I'm sorry, Derek; and ashamed.'

'You've nothing to feel ashamed about. Let's try and be objective before things really get out of hand. How do you feel in yourself?'

'I haven't been sleeping so good.'

'And how is Dorothy coping with all this?'

Naylor's face tightened. 'She's going mad. I can't blame her. It's the case, Derek, you see. It's the enquiry.'

'You think he's beating us, don't you?'

'Yes. He knows what he's doing does this one. I won't give up till he's caught, and then I'll take a short break.'

'A *long* break,' Oxley corrected.

'A long break, then.'

'I'm glad to hear it. The Ross murder has been bothering you unduly. You were at the crime scene, walking up and down that passage late last night.'

'You didn't see the body. I did. In my mind I visualise the surgeon coming towards me, leaving a broken body lying in that narrow stinking passage. Christian Purslow tells me about the injuries as if he's discussing a football match.'

'What are you talking about, George?'

'Bad dreams, Derek. I see faces I know, and a face I can't see. It's flat and featureless.'

'The killer's face?'

'Yes, yes, *his* face - the one who's ahead of us all the time. He's ripping girls to pieces. Ripping them up, do you hear?'

Naylor fell into silence and took on the appearance of a crumbling wreck.

'George . . . George.'

'Yes, Derek, what is it?'

'I take it you're not going home to rest.'

'I'll rest. I've got to do something rational for a change, if only to save my marriage.'

Oxley told him about Dean Cooney and showed him the file on suspect Number One. After ten minutes of quiet discussion the change in George Naylor became apparent. The inspector witnessed cerebral resuscitation in a patient dying from stress. The metamorphosis was unbelievable.

'I can't believe this man has not been investigated before now,' Naylor said.

'Priorities. We would have got to him soon enough, but let's not be too hasty.'

'Hasty? We won't waste any time on this one. You know what this means? It means we don't need a profiler telling us our job. Derek, we have our man.'

'Look George, he's a good suspect on the surface; but what we've got is circumstantial. There's no direct evidence of his guilt.'

'Not yet there isn't. We must get a search warrant.'

'We might not get the warrant. I've asked for 24-hour surveillance in the first instance. The chief super has given the go-ahead.'

Naylor got up and reached for his jacket. 'Well then, all is looking good.'

'You're off home?'

'I'll speak to Matthew first, and I'll see you tomorrow.'

They shook hands like two kids making up after a fight. Naylor went his way. Both men were hopeful that the end of the investigation was in sight.

Becky Watts managed to get Rivers' address from Lewis himself, in an innocuous sort if way. Lewis had no idea what she was really up to. And so her surveillance on Rivers began. On the first evening she had waited down the road from Rivers' house, situated in Clevedon, a few miles north of Blackpool. Nothing happened. The second evening saw her driving up and down the road a couple of times before returning home to be with her son, Johnny. Already fed up, she had no intention of prolonging her surveillance on a detective constable - even if he *was* dodgy. This was the last try, even if it meant sitting in a car for a few hours on a sultry evening.

Sheridan owes me one for this, she thought. She pictured him in her mind, the plain mild-mannered guy who looked anything but a private detective. He struck her as being a burned-out PI, searching in vain for the killer of a daughter he never knew he had. And to become a suspect himself. Not to mention the target of an ex-con's revenge. But she prided herself on bringing Dawson down. She re-ran the memory of his fall after she had kicked him in the groin.

All the same, she felt sorry for the old-style detective - the pen, pencil and notebook PI with his crinkled newspaper cuttings and a creaky chair positioned next to a window overlooking a busy street. To her, he came over as being a bit sad. Or was she moulding the character of Jim Sheridan to suite her own purposes? She *had* to help him, but not in the way he would have expected.

Becky fancied older men. The sympathy running through the fibres of her mind was a kind of excuse. She was succumbing to her primal desires.

Her daydreaming evaporated. A man was standing in the driveway of his house. She wound the window further down to let in more air, and took a hard look before he got into his Vectra. Sheridan's description was simple and accurate: mid-thirties, dark hair, paunchy.

Rivers drove off. Becky followed, hoping he wouldn't get suspicious. *What if he realises he's being tailed?* She thought it through. *Even if he stops, I can drive on and go home. He might be going out to buy a pizza or something. And then back to his home. Job done. Nothing to report.*

But Rivers kept going.

He drove cautiously, keeping to the speed limit. She kept a safe distance, closing in only when he approached a traffic light, lessening her chances of having to go through on red. He hit the main road into Blackpool. A couple of drivers managed to squeeze in between them. She kept a close eye on the Vectra. He took a left turn and headed for Wichonstall, a market town to the East of the resort. The other cars travelled on, leaving her a clear view. Suddenly, he accelerated to a speed that was too dangerous for her to contend with. Rivers' cigarette butt disintegrated into a spray of sparks as it hit the road. Becky pressed on, trying to close the gap. Rivers decreased his speed as he passed the Wichonstall signpost, brake lights flashing. She thought he was about to stop. He eyed the pedestrian, consumed by a powerful sexy image: short leather skirt and thigh-length boots. He suddenly accelerated and turned sharply into leafy Sherbrook Lane, an area consisting of immaculate detached houses with well-lit driveways. BMWs and Mercs spoke of rich men.

His car turned sharply into the grounds of a large detached house, surrounded by an eight-feet high wall. Becky pulled up, got out and peeped around the stone pillars that marked the entrance to the driveway. Two Victorian-style lamps illuminated the stone steps that led to a sturdy oak door. She snapped several photos of Rivers going up the steps. She wanted to get closer, but noticed the CCTV cameras on the walls of the house. Rivers pressed the buzzer. Thirty seconds later his knock was answered by a short, plump woman who obviously recognised him. Becky took another shot before he closed the door behind him. Then she saw a movement. Her eyes were drawn to the windows on the second floor, each one filled with a different coloured light penetrating the evening darkness.

Becky caught a fleeting glimpse of a shadowy nude figure. She kept her eyes on the window.

Seconds later, the coloured light faded into blackness.

Job done.

Time to go home.

TWENTY-FIVE

Enquiries confirmed that Dean Cooney still resided at Wilkes Parade. Teresa Moore had moved on to another address in the resort. She was claiming housing benefits. It wasn't difficult to trace her.

Cowley Park estate was a run-down, crime-ridden, festering hovel of a place. Its residents were rowdy, uncontrollable and unemployable.

DS Tanya Lambert and DC Rick Palmer were travelling to the address.

'Cowley Park estate,' Palmer mused. 'So, that's where Moore lives. They're a law unto themselves that lot.'

'How would you know, Rick? You haven't even been in Blackpool that long.'

'Steve Rivers told me. He knows what goes on at these places.'

'He's your usual partner, isn't he?'

'You know him?'

'Everybody knows him. Wild character is that one. Pushes his luck a bit too far at times. He ought to be more careful.'

'How do you mean?'

'Steve Rivers is crude, insensitive. Don't tell me you haven't noticed . . . He's also a womaniser. It's about time he was settling down.'

'I can't imagine him settling down.'

'To be honest, neither can I. Has he got a girlfriend, do you know?'

'Not to my knowledge.'

Lambert waited a few seconds and asked if Palmer had a girlfriend. He said he had.

'Take my advice, Rick, don't invite him for tea. Give him half a chance and he'll have her knickers off.'

'He's as bad as that, eh?'

'You obviously don't know him that well. He used to be married but it didn't last.'

'I'd no idea he was married,' Palmer said surprised.

'His wife had a rotten time. He was cruel to her. He used to beat her up, so I've been told.'

Ten minutes later they arrived at Moore's house. Lambert jerked the handbrake, got out and adjusted her skirt whilst Palmer fumbled with the seat belt, eventually managing to unclip it.

Teresa Moore peered through her window. The formal appearance of the strangers worried her. She opened the front door and asked who they were.

'What's the matter? What's wrong?' she asked.

'There's nothing wrong,' Palmer said, gesturing with his hands. 'Can we come in?'

Moore led them into the living room and pointed at the settee. She was in her mid-thirties and ageing well. Everything about her smacked of the unemployed single parent, struggling to make ends meet. A dozen or so food stains patterned her black skirt, which stood in contrast to the off-white jumper clinging to her skinny body. Lambert noticed the fluffy pink slippers, the soles of which were hanging off.

'Does anybody else share this house with you, Miss Moore?' Lambert asked.

'Only the kids. What have they done wrong this time?'

'This is nothing to do with the kids,' Lambert continued. 'We want to verify details you passed to the incident room: details about Dean Cooney, the man you used to live with.'

'I didn't live with him. We were lodgers in the same house, the one on Wilkes Parade.'

'I stand corrected. How long had you known him?'

'A couple of years.'

'How well did you know him?'

'Hardly at all. He was quiet, never said much. I didn't like him.'

'Why was that?'

'He was a dirty git. He asked me up to his room a couple of times and tried to get me to watch porno vids.'

'Did you?'

'Sometimes. I told him to grow up and find a woman. He didn't have a girlfriend. He never asked me out. I wouldn't have gone with him, anyway.'

'Did you ever go anywhere in his car?'

'No.'

'Did he ever lose his temper with you?'

'No.'

'Let's get back to the videos, Teresa,' Palmer said, leaning forward. 'What sort of videos did he watch?'

'I'm not sure how to describe them.'

'Were they videos featuring men and woman having normal sex?'

'Yes.'

'Okay. Now, how about his hobbies?'

'He liked taking photographs. Well, at least I think he did. He had lots of photos in his room.'

Palmer raised his eyebrows. 'Photographs?'

'Yes, photos of women. I saw this bundle of photos once. They showed women on the streets just walking along, and some were women and girls jogging.'

'Did *he* go out jogging?' Palmer asked, eager to press on.

'I don't think he ever did. He once told me something about women joggers.'

'Can you remember what it was?' Lambert asked.

'It was something to do with showing off their bodies and how that bothered him.'

'What was it that bothered him?' Palmer asked.

'I'm trying to think . . . No, can't remember exactly what it was. I got the feeling he was frustrated by these women who went out running.'

They were intrigued by her answers. Now it was time to get to the main points. Palmer continued. 'I want you to think about the time when Elizabeth Collinson was murdered. You remember when that was, do you?'

'That was about three months ago.'

'More like four,' Lambert corrected. She glanced at Palmer, leaving the way open for his next question.

'What happened on the night of the murder?'

'I was asleep when Cooney knocked on the door. I didn't let him in. I just asked what it was he wanted. He said he was in trouble and I told him to go away.'

'Did he say anything else?'

'No, but his voice sounded weird, as if something was wrong.'

'What happened next?'

'He went away and I fell asleep again. I woke up at half ten and went to make some corn flakes. There was no milk, so I went to Cooney's room and asked him for some.'

'You went *into* his room?'

'Yes. I knocked and walked in. He tried to cover himself up. I noticed blood on his shirt and hands.'

'Did you ask him what had happened?'

'I asked him if he had hurt himself. He said he was in trouble and I hadn't to tell anyone what I had seen. He must have meant the blood.'

'And that was all?'

'Yes. I didn't bother about the milk. I went back to my room. The night after that I remember reading about the murder.'

'Can you remember what you thought at the time?'

'I became suspicious about him and I kept thinking things over. In the end I phoned the police. I got this feeling that he wanted to tell me something.'

'What do think he wanted to tell you?' Lambert asked.

'I think he wanted to tell me he'd killed that girl. I think he wanted to get it off his chest.'

Palmer straightened himself and asked if she thought Cooney was capable of murder. She replied without hesitation. 'I'm sure he is; and he used to be a butcher, so blood wouldn't bother him. He's a sheet metal worker now.'

Lambert made a note of the company name.

'Anything else you can tell us about him?' Palmer asked, pressing for more information.

'He has a computer. I'm not sure what he uses it for.'

'Did he often go out at night?'

'He went drinking quite a bit. I don't think he had many friends, though.'

Lambert asked if Cooney had ever been to The Elms or The Unicorn. Moore had no idea. Then Palmer asked her to describe him.

'He's medium build, average height, blue eyes, and short brown hair.'

'Has he ever had a moustache?'

'Not while I've known him.'

Cooney didn't match the e-fit. Lambert took over with the questioning.

'You called the incident room again a few weeks later. Can you remember what you said?'

Moore thought for a while. 'I remember going into Cooney's room. I noticed some sheets of newspaper on the floor They were all about the murders.'

The detectives looked at each other, their eyes registering a deepening conviction in Dean Cooney's involvement with the crimes.

'I told Cooney he was an oddball for keeping the papers. He kept staring at me and then he said he was on the park when it happened.'

'He told you he knew where the body had been found?'

'Yes. He said he'd show me where it happened, so I could see for myself. I said I wasn't interested in going there, and then I left.'

'Did he mention about going there again?'

'No, Miss.'

'Do you remember the night of May 19, when Angela Ross was murdered?'

'I remember it clearly because he told me he'd had a great night following women about in all that fog.'

'Where had he been?'

'He never said.' Palmer was standing by the window. Moore kept her eyes on him.

'You're sure there's nothing else you can tell us?' he asked.

'I don't think there's anything else . . . Do you think he's done these murders?'

'I've no opinion at this stage, Miss Moore. What you have told us seems to implicate him, doesn't it?'

'Well, I wouldn't be surprised if he'd done it. He always struck me as being a bit crazy.'

'Thank you very much for talking to us,' Lambert said. She stood up and signalled Palmer it was time to go. Teresa Moore kicked off her dilapidated slippers and showed them to the door. Before they reached the car Moore asked if the reward was still on offer. Lambert answered that, as far as she knew, it was.

'If he's the killer, do I get the money?'

'I suppose so,' Lambert answered. 'As long as we can prove it.'

On the way back to HQ Palmer asked outright if she thought Cooney could be the responsible for the crimes. Lambert took some time before answering.

'It all sounded promising, until she mentioned the reward.'

'You think she's making it up?'

'Some of it, yes. It all fits too perfectly. If it's true what she said, why should Cooney practically admit to being the killer?'

'Perhaps he's stupid. Maybe he's pushing his luck. Who knows?'

'Let's not forget what Simmons told us. Whoever it is, he's forensically aware, doesn't leave any clues. And consider his mind-factor judgement. He reckons the killer scores a seven. I'm beginning see Cooney as one of life's sad characters - a nobody trying to be a somebody.'

'But Teresa Moore's recollections of what she saw are the same as what she reported. That's important.'

'You think he's the killer, don't you?'

'My gut reaction says he is, and I reckon we'll find something in that flat that nails him for the murders.'

Lambert and Palmer reported to Naylor as soon as they reached headquarters. The information gleaned from Teresa Moore was the confirmation needed to signal the go ahead for a surveillance operation. Palmer was pleased with developments. Lambert believed that Moore had partly fabricated her story in order to make Cooney look more plausible. She believed that Moore was putting herself in line for the reward.

When the two officers left the office, Naylor called Oxley and told him the outcome of their visit.

'At long last we seem to be getting somewhere. What do you say, Derek?'

Oxley's mouth twitched. 'There's some mileage to go yet, but I'm confident we'll have him.'

TWENTY-SIX

Sheridan was admiring his reflection in a shop window. He straightened his black waistcoat and pulled the brim of the Stetson a little further towards his eyes. Darren caught sight of his friend sauntering in the direction of Central Drive. 'Jim! Is that you?' he shouted.

Sheridan turned around. 'I was hoping you wouldn't see me like this.'

'I couldn't believe my eyes. For a minute I thought you were Gary Cooper,' he joked.

'I'm surprised you've heard of Gary Cooper. He died years ago.'

'Oh, all right. Clint Eastwood, then.'

'Not tall enough to be Clint Eastwood.'

Darren moved closer to him. 'I'm baffled. Why are you dressed like that?'

'Irene keeps asking me to join her at the Bloombury Club. Thursday night is Line Dancing.'

'I hope you enjoy yourself. Where did you get the hat and waistcoat from?'

'I didn't. She left them on my desk, with a note. I was out when she called.'

'What time does it start?'

'Half past seven. I'm an hour late.'

'I'd get a taxi if I were you. It would be faster than a horse.'

Sheridan laughed.

Ten minutes later a taxi dropped him off at the club.

The sound of Country music filled the air of the Bloombury Club. Sheridan felt self-conscious as he entered the building. A committee man asked for the three pounds admittance charge. No fuss. No bother. To him, Jim Sheridan was another crazy cowboy who liked dressing up as John Wayne . . . or Gary Cooper. 'High Noon' and 'A Fistful of Dollars' were the films being re-enacted in the minds of the cinema-icon gun fighters standing at the bar.

One 'cowboy' had even carved notches in his gun grip in recognition of the movie *The Fastest Gun Alive*, featuring Glenn Ford. The occasional glass of whisky slid along the bar and gun smoke hung in the air. Crazy Pat's Rodeo Disco entertained the crowd with Country's greatest Line Dancing songs: 'Black Coffee,' 'Dance the Night Away' and 'Holdin' Heaven.' This was another world - great escapism for one evening.

Sheridan strolled into the cabaret room. Irene spotted him immediately and waved to him. She appeared younger and prettier. A sense of normality was at last coming back to her.

'You made it, then,' she said, getting up from her seat. 'This is my friend, Jenny.'

'Pleased to meet you . . .You look great,' Sheridan remarked, admiring Irene's black straw hat.

'I'll get the drinks,' Jenny said. 'What's yours, Mr Sheridan?'

'I'll have a small whisky, please.'

'The usual for me,' Irene added.

Sheridan took the seat opposite Irene.

'I didn't think you would wear the Stetson and waistcoat,' she said. 'Do you like them?'

'They definitely serve a purpose. Thanks for buying them for me'

'It was a pleasure. Are you going to have a dance with me, later? I'd love to have a dance, Jim, like the old times. Remember the old times?'

'I do. I was a lot younger then. I'm beginning to feel my age.'

'Come off it. You don't look anywhere near thirty,' she joked, taking hold of his hand. 'I haven't seen you for quite a while. Are you still looking for this killer?'

'Well, sort of. There's very little to go on. Lewis and I are checking advertisements in various magazines. We think the killer is a sadist who might have used prostitutes to satisfy his urges.'

'Good luck to you both. I hope you find him.' She looked to the bar. Jenny was still waiting in the queue. 'I got talking to your friend, Bert Davies. He brought me home from town in his taxi. He mentioned a magazine article called "Parlour's House," or something like that.'

'Oh, yes. The murder of Patricia Burke. It's the only real clue we've got.'

'It's a bit flimsy. You're clutching at straws.'

'Let's forget about the investigation, Irene. How are you getting on?'

'It's not been easy . . . Remember when I told you that I could hear Elizabeth's favourite tune, the theme from *Titanic*?'

'I remember. You could hear it coming from her bedroom.'

'I still hear it now and then, but not as clearly. It's becoming fainter. As time moves on there'll be nothing left of it. Her spirit is waving goodbye.'

Jenny returned with the drinks. Twenty minutes later a hit-record by Shania Twain had the country music lovers line up in rows. Irene and Jenny were eager to join them. Sheridan watched the line dance with interest. He was beginning to loosen up and felt glad he'd made the effort to escape the confines of the office.

As the evening progressed the DJ began playing the ballads. Charlie Rich's 'Behind Closed Doors' made an impression on the country music fans. Irene was dying to have a smooch with her ex-lover. If he ever had any love for her in the past, she wanted to rekindle it.

Irene Collinson was falling in love again.

The evening drifted on. The lights were subdued, the atmosphere relaxed. With only twenty minutes to go, Crazy Pat called, 'Last orders at the bar.' Irene's glass was empty. She didn't want to risk losing the opportunity of asking him to dance with her. Jenny could sense her friend's intention. She offered to buy another round: the usual for Irene and a Jack Daniel's for her partner. Sheridan thanked her for the offer. Irene refused. She knew that she had had enough.

Jenny went to the bar and joined the queue.

Meanwhile, Crazy Pat played Anne Murray's emotional rendition of the classic, 'Could I have this Dance?' Irene loved that song. She placed the Stetson on Sheridan's head and held out her hand. He escorted her onto the dance floor. She wrapped her arms around him tightly and wondered if he would take her home. She could ask him outright. Somehow, it didn't seem the right moment. *Later, maybe,* she thought. She looked into his eyes and sang the words to the song: 'Could I have this dance for the rest of my life? Would you be my partner every night? When we're together it feels so right. Could I have this dance for the rest of my life?'

She managed to sustain her firm embrace. Sheridan had been on her mind ever since the day she visited him at his office. She knew he was the one person who could fill the emptiness in her life.

The song ended. Jenny had returned. She pointed to the glass of whisky standing among the empty bottles.

'Cheers,' Sheridan said. He downed it in one, then fanned himself with the hat. 'The heat's almost unbearable.'

Irene removed her hat and did the same.

'Wouldn't mind another one of those,' he said, as the bar shutters came down.

'Too late,' Irene said, content with knowing that Sheridan was beginning to chill out.

Jenny was happy for her. She thanked them both for a pleasant evening and said her goodbyes. Irene waited until she had left the room. She offered Sheridan a cigarette and told him she had some whisky at home. He refused the offer of the cigarette and accepted the invitation. At last she had someone to go home with, someone to talk to, someone she might be able to share her life with.

'I'll go and order a taxi. I won't be long.'

The phone was in use. Irene waited patiently. Sheridan checked the glasses to see if he'd left any liquor. He was out of luck. He leaned back and closed his eyes. He hadn't a care in the world.

'Don't fall asleep, will you? There's work to be done, Mr Sheridan.'

He opened his eyes and sat upright. Becky Watts was facing him. Sheridan was stunned by her appearance. Her long blonde hair was caressing her powerful shoulders. The carefully applied eye shadow accentuated the blueness of her eyes. The shiny gloss accentuated her full lips.

'Miss Watts. I'm surprised to see you here.'

'You were hard to pinpoint amongst all these cowboys.'

' I bet I was . . . Now don't tell me - Darren told you I was here.'

'Darren?'

'The lad who works below my office.'

'That's right, but I didn't come here straight away. I've been into town, with a friend for a few drinks and a laugh.'

'Anyway, it's good to see you.' He looked towards the door to see if Irene was coming back, then asked Becky what it was she wanted.

'Remember me telling you about that place Rivers went to?'

Sheridan had to think. 'Ah, yes. Some place in Wichonstall.'

'Well, I've found out what goes on there. I want to take you to it.'

'You want to go there now?'

'Right now, Mr Sheridan.'

'I'm tired and I'm not driving tonight.'

'It won't take long. We'll go in my car.'

Sheridan didn't want to give Becky the impression he was unappreciative. She had followed Rivers as he asked her to. He got up just as Irene was on her way back. She wondered who the blonde was, and couldn't help but notice the denim hot-pants and tight-fitting white top.

Sheridan introduced them to each other.

'I've got to go somewhere, Irene. Miss Watts has discovered something that might be important.'

Becky's untimely arrival had put him in an awkward position. Irene's expression became stern. She wasn't going to let him walk out of the club with another woman.

'A lead? What are you talking about?'

'Miss Watts is a private detective.'

'Disguised as an escort girl?'

'Don't be like that, Irene. She works for BBI.'

'I don't believe it. How does she come into all of this?'

'It's difficult to explain.'

'Look Jim, you're supposed to be coming home with me.'

'We're only trying to help, Miss Collinson,' Becky interjected, hoping to subdue Irene's anger.

'Is that so? And what do you expect to get from this case, Miss Watts? Are you hoping to arrest a psychopath and land yourself a load of money? Because that's all Carl Lewis is in it for.'

Irene marched off in a huff, pushing her way through curious onlookers. Sheridan followed and caught up with her.

'Don't go, Irene,' he pleaded. 'Miss Watts really is trying to help me. I'll see you later on, then I can explain what's happening.'

'Don't bother, Jim. You and your pathetic friend carry on playing hunt the killer, because you'll be hunting him for a long time.'

She left him standing alone and speechless. Becky came to his side. 'I think we'd better go, Mr Sheridan.'

He followed her outside. Irene was waiting for the taxi, pacing up and down in her anger. Sheridan kept his head low as they passed. Becky unlocked the car door and noticed Irene scowling at them.

Sheridan threw his hat onto the back seat, annoyed with Becky, and yet he couldn't let her down. He felt awful, too, having to leave Irene at such short notice.

'Where, exactly, is this place situated?' he asked.

'Off the main drag. It's a big house, like a mansion. It's supposed to be a massage parlour. In reality it's a high-class brothel.'

'That's interesting.'

'It is, considering Rivers is a copper. I was quite surprised when I found out about it. You can pretend you're a punter, find out what Rivers gets up to. That's the general idea, isn't it?'

'Yes, and I'm grateful to you. The trouble is, I'm feeling a bit unsteady, if you know what I mean. Right now I'd rather go home. I'll go to Wichonstall soon, when I've sobered up. I hope you don't mind.'

'I take your point. It's fine by me.'

Five minutes later she was in his living room watching him pour a whisky.

'Can I have one of those?' she asked, fanning her face with a newspaper.

'Certainly you can.' He poured a small measure which she downed in one.

'I wouldn't bother going to Wichonstall during the day if I were you,' she said, leaning back in the chair.

'Why is that?'

'You wouldn't get in during the day. They only operate at night.' Becky crossed her legs and smiled. Sheridan drank more whisky and couldn't stop his eyes focusing on her brown muscular legs. There was something suggestive in the way she was looking at him. *If only I was twenty years younger. Who am I kidding?*

'We'll have to discuss this some other time,' he said. 'It's getting late and I don't want to keep you longer than necessary.'

'Well, thanks for the drink. Can I use your bathroom?'

'Certainly. Go up the stairs and it's straight ahead.'

When she'd left the room Sheridan laughed to himself for being stupid enough to think she was giving him the come-on. Five minutes passed. He wondered what might be taking her so long. 'This is getting ridiculous,' he murmured, making his way upstairs.

The bathroom was in darkness. He thought she might have sneaked off home without saying goodbye, then he noticed that the bedroom door was ajar, a faint light shining from within. Sheridan stepped inside, his mind too dull to understand the reality of what was happening.

Becky was standing erect in all her naked glory, running a comb through her luxurious hair. She turned to face him. Sheridan was right after all. The glint in her eyes *was* for real.

There could be no turning back.

The age difference meant nothing now.

He admired the shape of her perk breasts, the curve of her slim waist and hips, the fullness of her lustrous lips. His burning guilt suddenly evaporated, his sense of morality drowning in a sea of alcohol. He undressed, and now she was lying on the cool bed sheets, beckoning with her stunning body, waiting for him to take command. He knelt between her open legs, delirious with anticipation.

Becky got what she wanted.

TWENTY-SEVEN

Midnight had passed. Whilst Jim Sheridan wrestled passionately with Rebecca Watts, DCs Tom Rice and Helen Burrows had taken on the role of a courting couple, following Cooney from one town centre pub to another. Both officers were in their twenties and blended in with the parched, beer-swilling punters.

Rice returned from the bar with a couple of 'boring' drinks. Burrows told him not to keep checking his transmitter in case he attracted attention. They tried to look innocuous. Cooney was the Number One suspect. They had to take note of what he was doing and where he went. They couldn't afford to let him out of their sight, but Cooney was swallowed up by the crowd.

'What's happened to him?' Burrows asked.

'I don't know. He could have gone to the toilet.'

Burrows told Rice to check the toilets, but they caught sight of their suspect leaving the pub. They rushed into the busy street and followed him along the Promenade. The sight of unruly drunken youths and the noise of shouting and jeering was an aspect of the famous resort that many of the older visitors regarded as too menacing. Even Rice and Burrows felt vulnerable.

A group of eight hen-party girls were coming towards them, supping out of bottles and singing the still-popular Gary Glitter song, 'Leader of the Gang.' Cooney sang along to the raucous rendition and laughed as two of the girls raised their T-shirts to expose their naked breasts. He cheered and threw his arms in the air as if the Seasiders had scored a goal. Rice laughed too. Burrows shook her head in disgust.

'I don't know why you're laughing. They're asking for trouble.'

'There's no sense of dignity nowadays,' Rice said, straightening his face. 'I must admit, I'm beginning to enjoy myself.'

Suddenly, Cooney dashed across the road, narrowly missing a black bomber taxi. The officers nearly lost him. Luckily, Burrows saw him urinating in a shop doorway. He had decided to go home.

They followed him inland, and away from the bustle of the town's night life.

'Wilkes Parade isn't far from here,' said Burrows.

'Good. It's been a long hot night.'

Cooney ignored the turning into Wilkes Parade, his attention focused on a lone female.

'Tom, you see that girl in front of him?'

'How could I miss her? She's semi-naked. No wonder he's latched onto that one.'

Cooney quickened his pace and walked beside her. Burrows felt a rush of adrenaline. 'Come on, Tom, let's get closer.'

'Not so fast, Helen. Let's see what happens.'

Seconds later, Cooney and the girl started arguing. The girl told him to knob off, and he turned around into the path of the officers.

'Okay, Helen. You go after the girl, find out what you can.'

Burrows responded. Rice waited for Cooney to reach him. He blocked his path and flashed his ID card.

'Stop, right there,' Rice said.

'What's up? I haven't done anything wrong,' he protested.

'Nobody said you had.'

When Burrows had returned, Rice carried on questioning him. 'What's your name and address?' he asked.

'Dean Cooney,' he replied, looking to the ground. 'I live on Wilkes Parade.'

'Lift your head up. I want to see your face. That's better. Who is the girl you were talking to?'

'Dunno.'

'Are you in the habit of bothering girls who you don't know?'

'No, I'm not. What's all this about?'

'Answer the questions, please. What did you say to that girl?'

'I asked her where she'd been, that's all.'

'You must have said something else. What was it you said?'

Cooney shrugged.

'Did you ask her where she lived?' Burrows asked.

He looked shiftily from one to the other. 'Yeah, I did.'

Rice told him to take his hands out of his pockets, then frisked him. 'Okay, you can go now.'

'Tossers,' Cooney shouted, running off.

'His pockets were empty,' said Rice.

'At least we know he wasn't carrying a knife. Well, that's it, we've done our bit. He didn't harm the girl, and she had no complaint against him.'

DC Rice called the incident room and spoke to Oxley. He told them to wait for their relief, then report back at the station.

Sheridan woke with a bad hangover. The time was 8.30. The smell of bacon had drifted into the bedroom. He threw off the thin blanket and got into his dressing gown and slippers. The phone rang. He went downstairs as fast as his sensitive head would allow him to.

Becky was fully dressed. She picked up the phone and spoke briefly before handing it to Sheridan. 'It's a woman,' she said. 'She didn't give her name.'

'Jim Sheridan speaking,' he said softly.

'It's Irene. Who answered the phone?'

Sheridan detected a hint of aggression in her voice. 'That was . . . uh . . . Rebecca Watts. She called to see me about the investigation.' *Wait for it,* he thought, *she's going to fly off the handle any second now.*

'You're telling me lies, Jim, aren't you?'

Irene knew that something had gone on between him and the girl from BBI.

'Listen to me, Irene—'

'You bastard. I never thought you would do a thing like that.'

'Hello . . .'

Becky came in with a few more bacon sandwiches. 'Who was that?'

'Irene. She was annoyed because you answered the phone. She's put two and two together.'

'I'm sorry. I didn't know you were intimate with her.'

'We're not intimate.'

'What's the problem, then? You're working on a case and I'm helping you.'

'It's not that simple, Miss Watts.'

'How do you mean?'

'I've known her for a long time. Things were developing between us: emotionally, I mean.'

'You should have told me, shouldn't you? And you don't have to call me Miss Watts anymore. It sounds stupid.'

'All right, it's "Becky" from now on.'

'And I'll call you "Sheridan." It suits you best.'

'What was last night all about, then?'

She took the chair opposite him. 'You don't need me to spell it out do you, Sheridan? It's called, sex.'

'Sex, with an old-timer like me?'

'I like older men. You find me attractive, don't you?'

'You're a bonny girl. I think it's one of the reasons why Irene won't forget this in a hurry. Please don't do that again.'

'You poor man,' she said with an expression of pity. 'Okay, I'll try not to do that again. You sleep downstairs next time; but remember, it takes two to tango.'

He shook his head and ate his bacon butties. Becky waited until he had finished eating and asked if he wanted anything else.

'No thanks. Have you eaten?'

'I'll grab something, later. Mum's looking after Johnny. They'll be expecting me home soon.'

'Your mother will want to know what you were doing last night, won't she?'

'I'm a big girl now. Anyway, don't you want to know about this place Rivers went to?'

'Oh, of course. I nearly forgot all about Rivers.'

'I'll carry on from where I left off. Last night I followed him to this house in Wichonstall. It's like a mansion, with ornamental lights in the driveway and steps leading up to the front door.'

Sheridan raised his hand. 'Before you go any further, are you certain Rivers didn't see you?'

'Positive. I managed to snap a couple of photos of him speaking to the owner. She's called Diana Humble.'

'I'm impressed. How did you find this out?'

'A friend of mine knows a woman who used to work there. I spoke to her and got some info on the place. It used to be a massage parlour, but it's more than that nowadays. They cater for businessmen and the like.'

'People with money?'

'Yes. Each girl has her own room. There's all kinds of weird music constantly playing. Each room has its own coloured light which makes the girls look different. It's supposed to protect their identities.'

'What's on offer?'

'Usual stuff, I suppose.'

'Anything kinky or sadistic?'

'I don't know. I see what you're getting at. Carl told me that you're trying to locate sadistic punters.'

'That's right. It was an idea we came up with. By the way, you didn't tell Lewis about your trip to Wichonstall did you?'

Becky shook her head. 'Carl might not even know about Rivers' escapades.'

'But I need to know why he goes there, what he does.'

'This is not going to help you catch your daughter's killer.'

'I agree.'

'You want to dig up some dirt because of the way he treated you. Is that it?'

'I'm not the vindictive type. I'm interested to know if he's following the same line of enquiry as Lewis and I. Maybe Lewis has told him about our interest in prostitutes and sadistic punters.'

'I doubt it,' she said, standing up. 'When Carl is working on a case he doesn't tell anyone what he's doing.'

Sheridan considered. 'I think I'm going to have to pay Diana Humble a visit. What do you say?'

'She doesn't accept visitors. You have to ring first, and you need to know the password or they will treat you as a normal customer and offer you a straight massage for a hundred quid just to put you off. At one time the password was "Humble Pie."'

'Humble Pie?'

'Yes. It has a certain ring to it, don't you think: a bit like, Parlour's Dolly House?'

'Yes, it does. Try and locate the woman who used to work there and see if she knows anything about Rivers. You might save me a trip.'

'And a lot of money.'

'Of course. Don't mention any of this to Lewis.'

'I'll carry out your orders. I'm sure your intentions are good.'

He showed her to the front door. She got into her car, started the engine and wound the window down. 'Thanks for a great night. I enjoyed it.'

Sheridan waved and returned to his comfy chair. He thought about the previous night's events. The shame of his amorous fling was already gnawing at him, and he had upset Irene more than he dared to think.

Palmer checked his watch for the tenth time.

'Look Rick, just pack it in will you?'

'I can't help it, Steve. There's only five minutes to go, then we move in.'

5 p.m. was the deadline. Police officers had been granted a warrant to search Cooney's lodgings. An arrest was imminent. The investigation - code-named, Stamford - had reached its most crucial point since the beginning of the enquiry.

DCs Rivers and Palmer waited in their vehicle. Uniformed officers were stationed close by, watching for the signal to move in.

Palmer was becoming fidgety. 'What do you reckon, Steve? Do you think he's the murderer?'

'Who knows? He sounds like a good contender to me. Don't forget what I said. You read his rights while I have a look round; and remember, he's being arrested on suspicion of murder. Make sure you get it right.'

'Don't worry, I will . . . Steve, look at the time.'

Action-time had arrived.

They got out of the car and walked briskly to the front door of the house, Uniformed coppers following behind. Rivers raised both hands and bashed the door. A middle-aged woman answered, looking bewildered. Rivers asked her to take them to Cooney's room. She led them up the stairs and pointed to a door. Rivers burst into the living quarters and looked around furtively. Barefooted Cooney rushed out of the tiny kitchen in his dark-blue dressing gown. Palmer nervously edged his way towards him and made the arrest.

Cooney's computer was operational. Rivers sat in front of it.

'Get dressed,' he ordered. 'Rick, you stay with him.'

Palmer followed him into a small room containing a single bed, a table, chair and a wardrobe. Cooney turned his back towards Palmer and started to dress. Meanwhile, Rivers searched for the websites that the suspect had visited.

A few minutes passed and Cooney entered the room looking white as snow, and became agitated when he saw Rivers at the computer.

'Leave that alone,' he said. 'It's got nothing to do with you.'

Rivers leapt up and slapped his face. Palmer grabbed his partner's arm before he could deliver another blow.

'You'd better cut that out, Steve.'

Rivers composed himself. 'You're under arrest, Cooney. It's not in your best interests to tell *us* what to do.'

'You'd better tell me what this is about,' he said.

'Shut your mouth, or next time I'll break your nose,' Rivers said, pointing at him. He resumed his position at the computer. 'You have some unusual tastes, don't you? . . . Let's see what we've got here. Oh, a series of videos for sale.' Rivers silently read the titles: *Goo Guzzlers*, *Bizarre Fetish* and *Obscene Desires*. 'This is disgusting stuff, Cooney,' Rivers said, smirking. He forward-paged whilst Palmer peered over his shoulder to get a closer look. 'Here we are,' Rivers continued, 'some more crap from a magazine called *Slave Sex*. It says, "He hypnotizes her into undressing before him. Her back stiffens as she gazes at the mirror hanging from the ceiling. She raises her bottom high, waiting for his command."'

Rivers switched the computer off and gave the order for Cooney to be taken to the station. Palmer waited until officers escorted the suspect off the premises.

'All that porn doesn't count for anything, Steve,' he said, pointing at the computer. 'Millions of people watch it everyday of their lives.'

Rivers ignored the remark. He got up and noticed Cooney's book collection. 'You're probably right, Rick,' he murmured. He slowly ran his eyes along the books, reading each title. 'This one's interesting.' He showed it to Palmer. The cover read, *Midnight Stalker*. Rivers flicked through the pages. 'What's this?' he said. He took a tissue from his pocket and used it to remove a photograph from inside its pages. Palmer felt a jolt of excitement when Rivers showed it to him.

The girl was lying face down, close to a bush, stab wounds visible on her back.

'Cooney has some explaining to do,' Rivers said, dropping the photograph into a small plastic bag.

TWENTY-EIGHT

'They're checking the photograph for clues. You know we can't see it until Forensic have finished,' Oxley explained.

Naylor was pacing the room and chewing his fingernails. 'I know that,' he said. 'We need to see it as soon as possible.' He dragged the chair from beneath his desk, then kicked it back under again. 'Why is everything taking so long?'

'Look George, I'm just as eager to examine it as you are.'

'I know, I know.'

'You did tell them that the photo was a priority job?'

'Of course.'

Oxley looked at his watch. 'How time flies when you most need it. By half past five this afternoon the twenty-four hours will have expired. A lot depends on the house search, and that's going to take time.'

'I realise that . . . How is the interview proceeding?'

'If Cooney is the murderer, he's not ready for admitting to it. He's nervous. I think he'll crack sooner or later.'

'Sooner is better than later. Everything fits. Even your so-called profile makes some sort of sense.'

'Do you think the profile has been useful?' Oxley asked with a searching glance.

'Has it buggery. It could have been useful, I'll admit that. Turns out we didn't need it after all, but I've glanced through it. Cooney is the right age, according to Simmons. He lives alone and he stalks scantily-dressed women. That's about as far as it goes.'

'He has access to Internet porn, don't forget. One of the advertised videos features a woman who is forced to endure anal degradation.'

'*Anal degradation.* Yes, yes. That's what the killer seems to like doing.'

'You know, George, the success of this investigation might hinge on the photo that Rivers discovered.'

'Yes, Rivers has done a good job for a change.'

The phone rang. Naylor snatched it, eager to learn of any new developments. The press officer said he was sorry to bother him, but the local newspaper's head office was pushing for a press release. Somehow, information had seeped through regarding the suspect - the prime suspect whom everybody wanted to know about. The superintendent resigned himself to the fact that news travels fast. He was optimistic that the end of the murder hunt was in sight and he agreed to a press conference. When the conversation ended he stood up and looked out of the window.

'You said the killer could be local. You may be right, Derek.'

Oxley was pleased with himself. He followed his boss to the display board in the incident room.

'Is that him?' Naylor asked, looking at the e-fit. 'Is that supposed to be Dean Cooney?'

'It looks similar, except for the moustache.'

'A moustache can be shaved off in no time at all.' He laid his hand on Oxley's shoulder. 'I'll let you know as soon as the photo arrives. You check with Forensic. I want to know if anything significant has turned up in Cooney's car.'

Davina Mullen crossed her legs and lit a cigarette. She swept her auburn hair away from her eyes. Her good looks were marred by worry-wrinkles under her eyes. Her cheeks had lost their fullness, adding extra years to her once youthful, vibrant features. She blew smoke rings in the air.

'I left Diana Humble's employ about a year ago,' she said, in reply to Becky's question.

'What was it like working there?'

Mullen drew deeply on the cigarette and exhaled in short bursts. 'It was a job, like any other.'

'Come on, Davina. Prostitution isn't the type of job most women would want to consider.'

'What can I say? You don't think about what you're doing. You get on with it and collect your wages to pay for the rent or whatever.'

'Was it well paid?'

'Good money for lying on your back, I suppose.'

Becky suppressed the urge to laugh. 'What kind of punters did you receive?'

'Blokes in their thirties to fifties. Usually well-to-do, plenty of cash. We'd get married and single men, ugly ones and nice ones.'

'Did any of them have unusual tastes like bondage or whipping?'

'I don't think so.'

'Okay. Let's talk about Steve Rivers. Was he one of your, how can I put it - customers?'

'Rivers? That wasn't the name he used. We all knew he was a copper.' She awkwardly stubbed out the cigarette. 'Yes, I slept with him a few times.'

'Did any of the other girls service him?'

'Most of them. Sometimes he had two in one night.'

'That would cost a lot, wouldn't it?'

'Depends on what you ask for. A bloke could pay as much as five hundred pounds to spend all night with the girl of his choosing.'

Becky gave a look of surprise. 'How often did Rivers go there?'

'Sometimes twice a week, but he wasn't paying for the services. I believe he used to work for the vice squad. He struck a deal with Humble.'

'His silence for free services?'

'That's right. You're not going to mention my name, are you? I mean, I don't want any trouble.'

'Of course not. I only want to know what Rivers was doing there,' Becky said, ready for the important question. 'Did he involve the girls in any sadistic acts?'

'Not to my knowledge.'

'Did he show any violence at all?'

'I think he once punched a girl for being too noisy.'

'Any anal intercourse?'

'That sort of thing was forbidden. Humble kept strict rules. If Rivers wanted some anal he could have offered a bribe, maybe in the form of drugs. He had access to cannabis. He gave it to some of the girls every now and then.'

'Did he say where he got it from?'

'A dodgy copper was stealing drugs obtained from raids. He passed it onto Rivers, who then sold it.'

'But why should he mention all this? It could have landed him in hot water.'

'Rivers had power over everybody, including Humble. He loved to brag about the things he did. He was nasty, too. Said he would have the place closed down if any of us grassed on him.'

Becky had got what she needed. She stood up. 'Thanks for talking to me, Davina. You've been a great help.'

'Why are you so interested in Steve Rivers?' Mullen asked when they were outside the house.

'We're investigating a murder.'

'How does it involve him?'

'It's a long story.'

'I hope everything works out for you. I never did like Rivers. He was a pure bastard.'

Becky waved and said goodbye. She got into her car and pressed the rewind button on her micro recorder.

Her conversation with Davina Mullen had successfully recorded.

Oxley had given orders for an identity parade to be assembled. Eight men, eight faces. Each man held a card with a number on it.

Karen Lawson's dyed blonde hair was back to its original black colour, enhancing the pallor of her skin. Her haggard features spoke of a haunting sadness. The grief of losing her best friend, Angela Ross, had proved difficult to come to terms with.

Naylor approached her. 'You are Karen Lawson?' he asked.

'Who else did you expect?'

He shuffled uncomfortably. 'We want you to look at these men,' he said. 'Look at them carefully. It's important you take your time. If you recognise the man who spoke to you and Angela Ross on the night of the murder —'

'I know what to do,' she said, glancing at the line-up through the glass panelling. 'You want me to touch him.'

'No. If you recognise the man, just remember his number. Go through that door, and begin when you're ready.'

Lawson stood at one end of the line-up. She closed her eyes and tried to visualise the face of the man who called himself Tony.

Naylor and Oxley were watching with deep interest, wondering how she would react to the fifth man - Dean Cooney.

She moved slowly down the line, passing the first two. She stopped at the third man, a civilian worker from the incident room.

'Oh, not him, please,' Oxley whispered.

She moved along to the fourth man and paused to study his features. She took a few steps back, then moved to the next one. Cooney's eyes met hers. She looked harder at him. She glanced at the men to her left and right, then back at Cooney again. Naylor was about to speak, then Lawson moved on, discounting the sixth and seventh. The last man - another civilian worker - was given a cursory glance. She turned and faced the officers who were barely visible through the darkened glass.

Oxley sighed. His boss walked away without speaking.

Lawson breezed into the room. 'Sorry,' she said. 'I can't make a positive identification. I think it might have been last man, but I can't be certain.'

She picked up her bag ready to leave. Oxley thanked her, disappointment showing on his face.

Oxley joined Naylor in his office. 'I thought she was going to pick him out, George.'

Naylor was clearly out of breath. He loosened his tie. 'I told you Derek, the man Lawson and Ross spoke to isn't the killer.'

'Well, perhaps we'll never know for definite whether it was him or not. What's that in your hand?'

'This might be the answer - the photograph recovered from Cooney's room.' He took a batch of crime-scene photographs out of the drawer and arranged them on the desk.

'This one, George.'

Oxley picked up a particular photograph showing the body of Elizabeth Collinson partly hidden by a holly bush. It became immediately obvious that Cooney's photograph showed a different body.

'They don't match, Derek. But we have our killer, I'm certain of that. One way or the other I'll get a confession from him. He'll tell us what we want to know. I'll make sure of that.'

'Don't you go pushing him too hard,' Oxley said, aware of Naylor's fragile constitution. 'Look, there's still some time left. Why don't you get off home and take a breather?'

'At a time like this? No way. When Forensic have finished their job we'll have all the evidence we need.'

171

'No doubt; but you need to have your wits about you. Your wife wants you home. She's been asking for you.'

'I'll call her. That's the best I can do. Dorothy will just have to wait, but it won't be for long.'

52-year-old Julian Francis had spent a pleasant evening entertaining a group of his 'believers.' The well-known psychic was renowned for his talents: palm reading, mind reading, cartomancy, clairvoyance and psychometry. People who paid for his services were mainly elderly women. And they adored him. If the curious were not impressed by his ability, they could hardly fail to be entertained by him. His camp mannerisms and speech - coupled with his short stature, pot-belly and curly grey hair - put him at the pinnacle of eccentricity itself.

11.45 p.m. The last of his flock had reluctantly departed. Francis locked the door, switched off the lights and went upstairs. He crept into his mother's bedroom to make sure she was comfortable. All was well. He washed and got into his comfy cotton pyjamas. The haloed moon was visible through the open curtains of his bedroom window. He got into bed and sat upright. He placed the palm of his hand against his forehead. Something strange and frightening had happened two months before, and it was happening again.

A powerful sense of foreboding erupted inside him, culminating in a paroxysm of utter fear and a feeling of helplessness.

He jumped out of bed and ran into the bathroom, the quick patter of his bare feet sounding off the wooden floor. He turned the tap on and threw cold water into his face. His eyes, exuding fear, looked back at him from the mirror. He could hear the blood surging in his head.

The disturbing psychic vision was taking shape, and there was nothing he could do to stop it.

He raced into his bedroom, opened the window, allowing the cool night breeze to caress his heaving chest. The energy drained from the muscles of his body. He slumped to the floor, his hands moving rapidly across his abdomen, protecting him from the silver flashes of the knife. He began to wriggle uncontrollably, arms thrashing, legs kicking, until total exhaustion quelled the desire to protect himself.

Then he suddenly froze, fingers stiff, arms outstretched. He was lying on his back, staring through the open window and preparing himself.

Cold blue eyes, staring.

Lightning-steel rips succulent flesh.

Strobe-like visions flashed in his mind. He saw naked blood-drenched bodies writhing in agony, open mouths yelling and screaming.

Devilish laughter was taunting him.

He saw his eyes changing to red, then back to blue, pupils mutating into tiny yellow moons.

His open mouth falls upon tempting breast. Red tongue darting in and out.

His teeth pierce the soft flesh, deeper and deeper.

His mind succumbs to evil passion, insane cruelty. He hates. He curses. The white serum of life is spurting incessantly.

The smile of death reveals crimson teeth. Intestines glow in the moonlight.

Her heart stops. The last breath expires.

The steel is ripping, stabbing again and again.

The violation is unfinished.

A portrait of horror waits to be discovered.

The fantasy lives on.

TWENTY-NINE

The sound of footsteps echoed down the corridor. The lock turned and the door to Room 6 swung open. Oxley slammed the door shut behind him. Naylor gave his name and rank, and pushed the photograph towards a pale, worried-looking young man. Dean Cooney was shivering with fear.

'Who is the girl in that photo?' Naylor asked. Straight into it. No soft talk.

'Don't know,' he replied, shrinking back.

'Where did you get it from?'

'It's a printout off the Internet.'

'You like that sort of thing, don't you? Mutilation is what I'm talking about.'

Cooney didn't answer.

'I'm waiting. Do you want me to repeat the question?'

'It's a photo, that's all. It doesn't mean anything.'

'What you mean is, you're not bothered that women are killed and mutilated; in fact, you like to see women being hurt.'

'It doesn't bother me.'

'Their suffering turns you on, doesn't it? That's what you're saying.'

'I wouldn't say that.'

'All right. Tell me about the other photographs. You took photos of hundreds of women: women walking the streets, girls out jogging.'

'I took them. There's nothing wrong in that, is there?'

'I don't suppose there is, Mr Cooney . . . You have problems getting on with the opposite sex. It's my opinion that you haven't got what it takes to form a sound relationship with a girl. I think you resent women because they're a threat to you, to your manhood.'

That's the way, Oxley thought.

Cooney raised a clenched fist and hit the table. 'You can't know that.'

'We know a lot about you. Why not tell us the truth, make it easier for yourself?'

'Tell the truth about what?' I haven't done anything wrong. Look, I've had enough. I'm tired. Just leave me alone.'

Naylor got up and stood behind Cooney. He grabbed a handful of hair and yanked his head back in one swift movement, causing Cooney to squeal like a pig.

'I'm tired too,' Naylor spat, releasing his grip. Cooney jerked his head forward.

'We're not leaving until you tell us why you killed those girls.'

'I don't know what girls you mean.'

Naylor returned to his seat. 'We found newspaper reports in your room: reports concerning two girls who were murdered here in Blackpool. You know who I'm talking about.'

'Plenty of people read articles and stuff like that. I'm not the only one.'

'You kept those articles because it reminds you of the excitement you felt when you killed them,' Oxley said, and continued with the questioning. 'Why are you being so evasive about all this?'

'I don't know anything. Just leave me alone. I haven't slept all night in that stinking cell and I'm tired.'

Oxley grabbed a chair and sat down. 'You will be tired, believe me, sonny,' he said, his voice full of threat. 'Let's talk about the first victim - Elizabeth Collinson. You remember the name, don't you?'

'I remember.'

'On the night of the murder, did you return to your flat with blood on your shirt?'

No answer. Oxley repeated the question.

'I don't know what I was doing that night.'

'Surely, you must remember returning home wearing a bloodstained shirt. How did the blood get there?'

'I never got blood on any of my shirts.' Cooney leaned back and took a deep breath, trying to ease his tension.

'You told Teresa Moore that you knew where the body had been discovered.'

'I might have done.'

A breakthrough at last. 'Did you tell her that you knew where the body had been discovered?'

After a long pause he said yes.

'And how did you know?'

'I didn't know. I was only pretending I knew.'

'You knew where the body was found because you killed her.'

Cooney frowned and shook his head.

'Why don't you tell us, get it off your chest? You've been in trouble before. We know all about your previous convictions.'

'I've said all I want to say.'

Naylor decided on a different approach. 'Listen carefully,' he began. 'Our forensic team have discovered a bloodstain on an item of your clothing. They have examined it. The DNA contained within that bloodstain matches that of Elizabeth Collinson. How do you explain that?'

Cooney gave Naylor a suspicious look. 'Fair enough,' he said, at last. 'Get me a solicitor and I'll tell you the truth.'

Naylor looked into his colleague's eyes. They both knew it would be pointless to continue with the interview. They left the room and saw DC Tanya Lambert walking briskly towards them.

'You're an early bird this morning,' Naylor said.

'I'm surprised you're still here, sir. I've just received a report from Forensic. They're still examining Cooney's vehicle. They haven't found anything that ties him to the murders. Fibre analysis looks doubtful—'

'What about blood?' Oxley cut in. 'There must be a trace of blood in that car.'

'Not a single speck, sir. Nothing.'

In 1965 Blackpool's Mecca Ballroom opened its doors to the public. The three-storey, box-like structure - considered stylish for its time - could hold up to 3,500 people. In its heyday thousands of club-goers came to enjoy dancing and listening to live bands. The Mecca's pulling power was enhanced by a glitzy stage and revolving bandstand.

The 1970s saw the opening of more intimate venues. The discos and nightclubs began to flourish and the Mecca's popularity started to decline. In the 80s it closed completely having fallen into a state of disrepair. It was the end of a great era. The 'Mecca Dancing' sign was eventually torn down, and the building - still referred to by many as the 'Mecca' - reopened as 'Premier Ten Pin Bowling'.

The rear of the building remained the same, the central part retaining its original iron stairs, providing escape routes in the event of a fire breaking out. The deep recesses in the walls were covered with bird droppings from top to bottom. Strange patterns - aptly named, 'Urban Art' - adorned the cleaner surfaces, and porno drawings spoke of teenage boredom.

Behind the Ten Pin Bowling stood the offices and storage areas of the Blackpool Borough Council Illuminations Department. The pathway between the two buildings was littered with rubbish: broken glass, beer cans, paper, discarded metal and a couple of half-filled dustbin liners.

Alf Livesey signalled right and turned his taxi into the waste ground next to the Ten Pin Bowling, where he could read his Sunday newspaper whilst waiting for his next fare. He had stopped there many times before, but this time was different. He started to read the paper, but the words failed to sink in. He threw the paper onto the seat next to him. That fleeting image was bothering him: something he saw in the corner of his eye. *Could have been a tailor's dummy. Probably a prank set up by some local kids.*

Livesey got out of the taxi. The waste ground was deserted. Even at 8.30 a.m. he expected to see another taxi or a couple of parked lorries.

He walked towards the rear of the building, not knowing what to expect, and turned right at the entrance to the filthy passage. Something in the first recess stopped him in his tracks. His eyes were drawn to the bizarre, lifeless figure sitting amongst the debris, its back against the wall, legs wide apart. The head was bowed, resting on the chest.

He looked down the passage which led to Geary Road. Nobody in sight. He was alone, fear pervading his mind. He hoped he was looking at the result of a sick joke. He stuffed his hands into his pockets and moved closer.

A rush of panic blasted his senses. Livesey began to retch as he staggered backwards. He took several deep breaths trying to compose himself before looking at the body one last time. The battered blood-caked features of her face reminded him of a creature in a zombie film. Her chest had suffered a ferocious assault. The breasts had been savagely mutilated. Glue-like blood, splattered over the legs, was glinting in the warm morning sun. Soft flesh had been torn and ripped, stomach carved open, intestines lying over the left leg. Traces of her blood were visible on the wall. The leaves of the hedge mustard growing from the base of the recess were splashed red.

His sense of reality escaped him for a moment. He turned away from the grotesque spectacle and covered his face with both hands.

Alf Livesey would never forget what he saw that day.

177

'Another body has been found, sir,' Lambert said to Oxley. 'A taxi driver made the discovery. The super has been informed.'

'Where did this happen?'

'Behind the Ten Pin Bowling on Central Drive.'

He considered the location. The Ten Pin was a fifteen-minute walk from the police station, and a stone's throw away from the scene of the Ross murder which took place only two months previously. Oxley rushed to Naylor's office. He didn't budge when the door cracked open.

'George, why are you sitting there doing nothing?'

'Mind-factors, Derek . . .'

'What do you mean?'

'The killer has a mind-factor of seven according to the high and mighty Dr Simmons. Isn't that correct?'

Oxley closed his eyes in despair. 'Yes, George, the killer has a mind-factor of seven.'

'He was wrong. This one scores a ten. Do you hear me? Forensic have drawn a blank. Once again, the killer leaves no clues. Angela Ross's bracelet hasn't even turned up . . . Close the door. We need to talk things over.'

'No. There isn't time to sit and discuss this. We don't know for sure if this latest murder was committed by the same hand as the others. If Cooney *is* the murderer then the body has lain undiscovered for some considerable time.'

'Cooney *is* guilty. Don't tell me you're having doubts.'

'We can't start jumping to conclusions. I hope you're not going to sit on your arse all day.'

Naylor looked passed him as Chief Superintendent Greenwood came in.

'I heard that, Oxley. I didn't realise your respect for George had deteriorated so much.'

'I'm sorry, sir . . . I ought to be making my way to the murder scene.'

'Splendid idea. We had better go with him, George. We have another poor victim who, by all accounts, has been mutilated in a most appalling fashion.'

The waste ground and pathway behind the Ten Pin were sealed off with the familiar blue-and-white tape. Uniformed officers took up their positions to ensure complete protection of the crime scene and surrounding area.

Dr Charles Scott was ready to make his examination. 'So, it's our man again, is it?' he asked.

'We think it might be,' replied Oxley.

'He won't get another chance,' Naylor said.

Scott's eyes focused on Greenwood, then back to Naylor.

'What makes you so sure, George?' he asked.

'Because we have arrested a man on suspicion of murder. He's a good suspect and I'm convinced he's our man.'

'And what do you think, inspector?'

'I'm inclined to agree. It all depends on when this victim was murdered.'

'Quite so. I can, perhaps, give you an approximate time of death.'

The four men walked up to the barrier tape. The mutilated corpse was clearly visible. Oxley was grim-faced. Naylor shrunk back a few paces. Greenwood snatched a handkerchief from his pocket and covered his mouth.

Scott walked slowly towards the body, surveying the ground surrounding the victim.

Oxley turned to Greenwood. 'I can't believe what I'm seeing.'

'It's devastation, Oxley. How could anybody do that to another human being? It looks like he's pulled out her insides.'

'He must have been covered in blood and, as yet, we haven't found any blood on Cooney's clothes or in his vehicle.'

'Then who on earth is doing this?' Naylor snarled.

Scott joined them after several minutes had passed. 'She probably died within the last twelve hours.'

'You're certain about that?' Oxley asked.

'It's only approximate. The pathologist will be better equipped to answer that with more certainty.'

'What can you tell us?' Naylor enquired.

'She's young, possibly mid-twenties. She's been beaten about the face. Numerous stab wounds to the chest. Parts of the breasts have been cut away and appear to be missing.'

'Was she dead when all this happened?' Greenwood asked.

'I doubt it. I noticed defence wounds on her hands. I should imagine she was either dead or unconscious when he disembowelled her . . . By the way, her shoes are missing.'

Oxley contacted HQ on his mobile and asked for an update on the examination of Cooney's car, personal belongings and the contents of his flat.

Oxley ended his conversation. 'Nothing of significance has turned up,' he said, his voice barely audible.

'Then release him,' Greenwood ordered. 'He couldn't have committed this murder and, furthermore, we can't hold him on hearsay and the fact that has an unhealthy interest in women.'

'I agree, sir,' Oxley responded. 'We must find out who she is as soon as possible. Somebody may have seen her with the killer.'

'I hope that is the case. I have to admit, my concern for public safety has never been as intense as it is now . . . Where is George?'

But Naylor was nowhere to be seen.

Oxley took one last look at the broken body.

Three girls murdered, he thought. *Three murders showing an escalation in brutality and violence.*

Two words flashed through his mind - serial killer.

THIRTY

Oxley escorted him down corridor, towards the exit. Cooney kicked the door open and stepped outside.

'Better luck next time, inspector,' he said, grinning.

'If you step out of line again I'll personally see to it that you spend a long time behind bars. Got it?'

'I think I've got the gist.' He angled his head to one side. 'Can't stop me taking photographs, can you? Can't stop me enjoying myself. Not you. Not nobody.'

'You *are* a sad character, Cooney.'

'Yes, I suppose I am.' He walked down the concrete steps, hands in pockets. 'Bye, bye,' he said in a childlike voice.

'Before you retreat into your perverted world, tell me what you meant when you said you would tell the truth.'

'Don't you get it, inspector? I was tired, I wanted a kip. I knew you couldn't pin the murders on me. A good defence would have tore you apart.'

Oxley returned to the crime scene. Dr Christian Purslow was examining the body whilst forensic scientists prepared to search for clues. Oxley spoke to the coordinator of the search team. As yet, nothing of importance had surfaced. Ten minutes elapsed before Purslow approached the inspector, who was waiting for any additional information regarding the injuries.

'I expected George to be here,' Purslow said.

A sudden burst of sunshine reflected off the white screens surrounding the dead girl. Oxley turned his face away from the light, and thought for a moment. He didn't quite know how to explain Naylor's absence.

'I'm sorry. Nobody seems to know his whereabouts.'

'That is odd. I thought he'd be in on this one. Anyway, I can tell you now - it's the same killer.'

Oxley wasn't surprised. 'I was going to ask you . . .'

'About the anal assault?'

'Yes.'

'I thought you would. She has been brutalised. Her attacker forced a piece of blunt wood inside her. It resembles a piece of furniture, perhaps a broken leg from a chair or something like that.'

'How old is she?'

'Early twenties. The level of violence exhibited in this crime is extremely rare.'

'What's your initial impression regarding the nature of the attack?'

'Bruising to the face indicates she was beaten up before he took the knife to her.'

'The police surgeon said parts of the breasts were missing.'

'Yes, pieces of breast tissue *are* missing. The chest shows numerous wounds, and an incision has been made from the breastbone to the pubic region. Her intestines were wrenched out.'

'How long would it take to inflict the injuries?'

'A few minutes. The poor girl tried to defend herself, as is evident by the cuts to the hands. The abrasions and scuff marks on her back and legs are consistent with a struggle.'

'How long would the initial attack have taken?'

'Again, we're talking a couple of minutes at most.'

'Was she strangled?'

'No signs. I'll clarify that point later when I carry out the post-mortem.'

'Would the killer have much blood on him?'

'There are splashes of blood on the wall of the recess and on the ground surrounding the body. There are traces of blood underneath the body too, which means she was probably in a standing position whilst being stabbed. His clothes will be impregnated with her blood.'

'Any clothing missing?'

'Knickers and shoes.'

Oxley surveyed the waste ground. He remembered having seen long-distance lorries parked overnight. Taxi drivers also parked there when waiting for fares. *Could be a lorry driver like the Yorkshire Ripper was,* he thought. *Such men might carry tools such as pliers. They might have cause to use industrial tape, too.*

He returned to HQ. George Naylor's absence was causing problems. Oxley telephoned his wife. Dorothy had no idea where he might be. It seemed as if he had disappeared into thin air.

'Where is he?' Greenwood asked, as soon as Oxley replaced the receiver. 'Any ideas?'

Oxley expected the chief superintendent to be immersed in the investigation, instead of busy-bodying around like a mother preparing for the daughter's wedding.

'Perhaps he's fallen asleep somewhere,' he answered flippantly.

'Oh, really? I'm not happy, Oxley. George has always been an intelligent and dependable officer. I wonder what has got into him? He's taking it all too seriously, isn't he?'

'How else is a murder investigation meant to be taken, sir?'

'You know what I mean, Oxley. He mentioned the mind-factor of this killer. How can we interpret what he is thinking?'

'I know George better than anybody. This is not about what he thinks; it's how he feels.' The telephone sounded. 'Excuse me, sir.'

The chief superintendent returned to his office. Dorothy Naylor was on the line to Oxley, expressing her worries about her husband. And that wasn't all. He was working long hours with hardly any sleep. Naylor was living and breathing the investigation twenty-four hours a day.

Carl Lewis was standing at the window of his flat on Bank Street. He couldn't resist the commotion outside. Two girls were arguing over a packet of cigarettes given to them by a stranger in a pub. Then the fight started, embellished by an exchange of obscenities that would disgust most people.

The blonde pulled and tugged her friend's black hair, then repeatedly pulled her head from side to side. The black-haired girl crashed to the ground, skirt riding upwards revealing her white knickers.

Lewis had the music blaring out. He always treated himself to a loud music session on Sunday afternoons, but the fracas in the street was far more entertaining.

The fighting and kicking continued relentlessly. Lewis turned the volume down, grabbed his can of lager and returned to his spot by the window. Blonde was getting the better of Black. A moment later, Black retaliated with a well-aimed kick to Blonde's crutch.

'Oh, nice one,' Lewis crooned. 'What a cheetah.'

Blonde tried for a head butt. Lewis tilted his head back and poured the last drops of lager into his wide-open mouth.

Back to the fight.

Who was going to win? Lewis had a little bet with himself. He wanted Black to win. Black staggered back and fell to the ground with the force of two fist punches. Blonde took careful aim and let loose a feeble kick as Black tried, in vain, to raise herself.

Blonde dug her foot into Black's chest. Lewis shook his head. *Poor kid.* He ogled her shapely legs, and his eyes focused on the dark patch beneath her white knickers.

The phone rang. He ignored it; but Blonde gave up the battle and sauntered off. Black picked herself up and straightened her skirt. She caught up with her friend and the argument continued. Lewis watched them disappear around the corner.

The phone was still ringing. He switched the music centre off and lifted the receiver.

'Is that you, Sheridan? . . . How are you?'

'Not so bad.'

'I left a list of numbers for you to ring. Did you get it?'

'Yes. I tried them all. There are more sadistic punters out there than I imagined, but we're talking Blackburn, Bolton and Manchester.'

'Did you discover anything useful?'

'Nothing, really. Some of the women I spoke to were quite open about their customers. The only trouble is —'

'They won't reveal their names.'

'Right. They probably use false names. Even if we had their real names it wouldn't be any use to us.'

'Maybe I should get Rivers to do some snooping around for us,' Lewis confidently suggested. 'He'll do almost anything for the right money.'

'I wouldn't get too involved with him if I were you.'

'Rivers is cool. I don't want to miss out on any info he might be able to offer me.'

'You know best. I take it you haven't been listening to the radio.'

'No. Sunday afternoon for me means music and a few drinks. Why do you ask?'

'There's been another murder.'

'When was this?'

'I don't exactly know. The body of a young woman was found this morning behind the Ten Pin Bowling on Central Drive.'

'Are they linking it with the others?'

'Yes.'

'That makes it three. This guy is a serial killer.'

'Yes. Bad news, isn't it?'

'Wow. We've got a serial killer right here in Blackpool.'

'The murderer could live anywhere.'

'I suppose so . . . I'm interested. What do you say?'

'We can't carry on looking for perverts and the like. I'm fed up of ringing escorts and prostitutes. It's not happening, Lewis. There's nothing concrete to follow up.'

'Oh, come on. What about all that Parlour's Dolly House stuff? Remember?'

'I really don't know. Perhaps it has nothing to do with these murders.'

'That's not what you said.'

'I've had second thoughts.'

'I don't care what you say. We don't want to give up now.'

'I admire your tenacity. The best thing to do is give me a call if you come up with something.'

'Okay, if that's the way you feel. See you around.'

The reinforcements had arrived. Forty uniformed officers and twenty plainclothes detectives were waiting in the conference room for further instructions. Oxley was in the stuffy incident room with his team of dedicated officers.

'Simmons thinks the killer might be a local man,' said Oxley, addressing DS Lambert.

'How has he reached that conclusion?' she asked.

'Because the killer must have known about the secluded pathway behind the Ten Pin Bowling.'

'I must admit, I didn't know of its existence. There's a technique known as geographical profiling. Have you heard about it?'

'Yes, but I don't want to get into that sort of thing at this point in time. How do we know the killer isn't a lorry driver?'

'You said yourself he could be local to the area.'

'True enough. We'll stick with what we've got. George and I were convinced that Cooney was our man. We shouldn't have been so eager. Having said that, he was a good suspect. Even Simmons thought so.'

'What did he have to say?'

'He totally agreed with our concerns. He said we would have been foolish not to arrest him. What bothers me is Teresa Moore's account of his activities.'

'I think her information was part truth, part lies. She lied about the bloodstained shirt, and Cooney's supposed knowledge of the Collinson crime location. He was a good suspect and she knew it.'

'She made him appear more plausible as a suspect?'

'Exactly. Once her story became known, he was impossible to resist. She was hoping to get the reward.'

Oxley became aware of shouting coming from outside the building. 'You know what, Lambert, I didn't even consider that as a possibility . . . Hang on a minute.' Oxley raised his hand, signalling her to be quiet.

'What is it, sir?'

'Listen . . . Listen to that voice.'

They listened. They heard. The man in the street kept repeating the words, 'mind-factor.'

'Oh, no,' Oxley said, walking towards the window.

George Naylor was waving his fist at the officers looking down at him from the windows of the incident room. Rivers was one of them. He turned towards Palmer. 'Look at him, Rick. See how stupid he really is, the silly old bugger. He can barely stand on his own two feet.'

Palmer couldn't help but feel sorry for Naylor.

'It looks like he's spent the whole afternoon in the Watering Hole,' Rivers continued. 'Oh, look, he's staggering back inside.'

'You think it's funny, Steve. I don't.'

'It couldn't have happened to a nicer bloke.'

'You seem to be forgetting that we have a maniac roaming the streets, and we can't afford to lose good officers like him.'

Rivers shook his head and sneered as his partner walked off.

Oxley phoned Naylor's wife. He told her to meet him outside the Watering Hole public house.

Twenty minutes later, she arrived. The inspector and Lambert were waiting for her.

'Where is he?' she asked, looking drawn and troubled.

Oxley dreaded to think how she would feel when he told her the news. 'He's in there.' He pointed at the pub. 'You'd better come inside with us. I want you to take him home.'

Dorothy was visibly shocked. Lambert took her by the arm and escorted her into the popular beer house. Naylor was sitting in the corner of the room, sandwiched between two young girls. Oxley couldn't believe his eyes. He told Dorothy to wait by the door. She didn't hear him due to the loud music pumping out of the jukebox.

They approached him, Dorothy practically hiding behind the officers.

Naylor was pleased to see them. 'Derek and Tanya. Come and have a drink with us.' His words were barely decipherable. The sound of the music didn't help either. He raised his glass of lager as if to say 'cheers.'

Oxley was crestfallen. The superintendent had lost the plot, lost his mind. His spirit had gone bust. Naylor quickly stood up, knocking several empty glasses onto the wooden floor. The girls laughed loudly. He pointed at them.

'Remember what I told you,' he slurred. 'Don't let Jack the Ripper catch you.'

Dorothy was holding a handkerchief to her mouth. Her presence didn't seem to register with her husband.

He rubbed sweat from his forehead with the palm of his hand. 'Thanks for your company, wee lasses,' he said, wriggling his fingers as a goodbye gesture. He took one step forward, and slumped to his knees. Dorothy let out a mournful cry.

Oxley wrapped his arms around him and heaved him onto his feet. 'Come on, George,' he said, his mouth close to his ear. 'Go home. Go home with your wife and stay there. You're not well.'

The music stopped, giving way to the babble and chink of glassware. Oxley helped him to his wife's car and made sure he got inside it. Dorothy was too embarrassed to say anything. She got into the car and quickly drove off. Oxley was standing in the road and waited until they were out of sight.

'Will he come back, sir?' Lambert asked, with a searching look in her eyes.

'Not for a long time . . . We need him, Lambert . . . *I* need him.'

A vehicle pulled up behind them, its horn sounding.

'Come on, sir,' she said, gently squeezing his arm. 'The troops are waiting for us.'

They headed back to the station.

Oxley's head was bowed in shame.

He was consumed by a sadness that almost brought him to tears.

THIRTY-ONE

Lucy Beckett had been missing for six months. Initial enquiries failed to produce any significant leads regarding her whereabouts.

Her mum remembered saying goodbye to her. That was on a cold rainy night in January. Lucy left home carrying a white plastic bag. Mum didn't know what was in it. She never bothered to ask.

Lucy was now a partial skeleton lying in a wooded area close to Plymbey, the tiny village a few miles from her home. The inhabitants of Plymbey were mainly old folk like Jack Robson and his wife, Avril. Jack was still enjoying his pre-breakfast walks that took him close to the spot where Lucy was murdered. He had quite forgotten about the music cassette he picked up early one morning in January. It was the one cassette that Lucy had decided to keep for herself.

A cold shudder swept through Irene Collinson's body when she saw the newspaper headline. The words, 'Serial Killer - Third Body Discovered', ensured a sell-out edition. The paper contained a huge write-up on the murders.

Irene turned to the next page. There she was. Elizabeth's picture had been printed next to the one of Angela Ross. Elizabeth was wearing a blazer and school tie. She had given Sheridan the same photo when she first went to see him.

The third victim was unidentified. Irene couldn't bring herself to read about her daughter's murder. She read the rest of the report with a worried intensity. Further on the report ran the sub-heading, 'Man Released without Charge.' No name was given, no indication of where the suspect came from or what sort of person he was.

Julian Francis, the well-known psychic, got a mention too. Francis had, apparently, seen the face of the killer in a vision which occurred on the evening of the Collinson murder. Detectives were ignoring the psychic's offer of help.

Irene had heard about his marvellous powers and she wondered if Francis would be able to 'tune in' to the mind of the murderer, but it seemed pointless to ask for assistance of any kind. Sheridan had not spoken to her since their last telephone conversation. She might have been able to persuade him to visit the man referred to as, 'Super Psychic'. Maybe Francis could provide a new lead. She had been hoping to tempt Jim Sheridan back into her life. Maybe she had been too optimistic.

Irene folded the newspaper and went into the kitchen to prepare an evening meal. It wasn't long before the tears started rolling. She came to the conclusion that he was sleeping with her. Even though Becky was considerably younger than Sheridan she resigned herself to the possibility that he had fallen in love with her.

Chief Superintendent Matthew Greenwood raised his hand before Oxley could speak. Greenwood removed a piece of white cotton from his trouser leg. He carefully dropped it into a bin beneath his desk, straightened himself, and took a sip of hot tea.

'You wanted to see me, sir?' Oxley said.

Greenwood picked up his fountain pen and tapped it on the desk. 'A young girl, by the name of Jill Pemberton, has just left the incident room.'

He passed a photograph to Oxley. It was a snapshot of two girls in a nightclub, dressed in revealing outfits.

'One of these two is the murdered girl,' Oxley surmised.

'That photo was taken on Saturday night, here in Blackpool. The girl on the right is Jill Pemberton. The other girl is her sister, Elaine.'

'Local?'

'No. They're from Leeds. The parents are on their way here to make a formal identification.'

'Has Dr Purslow seen the photograph?'

'Yes. I had a copy sent through to him. He confirmed that the murdered girl is definitely Elaine Pemberton.'

'Did he say if there had been any sexual assault?'

'There are no indications, apart from the anal rape with the piece of wood. Purslow found evidence of sticky tape having been used to cover her mouth.'

'The same method as with Angela Ross.'

'Correct. The latest from Forensic is disappointing. There are no clues on or near to the body. He's careful.'

'Or lucky.'

'Luck is on his side. Purslow is concerned about the breast tissue. He can't understand why the murderer should want to remove pieces of tissue.'

'There's lots of things about serial killers that are incomprehensible to the likes of us. This one is a trophy seeker. He's taken shoes, and her underwear is missing. There's a point: Was she wearing any underwear?'

'Yes. One of our female officers asked Jill Pemberton to describe her sister's clothing. As you can see from the photo, she was dressed in a boobtube and short white Lycra skirt. She wasn't wearing a bra. Her underwear comprised a pair of those skimpy things that girls wear nowadays.'

'A thong?'

'Ah, yes . . . A thong.' Greenwood seemed almost too embarrassed to say the word. Oxley studied the photograph. The sisters' footwear was not showing. Greenwood anticipated the next question.

'Elaine Pemberton was wearing double-strap, white high heels. She bought them at Charnley's whilst her sister was with her. I want you to get an exact pair and publicise them in all the newspapers—'

'And on TV.'

Greenwood raised his eyebrows. 'The case has already been featured on *Crime Monthly*. George took part in that one. It's debatable whether or not they'll give it a second airing.'

'I'm going to put it to them. This is the largest investigation the force has ever seen. We need full publicity and a reconstruction.'

'You're right, of course. And let's not forget the reward. What does it stand at?'

'I think it's a hundred grand.'

'A tempting sum . . . All right, Oxley, I'll leave you to your duties. I'll see to the press conference.'

'Very good, sir. Do we know the name of the nightclub the sisters visited?'

'Yes.' Greenwood picked up a sheet of paper. 'The club is called, Razmataz. The hotel they stayed at was The Berona.'

The inspector scribbled a note in his pad. His superior reminded him that Elaine Pemberton had not been officially identified. Her murder was not to be publicised until the parents' confirmation of identity.

Oxley was ready for action. He had a plan. 'I'm going to organise late-night surveillance of specific areas. It shouldn't be too difficult with the extra manpower we've got.'

'Yes, I'll go along with that.'

'The profile says that the killer stalks scantily-dressed females. Blackpool is full of them, especially in the season.'

'There are many other towns where he could strike; it doesn't necessarily have to be Blackpool.'

'There's always that possibility, but three women have died here. The latest victim was killed in a secluded spot. I believe he's local.'

'Interesting observation. Very well, let us suppose he is a local man. What do you have in mind?'

'We log all registration numbers of vehicles seen in specific areas, from 11-o-clock to 2 a.m. We do that for a month, correlate the data, and compare it with criminal records.' ·

'Your plan sounds good, in theory. It's the only way forward. Operation Stamford has practically come to a halt. Surveillance it is.'

The task ahead was massive. Greenwood had been on the periphery of the case, but things were different now. George Naylor had been taken ill, and their main suspect turned out to be the wrong man. Media attention was beginning to focus on Greenwood and his murder squad detectives. The big question was, 'Who is the killer?' They had to find out. He had to be stopped. They couldn't afford to let another girl be butchered like a worthless animal.

Lewis breezed into the office at 9.30 a.m. He aimed his jacket at the hook by the door. 'Shot! Morning, Becky. A bit late this morning, aren't I?'

'Good morning, Carl. Yes, you are.'

He disappeared into the kitchen and switched the kettle on.

'Mine's a coffee,' Becky sounded, 'and don't forget the Jaffas.'

'You've already had a coffee.'

'I fancy another.'

A few minutes later he stepped into the office, cup in both hands and a couple of Jaffa Cakes wedged under his arm.

'Where are the other two?' asked Lewis.

'Chris is doing surveillance.'

'What? He's milking that one, Becky.'

'And why not?' You'd do the same for more money, I'm sure.'

'Yeah, sure. What's the other one up to?'

'Bob phoned in sick.'

'I'll swing for him. It's the second time this year he's gone sick. He's a weakling.'

'Leave him alone. He's an okay guy.'

'*Okay guy*, eh?' Lewis tapped away at the keyboard. 'Anybody would think you fancied him.'

She didn't respond.

'When are you going to get a boyfriend?'

'*Boyfriend*? I'm not a little girl, you know.'

'Never said you were.'

'I'm thirty, not thirteen. Besides, I could ask you the same question.'

Becky felt emotionally restrained. She was trying to be friendly with him. It was difficult. She knew how much he fancied her. How would he react if he knew what had happened between her and Sheridan? Still, that was her business. Her amorous evening with the veteran detective was a one-off, and she tried to push the memory to the back of her mind.

There was little work to occupy her. She entertained herself with a computer game. Ten minutes passed by and Lewis asked if anybody had called the office.

'Jim Sheridan phoned.'

'What did he want?'

'A chat, that's all.'

'With you?'

'Yes. I think he's quitting the investigation.'

'That's the impression he gave me.'

'Does that mean you won't see him again?'

'Maybe I will. Another body has been found.'

'Yes, I know.'

'And I have no intention of giving up.'

'There's easier work to be found, don't you think?'

He turned to her and offered a sarcastic smile. 'This one's a great challenge. I mean, just imagine the applause, the adulation, the admiration I'd get for catching a serial killer.'

'A fantastic achievement - if you could pull it off.'

Lewis's eyes narrowed. He knew she was leading up to something. 'It could be done, even without Sheridan's limited help.'

'Perhaps he knows when he's beaten. Have you ever considered him as a suspect?'

Funny question, he thought. 'What on earth are you getting at?'

'The police have, haven't they? I bet he felt awful when Rivers had a go at him.'

'Sheridan told you, eh? So what? He's in the clear.'

'What about you and Steve Rivers?'

'You know something.'

'I do. You ought to be careful who you are dealing with. Rivers is bent, and that means he's dangerous.'

'He doesn't strike me as being dangerous,' Lewis countered. 'Anyway, there's no need to make an issue of it.'

'I thought you would have had the decency to tell me about it.'

'Look, Becky, I've known Rivers a lot longer than I've known you.'

'Fine. But do you know about his visits to the brothel at Wichonstall? Do you know about his drug dealing?' Becky got out her pocket-size recorder. 'I want you to listen to something.' She told him about her visit to Davina Mullen's house, then played the entire interview.

A worried look matured across Lewis's face.

'You had no idea?' Becky asked.

'About the drugs?'

'And the sex.'

'No idea. Who is Diana Humble?'

'She runs the brothel.'

'This was Sheridan's idea, wasn't it?'

'Yes. He had a hunch about Rivers. He got it right.'

'You're stupid if you think Rivers is a murderer.'

'That wasn't the point of the interview. Sheridan wanted me to find out what goes on at Humble's establishment - if that's what you can call it.'

'This all sounds fishy to me. Something's been going on between you and Sheridan.'

Clever Lewis, she thought. 'I don't really know what Sheridan's intentions are. He would probably still be on the case if Rivers hadn't interfered.'

'Look, Sheridan was bound to have been questioned. We haven't fallen out with each other, you know.'

'You're not partners any more and that's sad.'

'Our enquiries haven't got us anywhere. It *has* been tough for both of us. He has given up, I haven't. I can buy info and follow up my own leads.'

'Carl, anybody would think you were Inspector Maigret. You won't ever catch this serial killer, not even with the help of Steve-the-bent-cop-Rivers.'

'I'm sorry, Becky. I didn't know Rivers was that bad. Honestly. Trouble is, I'm becoming obsessed with this case. I'm going to find out as much as I can.'

'It's a waste of time and energy,' she snapped.

Lewis took a sip of coffee, walked to the door and put on his jacket. 'I've got loads of free time. See you later.'

He closed the door behind him.

She listened to the fading sound of his footsteps.

Nothing would stop him now.

THIRTY-TWO

Norman and Betty Pemberton decided to stay in Blackpool whilst their daughter helped with police enquiries. Norman was the first relative to view the body at the mortuary. He knew straight away that it was Elaine. He knew what to expect. She was different now. Her hair looked darker and accentuated the pallor of her waxen features. Her beauty was tainted by the mind-numbing stillness of death.

When his wife stepped closer to look at her she broke down, trembling with grief. She turned to the open arms of her husband. He held her tightly. The sudden loss of their daughter had blown a massive hole in their lives. The killer wasn't just butchering girls for his own gratification, he was creating emotional devastation amongst families.

Oxley was waiting inside his car. He started the engine. Lambert climbed in, closed the door and formally adjusted her skirt.

'I stopped at the Ten Pin Bowling this morning,' she said. 'You'd never believe what I saw. Somebody was asking if he could park his van on the waste ground, close to where the body was found.'

'Don't tell me he was selling ice cream.'

'Hot dogs, tea and coffee for the officers, photographers and journalists, would you believe?'

Oxley drove up the ramp leading from the underground police car-park. 'I'd believe anything.'

'There's a lot of activity down there. Loads of adults and kids are nosing around.'

'So I observed.'

'Have you seen the tabloids?'

'Not yet. I haven't had chance,' Oxley answered.

'Listen to this,' Lambert said, opening a newspaper. "Blackpool holidaymaker slaughtered by the Ripper" . . . Here's another one: "Blackpool's SCU bring in extra officers in their hunt for Ripper-style killer."'

'Typical. I remember Christian Purslow mentioning that name. George was worried. He said the press would have a field day once they latched onto the idea of a Jack the Ripper stalking women on foggy nights.'

'Angela Ross was murdered on one of the foggiest nights we've ever had.'

'Exactly. We can do without that kind of reporting.'

'Surely, Dr Purslow wouldn't have mentioned the victims' injuries to the press,' Lambert continued.

'Pemberton's body was discovered by a taxi driver. He saw everything - her blood and guts all over the place.'

Lambert winced. 'No doubt his recollections of what he saw will spread like a virus.'

'Everybody's talking about it. Incidentally, how's the taxi enquiry progressing?'

'Ongoing. The company taxis are registered. They're the easy ones. We're having problems tracing the freelance drivers. It's going to take time. The overnight lorry drivers have been traced. They were parked close to the crime scene.'

'And that's were our luck ran out.'

'Yes. They were facing the wrong direction or were parked too far away. Saw nothing. Heard nothing.'

Oxley stopped the car on Central Drive, opposite the Ten Pin.

The previous two days had seen concentrated police activity in the area. Detectives were busy stopping and interviewing drivers in a bid to gain information that might prove beneficial to Operation Stamford. A uniformed officer became curious when he saw Oxley's vehicle. He decided to question the occupants. He backed off when he recognised the inspector.

'They're not leaving anything to chance,' Lambert remarked.

'It's part of the plan. We are logging every single car that passes here during the next couple of days.'

'I don't think the killer will come here again. There's too much activity.'

'That's exactly the point. Some serial killers visit the crime scenes. He would be too scared to come here during the day. When darkness falls there'll be no obvious police presence, but we'll be watching, all the same.'

Lambert was thinking about Elaine Pemberton's horrific injuries. 'I wonder why he does it? What makes a man do such terrible things?' she said.

'Why he kills them, you mean?'

'Not just the murder, but why cut away pieces of flesh and then disembowel the poor girl?'

'Nobody really understands *why*. The psychiatrist says there are elements of sadism in his personality.'

'I hope she was dead when he ripped out her intestines.'

'I suspect she was.'

'That's not sadism, inspector. He can't hurt his victim if she's already dead.'

Oxley shrugged. 'I'm as wise as you are. Perhaps he needs to go that bit further to fuel his fantasies. He probably gets a sexual kick out of doing it.'

'There's no evidence of sexual intercourse,' Lambert prompted.

'That's right. None of the victims were subjected to forced intercourse. That's the bit I can't get my head round. I can understand rape being involved, if you know what I'm saying, but this goes far beyond the activities of any rapist I've ever come across.'

'And he lives in Blackpool?'

'Well, he knows the streets, the secluded places, the quiet spots. He was in Blackpool when Ross was murdered. He took advantage of the fog, remember? He knows when and where to attack.'

'Pity about Cooney,' she mused. 'He's got form, and he's local.'

'George and I were absolutely elated when he stepped into the frame.'

The two officers sipped coffee. Five minutes went by without a word. Lambert broke the silence. 'What, exactly, are we waiting here for, sir?'

'We need to work out the best places for surveillance.'

'How are we going to do that?'

'We put ourselves in the murderer's shoes.'

She gave a restrained smile. 'Only certain people can do that.'

'I'll try anything. Let's put ourselves in his position and ask ourselves, what are the most likely places to find lone girls? Any ideas?'

'Not in the busy town centre. How about we survey some of the quieter roads that lead to the hotels, particularly roads that have secluded spots where he could take his victims.'

'Good thinking, Lambert. There are probably hundreds of secluded spots, but we'll have to try something.'

Oxley's mobile rang. Important information had been received in the incident room. He shot a glance at Lambert and said, 'A man saw Elaine Pemberton walking down this road shortly before she was murdered.'

'How can we be sure it was her?'

'His description matches perfectly. He saw a car stop by the Ten Pin Bowling. The driver got out and approached her. Black hair. Thirties.'

Lambert was mindful of the e-fit that was generated following the murder of Angela Ross. 'Did he have a moustache?' she asked.

'He can't recall him having a moustache, but he's certain he was driving a white Ford Sierra hatchback.'

'I've already told you, Lewis. I've had enough of the investigation.'

Lewis settled comfortably in the client's chair. He looked at the newspaper articles on the wall. 'You've kept your murder display.'

'I haven't bothered to take it down.'

Lewis didn't believe him. He was convinced that Sheridan didn't approve of his relationship with Rivers and was continuing with the investigation alone.

'So, what are you up to then?'

'Waiting for work to come in,' Sheridan replied, rubbing his forehead. 'I'm running out of money.'

Lewis pulled a bundle of notes from his pocket and tossed it onto the table. Sheridan felt the weight of it.

'This is a lot of money. How much, exactly?'

'Don't know. A couple of grand, maybe.'

'Do you usually carry this amount?'

'Always carry a bit of money around with me.' He smirked. 'Keep it.'

Sheridan threw the bundle across the table. Lewis shook his head and defiantly folded his arms. 'Judging by the state of that coat hanging on your door you could make good use of a couple of quid.'

No reply.

Lewis got up, finger pointing at Sheridan. 'I need you back on the case.'

'Sorry, the case is too big. You know that.'

'Disagree. We could still make a go of it, like we originally planned.'

'The answer is no. You've been in contact with Rivers.'

'Yeah, you're right. I'm on the edge of a cliff. Must admit, I didn't realise he was into so much wheeling and dealing. You're a shrewd guy. You underestimate yourself.'

'Why bother with him?' Sheridan said. 'You know he's corrupt.'

'More corrupt than I thought. You got Becky to snoop around. She played the interview with Davina Mullen, the ex-pro. I got the impression that Rivers became *your* suspect.'

'I don't see him as a suspect. I was curious about the Wichonstall brothel and the activities that go on there. Rivers doesn't seem violent enough to be a sadistic murderer.'

'And he wouldn't be passing info to me if he was the killer.'

'Guess not. I'm sorry I used Miss Watts to snoop around without your knowledge. I wanted to find out for myself what he's really like.'

'No bother. I understand where you're coming from. At least it gave her something to do.'

'How is she, by the way?'

'She's all right. Playing computer games at the moment. Not much work to do. One of the reasons why I'm still on the case.'

'You don't give up easily, do you? My enthusiasm has dwindled.'

'It might come back, who knows? Have you seen the papers? Full of this Ripper stuff. And we were right about him being a trophy hunter. The front page shows a pair of shoes, the same as Elaine Pemberton was wearing when she was murdered.'

'I haven't read the papers yet. What's with the shoes?'

'The killer took them. Interesting, eh? And that's not all . . .' Lewis leaned forward. 'This is confidential.'

Sheridan frowned. 'Rivers told you.'

'Listen . . . The killer performed anal rape on Pemberton. He used a piece of wood. It had some kind of green fabric attached to it.'

'Where did the wood come from?'

'Don't ask me. Another thing: he actually cut bits of her breasts away. That's confidential, too.'

'No wonder they're calling him the Ripper. Any suspects?'

'Detectives are talking to taxi drivers and everybody who lives in the area where it happened. They're trying to trace everyone who visited the nightclub she went to. It's the biggest manhunt since the Yorkshire Ripper.

You ought to read about it.'

'All this is interesting, Lewis; but what do *you* intend to do?'

'Visit the crime scene. Ask questions.'

'You'll have to be patient. Central Drive is crawling with police.'

'Yeah, I know that. Anyway, I'm off.'

He tossed an envelope onto the desk. Sheridan asked what was in it.

'It's—'

'Confidential?' Sheridan guessed.

'Yeah, keep it to yourself.' Lewis opened the door ready to leave. He'd already noticed the half a bottle of Glenfiddich standing on the windowsill. 'And don't sit on your arse drinking whisky all day.'

He closed the door behind him. Sheridan went after Lewis, clutching the bundle of money he had purposely left behind.

Too late.

Lewis is right about the whisky, he thought. The cursed habit was here to stay, and it was eating its way into what little savings he had left. Sheridan would have to start looking for another job. Each day was longer and more boring than the previous day. There was time to kill, time to think, time for reproach.

He reached for the whisky and took a swig, then opened the envelope which Lewis had given him.

'Confidential indeed,' he murmured.

Lewis had written a heading at the top of the photocopied report: Profile of Murderer. Forensic Psychiatrist - Dr Andrew Simmons.

Particular sections aroused his curiosity. He read them out loud:

'"Will watch and stalk females in their twenties or thirties. Victim type: scantily-dressed females. Likely to possess transport. Use of pliers - to torture victim - indicates planning. Bracelet taken as trophy. The murderer is an organised offender. The two murders are linked owing to anal injuries sustained in both cases."'

Sheridan couldn't remember Irene having said anything about anal interference. *The police must have kept that secret.*

He read on:

'"Likely to be involved with a trade - car repairs, electrician, handyman. Can sustain the ability to appear charming and helpful. Likely to possess magazines: crime, bondage, pornography, sexual sadism, torture . . ."'

The words 'sexual sadism' came to mind. And then he remembered about Leonard Bertram Haines and Celia Parlour's dolly-house girls.

He rummaged through his papers in the desk drawer.

'Ah, here we are,' he said, his eyes searching for the relevant details: "'Edward's real name was Leonard Bertram Haines . . . Haines was a sexual sadist . . . He offered large sums of money to Burke in return for prolonged periods of *sadistic sexual abuse* . . . His demands escalated to a new and dangerous level . . . Patricia Burke died from internal bleeding after Haines had thrust a thrust a wooden implement inside her rectum."'

The clues were coming together.

Elaine Pemberton suffered the same abuse.

The police now regarded the Karen Lawson e-fit as significant. A dark-haired man, in his thirties, was seen driving a white Ford Sierra close to the place where Elaine Pemberton was beaten, stabbed and mutilated.

He knew the streets of Blackpool.

He possessed knowledge of crime-scene procedure.

The killer was being driven by an unseen force.

He was a sadist who needed to torture, humiliate and mutilate young women.

He was hungry for his next victim . . .

THIRTY-THREE

DC Rick Palmer looked behind, checking that nobody was watching. He pushed the door open with his foot, careful not to spill the drinks he was carrying. He walked into the canteen to find DC Rivers waiting for him.

Rivers pushed a cup towards him.

'What's the matter?' Palmer asked.

'You know I don't like tea. You drink it. Give me your coffee.'

'No problem . . . Who's first on the list?'

'Some bloke who lives on Marshall Road.'

'That's not far.'

'Take your time with that tea. No need to rush.'

'This isn't a good time for a break, Steve. We should be on the job now.'

'There you go again. You worry too much. Nobody will catch us in here.'

'Certainly not George Naylor. You haven't got *him* breathing down your neck any more.'

'Nice one, Rick. You know, I get the impression you feel sorry for him. You actually like him, don't you?'

'I never said I liked him. I have respect for him.'

'Pull the other one.'

'It's true. You only dislike him because he got you suspended when you hit Cunliffe.'

'True enough. If I ever see him again, I'll break his neck.'

'You've been in enough trouble already. I'd tread carefully if I were you.'

Rivers had his cup to his mouth. He slammed it on the table, coffee splashing everywhere. 'Ouch! . . . What do you mean by that?'

'I mean, it's time you were keeping your mouth shut. You don't need to tell the newspapers what we are doing, like you told them about the profiler. Naylor wanted that kept quiet. You did it to annoy him.'

'Too right I did.'

'Listen to sense, Steve. We've got a big investigation on our hands.'

'Have we? Oh, I didn't realise.'

Palmer grabbed a kitchen roll and mopped up the coffee. Rivers shook his head.

'You'll never change, Rick. It's no good being Mr Prim and Proper if you want to succeed in this job. You have to be ruthless.'

'Telling newspapers what SCU are doing isn't ruthless. It's what I call stupid.' He looked at his watch. 'Time's moving on.'

Rivers shot up. 'Right. Let's get going.'

They headed for the car-park. Palmer wanted to know how many Sierra drivers they had to interview. He put the question to his colleague.

'We're doing the white ones first. There's quite a lot.'

'What happens if we draw a blank?'

'Hard to say. We might end up travelling further afield. The Sierra driver might even come forward to eliminate himself.'

'Do you think it might be the killer, Steve? What do you think?'

'Don't know. Anything's possible.'

Sheridan answered the door to Bert Davies.

'Come in, Bert. Good to see you again.'

'I dropped by your office. That young fellow, Darren, said you'd gone home.'

They took seats in the living room. Davies rested his hands on his chubby belly. 'Can't stay long . . . I've got some news.'

'About the murder?'

'Indeed. Detectives questioned me this morning. They're questioning all the taxi drivers - everyone.'

'I guessed they would. It was a taxi driver who discovered the body.'

'Not one of ours, but we're all suspects. They're checking computer records and CCTV film from town-centre cameras. They want to know if anybody has spotted a white Ford Sierra hatchback. I think they've got a hot lead.'

'What's the situation along Central Drive?'

'No more spot checks. The blue-and-white tape has been taken down. They spent days combing the area for clues.'

'Judging by the papers, they don't seem to be getting very far.'

'Maybe not. Who knows?'

Sheridan fell silent, having nothing positive to add to the conversation.

Davies asked the obvious question. 'What's happening with your side of things?'

'Nothing.'

'You mean, no leads, no suspects?'

'Bert, this is a job for the police. I've tried. I've failed.'

'And what's with Carl Lewis?'

'He's young and full of ideas.'

'He's going ahead with it. You ain't.'

'In a nutshell - yes. I can't see Lewis making much progress either.'

'There must be something driving him. What's he up to?'

Sheridan went over the details of Lewis's relationship with Rivers. He told him the confidential facts regarding the anal degradation and removal of breast tissue. Davies wasn't slow on the uptake.

'It all ties in with the man who spoke to Angela Ross. What was his name?'

'Tony.'

'And he spoke about Celia Parlour's Dolly House. Jim, you have your killer.'

'Well, there's a good chance it's him.'

'A good chance. So, this dodgy Rivers character is helping your mate, Lewis?'

'For a price.'

'Lewis could help you catch this fellow.'

'I'm against it. He's playing with fire. I told him so.'

Davies sat upright, his interest deepening. 'You're close, Jim. I can feel it. *Close.*'

'Not close enough. Let's suppose his name is Tony. Suppose he is a sadist, fixated on mutilating young women and sticking things inside them. What am I to do?'

His friend thought for a while. 'Try the nightclub where the girl went. Somebody could have seen or heard something.'

'A nightclub in Blackpool, and in the season? Hundreds of holidaymakers, most of them probably drunk, many of them from all over the country. Like I say, it's a job for the SCU.'

'You should explore all avenues, my friend. This was supposed to be your last case, and the biggest. You are a good private detective.'

'I *was* good, once over.'

'And what does Irene say? Surely, she wants you to continue. I mean, it was your daughter—'

'I haven't spoken to Irene for some time.'

'Any reason?'

'Not really,' Sheridan answered, too ashamed to give the real reason.

The subdued answer told Davies otherwise. 'Well, I'm off home for tea. If I hear any titbits, you'll be the first to know.'

They went to the front door. Davies gave him a friendly pat on the shoulder. 'Think about what I said. Get your brain cells into action.'

Sheridan waved and closed the door. For most of the evening he watched TV and drank away the small amount of whisky that was left.

11.30. Nothing of interest on TV. He was wide awake, listening to the seconds ticking away. He stared at the empty chair opposite and pictured Becky sitting there showing oceans of thigh. He had been seduced by her beauty, hypnotised by her long blonde hair, sensuous lips . . . not to mention the tight-fitting top that hugged her prominent breasts. *She could tempt any man.*

He had succumbed, but couldn't understand why she wanted him in such a way. *Fatherly figure?* Perhaps. *Sheer lust?* Could be. He doubted that she had any deep feeling for him. He knew Irene had.

Regrets.

Solitude.

The phone interrupted his contemplation.

'*Perfect Murder*,' Davies said, bursting to tell him about the book.

'What's that? . . . I'm sorry, Bert, I didn't know who it was at first.'

'Remember that book you gave me, the one entitled *Perfect Murder*?'

'I remember.'

'Chapter Six is all about the American serial killer, Bobby Ray. Heard of him?'

'I can't say I have.'

'Bobby Ray was operating in the late seventies. His crimes were vicious in the extreme. Amongst other things, he disembowelled a girl and cut away pieces of breast tissue.'

'Elaine Pemberton suffered the same degradation.'

'That's correct. Ray was trying to commit perfect murder. He was always careful not to leave fingerprints or fibres. He was into biting. He actually bit a victim's breast and cut out the bite marks left behind.'

'Eliminating the possibility of being identified by his own teeth.'

'That was the idea. Detectives were baffled at first. When they caught him he confessed to all his murders. He told them about his compulsion for biting. It could be that the man who killed Elaine Pemberton did the same thing.'

'It's feasible.'

'I thought you'd like to know. I'll sign off. Sorry if I disturbed you.'

'Not at all. Goodnight, Bert.'

Sheridan slid further down in his chair and began to wonder if he had given up too early. The Leonard Haines/Parlour's Dolly House article seemed to connect with the man who had callously slain three girls in the resort. That fact alone was enough to ensure that he would never forget this series of murders, and the depressive effect the investigation had had on his life.

The frustration of being so close was almost unbearable. His instincts regarding the killer's sadistic personality were not wrong. What could he do? Even if he told the police about the parlour maid reference they probably wouldn't be interested. He could contact the press and tell them about the killer's reference to a magazine article. He doubted it would help detectives with their enquiries. But why should he help the police? He had been accused. He was a failure. Everything had gone wrong, and the loneliness he had learned to live with seemed more poignant now.

He spent another hour turning things over in his mind. The hour was late. Time to retire. *No use*, he thought. *I probably wouldn't fall asleep until four in the morning.*

He reached for a cigarette. Empty packet. *Must get some ciggies.*

Sheridan swapped slippers for shoes, grabbed his jacket. The nearest garage happened to be on Central Drive.

The trip took less than five minutes by car. Sheridan purchased twenty L and B. He pocketed the change, returned to his car, started the engine.

Sudden change of mind. He turned left instead of right, and drove towards the Ten Pin Bowling. *A little excursion,* he decided. He was curious and felt the need to view the murder scene for himself.

He swung the car round, stopping on the waste ground. A taxi driver was waiting for his next fare. Three lorries were stationed for the night. He got out. No-one in sight. The spot where Elaine Pemberton died was in complete darkness, as was the pathway running along the back of the building. A short walk took him to the recess where the girl had taken her last breath of life. He hurried back to the car and returned with a torch. He knew exactly where the body was found. He shone the torch along the wall, moving the beam down to the ground. The area surrounding the recess had been cleared of rubbish by the forensic team. There was nothing to indicate that a brutal murder had occurred there.

He walked the length of the pathway, careful to avoid the broken glass, empty food cans and random piles of dog dirt. When he reached the end of the building he surveyed an area of weed-ridden, rough ground, beyond which Geary Road ran west, leading towards the Promenade. A faint smell of burning became apparent. He looked to his right and saw thin wisps of smoke drifting from a doorway. A few steps took him to the entrance of a room no more than ten feet square. He stepped inside, pointing his torch to the ground. Empty beer cans, old newspapers and magazines were strewn about the place. He wafted the smoke away from his face. A small fire was smouldering in the centre of a room that was once used for storage purposes.

He shone the beam across the walls and onto a filthy settee positioned against the wall to his right. It occurred to him that somebody was using the room as a temporary shelter. The settee, supported by short wooden legs, had seen better days. One of the front legs was missing and had been replaced by a couple of bricks to support the weight.

Something that Lewis had said came back to him.

Elaine Pemberton was violated. *The murderer had inserted a piece of wood into the poor girl,* he remembered. *Wood that had green fabric attached to it.*

The fabric of the settee was green.

One leg missing.

THIRTY-FOUR

A big leather armchair dwarfed Julian Francis. His dark-green eyes were fixed on Irene Collinson who sat opposite him, bemused, waiting for him to speak. For all she knew he could have been daydreaming.

Suddenly he coughed loudly. Irene gave a little cry of surprise.

'I'm sorry,' he said, his voice soft, girlish. 'May I call you, "Irene"?'

'You may,' she replied, knowing that he could sense her apprehension.

Francis kept perfectly still, didn't move a muscle. 'Call me, "Julian" . . . Yes?'

She nodded.

'The police investigators aren't interested in my help,' he continued, bringing his hands together as if in prayer. 'Mother says I should go along and tell them what I know, how I feel. But it won't do any good.'

'That's why I've come to you. You wanted to see the parents of the victims.'

He smiled, revealing a set of perfect white teeth. 'Yes. The newspapers have been quite helpful. I had a lovely young journalist visit me. He was simply gorgeous.' He chuckled like a mischievous little girl. 'If I help you, perhaps you can tell them what I've seen.'

'How do you mean, "seen"?'

'I see things, in visions . . . and dreams.'

'What have you seen?'

'Dear Irene, you are, indeed, a believer. You believe in me. You *must* believe in me.'

'Oh, I do, I do.'

'Then trust me . . . A man from the past has entered your life. You must help him.'

Irene felt a surge of excitement. How could he know such a thing? She asked him in what way could she help. He closed his eyes, raised his right hand.

'Please, try not to ask too many questions. At this moment I am receiving psychic vibrations.'

'Sorry.'

'This man faces the prospect of great danger.'

'The man you are talking about is —'

'No!' He raised both of his little hands. 'I require no facts. I rely on intuition only.'

'My intuition tells me you are frightened of the murderer.'

'Your intuition serves you well. I am in tune with his psyche. That is disturbing for me.' Francis jerked his head to one side and closed his eyes tightly. Images appeared in quick succession. He saw soft-looking white hands, a knife, blood dripping onto a holly bush. His eyes opened. He took a few deep breaths and ran his fingers through his curly grey hair. The vision was over. 'Elizabeth was overpowered by a man who is obsessed with pain and the destruction of young women. His fantasy is now a reality. His name is Tony.'

Irene now wondered if he was really genuine. What he said could easily have been gleaned from newspaper reports.

He pointed at her. 'You need not doubt what I have said. I don't have to read newspapers in order to convince.'

'You amaze me,' she said, stunned by his apparent ability to read her mind.

Francis wiped his face with a handkerchief, then pushed it up the sleeve of his black shirt. 'I must try to get closer to him.'

'If there is anything I can do to help.'

'You can my dear, dear lady. I need something that belonged to Elizabeth, something that she was fond of, perhaps an item of clothing she liked to wear. I can then step into his mind, his world, his fantasy.'

And that was that.

He slid out of the chair and she followed him to the front garden. Her time with him was over. There were so many questions she would liked to have asked him, but Julian Francis was a man who would not be pushed into doing anything that was contrary to his nature. Irene, deep in thought, was left with no doubt regarding his uncanny psychic abilities. Francis remained at the door.

When Irene reached the garden gate she turned to face him. 'I'll bring something of Elizabeth's for you to work with.'

'You will, my dear,' he said, bowing.

One burning question remained. She asked him if the man from the past would love her again.

'I'm afraid I can't give an answer at this point in time. The one thing I am certain about is that the killer's fantasy will continue. It has become the driving force. I have a sense of it, particularly when the victim meets her end. It happened with Elaine Pemberton, and I felt completely helpless. The visions are still with me. This man *must* be stopped.'

'Elaine Pemberton died over two weeks ago.'

'Yes, I know. The visions are becoming stronger. This man's hatred for women is absolutely terrifying. I am fearful for their safety.'

'The murders aren't going to stop, are they?'

'Bring the item to me,' he said, placing his hand over his heart. 'I will tell you about Elizabeth's killer.'

She pressed him for an answer to her question.

'There is no choice. He will kill again.'

Sheridan was out of luck. The phone wasn't ringing. No jobs. No work. His curiosity had not faded though. Since his errand to the garage on Central Drive he had revisited the derelict room several times and learned from the locals that a tramp called Albie spent much of his time there.

His luck was about to change.

10.30 a.m. Jim Sheridan found himself walking down Central Drive on an overcast rainy day. He saw a man - probably Albie, judging by his appearance - entering the room. His pace quickened. He paused at the entrance, then walked in, not knowing what to expect. The man inside shot up from the settee, obviously scared. He was at least sixty, and wore a dark filthy coat several sizes too big. His eyes were grey, his stare intense. This was Dickens' Fagin, complete with grey scraggly beard and wide brim hat. He shuffled towards Sheridan, and repeated the words 'smoke' three times. Sheridan guessed he needed a cigarette. Without hesitation he lit one and gave it to him.

'Your name is, "Albie?"'

'Albie it is,' he replied, his voice surprisingly clear and sharp. They sat down on the stained settee, Sheridan wondering if any of the filth would stick to his trousers. He had never been so close to a tramp, and felt strange, almost intimidated, in his presence. The man's face was tanned and heavily lined. Even in the poor light, Sheridan noticed the countless blackheads dotted over the entire surface of his face.

Albie offered him a drag of the cigarette.

'No, thank you.'

He grunted and sucked away at the cigarette, taking it almost down to the filter. He dropped the butt into a large tin can, stared at Sheridan and said, 'Can I have one?'

'Have what?'

'A smoke.'

'You've just had one.'

Albie smiled, revealing what few blackened teeth he had left. An assortment of nauseating smells filled the air. Sheridan wondered how long he would last in the presence of this harmless eccentric.

'I'd like to ask you a few questions. If you help me, I'll let you have these,' Sheridan said, tempting him with a packet of cigarettes.

'You're the police. What do you want?'

'No, I'm not from the police.'

'No? I don't like them. They looked in here, but I was gone.'

'You know that a murder happened near here?'

'You think I did it. You *are* the police,' Albie retorted, fear in his eyes.

'I assure you - I am not . . . Have they questioned you?'

'No. They don't know about me. Smoke, please.'

Sheridan lit another cigarette. Albie snatched it and puffed heavily. 'I've seen him,' he said.

'You saw the killer?'

He held out his hand. 'Packet of smokes, please.'

Sheridan obliged. Had to.

'You saw the killer?' he repeated.

'I have, and I've read about it in the papers.'

'You buy newspapers?'

'I find newspapers. Never buy them. I read them, and burn them.'

'Did you see the girl, on the night she was murdered?'

'No.'

'What about this man you saw?'

'It was him. They call him Jack the Ripper.'

'How long ago was this?'

'A few weeks, I think.'

'Tell me about him.'

'He was standing outside this room, next to his car.'

'What did he look like?'

'A black shadow.'

'Can you tell me anything? Age, height, colour of his hair?'

'Dark hair. Could be black. I don't know how old he is. He was a black shadow, just a shadow.'

'What time was it when you saw him?'

'Don't have the time.'

'Late at night?'

'Very late. I was trying to sleep. I heard footsteps and a noise. I kept quiet, and looked out to see what it was. He got into a car.'

'Do you know what sort of car?'

'I don't know about cars. It was white, like the moon. It wouldn't start at first . . . When he got it going he drove to the road opposite.'

'Geary Road?'

'Yes . . . The car stops, and he gets out and pushes it further down the road. Next thing, I come back to my settee and go to sleep.'

The police had missed a vital witness. Sheridan was convinced that Albie had seen the killer getting into a white car. Probably an old one.

He dropped the remains of the cigarette into the tin and patted Sheridan's shoulder. 'You're happy now, aren't you? You're my friend. You are welcome here.'

Sheridan smiled and thanked him.

'I'll have some more smokes off you, in return for what I've told you.'

'That's no problem. I'll buy you some smokes.'

Albie had never been treated so kindly. He hugged his new 'friend.' Sheridan winced as Albie's foul bodily odour hit him.

'I've a few more questions for you. How long have you had this settee?'

He screwed up his face, deep in thought. 'You can't have it. It's mine. I found it.'

'Don't worry, Albie, I don't want the settee. How long have you had it?'

'Months. I found it round the back.'

'The back of this building?'

'Yes, yes. You find some good things round there.'

'There's a leg missing. Was it missing when you found it?'

He gave a puzzled look, then said, 'The leg? Yes, it was missing. Don't need it, anyway. I use these bricks to hold it up.'

Sheridan stood up, ready to leave. 'The bricks do a fine job, Albie. I must be on my way. I'll be back, soon.'

'With the smokes?'

'Yes, Albie. I'll buy you some smokes.'

Sheridan spent the rest of the day at home trying to relax in front of the TV. Nothing could stop him thinking about what Albie had seen. His information could be invaluable to the police enquiry. Obviously, they hadn't noticed the settee, and even if they had they may not have realised its significance. Had they got to Albie first he would have been treated as a suspect. His beloved settee would have been removed for forensic examination. They would have learned nothing from it.

Sheridan couldn't resist the temptation to theorise. He closed his eyes, trying to work out what had happened on that fateful night . . .

The killer parks his car outside Albie's den, having seen Elaine Pemberton coming down Central Drive. He waits for his chance, then drags her into the darkness of the passage behind the Ten Pin Bowling. At some stage he looks around for an object with which to attack her. He sees the piece of wood - the missing settee leg - and uses it to brutalise her. But how does he notice that little piece of wood? The place was in darkness. It's unlikely that he's carrying a torch. So, what happens next? He disembowels her and removes pieces of flesh with his knife. He removes her shoes - not unless they've already come off - and walks back to his car. Albie hears a noise and creeps to the doorway to see what's happening. He sees the man getting into the vehicle. He fires the ignition until it starts. The car is white. The killer's hair is black.

I must phone Lewis.

'I thought you'd call me sooner or later,' Lewis said, happy to hear his voice.

Sheridan told him the news.

'Wow. Well done, Sheridan. So, you're back on the case?'

'Not necessarily. See what you can come up with.'

'You can count on me. It looks like the killer is driving some knackered car that's only fit for the scrap yard.'

'It's a possibility. The police will probably beat you to it.'

'I wouldn't put money on it. Must dash.'

'Good luck, Lewis. Keep me informed, will you?'

'Sure will.'

7 p.m. Sheridan ate a light meal and undressed, ready for a hot bath. The door bell sounded. He slipped into his dressing gown and opened the door, surprised to see Irene.

'I've come at a bad time,' she said, looking him up and down.

'It's all right,' he said, pleasantly surprised. He showed her into the living room and offered her a seat.

'I can't stay for long,' she said.

'Well, what can I do for you, Irene?'

She told him about her meeting with Julian Francis. Sheridan wasn't impressed. She wasn't in an amiable mood anyway, for obvious reasons. He decided to tread carefully.

'How do you think this fellow can help?'

'He's going to tell me about Elizabeth's killer. I'm interested in what he has to say.'

'Perhaps he should try telling the police.'

'They won't listen to fortune tellers.'

'I suppose not. You want me to come along with you?'

Irene looked into his eyes, sensing his remorse. He waited for the answer, hoping she would say yes.

'That wasn't the idea. Remember the earring I gave to you: the one Elizabeth was wearing when she died?'

'You want it back.'

'Only for a short while. Francis needs something to work on. It might help bring out his psychic powers.'

'It's at the office. I'll drop it off tomorrow morning.'

She nodded. He followed her outside, disappointed because she hadn't stayed longer. There seemed little chance of a reconciliation.

She moved closer to him, purposely invading his private space.

'How's your beautiful friend these days? Seen her, lately?'

'No. I'm not likely to see her again.'

She shook her head slowly, displaying her contempt.

'Just listen to me for a minute, will you?' he said.

'No. I'm not interested in your sordid little games.'

'Well then, I'll post the earring through your letter box. Bring it back when Francis has done his bit. It means a lot to me.'

Irene could feel a jealous rage coming on, but she could not deny him the possession of the only memento he was ever likely to have.

'Don't worry, you'll get it back.'

'One more thing - let me know what Francis comes up with.'

She got into her friend's car and wound the window down. 'I didn't think you believed in supernatural things . . . I'll think about it.'

Seconds later, she was gone.

Sheridan didn't believe in such things as fortune telling and palm reading. He hoped her forthcoming visit to the well-known psychic would, at least, give him the chance to rekindle their friendship.

THIRTY-FIVE

The atmosphere in the incident room was tense, and Oxley could sense a long and tedious investigation ahead of him. Murder squad detectives were giving no less than one hundred per cent effort. Most of them, including Oxley, were working seven days a week.

The pressure of the enquiry had already pushed George Naylor over the edge. Oxley couldn't afford to end up in the same pitiful condition. He was pushing himself hard and managing to stay in control. His objectivity and patience were serving him well. The worry, however, was always there. This was *his* chance to prove himself. There was bound to be a promotion waiting for him if he could catch the murderer, who had been dubbed by some tabloids as 'The Seaside Ripper.'

Police officers were back on the streets talking to people, warning women of the dangers of travelling alone at night. Central Drive was a different matter. Secret night-time surveillance of the area surrounding the Ten Pin Bowling was in operation.

Oxley had hardly moved from his desk all day, fighting the tiredness that ran deep through his body.

DS Lambert approached. The Ford Sierra lead had injected hope into a beleaguered investigation, and she had news for him. A white Sierra had been logged by the team. The driver had passed the Pemberton crime scene on several occasions, late at night. Rivers and Palmer had questioned a Blackpool man by the name of Ormerod.

She waited until he finished his telephone conversation. 'Ormerod's been eliminated,' she said bluntly.

Oxley's closed his eyes and let out a sharp breath of air. 'Why has it taken so long to interview him?'

'He was never at home, until today.'

'Are they certain he doesn't merit further questioning?'

'Absolutely, sir. He fits the description: black hair, early thirties.'

'Lives alone?'

'Common-law wife.'

Oxley raised his hand, finger pointing upwards. 'Simmons' profile. Remember?'

'Yes. Simmons says, lives alone or with single parent. You really believe that, sir?'

'I do, but we'll check all suspects, single or otherwise.'

'I hope it doesn't turn out to be a waste of time like it did with Dean Cooney.'

'If the Sierra driver isn't the murderer, why has he not come forward to eliminate himself?' Oxley asked, leaning back in his chair.

'Too scared.'

'I don't believe that.'

'Well, if the Sierra driver *is* the murderer we need to look further afield. We've checked every Sierra driver in Blackpool, Sedgeburn and all the other large towns in Lancashire. Some of those even matched the description of our suspect.'

'It could become a full-blown nationwide enquiry. What's more frustrating is the fact that the killer might have sold or even scrapped his car.'

'We're looking into all that, sir.'

'I know. Let's keep at it.'

Lambert turned to leave, then said, 'Might I ask, sir, what you intend to do about that private investigator, Jim Sheridan?'

'Nothing. Why?'

'The surveillance team spotted him snooping round the Pemberton murder scene late at night.'

'Sheridan has been checked. He was in Norwich during the period of his daughter's murder.'

'I think we should bring him in again. Let's face it, sir, we know nothing about him.'

Lewis questioned the hotel managers at the Promenade end of Geary Road, which was close to the Pemberton crime scene. None of them could recall any recent guests who owned a white Sierra hatchback. Nobody remembered having seen such a vehicle on the night of 15 July to early morning the next day.

Geary Road Social Club was another option open to Lewis. The club looked inconspicuous from the outside, and easy to miss if you didn't see the sign. Sunday lunchtime entertainment was in full swing. Local duo, Sunrise, were singing the biggest hits in country and western music, including the standards 'Your Cheatin' Heart' and 'Sea of Heartbreak.' Lewis heard the music from outside and decided to call in for a drink. He watched the duo for as long as his curiosity would allow. A couple of minutes was enough to convince him how feeble they were. He made his way to the overcrowded bar. The great weather was pulling weekend visitors to the busy cheerful resort.

The magic of Blackpool hadn't completely faded.

The bar steward served him a pint of lager in a grubby glass. They got talking. He mentioned the Pemberton murder, and the fact that he was from BBI.

'What's BBI?'

'Big Brother Investigations.'

'You're not a copper, then?'

'No. This is a separate enquiry.'

'Hang on a minute.' He served another punter, then came back. 'I don't think anyone round here can tell you anything you don't already know. Most of them are visitors.'

'Yeah, I realise that.'

The steward left him and went to talk to an old acquaintance. Lewis remained at the bar, drinking lager, listening to the duo. *Just the kind of music Sheridan would like,* he thought.

'You need to speak to Mavis Bradley,' a voice said from behind him.

Lewis spun round. 'Are you talking to me?'

The barmaid motioned him to come closer. 'Mavis is serving on the other side of the bar, in the snooker room. She's taken a big interest in these murders. She thinks she's seen him.'

'Seen who?'

'The Ripper, of course.' She pointed at a door. 'Go through there, and through the other door facing you.'

'Thanks.'

Lewis decided to check it out. In the snooker room the air was cooler, cleaner. The languid players were talking in hushed voices. Mavis was sitting on a high chair at the end of the bar. Her eyes lit up when she saw him. She smiled. He smiled back. He reckoned she was about forty. She had short blonde hair, sparkling eyes. Her thin lips, coated with cheap bright-red lipstick, gave them a fuller look.

He introduced himself and offered to buy her a drink. She poured a Tia Maria and added lots of coke. He gave her a tenner and told her to keep the change.

'A tenner. Are you sure?' she asked surprised.

He nodded and went on to explain his mission.

'How long have you been working on this case?' she asked.

'Since the first murder.'

She grinned. 'You're after the reward.'

'Who isn't? A hundred grand would go a long way.'

'It's gone up twenty grand. Didn't you know?'

'I didn't . . . One of the bar staff told me you've seen something.'

'That's right. Everybody round here thinks I'm stupid. They take everything I say with a pinch of salt.'

'I'd still like to know what it was you saw.'

'Would you?'

'Yes. I'll give you something for your trouble.'

'You don't need to pay me, love. I'll give you my telephone number.'

'Okay. Fine.'

'I don't live far from here.' She licked the top of her glass, then took a sip.

Lewis wasn't slow on the uptake. 'You want me to come to your place. Is that it?'

'When you've got time . . . plenty of time.'

'Right now, I haven't got much time.'

'You ought to slow down a bit. Good looking lad like you should be enjoying life to the full.' She took a pen out of her handbag and wrote her name and telephone number on a beer mat. She took a sip of her drink and winked at him.

'I'll ring you, soon as I've got time,' he said softly, trying to sound sincere.

'I hope you do, love.'

'Heh, this is Carl Lewis. I'll be there when the time comes, but I really am in a hurry. Are you going to tell me, or not?'

'Okay, Carl Lewis. I can see you're in a rush. I won't waste your time, just as long as you save some of it for me.'

'Promise.'

She leaned towards him. 'It was one o'clock in the morning when I left this club—'

'Hang on. When was this?'

'Couple of weeks back - Sunday the sixteenth. I remember. I'm good with dates.'

'How come it was so late?'

'Well, don't say anything to anybody. Some of us stay behind for drinks, after the club is shut. You keep that to yourself or I'll loose my job.'

'I won't say a word.'

'I left the club and started walking towards Central Drive, where the bowling place is. This car came along and stopped right opposite me.'

'Colour?'

'White . . . This bloke was revving the engine. I thought it was a taxi at first. I was wrong. Anyway, I caught a glimpse of the driver. He looked horrible.'

'In what way?'

'He looked menacing, as if he was real mad at me. It was scary, I can tell you. I stared back at him and he turned his face away. I carried on walking and the car set off again.'

'Tell me about him.'

'I'd put him at around thirty. Dark hair. He had these spots on his face. Couldn't tell what they were. Might have been blood.'

'What make of car?' Lewis asked, eager for as much information as possible.

'I'm not sure, but I noticed all this rust at the bottom of the doors and I'm sure there was a yellow sticker in the back window.'

'A sloping window?'

'Yes, I think so. I told my friends what I saw. They just laughed.'

Lewis wasn't laughing. He reckoned the police had already interviewed the murderer and eliminated him from the enquiry. He had the profile and a description of both driver and car. He knew where to start looking.

He gave her a big smile. 'You've been a great help. Thanks.' He made off towards the door.

'Carl Lewis,' she called. 'Don't forget to ring me.'

He winked at her. 'You can bet on it.'

When he reached his car he looked at the name and number on the beer mat. He laughed to himself and threw it away.

Irene Collinson was pacing the room, waiting anxiously for Julian Francis. She looked at old black and white photographs of the Francis family, then went and sat in the comfy leather armchair. The silence of the house was accentuated by a ticking clock. The smell of the room reminded Irene of old books in a library. She became aware of a creaking noise and the muffled sound of approaching footsteps. The door opened, and the little man walked in.

'My dear Irene, I am expecting visitors soon. There is little time to spare.' He took the chair opposite her.

'I don't mind coming again—'

'No, no. I'm sorry if I sounded rude. This session shouldn't take long. What have you brought me?'

She showed him the earring. He took it from her and held it close to his temple. 'This was your daughter's?' he asked.

'Yes. She was wearing it on the night she died.'

He held it in front of his face and closed his eyes. He told her not to say anything. A minute later his chest was rising and falling, his breathing deep and rhythmic. Suddenly, his eyes opened wide, revealing only white eyeballs.

Irene took a sharp intake of breath.

He was unaffected by her alarm. The vibrations were coming through already. His breathing became less laboured. His lips were quivering. He mumbled something incoherent then said, 'Elizabeth is limping.'

Half a minute passed without another word. Irene broke the silence. 'Where is she?'

'I see trees, a hospital . . . She has hurt her foot and is resting . . . Yes, she is resting next to an open gate.'

The gates of Aristor Park.

Francis was reliving Elizabeth's last moments.

'A man is crossing the road, coming towards her. He is consumed with hate.' He closed his eyes tightly. 'Elizabeth is speaking.'

'What is she saying?' she asked, assuming he was in touch with her daughter's spirit. Whatever was happening in his mind he could not hear Irene's voice.

'She is pointing at her foot.' Francis turned his head to the left, then to the right. 'He is listening out for the traffic . . . He looks beyond the gates and into the park . . . *He must have her.*' He grabbed his neck with his left hand, his other hand squeezing the earring. 'He is dragging her into the park . . .'

'What does he look like?'

'She is struggling, struggling violently.' Francis gasped. His eyes opened wide revealing the horror of the moment.

'What is it?' Irene shrieked. She held her arms out towards him. 'What's happening?'

'I see different faces, different people. I feel the power, the force driving him . . . Oh no, please, stop this . . . She is falling, falling, gasping desperately for air . . . She wants mummy to be there . . . She thinks it's all a dream. She can't believe it's happening.'

Irene was now sitting bolt upright, hands clenched tightly.

His breathing slowed down a little. His psychic revelation seemed to have ended. Seconds later, the breathing accelerated again. He fell back into his chair, as if an unseen force had pushed him. 'He is dragging her body . . . I see a holly bush . . . He his holding the knife . . . The urge to kill is irresistible . . . He is their disciple. The way has been shown to him.' Francis was sweating heavily. He ripped his shirt open, uttering the words, 'Queen of the Night beckons him . . . I feel his presence . . . He is coming closer and closer . . .'

Francis fell silent. The earring fell from his open hand. A few minutes later his breathing returned to normal. Irene retrieved the earring and waited for him to regain his composure.

'I have returned,' he said, at last, 'back to the world of reality.'

'Are you feeling all right, now?'

'Yes, my dear. When this is all over, you and I will be happier people.'

'I do hope you're right.'

They stood up and faced each other.

'You must go now. The tide of fortune will change for the better. Your anger, sadness and bitterness will subside.'

'Thank you, Julian.'

He took hold of her hand, squeezing it affectionately. 'I fear that I have not helped you much. The man who killed your daughter is filled with hideous desire. That is all I can tell you. I am at a loss to know exactly what is going on in his mind.'

'What did you mean when you said he is coming closer?'

'His presence is strong. That is all I know. There is danger all around.'

'You said the words, "Queen of the Night." What does it mean?'

'I am not sure. I can only assume that it refers to the Babylonians. They worshipped the moon. The moon can be a strong influence on people, you know. Whether or not this cryptic clue could be of use to the police is a different matter. Anyway, there it is.'

He showed her to the door where they said their goodbyes. She headed straight for home and immediately wrote down all she could remember about the night's events.

10.45 p.m. Lewis checked his desk to see if any messages had been left for him. He switched off the office lights, locked the door and skipped down the stairs. Seconds later he was driving back to his apartment on Bank Street. It had been the most significant day in his life. Since leaving the Geary Road Social Club there had been a dramatic development in his investigation. He could barely contain his excitement and couldn't wait to tell Sheridan what he had discovered.

The car sped along the cul-de-sac, tyres screeching as he sharply pulled up outside the garage behind his apartment. He left the engine running whilst opening the garage doors. He switched the light on, returned to the car and steered it into the confined space. He got out of his car, closed the door, and stood motionless.

What was that noise? he asked himself.

But before he could turn round the hammer came down onto his head.

He slumped to the ground, the warm crimson life force bubbling from the cracks of his shattered skull.

Strong hands rolled him over onto his back.

Lewis saw a featureless face hanging above him, the merest hint of a black hairline, and a hideous grin that began to fade as he slid silently into eternal emptiness.

THIRTY-SIX

'Slow down,' she said loudly. 'There's a phone near that pub.'

He stopped the car and sat in silence.

'Go on then, Dave,' she urged. 'Ring them.'

'Can't *you* tell them?'

'I'm no good at that sort of thing. Anyway, you saw it first.'

'We both saw it at the same time . . . Oh, all right, I'll do it. What am I going to say?'

'Just tell them who you are. You were out walking in those woods with your girlfriend. Tell them we came across a hand sticking out of the soil.'

'I can't say, "a hand," can I?'

'Yes, you can. Tell them you think it's a skeleton.'

He made the call and they waited patiently, counting the minutes and watching the seconds tick by.

When the police arrived, an officer asked who they were, what they were doing. The couple then got into a police vehicle and the girl gave directions. A few minutes later the officer drove down a narrow leafy lane that ran for a hundred yards before metamorphosing into a jumble of bushes and weeds. They showed him the exact location of the corpse, and watched as he carefully examined the fragile remains.

When Sheridan reached his office Darren gave him a sealed envelope that Irene had delivered by hand. The little hard lump could only have been his daughter's earring.

He prepared coffee, sat down and eagerly tore open the envelope. He held it upside-down. The precious memento fell onto the desk. He looked inside the envelope. Irene had written a letter to him which began, 'Jim, I have been to see Julian Francis. Gave him the earring. I'm not sure that his help would be of any use to the police. I have written down most of what he said and I believe him to be genuine. You asked me to let you know what he said, so, here it is.' The letter ended, 'Take Care - Irene.'

If only I had arrived a bit earlier, he thought.

Sheridan would have been able to speak to her, smooth things over.

He paced the office, cup in one hand, letter in the other. He read the rest of it with scepticism, ruminating over various sentences: 'He is holding a knife.' *Any fool would know that*, he surmised. 'I see a holly bush.' *The bush was probably mentioned in a newspaper.* 'He is their disciple. Babylonians worshipped the moon. Francis saw different people, different faces, in his vision.' *What's all that about? Is he saying there is more than one killer?*

He threw the letter onto the desk, then heard voices from outside. He looked out of the window and saw Darren standing next to a police car, talking to a man and a woman. A uniformed officer was also present. Sheridan could sense trouble. Minutes later, the door cracked open.

'It's good to see you again, Mr Sheridan,' Steve Rivers said.

DS Lambert scanned the room, her eyes falling on the map and news reports which Sheridan had stuck on the wall.

'Good morning, DC Rivers,' Sheridan said, unimpressed by his condescending attitude.

'I'll get straight to the point,' Rivers said, eyeballing him. 'Where were you last night?'

'I was at home all night.'

'Do you mean, here?'

'No. This isn't my house, this is an office.'

'An office, eh? It's not what I'd call an office. What were you doing at home?'

'Not much. I fell asleep watching the tele.'

'Oh, yeah? And what time did you fall asleep?'

'I'm not sure. Early evening, I suppose. I had a few drinks.'

'Been on the piss, you mean?'

Typical of Rivers, Lambert thought.

'I had a few, yes.'

'Who was with you?'

'Nobody.'

'Did you speak to anybody?'

'No. It must have been about half-ten when I went to bed.'

'So, there is nobody who can verify this?'

'That's right. If you don't mind, I'd like to know what this is all about.'

Lambert stepped forward. 'A body was discovered this morning. It's not been formally identified but we are certain it's Carl Lewis. He was murdered last night.'

Sheridan shuffled to the other side of his desk and fell into his chair, physically drained by the emotional shock of what he had heard.

'It looks like the motive was robbery,' Rivers said, without even a hint of remorse.

'You're going to arrest me aren't you?' Sheridan responded, picking up the letter and earring.

'Leave those where they are and come with us,' Lambert said.

He followed her to the landing where a burly constable was waiting. Rivers closed the door and stayed in the office. Lambert made the arrest and cautioned him. He didn't say a word. The arrest meant nothing to him. He was too upset for that, and didn't believe for one moment that the motive for his death was robbery. Sheridan believed that his one-time partner had come face to face with his daughter's killer.

Rivers was still rummaging around the office, and came upon incriminating evidence. He opened the office door. 'I see you have resorted to fortune tellers,' he said. 'You must be desperate. I have to say, we don't believe in that sort of nonsense.'

'Neither do I. You're wasting time arresting me. I didn't kill Lewis. He was my friend.'

'Was he, indeed?' Rivers said, waving a bundle of twenty pound notes. 'How much?'

'Now, wait a minute—'

'How much?' he repeated angrily.

'About two thousand. If you let me explain—'

'You've been cautioned,' Lambert said. 'I wouldn't say anything if I were you.'

Becky told detectives what she knew about Lewis's investigation, and his relationship with Sheridan. They didn't learn much. The other BBI men, Chris and Bob, were not available. They would face questioning at a later stage.

Becky was alone now, wandering about the office, ignoring the telephone whenever it rang. She didn't realise, until now, just how attached she had become to Carl Lewis. In the few years she'd known him they never really fell out with each other. He was easy going, humorous, always pleased with her work. Although he was in charge, there had been occasions when she more or less told *him* what to do.

He fancied her right from the start, that was for sure. That was never a problem. Lewis wasn't a bad looking guy. She never fancied him, though.

And now it was all over. No more Lewis. Gone forever. There was nothing to remind her of him. Not even a photograph.

The bad news came as a huge shock. Suddenly, her grief exploded. Becky's blue eyes unleashed a torrent of tears.

She sat at his favourite spot by the window and cried her heart out.

The tiny inconspicuous camera in Room Six was operative. Oxley was glued to the TV screen in the next room, watching private detective Jim Sheridan's every move.

Lambert told him that Sheridan and Lewis had been working together for some months. Although Oxley thought he was an unlikely suspect, he wasn't entirely happy with the arrest. He rose from his chair and faced Lambert. 'Why should he want to kill Carl Lewis?' he asked.

'Perhaps it was for the money, sir.'

'And you think he's been killing these young women?'

'I don't know about that. He was observed at the Pemberton crime scene.'

'It doesn't make sense. Why should he kill his own partner for a couple of grand?'

'Two grand could be a fortune to someone like Jim Sheridan. Not unless . . .'

'What?'

'Not unless Lewis became suspicious. Maybe he confronted him with some evidence. Sheridan kills him and makes it look like robbery.'

Oxley considered. 'I'm not convinced. I'll give it straight to you, Tanya - Sheridan's not a serial killer. Whether or not he killed Lewis is a different matter . . . What's with the solicitor?'

'He waived his rights.'

'Has he, now? Well, he must be confident. You'd better get the tapes rolling. Who's conducting the interview with you?'

'DC Rivers. He's questioned Sheridan before.'

Oxley turned away from her and sat in front of the screen. Lambert left him and entered Room Six, accompanied by Rivers.

Sheridan lit a cigarette and calmly exhaled the smoke. It was impossible to tell that Lewis's death had deeply upset him. Rivers switched the cassette recorder on. Lambert announced the time and details of who were present. Again, Lambert asked him about his whereabouts during the previous evening. The answer was the same as before. Nobody could verify his alibi.

'How long had you known Lewis?' Lambert asked.

'About four months. He was helping me find the man who killed my daughter.'

'How far did you get with your enquiries?'

'We made no progress at all.'

'Did you have any disagreements?'

'No. I have to point out that he came to me in the first place. It was his idea to join forces. We got on well.'

'What lines of enquiry did you pursue?'

'We came to the conclusion — '

'This isn't relevant,' Rivers snapped. Lambert looked at him over the top of her glasses. Rivers was seemingly somewhat agitated. Sheridan knew why.

'Let's talk about this money,' Rivers urged. 'Where did you get it from?'

'Lewis gave it to me.'

'I doubt it. Two grand is a lot of money.'

'Lewis had plenty of money. He knew how to use it to his best advantage.' Sheridan gave a combined raised-eyebrows-nodding-of-the-head gesture: a warning that Rivers couldn't ignore.

'Why should he give you such a large sum?' Lambert asked.

'I don't have a lot of money. Lewis was merely trying to help me. He insisted — '

'That's a lie!' Rivers interrupted. 'You waited for him to return to his flat, then you killed him. Nobody gives two grand away just like that.'

Sheridan took the last couple of drags of his cigarette and casually stubbed it in the ashtray. 'I wouldn't kill a person for any amount of money; even if I did, I wouldn't be stupid enough to leave it in my office drawer. Anyway, you're welcome to search my house, car, clothes - anything you like. I didn't kill Carl Lewis. You're barking up the wrong tree.'

Rivers kept silent. Lambert felt they had gone as far as they could with regard to Lewis's death. She went on to say that the surveillance team had spotted him snooping around the Pemberton crime scene. She asked for an explanation.

'I ran out of cigarettes. I went to the nearby garage to buy some and then decided to take a look at the scene for myself.'

'Why should you want to revisit a crime scene?'

'Sorry, DS Lambert, but I didn't *revisit* the crime scene. It was my first visit. I went there because I was curious.'

Lambert's intuition told her he was holding something back. She decided to dig deeper. 'We know that you were, allegedly, in Norwich when your daughter was Murdered.'

'I *was* in Norwich,' Sheridan exclaimed.

'Can you tell us what you were doing on the night of July 15?'

'I was at home on that particular evening.'

'Can you prove it?'

'You have my word. I stayed in all night.'

Lambert stared him straight in the eyes. He remained placid, didn't move a muscle.

'Okay, Mr Sheridan, I have no further questions at this point in time.'

'Wait a minute,' Sheridan said. 'I've been in regular contact with Lewis since these murders began. I think he was onto something.'

'Any details?' she asked.

'Terminate the interview,' Rivers ordered. 'This is irrelevant, nothing to do with the murder of Lewis.'

Lambert shrugged her shoulders and officially terminated the interview. Rivers was vulnerable now. Before anyone could speak the door burst open and Oxley came in. Sheridan looked at Oxley, intrigued as to why he had come in so suddenly.

Payback time had arrived. Rivers kept a stern face, trying to suppress the guilt that was simmering inside him.

'If Lewis was onto something, as you put it, I want to know what it was.'

Sheridan knew all along that the interview was being monitored. 'I'd like to know who I'm speaking to.'

'Inspector Oxley. I'm in charge of this investigation. I don't have to tell you how difficult it's been. We need all the help we can get. What can you tell us about Carl Lewis?'

Sheridan cleared his throat. 'Lewis was an intelligent private detective. Don't ask me how he did it, but he came up with his own profile of the murderer.'

Oxley leaned against the wall, folded his arms. The word 'profile' was all it took to gain his full attention. Rivers was alarmed. He knew Oxley detested him. He also knew that Sheridan was playing games with him.

'Tell me about this profile.'

'Well, to be honest, I can't remember much about what he said. He talked about the killer being both organised and disorganised. He reckoned the killer was some saddo who was abused as a kid. He talked about him having these violent fantasies. He's a man who hates women, you see. He probably spent much of his youth visiting brothels, paying for sadistic sex, and that was the trigger for part of our investigation.'

'The trigger? So, what was the follow-up?'

'I personally made numerous phone calls, ringing escort agencies and magazine advertisements. Lewis decided to concentrate on the brothels, but there's only one as far as we could ascertain.'

'Which one?'

'There's a place in Wichonstall. It's run by a woman. Now, what is her name? Let me think . . .'

Rivers was sweating. His job was on the line.

'Diana Humble. Yes, that's her name. She runs the place.'

'Did you discover anything of interest?'

'No. We managed to get the names of all the punters who visit the place. It was a disappointing exercise.'

Inspector Oxley didn't attach any significance to his answer, his veiled threat to Rivers.

'I have nothing else to add,' Sheridan said.

Rivers breathed a sigh of relief.

'Any ideas as to why anyone should want to murder Carl Lewis?'

'Catch the man who is killing these girls, inspector. He's the one you want. He's the man who killed my partner.'

Jack Robson settled in his chair and watched the national news on TV. His wife, Avril, was in the kitchen busily drying the pots and pans. When the news reader mentioned the discovery of a body in Plymbey, he called his wife's name and turned the sound up.

'What do you want?' she asked.

'Look at this. The television people are down by the wood.'

The news reader began: 'And now for the main story we can go live to our crime correspondent who is at the scene of the discovery in Plymbey.'

The correspondent brought the microphone closer to his face. 'This is woodland in Plymbey, on the outskirts of Sedgeburn,' he began. 'Earlier today a couple, who were out walking, came across a skeletonised hand protruding from the soil. Behind me, forensic scientists and a Home Office pathologist are making a preliminary examination of the scene and the remains of what appears to be the body of a female.'

At that point he was joined by Detective Superintendent Mike Rogers of the Sedgeburn Police. Rogers carried a grim expression and spoke in a deep voice. He was asked for further details.

'The body is that of a female. We are unable, at this stage, to say how old she was when she died. The body is partially clothed and the Home Office pathologist has just informed me that although the majority of the major organs have decomposed, several structures are still intact.'

'Can you tell how long the body has been there?'

'First signs would indicate several months.'

'Is this being treated as a murder?'

'Yes. There's no doubt at all that she was murdered before being buried. Our first priorities will be to determine the cause of death, and put a name to the body. Thank you.'

Jack switched the TV off. 'I can't believe it,' he said. 'I pass by that wood nearly every morning.'

'It's frightening to think someone might have been murdered down there,' Avril added, feigning a shiver.

'Right on our own doorstep,' Jack added.

THIRTY-SEVEN

6 p.m. Irene Collinson sat down to read the local news. The front-page headline startled her: 'Private Detective Murdered.'

Although deeply shocked, she gave a sigh of relief when she learned it was Lewis, and not Sheridan, who was dead. The report was brief, giving scant details about Lewis's interest in the crimes. Sheridan's name didn't appear. *Curious,* she thought. She had no idea that Sheridan had been arrested. The thought occurred to her that Lewis had come close to catching the killer, but the last paragraph stated detectives were working on the theory that robbery was the most likely motive.

Irene was chilled by an enveloping sense of evil. She recalled Julian Francis saying, 'He is coming closer. There is danger all around.'

She wanted to know more about the BBI detective.

She grabbed the telephone, punched in Sheridan's office number.

No reply.

She tried his home number.

No reply.

George Naylor was under strict orders to take it easy. Dorothy made sure he did. She also made sure he took his tablets according to what the label read. She accompanied him everyday for a brisk walk by the sea. The break was doing him good. He was beginning to converse more and was appreciating the time that was his to enjoy.

And that made her happy.

Not once had he mentioned the investigation, not until he became acquainted with the recent events aired on TV. The old 'grey matter' started to effervesce once again.

He picked up the newspaper and read the article for the second time. Dorothy knew what was on his mind. 'George, you're doing ever so well. Don't start troubling yourself over these murders. It's not your job any more. They'll catch him in the end. Just you wait and see.'

'I hope they do. I wish I could be there on the day it happens . . . I wonder how Derek is coping?'

The pensive look said it all.

'No you don't, George,' she said firmly. 'Don't even think about ringing him; not until you've fully recovered.'

'I won't,' he assured her. 'Promise.'

George Naylor kept his promise.

Detective Superintendent Mike Rogers was leading the investigation into the murder of the unknown female. He was well acquainted with the pathologist, Dr Christian Purslow, and was eager to obtain any clue that could put a name to this unfortunate victim.

The latest case was a refreshing change of pace for Purslow. Previously, police had asked him to confirm what they believed was an accidental death. A man in his seventies had, apparently, fallen off his step ladders at his home. During the initial examination of the scene Purslow noticed a greyish smear on the wall close to the body. The smear was brain matter. He knew that it took more than a fall off a five foot step ladder to cause such an injury. A murder had been committed, and the astute pathologist received a commendation from the senior investigating officer who led the hunt for the killer.

The body retrieved from a woodland grave in Plymbey presented difficulties of a different kind. Putrefaction had done its work, obliterating any obvious clues that might otherwise have presented themselves for interpretation. Nevertheless, Purslow's keen eye for detail had revealed an injury that could easily have passed unnoticed.

Rogers circled the body like a bird of prey waiting its chance to devour a carcass. Purslow was sitting at a table several yards away, hunched over an optical microscope. Eventually, he straightened himself and turned round.

'You shouldn't have much trouble identifying her,' he said, adjusting his rectangular glasses. He held a small plastic bag in front of his face. Rogers joined him. The bag contained a discoloured gold chain and letter 'L.'

'That was found with the body,' Purslow said. 'You have the initial of her Christian name.'

'I'm amazed the murderer didn't take it with him.'

'Perhaps he didn't know it was there.'

'H'm. Perhaps he thought the body would never be discovered.'

'Good point, superintendent. Shallow graves inevitably attract all sorts of wildlife. I read of a similar case only recently. A young girl was abducted, sexually assaulted and killed. Her abductor buried her in a wood not far from where she lived. Several months later her bones were found scattered over an area covering fifty square yards.'

'I remember the case,' Rogers said, closing in on the skeleton. He asked Purslow if he had been able to determine her age.

'Teeth and skull analysis indicate mid-twenties. Of course, it's impossible to say if a sexual assault took place. I find it interesting that the jumper and blouse have been cut through. This may be indicative of sexual intent.'

'Any clothes missing?'

'I don't think so. The thick coat that she was wearing is suggestive. It's the type of garment one would normally wear in cold weather. This confirms my estimation that she was buried several months ago.'

Rogers picked up a bag containing a pair of knee-length, black boots. 'I'm sure that her clothes and the L-chain will help to identify her,' he said.

Purslow waved him over to the microscope and said, 'I'd like you to take a look at this specimen. It was taken from the body.'

Rogers looked through the lenses and adjusted the focus.

'What you see there is a bony structure of the neck: the thyroid cartilage. It would probably have been one of the last structures to decompose.'

'There are two halves,' Rogers remarked.

'That is significant. Can you see the darker colour along the edges of the cut surfaces?'

'I can.'

'That was caused by haemorrhage. In the region of the cartilage I found a blood vessel that is consistent with a severed artery. The artery has decomposed.'

'What does it tell us?'

'Her throat was cut. It may have been the cause of death.'

'I see. We have some useful clues thanks to you, doctor. I'm grateful. First thing tomorrow morning I shall consult our missing persons records.'

Sheridan was sorely tempted to let Jack Daniel's Tennesse Whiskey take care of the sadness and shock. So be it. He opened the cupboard and reached for the square bottle. He pressed the open bottle against his lips, watching the brown nectar flow towards its final destination. Suddenly, he slammed the bottle onto the coffee table. He decided there and then not to touch another drop. Not now. Not ever. He marched into the kitchen, pulled the lid off the waste bin and flung old 'Jack' into it as hard as he could.

He felt better for that. He knew there must be other ways of dealing with feelings of sadness and anger. And he *was* angry: angry with the way the police had treated him; angry because he believed he could have done more to catch Elizabeth's killer and the man who had callously taken his partner's life. But he was home now and free to do as he pleased. He removed his jacket, switched the kettle on and waited for the steam to drift through the spout.

He thought he heard the doorbell ringing. It was 11 p.m. *Nobody calls at this hour,* he thought. *Not unless it's important.* He made his way to the front door, thinking the police wanted to question him again.

Becky Watts was standing there. The night breeze was blowing her hair across her face and cooling her bloodshot eyes. He stepped back to let her in. She walked straight into the living room and sat down. Sheridan joined her.

'You know why I've come?'

He nodded slowly. 'I was arrested this morning. They said they had to formally question me. They eventually let me go. An inspector called Oxley doesn't believe that I killed Lewis.'

'Arrested you?' she said in disbelief.

He recounted the morning's events, including the brief search Rivers had made and the discovery of the money Lewis had given to him.

Becky was offended by their ineptitude. 'Didn't you tell them about Rivers?' she said angrily.

'You mean his visits to the brothel?'

'And the drugs.'

'Becky, it wasn't the time and place to go into all that. I was there to answer questions, not to make allegations about one of their officers.'

'What are they playing at?'

'They're looking at every possibility, I suppose. They think Lewis might have been robbed, but I know different.'

Becky became emotional. 'His parents are on holiday in Florida,' she said, wiping her eyes. 'I made the identification before they contacted them. They also questioned me about his recent movements.'

He waited until she had composed herself. 'I'm sorry, Becky. I'm really sorry.'

She sat in silence for a few minutes, staring ahead, picturing Lewis laughing and joking. 'It's happened so sudden. Nobody hated Carl. He never hurt anybody. And now his life has been taken from him.' She composed herself and said, 'Tell me what you know.'

'Becky, this can wait. You need to rest.'

'I'll be all right, Sheridan. I *will* rest, but I need to know what's been happening.'

'Okay, I'll make it brief.'

He told her about his visit to the Ten Pin Bowling, the tramp's den, his subsequent meeting with Albie and the discovery of the green settee with one leg missing.

'What's so important about a settee with a missing leg?'

'Lewis told me that Elaine Pemberton had a piece of wood thrust into her rectum. The wood had some green material attached to it. It's my belief it came from the settee. On the night of the murder, Albie heard sounds coming from outside his den. He saw a man standing next to a white car.'

'The police are looking at drivers of white Sierras.'

'Correct. Albie saw the killer. Unfortunately, he couldn't describe him in any detail. Needless to say, I didn't mention any of this to the police. When I told Lewis about the tramp he became excited.'

'How did Carl know about the piece of wood?'

'Think about it.'

'Steve Rivers.'

'Right. He also sold him a psychological profile of the murderer. I've got my own copy. Good job I brought it home. If Rivers found it, I'm sure he would have confiscated it.'

'Carl didn't mention any of this to me. Do you think he located the murderer?'

'I'm absolutely certain he did. Lewis got to him all right. He must have spoken to him and aroused suspicion. The murderer thinks his time is up, so he follows him back to his flat and kills him.'

'If he met the murderer he wouldn't have said anything to arouse suspicion. He was a pretty shrewd guy, believe me.'

'Well, something went wrong. Did he contact you or leave any messages?'

'No contact at all; but he must have returned to the office because some papers had been moved around.'

'Could anybody else have moved the papers?'

'There's only Chris and Bob. They were out all day.'

Sheridan couldn't understand why Lewis didn't contact him during the course of his investigation. There *had* to be a way forward.

It came in a flash.

'There is one possibility,' he said, hope in his voice. 'I remember him carrying one of those small recorders. He told me he used it for taping interviews.'

'I forgot about that.'

'There's one problem. He was robbed.'

'The murderer took it with him.'

'And if he didn't . . .'

'The police have got it.'

'Right you are, Becky. They won't hesitate to play it.'

'There's a chance he left it in the office. I'll have a look round.'

'I'd be grateful.'

They stood up and moved closer to each other. Becky's sad beautiful eyes were burning into him.

'Sheridan, I feel lonely. I want to stay with you tonight.'

He closed the gap between them and put his hands on her shoulders.

'Becky, right now the best place for you is home. Go home to your mother and son.'

Her eyes melted into tears. He held her tightly.

'Go now and get some rest. You can call me in a few days' time . . . I'll be here, won't I?'

Becky kissed him on the cheek and left him with his thoughts.

She drove passed BBI on her way home and looked up at the window where Carl Lewis had spent many an hour. She thought about the times she used to go out to buy his dinner. He would smile at her, sometimes pull a funny face like child. When she heard the dreadful news she felt like a part of her had died. She wanted somebody to hold, somebody to cry with, somebody who could share her grief. Somehow, her closeness to Sheridan helped to ease the burden of the emptiness and sadness that threatened to turn her life upside down.

Becky Watts believed that things would get better as time marched on.

But worse was to come - more than she could ever have dreamed in her darkest nightmares.

THIRTY-EIGHT

A week had passed by since 26-year-old Lucy Beckett's skeleton was finally removed from its damp insect-infested grave. The description of her clothing - contained in her Missing Persons file - exactly matched the garments recovered at the burial site. The knee-length black boots and L-chain were the key factors which confirmed Rogers' belief that Lucy was indeed the missing girl who had been murdered and buried only a few miles from her home in Sedgeburn. Comparison of dental records provided positive identification.

For six agonising months Lucy's mother, Anne, had been living in hope, waiting for her to walk through the door or telephone to say she was all right.

Lucy Beckett's loose morals were well known in the area where she lived. The local gossip being fed back to her mother was often hurtful. It wasn't far from the truth. Lucy had many male friends in her life and was a happy-go-lucky girl, just like her mother had been in her younger days.

Anne told detectives that her daughter could have gone off with somebody without thinking it through. 'It definitely wasn't planned,' she said.

Lucy left home to meet someone on 21 January. She didn't say where she was going or who she was meeting. Anne never asked her but she remembered the night in question. She couldn't understand why her daughter wanted to venture out on such a cold, wet evening. She also remembered Lucy taking a white carrier bag with her. She was almost certain that the bag contained music cassettes.

Seaside Ripper. Two words that, separately, evoke entirely different thoughts and images. And now those words were firmly embedded in the public' conscience.

The incident room had gone frantic with incoming calls after the police questioned Mavis Bradley and went on to create an e-fit. Operation Stamford was revitalised. Oxley and Greenwood welcomed the response from an eager public whilst remaining mindful of Simmons' assessment of the killer's mind-factor. As a result of this they made a last-minute decision not to release details of the white car with its rusty doors and yellow sticker, in case the killer decided to alter its appearance or sell it.

Recent developments had taken a turn for the worse. *The Gazette's* headline read, 'Seaside Ripper Enquiry - Police Release Suspects.' Two men, from entirely different backgrounds, had been arrested and questioned for several hours. Two men, with previous convictions, came under intense scrutiny. It looked like the investigation was getting somewhere. They were regular visitors to Blackpool; they owned white Ford Sierras; they were of the correct age and background - according to the profile - and were regular users of Internet pornography. Oxley became aware of other factors which catapulted these men to the top of the suspect list. Subsequent enquiries ended with the all-too-familiar dead end. No charges were brought against them. Oxley was more than disappointed, and pushed himself even harder.

Each evening, after a fifteen-hour day, he visited the various surveillance locations to ask about the latest updates. There was nothing to report, nothing suspicious. Oxley became deeply concerned during his late night excursions. Lone scantily-dressed females were still walking the streets regardless of the danger.

At Oxley's request police officers visited the offices of Big Brother Investigations and took Lewis's computer away for examination. He wasn't leaving anything to chance. If Carl Lewis *had* solved the mystery of the Ripper's identity he may well have left some clue as to his movements during the last day of his life. The other BBI detectives, Chris and Bob, were eventually questioned by police. They could throw no light on Lewis's investigation. Becky thought as much. They came to see her for the last time and said they were seeking new employment, even if it meant moving to another town or city. She thanked them for all their help and said she was staying in Blackpool with the aim of helping Jim Sheridan find his daughter's killer.

Darren kindly offered to carry the computer up the stairs, with Becky following behind, ready to support him if he lost his balance. He lowered the computer onto a table in the corner of the office. Becky inserted all the cables into their respective sockets. As Darren was leaving she asked him to fix the noisy step on the stairs.

'The one that creaks, you mean?' he asked.

'Yeah.'

'Sorry. Jim says not to touch it. He likes it that way.'

Becky smiled and shook her head. At least she felt a sense of purpose. She had a friend, a partner she could trust. Sheridan's determination to solve the case fuelled her with courage and strength. He had happily accepted her suggestion to move into his office, even knowing that Irene might turn her back on him forever.

When Darren got to the bottom of the stairs he met Sheridan on his return from the town centre.

'Jim, is that really the girl who's moving in with you?' he asked, curious as hell.

'She's sharing the office with me, that's all.'

Darren exhaled slowly. 'You jammy old bugger. She's as fit as a butcher's dog. How did you manage to pull it off?'

'It's a long story,' Sheridan replied, then climbed the stairs. Becky was polishing the few bits of furniture that comprised his working environment. 'I got the tea bags,' he said. 'Enough to last a month.'

'You got the Jaffas?' she asked.

'I did.'

'Make some tea, then. I'll finish cleaning this place.'

'Yes, madam,' he said jovially, wanting to please her.

A short while later he came in with the tea and biccies and sat at his usual place by the window. Becky stayed by the computer situated on her own desk. Sheridan had never used a computer and asked her what she intended doing with it.

'Input all the information we have on the murders. I can enter names, dates, locations - anything that might be useful . . . Did you keep the newspaper reports?'

He opened the drawer and took out a blue folder. 'Everything is in here, including the profile and an article from a crime magazine.'

'Which article?'

'It concerns the murder of a prostitute called Patricia Burke, and Parlour's Dolly House.'

'Parlour's Dolly House,' she repeated. 'I seem to recall the name. Tell me about it.'

Sheridan told her about his visit to The Elms public house where he learned about the obscure reference to the Patricia Burke article. Becky was now standing by the display on the wall, comparing the e-fits created by Karen Lawson and Mavis Bradley. 'Have you spotted the similarity?' she asked.

'There's a certain likeness in the features.'

'I wonder if the police think the e-fits depict the same man?' she said, thinking out loud. She read details of the Ross and Pemberton murders. 'The name "Tony" doesn't appear in the article about Elaine Pemberton.'

'Maybe they don't attach any significance to it. Julian Francis did.'

Becky sat on the edge of the desk, her eyes asking for more information.

'Supposedly well-known psychic,' Sheridan said. 'Irene went to see him. She took Elizabeth's earring for him to use as a communication tool. You know how it is with these guys.'

'Well, what did he say?'

'In my opinion he came out with a load of nonsense. Irene wrote it all down in a letter. I wanted to know what the outcome was, out of interest, you understand.'

'Of course, Sheridan. I'd like to see it, please.'

'It's all in the blue folder. I take it you're a believer, then?'

'I didn't say that.' She picked up the folder and returned to her desk. 'Are you and Irene on friendly terms now?'

'No. She's sore because of what happened between you and me. Anyway, that's all in the past.'

'It's all in the past,' she echoed. 'We have a job to do. I want to know who murdered Carl and all those girls.'

'I intend to find out. As a matter of fact I went along to the police station this morning and asked to see Steve Rivers. They wouldn't let me see him, which is what I expected. When Rivers finds out I'm looking for him he'll start to worry. That's what I want him to do. He knows I can ruin his career, and I will if he doesn't help me.'

'I don't think Rivers is even bothered about his career.'

Sheridan took a gulp of tea, then lit a cigarette. 'You interviewed an ex-pro called Davina Mullen. She said Rivers had been to that brothel in Wichonstall, the one run by Diana Humble. He got free sex in return for his silence.'

'He also sells drugs too, don't forget.'

'Yes. He's a naughty lad, and now he's going to tell me what I want to know in return for *my* silence. That's the plan.'

'He might call your bluff. He probably doesn't care about hearsay, not unless you can offer proof.'

'That's already crossed my mind.'

'When are you going to see him?'

'Tonight. Can you remember the address?'

'It's in the computer. I still have the photos I took of him talking to Humble, and the recording of the Davina Mullen interview.'

Rivers stuffed his mouth with king prawns and curried rice, occasionally swilling it down with a cheap supermarket wine. When the feast was over he grabbed the TV handset and switched channels to see if there was anything worth watching. It all seemed pretty crap viewing. There was no violence, no nudity, nothing to hold his attention. He switched the TV off and took the dirty dishes into the kitchen, tossing them into the basin. Then he went to answer the front door to see who it was.

'Please may I come in, Mr Rivers?'

'You've got a nerve.'

Sheridan's big foot prevented the door from closing. 'I need to talk to you,' he said, with a sense of urgency. Rivers pushed harder, hoping he would back off. He knew Sheridan had been enquiring after him at the station. He gave the matter some thought. If there was to be a confrontation, better to have it now in his house.

The door slowly opened. Rivers poked his head out and looked to see if anybody was hanging around. Nobody else was in sight.

Detective constable and private investigator sat opposite each other in a cosy room.

'You shouldn't have come here. We still regard you as a suspect for Lewis's murder,' Rivers said, hoping to put him on the defensive.

'I won't face a murder charge. You have no evidence.'

'You had motive.'

'It may appear that way to the likes of you. You're unprofessional, to say the least.'

'Now look here, don't start smart-mouthing me in my own home. I'm not in the mood.'

'And I'm in no mood to be made a fool of.'

Rivers' eyes became narrow and angry. Sheridan could sense his unease, his agitation.

'You sold confidential information to Lewis. Elaine Pemberton suffered anal assault with a piece of wood, and the killer cut away parts of her breasts. Only the police know that.'

'So, what's the big deal?' he said, trying to appear unconcerned.

'You're not stupid, Rivers. I could end your career if I wanted to.'

'Nobody would believe you.'

'Even if I had proof?'

'You ain't got no proof. Lewis is dead, so there's an end to it.'

'I have proof. Lewis gave me a copy of a psychological profile. I might show it to your inspector.'

'You can't prove that I had anything to do with it.'

'We'll see.'

'You're nothing but a cheap, burned-out private eye. Nobody's interested in what you have to say. If I were you I'd stick to divorce cases and helping old ladies cross the road. Your time has run out. I'll show you to the door.'

Sheridan remained seated and offered Rivers a cigarette. He declined the offer and said, 'You don't get it, do you? You'd better leave now, otherwise I'll throw you out.'

'The fact that you sell information - not to mention your visits to a brothel in Wichonstall - doesn't bother me that much. It's your coldness and lack of emotion towards Carl Lewis that stands out more than your bent ways and sordid life style.'

Rivers was angry. He resisted the temptation to land a punch on Sheridan's chin. 'I'm a detective,' he said. 'We deal with murders all the time. We get paid to do a job. Feelings don't come into it.'

'You really are a heartless, grabbing, self-centred coward. And now, you're going to do something good for a change. You are going to help me catch Lewis's murderer - the man who took my daughter's life and the lives of the those other unfortunate girls.'

'You must be out of your mind.'

Sheridan shot up like a spring. For once in his life, Rivers felt intimidated.

'Listen to me, Rivers, and listen carefully. I have the means to ruin you, and I will unless you co-operate.'

He sat down again and tossed a brown envelope onto Rivers' lap. He opened it, hands visibly shaking, and took out the photos which Becky had secretly taken in the grounds of Diana Humble's high-class brothel.

'These photos don't prove a thing,' he said, throwing them back. 'Do what you want with them.'

'You could be right,' Sheridan said nonchalantly. He reached into his trouser pocket and pulled out Becky's microcassette recorder. 'Do you know a prostitute called Davina Mullen?'

'Never heard of her.'

'You surprise me.'

Sheridan played the entire interview. Rivers' expression remained flat. He recognised the voice of Davina Mullen and regretted having been so foolish, so reckless and arrogant. Sheridan had the upper hand. Mullen's recollections were enough to ensure an end to his career, and a stiff prison sentence.

'Powerful stuff, Rivers. Difficult to explain away, wouldn't you say?'

He shrugged. 'I can't deny it. I *was* selling drugs; but that was a long time ago.'

'What about the cannabis you gave to Humble's girls?'

He said nothing, his guilty look conveying the answer.

'So, we can strike a deal?' Sheridan said.

'What is it you want?'

'To begin with, I'm convinced that Lewis found out where the murderer lives. He was looking for a white Sierra. Simple fact is, he wouldn't know where to start looking. You see what I'm getting at?'

'Well done, Sheridan. You don't miss much, do you? I gave him a printout of names and addresses. There are thousands of white Sierra owners, so I don't see how Lewis could have succeeded.'

'He paid you for this?'

'As always . . . Look, I don't go along with your theory. All the Sierra owners living in this county have been eliminated from the enquiry.'

'That may be so. I don't know what Lewis did with his printout. I want you to get me a copy as soon as possible. Understand?'

Rivers shot up from his seat. 'All right, all right. I'll do it.'

Sheridan made his way outside. Rivers joined him and said, 'I'll drop it off at your office.'

'Don't make me wait too long. By the way, is there anything else you can tell me about this vehicle? Any distinguishing marks?'

'The report given to us describes it as having rusty doors and a yellow sticker in the back window.'

Sheridan started walking to his car.

'We checked them all,' Rivers added. 'There's plenty of Sierras with rusty doors. We didn't come across any with yellow stickers. It looks like you're in for a long search.'

Sheridan breezed into the office at 10 p.m. He was surprised to see Becky tapping away at the computer keys.

'At last, we are getting somewhere,' he said, falling into his chair. He noticed Lewis's microcassette recorder next to Becky's computer.

'You found it, then?' he said.

'Don't get too excited. I came across it by chance. Carl must have forgotten to take it with him. I listened to the entire tape. Unfortunately, there's nothing on it except for some routine matters he was dealing with.'

'No clues at all as to where he went?'

She shook her head and asked if he had been to see Rivers.

'Yes. I showed the photos to him, played the interview. I told him straight that I'd use it against him if he refused to help me. Lewis paid him for a printout of Sierra owners. It's extensive. The police have already checked all the owners in the county.'

She considered for a moment. 'I can think of only two possibilities. The murderer lives miles away and, as yet, hasn't been located, or he lives within the county and has slipped through the net.'

'That's unlikely.'

'It could happen, especially if he has a watertight alibi for the night of the Pemberton murder.'

Sheridan gave her a long, lingering look. 'You know what Becky, I'm beginning to have my doubts about this white Sierra. False leads are commonplace in major murder investigations.'

'But let's not forget about the horrific attack on Carl, supposedly carried out for theft of his money and belongings. That sort of attack isn't commonplace. It was brutal in the extreme. Somehow, he got to the murderer. He had the all-important printout. The success of this investigation lies in its contents.'

'Let's hope you're right . . . Cup of tea, Becky?'

THIRTY-NINE

July drifted into August, bringing sunshine, hot weather, and an army of unruly fun seekers. Female attire had suddenly changed. Skimpy outfits of every description were being worn, and lustful men were on the prowl. Unfortunately, there existed a minority whose aim was to partake in a monumental booze-up and create public nuisance offences.

During the sultry weekend nights the pubs and nightclubs were swollen to capacity, becoming hot spots for the hunting male species: the ten-pints-and-a-curry merchants; the curious young local lads who wondered what fresh talent was in town; the older single gentlemen-type who had money to spend. Most of them were on the 'pull.'

The town centre had become an erupting volcano of bustle, excitement, dance fever and sexual intent.

Oxley was standing close to the sea wall. The blood red sun, sitting on the horizon, projected its rays across a calm Irish Sea. A delightful sight for those partaking in an evening stroll.

A TV crew had raced to Blackpool to make an half-hour special programme on the most talked about series of murders since the reign of the Yorkshire Ripper. Earlier in the day they had filmed the crime-scene locations at Aristor Park, the covered alley close to Seaforth Road and the passage behind Central Drive's Ten Pin Bowling.

Chief Superintendent Matthew Greenwood had allowed the camera crew into the conference room after addressing the press conference, when he openly admitted that the investigation was hampered by a singular lack of clues. During the interview he spoke about the Ripper's apparent knowledge of forensic detection which could have been gleaned from TV documentaries, books and magazines. The killer was a dark-haired white male in his thirties. He owned a light-coloured vehicle, possibly a Ford Sierra. Greenwood displayed a similar bracelet to the one Angela Ross had been wearing, and a pair of white shoes identical with those worn by Elaine Pemberton.

Oxley's job was to hammer home the threat that the killer posed.

The cameraman, Len, started the next sequence by filming the famous Tower, a familiar sight instantly recognisable to millions of people. Joanne

247

Maclean, the field reporter, positioned herself opposite the inspector and waited for her cue. Her opening lines were smothered by the roaring grating sound of a passing tram. She waited a while then started from the beginning.

'Here we are on the Promenade, not far from Blackpool's North Pier. Looking round me it's hard to imagine that a vicious serial killer could be amongst the crowd of holidaymakers, many of whom come here every year to enjoy the shows, the circus, the Pleasure Beach and the Illuminations.

'I am joined by Inspector Derek Oxley, the man who is leading the hunt for Britain's most wanted criminal - a man who has already murdered and mutilated three young women here in the resort. It's one of the biggest manhunts ever launched, involving more than one hundred and fifty officers, many of them drafted in from other forces.

'Inspector, what are the chances of this man striking again?'

'In the light of what we know about this type of murderer, the chances are extremely high. I am not trying to sound alarmist. The simple fact is we are dealing with a serial killer who is concentrating his activities here in Blackpool.'

'Is it reasonable to assume that he lives here?'

'It is a possibility. Blackpool is a popular venue for millions of people and has become his stalking ground. The season attracts visitors, many of them young females.'

'Can you tell us anything about his method of approach?'

'It seems clear that he engages them in conversation for a short while before dragging them into a secluded area.'

'And the victims were alone when he approached them?'

'Yes. He is looking for single women who happen to be close to a secluded place that offers some sort of cover. He could attack at any time during an evening. It doesn't have to be late at night.'

'So, your message is to stay in pairs.'

'That's right, up to a point. Women are safe as long as there are other people around. It's the high season now. Many girls are coming to the resort. We don't want to see them alone at night. That is asking for trouble.'

'There have been some recent arrests. Can you comment on that?'

'Arrests have been made. The men in question have all been released without charge.'

'The chief superintendent spoke to us earlier today. He talked about a light-coloured vehicle, possibly a white Ford Sierra. How important is this?'

'The Sierra enquiry is ongoing and could be vital to solving this case. We are fairly certain that the offender is in his thirties. As you know, he takes items of jewellery and clothing from his victims.'

'Viewers were shown a bracelet and a pair of white high-heel shoes.'

'We desperately need to trace those items.' Oxley turned to the camera. 'I am asking people to think about the things we have talked about. This man is, in a sense, isolated. There will be something odd about him. If the pieces of the jigsaw fit together do not hesitate to make that phone call. There is a huge reward waiting to be collected.'

'Thank you, Inspector Oxley . . . We will be showing the incident room telephone number towards the end of the programme.'

Maclean wished him luck. It seemed an odd choice of words. If anything, the investigation was in dire need of a lucky break.

The camera started rolling again.

'And so, the hunt for the Ripper goes on,' Maclean began. 'But what do the locals and holidaymakers think? Are they aware of the danger? More importantly, do they care? . . . Well, let's find out.'

The team hurried across the busy road and joined the line of human traffic. Maclean spotted a noisy group of teenage girls bustling along. The camera and microphone attracted their attention.

'Are you lot together as a group?' she asked.

'We're on a hen party,' the hefty blonde replied.

'How long are you staying for?'

'We're going back on Sunday.'

'Where are you from?'

'Shrewsbury.'

The girls cheered and squeezed closer to each other, waving and smiling for the camera.

'Are you aware of the murders in Blackpool?'

The blonde gave a look of puzzlement, then nodded. 'My dad told us to watch out for the Ripper. Anyway, there are too many of us so we should be okay.'

'Do you read the newspapers?'

'Some of us do, sometime.'

'What do you know about the killer?'

'Well, he's obviously a weirdo. He's what they call a serial killer, like the one they had in London.'

'You mean, Jack the Ripper?'

'Yeah. This one cuts them up the same way. Horrible!'

'Are you taking precautions?' Maclean asked finally, aware that the filming was causing an obstruction.

'We certainly are,' the blonde answered, with a cheeky grin. 'We've got our condoms, just in case.'

The Shrewsbury girls moved on, waving and blowing kisses.

'I wasn't expecting that,' Maclean said to Len.

The crew shuffled along, discussing where they might get a bite to eat. They entered the town centre's busiest road. Four girls from Bath exited a taxi and surrounded Len as he pointed the camera towards them. A tall thin girl, whose never-ending legs were on show, took the lead. 'What are you filming for?'

Maclean seized the opportunity and asked her to move closer to the camera. 'We are making a programme about the murders in Blackpool. Where are you from?'

'Bath,' Miss Never Ending proudly answered. 'We're staying at the GR8 Hotel.'

'What do you know about these murders?'

The crowd started to swell with curious onlookers. Never Ending coughed and tried to look serious. 'You're asking me?'

'Yes. Do you know any of the details?'

'Let me think . . . It's a man who drives a white van. He grabs women off the streets, stabs them and cuts their fingers off.'

'Nipples,' one of the others said.

'Maybe it's nipples. I don't know.'

'Do you know how many he has killed?'

'Three or four,' Never Ending surmised. 'Could be five or six. My dad used to be a policeman. He told me about the murders.'

'What did he say?'

'We have to be so careful. The killer uses a knife and cuts his victims to pieces.'

'Do you think you are safe?'

'I think so. I'm not likely to wander off on my own.'

'My dad thinks he's an escaped lunatic,' the girl wearing a pink cowboy hat added. 'All he does is talk about the murders and how stupid the police are. Mum tells him to shut up.'

'You're not afraid to come to Blackpool?'

'No,' they all replied.

'What do you think the reason is for these horrendous murders?'

'He's a psycho, see,' Never Ending began. Her friends laughed loudly. 'Shut up a minute, will ya?'

'Tell us what you think,' Maclean urged.

Never Ending was beginning to enjoy the attention. 'Right. This man in the film *Psycho* hated his mother because she had a lover—'

The name, 'Norman Bates,' sounded.

'Right, Allison. Norman bleedin' Bates. Bates grows up hating women, and he kills them in showers and cellars.'

'So, you think the murderer is a Norman Bates-type character?'

'Definitely. He hates women because he hates his mother. He takes his frustration out on us girls. They'll catch him in the end. They always do.'

Maclean stepped back to allow passage for several lads wearing women's dresses stuffed with enormous fake boobs. The Bath girls were swept along with them.

The crew moved on and shot the final sequence in a relatively quiet area in front of the Central Library.

Maclean gave a résumé of Greenwood's main points and repeated Oxley's warning . . .

'The police say the murderer will be caught. Meanwhile, if you harbour any suspicion about a particular person, call the incident room here in Blackpool or contact your local police station. Remember, serial killers don't stop until they are caught. Most people here seem to be aware of the danger, but with an ever increasing input of holidaymakers to the resort the opportunity for him to kill again is greater.'

With those chilling words Len aimed his lens towards the top of the illuminated Tower. A reminder that life goes on as normal.

Sheridan flicked the light switch on and laid his pizza on the desk. He breathed a weary sigh and threw his jacket over the client's chair.

Another disappointing day.

Rivers' Ford Sierra printout was comprehensive. The task of checking vehicles with their owners - to see if they matched the e-fits - was problematical.

Without thinking he went to the kitchen, switched the kettle on and returned with knife and fork. The phone's flashing red light caught his eye. One message had been recorded. He hoped it was from Irene, but it was Becky's voice:

'Hi, Sheridan, it's me. Remember the old black and white film *The Wolf Man*, with Claude Rains and Lon Chaney? It used to scare me to death when I was a kid. Mum used to say I had a look of Evelyn Ankers. She was in the film too. Claude Rains recites a poem: "Even a man who is pure in heart and says his prayers by night, may become a wolf when the wolfbane blooms and the autumn moon is bright."

'Check the dates when the murders occurred. There's a pattern. I spent some time reading the stuff in your blue folder. Julian Francis said the words, "Queen of the Night." I wondered what he meant. Then I remembered something you said about the Pemberton crime scene. It was in total darkness when you went there. How could the murderer see what he was doing? How could he find a piece of wood in all that darkness, and do the things that he did? . . . See you soon.'

FORTY

Jack Robson groaned as he reached for the cassette that had fallen off the shelf. *Funny,* he thought. *I don't recognise this one.* The writing on the cover was difficult to read, except for the word 'Saxon' which had been written on the cover in capital letters.

'What does it say on here?' he said, passing the cassette case to his wife.

She struggled to read the almost illegible scrawl. '"Death Pledge" . . . "Angels Come Closer" . . . and, I think it says, "Horns of Satan" . . . Such unusual titles.'

Jack suggested that their son could have left it during one of his visits. Avril thought it was unlikely to belong to him and, in any case, it wasn't his handwriting. Jack took it from her and dropped it into the waste bin. She returned to the kitchen to continue with her baking. Five minutes later she appeared in the doorway separating the two rooms.

'Jack, wasn't that the cassette you found on one of your walks?'

He thought for a moment. 'Oh, now that you mention it.' He retrieved it from the bin and looked at it again. 'I seem to remember playing this. What was on it? . . . Let's find out.'

'Don't have it too loud,' she ordered, returning to her chores.

He switched on his music centre and inserted the black cassette. He pressed the play button and leaned back in his chair, listening to screeching guitars and male voices repeating a phrase in Latin. The music was impossible to categorise. Jack found it irritating and switched it off. A few minutes passed, then he realised that there was something unusual about that cassette. He couldn't figure out what it was. It couldn't have been just the weird music. Something had occurred when he played it for the first time. He pressed the rewind button for a few seconds. He played it again, and moved closer to the speaker. The music stopped. A man's voice sounded through the speakers, saying, 'Don't leave me, Lucy . . . Stay with me, forever.'

'Avril, come here a minute, will you?'

She rushed into the room. 'What is it, Jack?'

'Listen to this.'

She listened, and when he played it a second time she could hear her heart beating.

'It's her, isn't it?' she whispered. 'He's referring to that girl who was murdered and buried in the woods. He's referring to Lucy Beckett.'

'They reckon the body was buried about eight months ago,' he said. 'I must have been a matter of yards away from the grave when I found that cassette.'

Avril sat down and fanned her face with a newspaper. 'Oh dear, I've gone all hot. What are we going to do?'

'I'm going to inform the police. The man who made that recording could be Lucy Beckett's murderer.'

Sheridan settled himself by the window overlooking Chapel Street. Becky had been busy working at the computer most of the afternoon. She was glad to see him.

'You look exhausted,' she observed.

'Sierra drivers are causing me problems.'

'How is that?'

'I go to an address and what do I find? Nobody's there. So I wait a while to see if a Sierra pulls up. If I'm lucky, it does. I thought I was on to something when this particular man turns up in a rusty Sierra. He looks like the recent e-fit and appears to be the right age. I find out that he's already been questioned and eliminated.'

'Who told you?'

'I phoned Rivers. He left his mobile number when he dropped the profile off. He's playing safe, doesn't want me calling at the station or paying him a home visit . . . By the way, is there any news regarding Lewis's murder?'

'I'm afraid not. I telephoned his father this morning. The police have released his body. He's to be buried in Kent, close to where his parents live.'

'Are you going to attend the service?'

'I'd like to, but I've decided to stay here. From what I can gather it sounds like they want it to be a family affair.' Her tears began to fall. She looked to the floor and then straightened herself. 'Sorry. I'll be all right in a minute.'

'You don't have to be sorry. I understand how you feel.'

Becky blew her nose and smiled faintly.

Sheridan pulled a face. 'I feel a bit awkward about the money he gave to me.'

'The two grand?'

'I think I ought to return it to his family.'

She shook her head. 'It wouldn't be appreciated at a time like this. Carl gave *you* the money and he meant you to keep it.'

'It was kind of him. You know, if I hadn't given up so easily — '

'You tried your best. It's no use talking about what might have been. What's happened has happened. Carl respected and admired you. Nobody's blaming you, least of all me.'

She left the office and returned with a bottle of champagne and two glasses.

'What's all this in aid of?'

She popped the cork. 'It's our treat.'

'Our treat?'

She poured the drinks. 'To us, Sheridan - our success, our friendship.' She took a sip then said, 'Even a man who is pure in heart . . .'

He raised his glass. 'And says his prayers by night . . .'

'May become a wolf when the wolfbane blooms . . .'

'And the autumn moon is bright.'

She squeezed his hand. 'Thank you. Thanks for everything you've done. You're a great guy. I don't know what I'd do without you.'

'The same applies to you.'

She let go of his hand and refilled his glass. 'You've seen the film, too?'

'I saw it many years ago. You know, I've been thinking about this theory of yours. It's interesting. All the murders were committed when it was a full moon. It was a clear night when Elaine Pemberton died.'

'It explains how the killer could see what he was doing.'

'You are a perceptive girl. Unfortunately, I'm not convinced.'

'You think it's a coincidence.'

'Could be.'

'Julian Francis got it right. He couldn't have known about the murders coinciding with the full moon. It fits together, don't you see?'

'Becky, he's a fortune teller. It's all kidology, mumbo jumbo.'

'I can understand your scepticism, but let's suppose — '

'You're getting carried away with all this fortune teller nonsense.'

'Will you let me have my say?'

He laughed a little. 'Anything to please you.'

'Right, just listen for a minute. I've been doing some research into lunar cycles and violent behaviour. Psychiatrists in America have been studying the relationship between the lunar synodic cycle and human aggression.'

'What does synodic mean?'

'I think it means the conjunction of celestial bodies, like the moon and the sun.'

'I see.'

'The studies show that murders and suicides all show lunar periodicities. Statistics highlighted the fact that murders occur in a cluster which coincides with the full moon.'

'H'm. That's statistics for you.'

'You still don't believe me?'

'There might be a possibility of this happening but, hang on a minute. Thousands of murders are committed every month, so there's bound to be an overlap.'

'But—'

'Furthermore, what about the dates of the other full moons when he didn't commit murder? By now there should be five victims instead of three.'

'Maybe he didn't get the chance to do a murder. This serial killer doesn't take unnecessary risks.'

'And how are we supposed to utilise your full moon theory?'

'We give it to the public and see what happens.'

'How do you propose to do that, Becky?'

'I've already done it. Prepare yourself for a big day. I'm talking about tomorrow.' She handed him a sheet of paper.

'Tomorrow?' he asked, glancing at the notes she had made.

'Yes. Private investigator, Jim Sheridan, is to appear live on TV.'

'What do you mean?'

'There's no escaping. You are due to appear on the half-hour chat programme hosted by Nicholas Bryan.'

'I've . . . I've never been on TV before.'

'Don't worry about it. The day after tomorrow you're doing an interview for a magazine called, *How About It?* It's a big nationwide seller. Loads of women buy it, including me. They print all kinds of stories like infidelity, unwanted pregnancies, drug abuse - you name it. The next big feature is about a PI in search of his daughter's murderer. It will sell in the millions.'

'Becky, I'm not sure about all this.'

'You'll do it,' she said sharply. 'All the details are on that sheet.'

'I could be making a fool of myself.'

'You won't. Here's your chance to tell the world about your investigation, the ups and downs, the frustration. You tell them how you got started. Give them your opinion on the killer's state of mind. Get the public to help you find him: the killer who is influenced by the full moon. Let your feelings be known. You'll be surprised at how many people will want to help.'

'I appreciate what you've done. A magazine article may help, but I'm not too happy about going in front of the cameras and talking about a serial killer whose murderous predisposition is influenced by a full moon.'

'Remember when I followed Rivers for you?' she asked, folding her arms.

'I remember.'

'I wasn't very keen on following a detective, only you had a hunch about him and it paid off. This is more than a hunch. There's evidence to back it up. So let's not be too hasty.'

'I've done some unusual things in my time . . . Okay, I'll do it, if only to prove you wrong. I'll receive loads of crank letters, you know.'

'That's to be expected.' She raised her glass. 'One more time, Sheridan. Let's drink to our friendship and a successful investigation.'

They repeated the toast. Becky licked her lips and said, 'Lovely champagne. We must do this more often.'

'Agreed.'

'By the way, don't drop yourself in it when you're on television. If you say anything that's not in the public domain you might be arrested again.'

'I'll be careful. I might mention Parlour's Dolly House. Somebody out there might know something.'

'Sure, give it a try. You've nothing to lose. Bertram Haines was a sadist and so is the Seaside Ripper. That's what the papers are calling him.' She reached towards her desk and grabbed an A4-size notepad. 'The Internet is loaded with stuff about serial killers. I've been trying to work out exactly what kind of person is committing these crimes.'

'You *have* been busy. Becky the PI turns profiler. What have you discovered?'

She glanced at her notes. 'The profile that Rivers obtained gave me my starting point. It says the offender is a lust serial killer. He is motivated by sex. There are different types of serial killers, so you have to be aware of certain parameters when trying to analyse them. You've heard of organised and disorganised offenders?'

He nodded. 'One plans his crimes, while the other is more impulsive and spare of the moment.'

'In a nutshell - yes. The murders show both kinds of offender. There are other distinctions, too.'

'Such as?'

'Some serial killers like to torture their victims. They get turned on by the suffering they cause. Others kill their victims fairly quickly by strangulation or stabbing. These types aren't interested in prolonging the distress and suffering. Some killers use both methods.'

'My daughter was killed quickly; there was no evidence of torture. The second victim, Angela Ross, *was* made to suffer. So, what does that tell us?'

'The man we are searching for is like different serial killers rolled into one. Julian Francis said something which gave me this idea.'

'Not him again.'

'*Him again*. During his psychic vision he said, "He is their disciple" and "The way has been shown to him."'

'Could he be a religious freak?'

'I don't think so. It's almost as if he's being influenced by other murderers. Haines thrust some object into Patricia Burke. Elaine Pemberton suffered the same and she was disembowelled in the same way as Jack the Ripper's victims.'

'Excellent, Becky. I congratulate you on your remarkable observations. All this makes me wonder just how far the killer is prepared to go. I mean, the crimes are becoming progressively worse.'

'I dread to think what he might do to the next one.'

'Let's hope they find him before that happens,' Sheridan said, yawning. 'I'm going home. I must prepare for tomorrow; then it's off to bed.'

'I'd like to stay here a while longer. Do you mind?'

'Not at all. Make sure you lock the doors on your way out.'

'I will . . . Good luck for tomorrow.'

'Thanks. You take care. Don't be staying up too late.'

He drank the remainder of his champagne and left Becky to mull over her serial-killer profile.

FORTY-ONE

The lights seemed to be on red for ages. Dr Christian Purslow glanced at Sedgeburn's stately Davenport Hotel, situated in the heart of the busy town centre. He drummed his fingers on the steering wheel, waiting patiently. Another minute went by. He fanned his face with a magazine. It had been a long hot day. Purslow wouldn't allow himself the comfort of loosening his tie and undoing the top button of his crumpled white shirt. Police headquarters was less than a quarter of a mile away. Apart from being tired, he was in a hurry to return home. Luckily, he was fairly close to Sedgeburn when an excited Detective Superintendent Mike Rogers phoned and asked to see him with regard to the murder of Lucy Beckett. True to form, Purslow assured him he would be there within the hour.

Rogers was seated at his desk in the incident room when the eminent pathologist breezed in. He seated himself in front of the fan and sighed with relief.

'Sorry to bother you, but we've got an important lead.'

'So soon? That *is* encouraging.'

Rogers explained who Jack Robson was and where he resided. He played the crucial extract from the cassette.

'Robson takes a walk every morning. He found this cassette tape sometime in January, close to Lucy Beckett's grave. He can't remember the exact date.'

He played the extract again and asked Purslow for his opinion.

'There must be a connection between Lucy Beckett and the man whose voice is on that tape,' Purslow pointed out.

'I agree. The mother doesn't seem to think it's one of Lucy's tapes and, somewhere in the back of her mind, she recalls her daughter having mentioned a man - probably an acquaintance - who may live in Blackpool.'

'So, there is a chance he is the owner of that cassette. It seems straightforward enough. All you need to do now is release details.'

'I shall, doctor.'

Purslow moved closer to the fan. 'Well, if that's all you want me for I'll be on my way. Sorry if I seem to be in a rush.'

'No problem. There is one more thing I'd like to know. During your examination of the skeleton you discovered faint incisions on the breastbone that could have been made with a knife.'

'In all probability.'

Rogers gave a pensive look. 'I wonder if Lucy Beckett's murderer is the same man who is operating in Blackpool. It's a thought that occurred to me. What's your opinion?'

The answer to his question came straight away. 'I doubt it. You see, the Ripper's victims were left on display. There was no attempt to hide the bodies, only partial concealment with respect to Elizabeth Collinson. I'm afraid there are two killers on the loose.'

Julian Francis clasped his hands together tightly. 'That man is on the hunt again, mother.'

Elsie Francis, minus wig and false teeth, looked more like an Egyptian mummy than a mother. She looked across the table at her son.

'Concentrate on your meal, Julian. Don't let him bother you.'

He shook his head, hoping to subdue the tingling sensation in his head.

'Lovely tomato soup, mother.'

'I always make good soup, don't I?'

'Always, dear mother.'

He picked up a piece of bread roll. Elsie didn't notice his trembling hand or the change of colour in his face. He dipped his bread into the soup and succumbed to a terrifying psychic revelation.

He lifted the heavy bread out of the crimson gaping gash in her abdomen.

He gasped loudly. Elsie knew what was happening. He lowered himself from the chair and trotted to her side, hands clinging to his chest.

'That man is here again, isn't he?' she said.

He fell to his knees and wrapped his arms around her. 'I thought he'd gone away,' he whimpered. Francis tried in vain to stand up. Elsie looked on helplessly as he reeled backwards, falling to the floor with outstretched arms, his face contorted with fear and disgust.

He saw a clear blue sky and tree tops that looked two dimensional like a painted scene. A force yanked his arms backwards. He gave a scream of hellish torment.

Elsie got down from her chair. She sat beside him, held his hand and began praying for his 'vision' to end quickly.

'Breath deeply, Julian.'

He sat upright, his head flopping onto her chest. She cuddled him, her little child, comforting him as best she could.

A muffled scream rang in his ears as her naked body rose from the ground, feet dangling, neck horribly elongated.

Elsie caressed his head and called out his name.

Her voice fell on deaf ears.

His eyes could see only lush undergrowth and black ominous trees.

The essence of *his* evil was all around, permeating every leaf and blade of grass, every blood red flower. Francis strained himself, lifting one leg in front of the other, trying to run away from the figure standing behind him. A few steps left him exhausted and soaking with the stinking sweat of fear.

His lips curled into a hideous smile.

Francis mouthed silent cries for help, trying to free himself from the depths of a psychic vision, the like of which he had never before experienced.

'How can I help you, sir?' asked the unseen, charming man.

Francis straightened himself. A cool breeze sailed through the shrubs, evaporating the sweat from his face. 'Are you here to help me?' he asked, confused and agitated.

'Of course I am,' the man replied in a familiar voice. 'I assume that you are lost.'

'I am trying to escape, don't you see?' he said indignantly, his burning fear subsiding. *I know that voice. I must confirm.* 'Where have you come from?'

'I am here, now, as we speak,' the charming man replied soothingly.

'Mother?'

High-pitched mocking laughter emanated from the man's throat.

'Is it you, mother?'

'My dear Julian, turn towards me and see for yourself. You have nothing to fear.'

Mother's voice. He speaks in mother's voice. Can I escape? Is it really her, or just a trick?

'Turn to me, dear son, and you will be free.'

'I'm not sure I can trust you,' he said tearfully.

'See how the trees have come alive once again. The birds are singing for you . . . Your legs are no longer heavy. There is nothing to stop you now. Trust me, my son. You have always trusted dear old mother.'

'I can't do it. I can't look at you. You are not what you pretend to be.'

'Trust me and be free. You cannot escape on your own. You *must* look upon me, Julian. It's the only way out. You don't want to be trapped forever, do you?'

'You can't help me!' he cried.

'This will soon be over. You must do as I tell you.'

Francis yielded to his command. 'All right, then . . . I will look upon you.'

He turned slowly and saw the ankle-length, black plastic coat fastened tightly around his neck.

Black hair. Cold blue eyes, staring.

'Mother is with you,' he whispered, pointing with his long bony finger.

He looked in the direction indicated, his mind swirling in disbelief, his stomach muscles tightening with shock. He gulped air, trying to catch his breath. Then the sobbing started and the words, 'No, no, no,' burst from his mouth.

Her naked shredded body was dangling from a tree . . .

'That's how it's done, Julian,' said the man, unperturbed. 'That's how you take care of them.'

. . . and her belly erupted, scarlet guts spewing onto the ground, hot blood seeping into the grassy soil.

The man's mouth opened wide, expelling an insane cruel laugh that echoed all around. Her body was slowly rotating. He looked in horror at the lacerations to her back and legs, and the blood dripping onto her fetid organs covering the ground beneath her.

Francis spat at him and screamed. The laughing ceased. The man raised his arms and came at him, head bowed, leaping high in the air, calling his name over and over.

The spectre of death was upon him, his foul breath polluting the air as he faded from Francis's overwhelming subconscious terror.

'Julian . . . It's over now. He has gone away.'

Dear old mother looked like an angel. He felt safe in her arms.

Later that night they prayed and asked God to vanish the evil that had no place in this world or the next.

Hadden Creek, on the outskirts of Wichonstall, comprised the River Doy and thick woodland interspersed by a network of footpaths. The river itself, often swollen during heavy rainfall, served as a base for numerous sailing vessels sitting idly against its muddy banks. Yellow crusty xanthoria lichen covered broken dilapidated jetties, some of which could only be reached by crossing a row of planks that covered marshland laced with mauve coloured Michaelmas daisies. The woodland could be reached by travelling down a narrow road which curled between the Doy and a row of splendid lime trees.

Hadden Creek had seen many a courting couple, walkers and young school kids who were often enchanted by its varied smells and rich habitat. Today, its serenity and beauty were tainted by the sound of the police helicopter hovering above.

Greenwood and Oxley sat in silence during the journey to the Creek. The driver braked hard on entering the parking area. Oxley jumped out of the car and checked his watch. It was almost 9 a.m. Other police vehicles followed them in, throwing up clouds of dust. The activity was becoming more intense by the minute.

A stern-faced officer entered their names in his log and indicated the path which led to the crime scene. Both men were struck by the beauty and isolation of the setting - a place where the Ripper could unleash his sadistic rage without fear of being seen. The resort's obvious police presence had proved too hot for him.

When the clearing came into view, Dr Charles Scott moved out of their line of site, and they saw what he had done to her. The body was hanging from a tree, the rope biting into her delicate neck. The young woman, dangling like a butchered carcass, had been sliced down her middle. Her entrails - cut from their attachments - were lying beneath her.

'It's definitely the Ripper,' Greenwood murmured, turning away in revulsion.

'It must be,' Oxley returned. 'This can only be the work of one man.'

Greenwood had no intention of staying there a minute longer than was necessary. 'I'm going back to headquarters,' he said, hand to his mouth. 'Scott shouldn't be too long. Get what you can from him.'

'Yes, sir.'

'I want a thorough search of this wood. Every inch of the place. Every inch. The pressure from above is overwhelming. We have the deaths of four girls to contend with as well as the murder of Carl Lewis . . . And keep the press away from this area. They'll be down here like a swarm of bees.'

Oxley stared at the corpse, unable to understand the reason why such appalling injuries needed to be inflicted. The quiet stillness of the place was unnerving, as if locked in time.

Scott finished his work, and plodded wearily through the grass and weeds, stopping a few feet from the inspector.

He removed his glasses. Tears were visible. 'There's not much else I can do round here.'

'Are you all right?' Oxley asked.

The helicopter was hovering overhead. He waited until the sound died away. 'Police surgeons see many terrible things. This isn't just a murder, it's desecration beyond human understanding. I'd be careful if I were you. Don't let your officers get close enough to scrutinise the body.'

'I'll take your advice. The man who made the discovery was almost incoherent when he called us. It must have been a terrible shock.'

'Enough to shock anybody. I'm afraid I can't pinpoint the cause of death. She was probably killed about twelve hours ago. The weapon used was a knife with a stout blade. There are a dozen deep wounds on her back. She was still alive when the cuts were made. You'll find blood on his clothes - if you ever do catch the monster who did this.'

Oxley looked at her butchered body for the last time. 'This can't go on. Somebody must know something.'

'Be careful, inspector.'

'What do you mean?'

'Don't drive yourself into the ground like George did.'

'I don't believe I have a breaking point.'

'Everybody has a breaking point. Anyway, time for me to go . . . Oh, incidentally, the murderer stuffed something inside her mouth. I'm not sure what it is or why he put it there.'

Scott left the inspector to do his job. Ten minutes later Oxley followed the path back to the cordon, pondering over the crime location. *Secluded spot. Therefore, he must be familiar with the area. Why have we missed him? Every male who owns a Ford Sierra has been checked. Where do we go from here?*

Greenwood grimaced when Scott told him about the torture. They turned to face Oxley, who quickened his pace when he saw them.

'I am certain the killer knows this area,' he announced.

'Are you, Oxley?'

'I am indeed. The Sierra owners, who live in Wichonstall and Blackpool, are going to be checked again. I want to know what they were doing yesterday, where they went and who they spoke to.'

'I don't agree,' Greenwood said. 'They have been checked and eliminated. I'm not happy with this business of going over old ground.'

Greenwood was on a loser.

'I'm going ahead with it, sir,' Oxley said defiantly, making off towards the police incident vehicle.

Greenwood folded his arms. 'Oh dear. The investigation is getting on top of him,' he said, under his breath, 'and now he's telling me what to do . . . What a lovely day it is here at Hadden Creek . . . What a lovely, horrible, stinking day. '

FORTY-TWO

Detective Superintendent Mike Rogers' appearance on national television had worked a treat. The message was clear: listen to the voice on the tape. Do you recognise it? A freephone number was set up for anyone to ring, anytime night or day.

The recording was the best clue they had. Only eight words were spoken - enough for dialect experts to say the accent originated in the north-west of England. The age of the speaker was estimated to be late twenties to early thirties. The voice was distinctive, and senior police officers were hopeful that somebody would recognise it.

Rogers was sitting at his cluttered desk in the incident room. He listened to the recording, as he had done many times before, then studied an enlarged copy of the handwriting on the cassette cover. The handwriting had also been displayed in the newspapers, some of which were speculating the possibility of a connection between Lucy Beckett and the Seaside Ripper. Rogers now attached little credence to this speculation.

The phones were ringing.

The tip-offs were coming in.

'I'm sure this is going to work,' Becky said confidently. She tore off small pieces of Sellotape and proudly stuck the article onto the wall. She stepped back a few paces and admired it. A head-and-shoulders photo of Sheridan accompanied the feature, 'Blackpool Private Investigator Hunts Full-Moon Killer.'

'I'm putting my reputation at risk,' Sheridan joked, from behind his desk. 'It makes me sound like I'm a psychic detective.'

'Maybe so,' she said, taking the seat opposite. 'But look at all these letters addressed to you.'

'So far half the ones I've read are from cranks with nothing better to do than write tall stories. Listen to this one . . . "My husband makes me dress in a black bra, suspenders and knickers. He insists I wear pale make-up and bright red lipstick to make me look like a vampire. He makes me bend over so that he can whack my bottom with a cane. When I beg for mercy he insists on having hard sex. He pumps me again and again. There is no stopping him. This behaviour only happens on the night of a full moon." And she goes on to say, "He has read about the murders and says he doesn't want to see the killer get caught. Maybe he is doing the murders. I think it's him."'

'Pumps me again and again,' she mused. 'Some stud.'

He dropped the letter into the bin. 'It's not funny, Becky. Some of these writers are wasting our time. In fact, I'm beginning to think the whole exercise was a waste of time.'

'Like your Sierra investigation?'

'I guess so. I've managed to track down a dozen cars and none of them have yellow stickers in the back window.'

'There's loads more to go at. You've only scraped the surface.'

'Indeed. There's only several thousand left to do. I should have the job finished by the time I'm eighty.'

'Then tell me how Carl managed to find the right car in less than a day?'

'Maybe he knew something we don't know.'

'I doubt it. Anyway, what we do know for certain is that the Hadden Creek murder took place on the sixteenth.'

'During the period of a full moon, so you say.'

'Sheridan, I checked. It *was* a full moon on the sixteenth. It can't be a coincidence, can it?'

He shrugged. 'We're falling into the realms of the supernatural.'

'We know that some people are affected by lunar events. There could be a connection. Agree?'

'Improbable.'

'But not impossible.'

'Well, maybe not.'

'Even a man who is pure in heart —'

'Yes, yes. Go and fetch me a cold drink.'

Becky stood up and saluted. 'Apple and blackcurrant, or Kia-Ora?'

'Anything will do,' he replied, rolling his eyes.

He picked up a handful of letters and shook his head. 'What a load of rubbish,' he said, dropping them onto the desk.

'Fan mail?'

He looked up to see Steve Rivers standing in the doorway.

'I'm not that famous. What is it, Rivers? Have you come to arrest me again?'

Rivers sneered. Becky walked in, frowning. She passed the drink to Sheridan and sat by her computer.

'My, my,' Rivers said, ogling her shapely legs. 'I didn't realise you had such a gorgeous assistant. You must be Rebecca Watts. I'm pleased to meet you.'

'Can't say I feel the same way, Mr Rivers,' she hissed, snubbing his offer of a handshake.

'It's "Steve," by the way. Can I call you, "Becky?"'

'Certainly not.'

Rivers sat in the client's chair. 'Never mind. What's a pretty chick like you doing with an old-timer like Sheridan?'

'You cheeky git,' she said, pulling a face.

'Pack it in,' Sheridan snapped. 'What is it you want, Rivers?'

'I was just passing. I thought I'd let you in on things, seeing that you're desperate to catch the Ripper.'

'I see. What can you tell us?'

'The Sierra enquiry is completed,' he said, folding his arms. 'So don't bother wasting your time checking the list I gave you.'

'Thanks for that. Does this mean the murderer doesn't drive a white Sierra?'

'Not necessarily. He could easily have slipped through the net.'

'You're prepared to admit that?' Sheridan asked, surprised.

'Absolutely. After all, we're only human like everyone else. We've had some good suspects, I must admit.'

'And some bad ones. He was one of them,' Becky said, nodding towards Sheridan.

'Look, love, we have to consider family members and ex-lovers. In fact, everybody and anybody.'

'Should have considered yourself then, shouldn't you?'

'That's enough, Becky,' Sherdan said.

Rivers smiled at her. 'I understand your predicament. I'll leave if you want me to.'

'There's no need for that. Becky is a little tired, that's all. Anything else you want to tell me?'

'The girl at the Creek has been identified as Amy Tyler. She was eighteen years old and lived with her parents and brother at Wichonstall. Tyler was tortured and extensively mutilated.'

'Any anal assault?' Sheridan asked, curious.

'No. There's no doubt about it being another Ripper murder. Amy Tyler was in the wrong place at the wrong time. She went there to meet a friend, but she didn't turn up.'

Rivers was unusually informative. Sheridan took advantage while the going was good. 'What sort of place is Hadden Creek?' he asked.

'It's next to the River Doy. A few dozen sailing vessels are moored down there, and there's the wood close by. It's all right if you like walking.'

'A busy place, then?'

'Not really. It's a bit out of the way. Courting couples are fond of the place. It's nice and secluded, especially at night.'

'It could have been an opportunist attack.'

'I suppose it was.'

'Can you reveal the extent of the injuries?'

'I don't see why not. The pathologist found she had a broken leg. The theory is that he knocked her down with his car. She was dragged into the wood, undressed and hung from a tree.'

'What form did the mutilation take?'

'She was disembowelled.'

'He was running a big risk.'

'He could have been caught red-handed.'

'Did anyone see anything suspicious?'

'I was coming to that. We've got a new lead. You'll read about it in the newspapers. On the evening of the murder a man was seen running out of the wood. He got into a small red car.'

'Description?'

'Dark hair. Could be twenties to thirties. He drove away real fast. We've got a red car to deal with now, instead of a white Ford Sierra.'

'You've had some bad luck.'

'More than that - he's giving Forensic a hard time. He doesn't leave any clues. Amy Tyler's clothes and shoes are missing, and we haven't found the murder weapon. There's nothing to examine, except the girl's terrific injuries.'

'What's your next move?'

'Local Sierra drivers have been re-interviewed. No luck there. So now we're working on the small red cars . . . Any chance of a drink, Miss Watts?'

Becky glared at him.

'I guess it's not my lucky day. And what have you got to tell me, Sheridan?'

'Not much, I'm afraid.'

'The murderer only strikes when it's a full moon,' Becky said. 'I've checked the dates.'

Rivers got up. He walked to the doorway and turned round. 'Full moon, eh? I think you've been watching too many horror movies.' He checked his watch. 'I'll be on my way, then.'

'Wait a minute,' Becky sounded. 'Any news on Carl's murder?'

'Don't know. That's nothing to do with me.' He closed the door behind him.

'I don't understand him,' Becky said, frowning. 'Why should he come here to tell you about the police investigation?'

'He's no fool. We know a lot about him, remember. He's scared.'

'Not scared enough for my liking. Where are you going?'

'I'm off to Sedgeburn to check some more Sierras, for what it's worth. I'll be home late. What are you going to do with yourself?'

'Might as well read some of these letters.'

'Very good. I'll love you and leave you.'

'See you later . . . Good hunting.'

Derek Oxley answered the phone and found himself speaking to a scientist at the forensic laboratories in Manchester.

Elation prevailed.

Operation Stamford had taken a step forward.

'At last,' he cried.

'What is it? You seem pleased,' DS Lambert said.

'That was Dr Trainor. He's discovered something important.'

He turned to leave. Lambert grabbed his arm. 'Inspector, tell me what it is,' she begged. 'We're all down in the dumps. You know how it is.'

Oxley's mouth twitched. 'The killer has left a clue.'

'Something to do with the red car?'

He shook his head. 'Amy Tyler's killer stuffed a couple of tissues in her mouth. They are stained yellow. Trainor was puzzled at first, until a thought occurred to him. The yellow stains are, in fact, catarrh.'

'That's awful.'

'The killer blew his nose and stuffed the tissues into her mouth. It's a form of degradation.'

'What's so important about catarrh?'

'Trainor found leukocytes: white blood cells, to us. You know what that means?'

'I'm not sure.'

'Come on, Lambert. All human cells contain DNA. We've got a DNA profile of the murderer.'

The office light was still burning at 11.30 p.m. Becky was alone. She went to the kitchen and returned with a glass of milk and a handful of Jaffas. She sat in Sheridan's chair. A ten-minute break was all she needed. She munched on the Jaffas whilst admiring his wall display. *At least he had made an effort,* she thought.

And she wondered if it had all been a waste of time.

She had sorted the letters into three piles. The ones on the left were so ludicrous as to warrant throwing in the bin. The right-hand pile contained letters which were less easy to dismiss. The ones in the middle, fifty in all, were waiting to be read.

Becky decided to get the job done.

Thirty minutes had passed when she came to the twelfth letter, sent by a woman called Susan Rawcliffe who was a past resident of Sedgeburn.

Susan always kept a diary in which she wrote about important or interesting events in her life. The writing started when she was thirteen. One particular diary listed the dates of the full moons. Susan was an avid reader of magazines, including *How About It?*

When Susan read the article that featured Sheridan, unpleasant memories were rekindled. She looked through all her diaries and found the one she wanted.

One of her ex-boyfriends had dated her for eight months. It seemed a lot longer at the time. He wanted sex after the first week. She obliged. The sex became more violent, more perverse. She was subjected to beatings during sex, and the bite marks he inflicted on her, after sex, often lasted for days. She suffered the anguish of having a knife held to her throat while he took her from behind. That was bad enough. Then he introduced her to the wooden pole, her 'little anal friend,' as he used to call it. She pleaded with him not to use it on her. She was ignored. Susan was too scared to tell anyone. He threatened to kill her if she ever breathed a word about his sadistic sexual nature, which was extreme during the periods of full moons.

Susan couldn't get him out of her life, so she left town and went to live somewhere else. Luckily, he was unable to trace her.

Becky's tiredness had given way to an adrenaline rush. She ran through the letter again, her thoughts prompted by her insight into the murders. Certain relevant facts were beginning to emerge in her mind: *Rectal abuse using a wooden implement. Bertram Haines engaged in such activities. Susan Rawcliffe's lover inflicted deep bite marks after sex. American serial killer, Bobby Ray, bit his victims and cut the flesh away to remove evidence of teeth marks.*

Becky opened Sheridan's blue folder and rummaged through the papers.

'Here it is,' she said, practically shaking with anticipation.

She turned the pages of the car registration list. The car owners' names were in alphabetical order. She slowly checked the 'S' column. Her heart began to race when she read the name.

Susan Rawcliffe didn't know where he was living at present.

His name appeared in the letter and on the list.

He owned a white Ford Sierra.

He was living in Sedgeburn.

His name was Gary Swan.

FORTY-THREE

Sheridan was standing at the living-room window, gazing into the street and wondering whether or not to call Rivers. A few minutes past and his mind was made up. He fell into his chair, dialled the number. Rivers answered immediately.

'Is that you, Rivers?'

'How did you get my home number?' he asked, immediately recognising his voice.

'I got it from Becky. She must have got it from Lewis.'

'The lovely Rebecca Watts. Mighty hot stuff. What do you want?'

Sheridan told him about the Rawcliffe letter, adding that Gary Swan's name also appeared on the Sierra registration list.

'Sounds like a load of crap. Susan Rawcliffe's "Gary Swan" is likely to be someone else, not the guy whose name is on the list.'

'Possibly, but there are similarities between Swan's sexual perversions and some of the victims' injuries.'

'Look here, Sheridan, there are millions of blokes with sexual perversions, as you put it; and I'll tell you now, there are probably dozens of blokes called "Gary Swan." Some of them might have sexual perversions. If you think he's a killer because he knocks women about when it's a full moon —'

'I'm not suggesting that. All I'm saying is, the similarities are too close for it to be a coincidence. Surely you'd go along with that.'

'You've been listening to that blonde bimbo too much, haven't you?'

'She may have a point. I think Swan needs looking at more closely.'

'Impossible, Sheridan. He's been questioned and eliminated. It would take a lot more than a letter to a private detective for him to be questioned again. Full moons don't make men commit murder.'

'I appreciate what you're saying —'

'Look, we've had some good suspects during this enquiry. I spoke to one of them myself. He became our prime suspect. The SIO was convinced we had the Ripper. Turned out he was a weirdo, and that's all Rawcliffe's ex-lover is. Don't waste your time on him, and tell that blonde to stop playing detective.'

'I don't agree,' Sheridan said, offended.

'Look, I've helped you all I can. If you want to delve into someone's life on the basis of a crank letter then that's your affair.'

'Fine. Just thought I'd let you know what the position was.'

Rivers replaced the handset.

Sheridan considered. The seeds of doubt were sown.

Sheridan thought about Gary Swan, of Bouverie Road, Sedgeburn. He had been eliminated from police enquiries. There must have been good reason for such a decision to have been made. Swan could have been miles away from Blackpool when Elaine Pemberton was murdered. He could even have been at home with somebody who was willing to confirm his alibi.

He knew it would be a waste of time knocking on his door and asking questions. He thought about putting him under surveillance. He could watch the house, follow him, find out where he goes, what he does. But for how long? And maybe Swan would latch on to the fact that he was being followed.

Another idea flashed through his mind. He could easily take a photograph of him and show it to Karen Lawson. She was convinced she spoke to the murderer on the night when her friend was killed a short distance from where she lived. But would she remember his features after all this time?

He thought it through and came to the conclusion that there could be reason enough to suspect Gary Swan.

Sheridan had been to Sedgeburn, and it was only a twenty-minute drive down the motorway. He sank deeper into his chair and ran through the scenario:

Sedgeburn. First exit off the motorway, leading straight onto Bouverie Road. Swan's home address would have been the nearest one on Lewis's checklist. That's the reason why he accomplished his mission in a day. He visits a couple of addresses in Blackpool, then heads for Sedgeburn. He sees Swan's car in the driveway. He looks round, making sure the coast is clear. He enters the shrubbery next to the driveway and sneaks up to the Sierra. Swan must have seen him. He watches. Lewis finds that it's unlocked, looks inside and discovers incriminating evidence. He drives back to his office unaware that Swan is following amongst the slow-moving traffic that's heading for the holiday resort. Swan notices the BBI Detective Agency sign in the window. Swan knows he's in trouble. He waits for Lewis to come out and follows him to the garage behind his flat. He waits for his chance. He kills Lewis and takes the cash from his pockets, creating the impression that it's a robbery . . .

Sheridan didn't attach much importance to the Sierra on the day he walked past the entrance to the grassy driveway. He was looking for a Sierra with rusty doors and a yellow sticker in the back window.

Swan's car had neither.

Following an anonymous tip off, Sedgeburn detectives raced to an address in Blackpool. The caller was absolutely certain the voice on the tape was that of 27-year-old Nathan Walsh.

Walsh showed no concern when a sergeant and detective constable arrived at his house to question him about the murder of Lucy Beckett. He showed them into his small untidy bedsit. A pile of unwashed clothes and several pornographic magazines had been thrown into a corner. A huge stack of music cassettes filled the opposite corner. There were no tables, no chairs, no TV set. A two-seater settee stood in front of an expensive hi-fi system linked to a couple of massive speakers.

Walsh was sitting on the settee, shoulders hunched, hands on knees. The officers remained standing and fired questions at him. He was slow in giving his answers, as if struggling to find the right words. He persistently ran his long fingers through his dark thinning hair and never once looked at their faces. They could sense something quite odd about this character. What was he not telling them?

At first, he denied having known Lucy. The sergeant knew different. So did his colleague. They recognised his dry monotonous voice - the voice they had heard so many times before. The question was put to him: How did Lucy Beckett come into possession of a cassette belonging to him?

Walsh became agitated when the question was repeated. After a long pause, he looked at the floor and clenched his fists. 'She was the only girl I ever loved,' he said. He looked up, his eyes moving rapidly from side to side. 'She left me, you know. I knew she would. She was wrong to do that. I'm not to blame for it, am I? I mean, she *did* leave me, didn't she?'

The officers' eyes met. The detective constable nodded knowingly, and Walsh was arrested. He said nothing as they escorted him to their vehicle.

A constable stayed at the address, and guarded Walsh's red Vauxhall Corsa.

Bouverie Road had a row of detached and semi-detached houses down one side. The opposite side of the road consisted of a row of chestnut trees and hawthorn shrubs, giving way to acres of weed-ridden fields.

The three-storey, dilapidated building - built in the 1920s and subsequently converted into flats in the 1950s - housed an unemployable lazy couple on the top floor, an elderly retired couple on the first floor and a mother and son on the ground.

During the last four days Sheridan and Becky had taken turns at keeping the house under scrutiny. Their only vantage point was across the road, where they could hide amongst the shrubs.

The front of the house was obscured by a few trees and clumps of hawthorn. The area to the left of the driveway consisted of a mass of weeds and patches of rosebay willowherb.

The four-day period had seen nothing but rain. The white Ford Sierra hatchback hadn't moved in all that time, and Gary Swan was nowhere to be seen.

The fifth day started with a cloudless sky. Becky left home at 8 a.m. She told her mum not to worry if she didn't return for a day or two, and not to ring her mobile unless it was urgent. Mum understood. She was accustomed to her daughter's absences.

Becky didn't tell mum she was hoping to speak to a man who might be a serial killer. And that was the plan. She didn't tell Sheridan, either. No chance of that. He would do everything in his power to dissuade her. And who could blame him? Becky was determined to do the job the way she thought best. The Sheridan way was not hers. Her mind was made up. She had to know if Swan was responsible for committing the Ripper murders. If he *was* the killer then there was only one way to entice him.

Becky had studied the psychological profile. She remembered one sentence in particular: the killer will stalk scantily-dressed females.

She was dressed in short denim skirt, white high-heel shoes and a revealing low-cut top. She hadn't bothered to apply any makeup. She reckoned the killer wasn't particularly bothered about a woman's looks.

At 9 a.m. she plodded barefoot along the field that ran parallel to Bouverie Road. She didn't want to risk ruining her high-heel shoes. They were tucked away in her shoulder bag along with other important items: her mobile telephone, microcassette recorder, camera and a plastic sheet used for covering the damp ground.

She took her position amongst the shrubs and laid the sheet. Only a few minutes passed by, and she saw him standing next to the Sierra.

The moment had arrived. There was no time to lose.

Becky ran the forty or so yards back to the gap in the hawthorn. She climbed a wooden fence, separating the shrubs from the pavement, and quickly got into her shoes. She waited for a gap in the traffic, dashed over the road and ran as fast as her shoes would allow. She was breathing heavily, not so much from exhaustion but the anticipation of meeting a man who could well be the country's most wanted criminal. She waited at the entrance to the driveway. Was she doing the right thing? Was it really worth stepping into unknown territory from which she may never come out alive?

'Damsel in distress?'

His voice shattered her thoughts. She could feel her heart pounding. She ran her eyes down his body, trying to remember everything about him in case she decided to opt out.

She put him at five feet nine inches and in his mid-thirties. His shaven head showed the outline of dark hair. His clean shaven face was long, his eyes piercing blue. The pallor of his skin accentuated his dark eyelashes. Becky wondered if he'd applied mascara to them. The bottoms of his dirty baggy jeans covered scruffy trainers. His red T-shirt hung loose over an obvious paunch.

'Are you in trouble?' he asked. His voice was soft, his demeanour calm.

Go for it, Becky, she thought. *This is the only chance you'll have.*

'He's just thrown me out of the car,' she said angrily, desperately trying to arouse his curiosity. She threw glances up and down the road.

He frowned dramatically. 'Who has?'

'Oh, it doesn't matter.'

He gently pulled her into the driveway. 'If there's anything I can do to help,' he said, with a hint of a smile.

Becky rubbed her head as if flustered. 'He's supposed to be taking me up north to Carlisle, where I live. We've been on holiday for a few days, and on the way back he started this crazy argument over nothing.'

'You're sure he's left you?' he asked, feigning concern.

'Yeah, I'm sure.'

Becky glanced at the sloping rear window of the car. No yellow sticker.

'Where did he drop you off?'

'Dropped off? I was pushed out.'

'Nasty thing to do,' he said, dabbing his forehead with a filthy handkerchief. 'Where did he push you out, then?'

'About half a mile down the road.'

'I'll take you there if you like. He's most likely waiting for you to come back.'

'Not him,' she assured, shaking her head. 'He's probably halfway home by now.' *This isn't working,* she thought. *Maybe he's not the killer.*

'He wouldn't leave you stranded like this, would he?'

'He would - believe me. Anyway, I'm not sure I want to see him again after what he's done.'

Becky made a sad face hoping to create some kind of sympathy, perhaps excitement even.

He stuffed his hands into his pockets and looked towards the road. 'I was just thinking . . .' he said, turning to her. 'We have a telephone. You can phone home.'

'No point. I live alone.'

He glanced at her breasts like most men would do, then his eyes locked onto hers.

'I'm tired,' she continued. 'It's been a long journey. I need to get some rest before I set off home. Are there any hotels around here, anywhere I can get a room for the night?'

'Not round here,' he lied.

Becky smiled. 'Just my luck. Never mind, I'll find somewhere. Thanks for your time and consideration.'

She strolled towards the road, wondering if he would say something.

'Hang on a sec,' he said. 'You can stay here if you like. We have a spare bedroom.'

Becky turned to face him, then shook her head.

'It's no problem, honestly,' he said. 'If you like you can have a good sleep here and I'll take you to the train station.'

'It wouldn't be fair to impose on you like that.'

He closed the gap between them. 'You might get a hotel in the town centre, but they're expensive. You can stay here free of charge. I live on the ground floor with my mother. She won't mind. You can take a shower and I'll fix you something to eat.'

He fumbled in his pocket and pulled out a packet of cigarettes. He took two from the packet, lit one and offered her the other.

'No, thanks.'

'It really is no trouble . . . Well?'

He waited patiently. Becky was trying to assess his character. He seemed pleasant enough, didn't look particularly strong and aggressive.

But that didn't count for anything and she knew it.

'Thank you,' she answered. 'You're very kind.'

'Come on, then,' he said, heading towards the front door. 'I'll take you to your room.'

She followed him into the house and entered a dark dingy hallway. Already, she was beginning to feel uneasy. She glanced at the steep uncarpeted stairs in front of her. She turned left and sharp right, following him down the passage which ran between the stairs and living quarters. A thin worn carpet covered a wooden floor. The wallpaper was a disgusting orange colour, adorned with a spider-web pattern.

'This is the living room, followed by Mother's bedroom. And this is where I sleep,' he said, pointing at the door in front of him 'The one next to mine is the spare bedroom. It can be yours for a day or two, or whatever.'

Two bedrooms side by side. His and hers. The bathroom was straight ahead. Becky was curious to know what lay beyond the door directly opposite the room which was to be hers. 'What's in here?' she asked innocently.

'Stairs leading to the cellar.'

She followed him into the bedroom. A grey single-bed mattress was the first thing she saw.

'Don't worry, I'll sort some bedclothes out for you,' he said, placing a friendly hand on her shoulder. 'What's your name?'

'Annie.'

'Nice name . . . Well, I'll leave you to it. I've a few things to be getting on with. You won't see me for a while. There's plenty of hot water and towels.'

'Thanks. I appreciate all this.'

He stepped out of the room and popped his head around the door. 'I'm Gary. If you need anything, give me a shout.'

Off he went. Becky listened to the sound of his fading footsteps.

The plan had worked. She was on the inside now, next to his bedroom. She wondered what to do next. *First things first,* she thought. *I must ring Sheridan.*

At first he was pleased to hear her voice, but when she told him where she was he called her a fool. She confirmed the fact that the Sierra had no yellow sticker, hoping to appease his concern and agitation. It didn't make much difference. He told her to leave at once. No chance. Becky could be stubborn. In the end he had to resign himself to the fact that she wasn't going anywhere - not until she was satisfied that Gary Swan wasn't a killer of women. She wanted to know about his hobbies, his job - if he had one - and whether or not he had known a woman called Susan Rawcliffe.

Becky had already decided to speak to his mother.

Mother would never reveal much about him. Not to anyone.

Mother loved and feared her son.

Mother would do anything he asked.

She didn't know everything there was to know about him. She didn't want to.

Mother respected his privacy.

FORTY-FOUR

Becky checked that the bathroom door had a lock. She took a shower, got dressed and made her way to the kitchen.

'Did you sleep well, Annie?'

His voice made her jump. He was sitting at the table and had just finished eating his breakfast.

'Not too badly,' she answered.

She had hardly slept at all. The absence of a lock on her bedroom door meant she had to position a chair behind it. In any case, trying to get to sleep was difficult, if not impossible, due to claustrophobic heat.

He watched her closely, his eyes stripped of any emotion. Becky felt uncomfortable and wondered if he knew who she really was.

'I have to go out this morning. I need a few things for the car,' he explained. 'Help yourself to some breakfast. We've got plenty of cereals, bread, tea, coffee . . .'

'Thanks. I am a bit peckish.'

'I expect you need to phone your boyfriend.'

'There's no rush.'

'We have a payphone. It's on the right, as you come in through the front door.'

Becky kept quiet, waiting to see how he would react.

'It's playing up a bit, worse luck,' he continued. 'There's supposed to be someone coming to look at it. Do you have a mobile?'

She shook her head. 'I left it in the car. You forget about these things when you're in an argument.'

'I suppose so. When I come back I'll take you to the station.'

'I meant to ask . . .' she said, taking a few steps closer to him.'

'Ask what?'

'If I could stay a bit longer.'

'A bit longer?'

She nodded.

'No problem, Annie,' he said, with a searching look in his eyes.

He wants rid of me. He can sense I'm not who I say I am.

'Won't your family and friends start worrying about you?' he asked.

'My family live all over the country. I have a few friends, but I don't see much of them. I fancy having a look round the shops before I leave. I might find something to wear. You know what us women are like.'

She wondered how he would react to that. He got up and walked out of the kitchen without saying a word.

Strange behaviour. I Might as well grab a bite to eat, then see what his mother has to say for herself.

Oxley crunched hot buttered toast whilst his partner poured fresh coffee.

'What are you thinking about?' she asked, sliding the cup towards him.

'Nothing really,' he answered, shrugging.

'Oh, come one, Derek. You've been really quiet recently. I know you're overworking, but at least you got the extra men you wanted. How many officers are involved with the enquiry? Two hundred, didn't you say? The news reporters are practically on our doorstep. One day I expect to wake up next to a reporter. The investigation has become international news—'

'Okay, Liz, you've made your point . . . I spoke to Rogers last night . . .'

'The body in the wood?'

'That's the case. Sedgeburn police are focusing their enquiries in Blackpool. Some of our officers think it's a job for the Ripper squad. Lucy Beckett was stabbed, and Purslow found evidence of a cut throat.'

'You said that Nathan Walsh has been released. So, why all the fuss?'

'He's been released on bail, pending further enquiries.'

'No evidence to charge him with?'

'Not enough. However, Forensic discovered a smear of blood in his car. It could be important. Scientists are working on the DNA profile. It should be completed today or tomorrow.'

'A blood smear in a car, you say? A mechanic could have cut his hand.'

'Yes, Liz. A mechanic *could* have cut his hand.'

Oxley shot up, got into his jacket, finished his coffee in one gulp and walked briskly out of the house. Liz followed.

'We're looking for little red cars, don't forget . . . and men with dark hair.'

She watched him get into his car. He opened the sun roof and activated the automatic window.

'You don't have to tell me,' she called, anticipating his last words. 'I'll leave your supper in the fridge.'

Oxley blew a kiss and hit the accelerator.

Becky ate a simple breakfast of Weetabix and toast. She made coffee, sauntered out of the kitchen and into the hall.

The house was unusually quiet, as if uninhabited.

She went outside, coffee in hand. To her left, an eight-feet high fence formed the dividing line between the two houses. She descended the stone steps, turned sharp right and walked to the corner of the house.

She looked to the right. The sight of the Sierra was simply too much to resist.

She moved closer to the vehicle, casually sipping coffee as if she was taking the air, enjoying the sunshine. She ran her eyes down the bodywork, especially the doors. *Good condition for an 'F' reg,* she thought . . . *Looks like it's been resprayed . . . Another intriguing fact . . . Maybe a coincidence. If he is the murderer, why not get rid of the car? Why have it sprayed the same colour?*

Becky noticed a movement in the curtains. Mother was watching, puzzled by her apparent interest in the car.

She headed back to the house, oblivious to the padlocked hatch that led down into the cellar.

'No time to lose, Becky,' she said to herself.

She went back to the kitchen and left her cup by the sink.

A few steps took her to the living room.

She knocked. No answer. She turned the handle and let go.

'Who is it?' asked Mother, slightly irritated.

'It's me - Annie.'

'Come inside and close the door.'

Mother was standing by the window, clutching a handkerchief. She was a tall grim-faced woman who looked older than fifty-four years. Her black hair had given way to a preponderance of grey. The long dark-blue dress made her look thinner than she was.

The room looked pretty much like Becky thought it would: drab wallpaper, well-worn manky settee and matching chairs, old fashioned tiled fireplace beneath a big oval mirror. An upright piano stood against the wall to her right. Above the piano, a collection of books and magazines occupied two shelves which hardly seemed capable of taking the weight.

'I'd like to thank you for letting me stay,' Becky said, hoping to start a conversation.

'Take a seat . . . please,' she said, her youthful voice betraying her years.

Becky sat in the chair nearest to the piano.

Mother remained standing. 'You have been away on holiday, so my son tells me.'

'We had a few days at a place in Cornwall. It's marvellous this time of year. Have you ever been there?'

'I haven't been away since I was a child,' she replied, looking forlorn.

Silence.

The seconds drifted by.

Becky had to say something, if only to prevent an embarrassing situation.

She looked round and spotted a wedding photo on the fireplace.

'That's a lovely photograph. Is it of you and your husband?'

She moved silently across the room, towards the fireplace. She picked up the photograph and began polishing it with her handkerchief. 'He was my second husband,' she said, sadness in her voice. 'He died a long time ago.'

'I *am* sorry. Forgive me for being nosy.'

She turned and looked directly into Becky's eyes. 'Are you married?'

'I'm a single woman.'

'You seem to be a pleasant young lady,' she said. She moved slowly to the window again, seemingly isolated and somehow out of touch with reality. Becky's intuition told her to stay put and fish for more information.

'I'm sure I will get married, when the time is right.'

'This boyfriend of yours . . .' She paused, as if uncertain whether or not to continue.

'I don't think he's the one for me. What I mean is —'

'Did he hurt you?'

A telling question. 'No, but there *have* been occasions when he lost his temper.'

Something was bothering her. Becky decided to probe.

'Why did you ask if he hurt me?'

'It doesn't matter,' she answered sternly.

Time to change the subject. Becky looked around the room. 'That's a nice piano. Do you play?'

'Nobody plays it. It was there when we came to live here.'

'And how long have you lived here?'

'No more than five years. Do you play the piano, my dear?'

She got up. A few steps took her to the piano. 'I wish I could,' Becky answered, opening the lid. She played random notes whilst running her eyes along the bookshelves, then asked what sort of work her son was involved with.

'He's unemployed at the moment.'

'Pity. It seems more and more difficult to find a decent job these days . . . Was he involved in a trade?' she asked, desperate to learn more about him.

'He was self-employed at one time, doing odd jobs, electrics, decorating. He used to try his hand at anything. Why are you asking these questions about my son?'

Becky closed the piano lid and made a gentle smile. 'No reason. He is such a charming, considerate man. It makes a change to come across somebody who is willing to help you.' She took a deep breath, trying to extract more oxygen from the stale air.

Mother murmured an apology and said she was retiring to her room for a rest. She walked towards the door, taking short steps in a dress that was too tight to allow any appreciable movement.

Becky interrupted her exit. 'By the way, I thought I heard a voice during the night. It sounded like someone screaming. I got the impression it was coming from the cellar.'

'You must have been hearing things,' she said nervously. 'Nobody goes down there. It's not used any more. The wiring is all loose.'

She closed the door on her way out. Becky couldn't believe she had the room all to herself. She flicked her hair back and turned to the bookshelves.

The bottom row was filled with mass market paperbacks including the authors P. D. James and Agatha Christie. The books on the top shelf aroused her curiosity. She couldn't afford the time to read all the titles. The four titles she picked were enough to give some indication of the reader's interest: *Criminal Intent, A Sex Killer's Paradise, Wicked Crimes in History - Sadism, Sex murder and Necrophilia,* and *Forensic Detection.*

Her eyes drifted along the collection. Several dozen well-thumbed magazines were stacked at the end of the shelf. She lifted half of them onto the piano lid, and cursed as they slipped from her hands and onto the floor. She started picking them up when she heard the front door slam shut. His footsteps came closer, too close for her to put them back in time. *Act casual,* she thought. *Just tell him you were looking at the books and mags. He won't bother. Why should he?*

He stopped outside the living room. Becky breathed as quietly as she could, too scared to wipe the sweat that had run into her eyes. A few seconds passed. He continued along the hall, turned right and opened the cellar door.

Becky mistakenly believed he had gone to his bedroom. She had enough time to gather the magazines together and see what they were all about. The front page of each one depicted the face of a killer. There was a name and a caption for each one. She didn't recognise the face of the innocuous, bespectacled bank manager. His name though was familiar to her. The caption read, 'Leonard Bertram Haines - The sadist who went too far.' She turned to the page in question and saw the tenuous clue that Sheridan had attached so much importance to.

She skimmed over the passages, picking out the key names: Celia Parlour, Patricia Burke, Parlour's Dolly House. All the clues were staring her in the face.

And now she knew for sure that Gary Swan was a sadistic killer of women.

She replaced the magazines and headed back to her bedroom, oblivious to the regular metallic sound of the hammer blows coming from below.

Becky ignored the immediate danger, and mused over the profile. Everything she had learned seemed to be making sense. Gary Swan and the profile were becoming inseparable. She recalled significant details: *The offender is forensically aware and is likely to be involved with a trade, for example, electrician. He is likely to keep crime magazines. He lives with single parent, or alone.*

Becky could walk away from the house forever, and she thought about doing just that. She knew there was enough information to initiate a full investigation into the life of Gary Swan but felt compelled to stay a little longer if only to discover what had caused the faint sickening screams she heard in the sultry night.

She had to know.

A feeling of nausea came over her. She was in hell now, and had decided to stay longer. She went outside, away from the oppressive atmosphere of the house.

A few minutes later, he joined her.

'Annie, how are you doin'?'

'I'm taking in some fresh air. It's so hot.'

'Sure is. I've some good news for you. I'm travelling up to Penrith tomorrow.'

'Really?'

'I've got an uncle up there. I usually visit him a couple of times a year and I don't mind going that bit further. I'll take you to Carlisle, if you like.'

'That would be great,' Becky said, knowing that any other reply might arouse suspicion.

'You be ready, nice and early.'

'What time?'

'Seven o' clock. Breakfast first, then away we go.'

Rivers phoned Sheridan at 10 p.m. At 10.30 p.m. Sheridan called Becky. Her mobile was hidden under the pillow of her bed. She was almost asleep when it rang. She answered, speaking quietly, making sure that nobody could hear her.

Sheridan was relieved to know she was okay. He was annoyed, too, considering she hadn't replied to any of his text messages, most of them telling her to ring him. She let him have his say, and updated him with the latest developments. She was unable to confirm a previous relationship between Swan and a Susan Rawcliffe. That didn't matter to her. She was suspicious over his shaven head and the fact that his car had been resprayed. She told him about the books and magazines featuring infamous murders, and it was highly likely that he knew about Leonard Bertram Haines and Celia Parlour's dolly-house girls. Then there was his interest in forensic science. He lived with his mother, and Swan had served an apprenticeship to work as an electrician. In short, Gary Swan had stepped into Dr Andrew Simmons' profile of the Blackpool serial killer.

Sheridan told her there was no need to stay a minute longer at the house on Bouverie Road.

An arrest was imminent.

Rivers had told Sheridan about Nathan Walsh.

Operation Stamford was drawing to a close.

The blood smear found in Walsh's red Vauxhall Corsa contained DNA matching that of the Hadden Creek victim, Amy Tyler.

FORTY-FIVE

Irene Collinson was standing by the holly bush where her daughter had died. The decision to go there hadn't been an easy one. The thought of visiting Aristor Park had been festering in her mind for some time. She felt better having seen the place where it happened. Five months earlier she had viewed the floral tributes from a distance. Her closest friend told her that some of the sympathy cards were from people she had never heard of. That was a comfort to Irene.

She made her way towards the boating lake, bending low to avoid the leafy branches. She followed a footpath which was almost obscured by a rich growth of weeds and grasses, parched by the August heatwave.

The lake was smooth as glass. Irene stood at the water's edge, thinking about Jim Sheridan and whether or not she really did love him all those years ago. She analysed their early days together and realised that it was her immaturity that forced them apart.

She started blaming herself for the way things had turned out. She was always the dominant one, always making the decisions. Sheridan was the bystander, never dogmatic or intolerant in his attitude towards her. That was the trouble with him. He was too easygoing, especially with pretty females.

Irene's anger was still simmering over his relationship with Rebecca Watts. She didn't hate Becky - she didn't know her well enough to be able to experience such a strong emotion - and maybe she had been too hasty in condemning her worth as a private investigator.

Too late for regrets, she thought. *Maybe he drank too much when he came to see me at the Bloombury Club . . . But why did he go off with her? Was he really so wrapped up in the investigation, or did he find her too irresistible?*

During the journey home she thought about her future. She admitted to herself that it didn't seem so promising. She recalled her visits to that peculiar psychic, Julian Francis, and remembered asking him if the man from the past would love her again.

He declined to answer.

Was Francis aware of something he couldn't put into words - something too dreadful to contemplate?

Becky pulled the damp T-shirt away from her body for momentary comfort, and used an old newspaper to fan her face. The summer heat was merciless and she was longing for a cool refreshing shower. Her watch showed 7.15 a.m.

She switched her mobile off and dropped it into her bag along with the high-heel shoes. She wanted a quiet exit. No point in alerting the others. She eased the chair away from the door and opened it slowly, listening for any sounds. An ominous silence greeted her. She peeped around the corner and stepped into the passage separating her bedroom from the cellar door.

Becky made a conscious effort to breath quietly. She could walk out of the house if she wanted to, or make a run for it. But she wasn't satisfied. There wasn't enough evidence to satisfy the police - only the culmination of a few tantalising facts that seemed to point to Gary Swan's involvement in the murders.

The cellar door was in easy reach. The handle turned easily. The door opened quietly. As if in a nightmare Becky stepped into the black opening, unable to resist the urge to discover exactly what had caused the dreadful screams she knew had come from the cellar.

She nervously pressed the light switch at the top of the stairs and a naked bulb illuminated the way. The wooden stairs took her weight, creaking with every gentle step that she made. When she reached the bottom she took a right-hand turn. She stopped and looked down the dingy passage ahead, her eyes drawn to the two rooms separated by a dead-end passage.

She crept forward, listening for any movement from above. She stopped outside the first room and wrapped her fingers around the door handle. She hesitated, then pushed the door open. The light from the passage was too weak to penetrate the gloom. She stepped inside and froze. A pale motionless figure was standing in the darkness. She stood her ground and ran her hand across the wall, feeling for the light switch.

A spotlight came on, its beam directed towards the bald mannequin dressed in black T-shirt, short red skirt and wearing double-strap, white high-heel shoes. A metal rod, fixed into a concrete base, ran between its legs and into the crotch.

Becky was focusing on Elizabeth Collinson's earring dangling from its ear. Her eyes followed the length of its long thin arm, finally focusing on Angela Ross's bracelet.

Becky's chest was heaving from the fear and panic. She tried to calm herself as the horror of what she was seeing began to overwhelm her.

The shocking revelation confirmed her suspicion.

The walls of the room held framed photographs and newspaper cuttings - further proof of Swan's interest in serial murder, further proof of his guilt.

Becky could barely believe what she was seeing. As she moved closer to the bizarre figure, a sound came from behind. She spun round and gasped loudly.

He was standing in the doorway like a spectre of death, feasting his cold blue eyes on her glistening body. His lips, smeared with red lipstick, stretched into a hideous grin. He unfastened the top button of the long black plastic coat that covered his naked body.

'Want some of this?' he said, waving a razor-sharp kitchen knife. 'Don't scream, or I'll cut you here and now. Understand?' He locked the door and switched on the other spotlights which were directed at his photographs and newspaper cuttings. 'Put the bag down,' he ordered.

'What on earth are you playing at?' she said trying to be brave, hoping to appeal to any rational senses that he might have.

'Put the bag down and sit on that chair behind you,' he repeated, stepping closer, pointing the knife at her.

Becky was scared, but not scared enough. She waited for him to lower the knife, then she would pounce.

The chance never came.

Without warning he raised his leg and drove his heel into her stomach. She hit the floor and curled into a ball, moaning and gasping for air.

He stared dumbly, whilst releasing the remainder of the buttons on his coat.

'Get into the chair,' he repeated.

He waited for her to recover. She struggled into the chair, badly winded and in no fit state to put up a struggle. And now she knew there was little chance of leaving that house alive even if she told him who she really was and the reason for her lie about being ditched in Sedgeburn.

He ran his hand over her shoulder as if caressing her, then yanked her head back, his rage intensifying like a gathering storm.

'Do you like the lipstick, Annie? I found it in your bedroom this morning. I was going to bring you down here last night but you blocked the door with a chair. Can't trust anyone, can you? . . . Anyway, I enjoyed the taste of your lipstick. I'll use the rest on the dummy.'

Becky ignored him and was rubbing her stomach, trying to ease the nauseating pain he had inflicted on her.

He released his grip, and held the blade an inch from her face. He straightened himself, revealing his solid erection. He gripped the knife between his teeth, took a length of washing line from his pocket and tied her wrists. He bent down, watching her closely, his expression flat, unaffected by her obvious distress.

She was his slave now and he could do anything that took his fancy. She was an ideal victim, and now her voluptuous body was his to destroy.

Nobody knew where she was. He would tell mother that she left the house of her own accord. Mother would have to believe him. She would have to cover for him as she had done in the past.

He completed the final knot and put the knife on a table in the corner of the room. He opened a drawer and took out a roll of black masking tape - the same tape he had used to silence Angela Ross and Elaine Pemberton.

He dried her mouth with a handkerchief, tore a strip from the roll and stuck it firmly into position.

'Just in case you're wondering, I am a serial killer - *the* serial killer. You might have heard about the murders in Blackpool. All those bangtails ripped and mutilated. It was me who did it. Me.'

He positioned the chair so that Becky was facing the mannequin.

'I want to tell you about what I've done. I've never had the chance to tell anybody before now. Somebody needs to be told about my accomplishments, and you're just the right person.

'You know, Annie, just looking at the dummy brings back all the memories of the kill.' He picked up the knife and held it in front of her face again. 'Lucy Beckett was the first. I was driving my car when I picked her up one night outside this very house. She was so gobby and had no sense of humour. She got stroppy with me so I showed her a thing or two. I was going to kill her anyway but I couldn't decide which serial killer I was going to be. I bit her, stabbed her a few times and ripped her up. She was my practise session.'

His chilling words, spoken calmly, added revulsion to her paralysing fear. Her heartbeat was racing, her breathing frantic, her body shaking as if every nerve fibre had been pumped with electricity.

'Ever been to Blackpool, Annie? Plenty of damsels there, especially in the season. I came across the second one quite by chance. The high season was months away, so I decided to have a drive round and get to know the places where I could start my work. I was driving near a park when I spotted her. It was the bright yellow shorts that caught my attention. You couldn't miss her, you know. I stopped the car and waited for her to pass by. I so much wanted to stab her. The thought of it gave me an instant woody. I watched her running along. Her ankle gave way and she started hobbling. This bloke tried to help her see, then he got into his car and drove off . . . I couldn't resist the temptation. I was lucky wasn't I? I mean, there was a hospital car-park up the road so I left my car there. She was approaching the park gates when I reached her. I dragged her into the park, see, and did it there . . . I could have done more to her but it was risky: not dark enough to hang around for too long. I strangled her and she fell down like a baby. I couldn't just leave it at that, Annie. She was asking for it, you know, like all the others. I can't tell you how powerful I felt when I was destroying her. It happened so quick, but it was worth it. I pulled her shorts up before moving the body. It confuses the police when you do stuff like that . . . See the earring on the dummy? It belonged to her.'

Somehow, Becky managed to calm herself. She kept perfectly still, not wanting to provoke him into hurting her again.

'I met the third one in a pub. Big chunky thing she was. Her name was Angela. Thought she looked great in that trashy outfit she was wearing. I gave her what for. I beat her up first, then I thought I'd use the pliers. Some serial killers are just too boring, you know: no imagination, no creativity. That's her bracelet right there.' He grabbed a handful of Becky's hair and pulled hard. 'Are you listening?' he growled.

Becky tried to nod.

'You're sweating like a big stinking sow. Do you want a drink? I'll get you some water a bit later. Always wanting something you women. You think you've got it made, don't you? . . . I'll carry on; no use stopping now . . . Damsel Number Four was a drunk girl called Elaine Pemberton. She didn't even live in Blackpool. What a great holiday she had. She got a bit too noisy so I beat her up. It was a great night for it. Nice and hot. Moon shining bright. She put up a bit of a fight. That made me mad, I can tell you. You wouldn't believe what I did to her, Annie - all in the name of fame. Don't you agree that the dummy looks good in those shoes of hers? Even the papers mentioned the shoes, and they talked about how shocking the murder was. All this talk about the Ripper made me feel invincible . . . I hope you are taking all this in.'

Becky couldn't speak. She was pulling hard, trying to loosen the bindings around her wrists.

'I had car trouble that night,' he went on, 'and had to mess about with the engine. It kept stalling, see. I managed to get it going, then some woman saw me. I would have cut her voice box out if I'd had the chance.

'Not long after that some private detective comes here and gives my car the once-over. He must have fancied his chances of catching the world's greatest serial killer, but I was watching him. By this time I was in all the papers. See all those cuttings on the wall?' He walked to the display and pointed with his knife. 'These are my conquests, including this idiot private investigator who happened to find Pemberton's thong in the boot of my car. He took it with him. Smart move, for an idiot. It had her blood on it, see. That would have proved my guilt. I had no option but to follow him and kill him. At least I managed to get the thong back. He'd left it in his pocket, luckily enough.

'After killing Pemberton I had to change tactics. Blackpool was swarming with police. I wanted a quiet spot for my next game. I found the right one: a quiet place with a river close by. So scenic, Annie, and not too far from here. I had this coat on and a ridiculous wig when I butchered that one. I ripped her like a pig at market.'

He ordered her to stand up, then positioned the chair in front of the framed photos that hung on the wall.

'Sit down here and take note,' he said, his features showing no sign of shame or remorse.

'Meet the gang - my masters,' he said jovially. He pointed to the photograph on the left. 'This smartly-dressed gentleman is Peter Kürten . . . Don't worry, Annie, I won't bore you with family history or birthplaces. *Kürten.* What a character, what a genius. He liked stabbing people, and animals too. He did them all. His preferred weapon was a knife. I used the Kürten effect for the park murder. It was a split-second decision to kill her that way . . . Kürten was clever. He used a hammer on one of his victims. The police were confused. They thought the killings were the work of two men. I thought of Peter when I bludgeoned the private investigator . . . The lump hammer is a marvellous weapon when used properly. I can't say I enjoyed that murder very much. I just had to get rid of him.'

Becky was practically melting due to the suffocating heat, fear and panic. She was still trying to free her hands from the bindings, but Swan had secured them with ferocious intent.

He pointed at the next photograph. 'This is Malcolm Sargent. Not many people have heard of him. He could have been one of the greats but got caught after his second murder . . . Sargent liked to inflict pain. He was one of few men to use pliers, so I used pliers before I killed Angela Ross. It was my tribute to Mr Sargent.' He went to the table and picked up a large hammer. 'Don't fret, Annie. I'll wash you a bit later.' He held the hammer in front of her face and smiled. 'This is to make sure you don't cause any trouble.' He turned to the third photograph which was a blow-up of a book cover depicting the silhouette of a man carrying a Gladstone bag and wearing a top hat. 'You've heard of Jack the Ripper? Who hasn't? He was the greatest Ripper of all time - the Victorian criminal genius. But he wasn't a criminal. We do what we have to do, that's all. People just don't understand, do they?

'Nobody knows who Jack really was. I think he was an angry medical student who caught a dose of the clap from some stinking filthy whore. They got what they deserved. It's such a bloody business trying to be Jack the Ripper. He's the main chap. He's my inspiration.' He took a step forward and pointed at the next photo. 'Meet Bertie Haines, abuser of prostitutes, fetishist, sadist. Delightful character. I've known about Bertie for a long time. I thought I'd inject a bit of his charm into my murders, just to add a bit of spice.

'And here we have Bobby Ray, known to some as "The Vampire." He was always trying to be one step ahead. He was quite brilliant at it too. I learned about the forensic side of things from him. Ray was forever dreaming about stabbing and ripping and biting. *Biting.* Now that was his speciality. Ray's teeth were crooked so he cut out his bite marks in case they used the impressions to identify him. Ingenious, don't you think?

'And finally, Ted Bundy, one of America's greatest serial killers. Bundy was master of disguise. It was his antics that gave me the idea of shaving off my tache and becoming bald . . . Good old Ted. Pity he was executed.'

Swan pulled a large pair of scissors from the coat pocket. 'Your white bag and lipstick will look great on the model, but there's one thing missing . . .'

Becky closed her eyes as he snipped away at her lovely hair.

'There we go,' he said, dangling it before her eyes. 'Looks a bit like a horse's tail, eh?'

Swan licked the hair, stuffed it into his coat pocket and raised the hammer. Becky's mind suddenly exploded with the sickening pain from the hammer blow to her big toe. She raised her leg, rocking to and fro in agony, her cries straining against the masking tape. He remained calm, playing with himself whilst enjoying her torment.

Five dreadful minutes passed by. Five minutes that seemed like forever.

He knelt beside her and ripped the tape from her mouth. She could not speak, and she was too incapacitated to cry for help.

He unlocked the door and said, 'Hope you enjoyed your stay. Your bedroom used to belong to Nathan, my half-brother. He's not here any more. Poor old Nathan wants to lead what you would call a normal life. It's one of the reasons he left this house. He wanted to get a girlfriend, you know; and he did. He likes women. I hate 'em. You know, he's too brain-dead to realise I'm playing all these games. Even if he knew, he'd be too scared to tell anyone. Mother is scared too. I think she has an idea I'm the Ripper. She won't say a word to anyone. She won't admit it, not even to herself. At least she lets me get on with what I'm doing. I'm going to be the greatest, Annie. I'll be remembered as the most infamous serial killer of all time.'

He left her alone in her misery and terror, unable to bear the thought of the suffering she was about to endure.

FORTY-SIX

Julian Francis was lying in a bath of cold water, looking up at his mother. 'I'm so hot,' he whimpered. 'My skin feels like it's on fire. Bring some ice cubes, will you? I feel terrible.'

'You're going to be all right,' she said soothingly. 'The hot weather is causing the discomfort.'

'The weather is not causing discomfort, mother. I told you this morning. That man is going to kill again.'

'I don't understand. Perhaps you have caught one of those viruses.'

'Just bring the ice, mother. Do as I tell you - please.'

Old Mrs Francis left him alone and went for some ice cubes. By the time she returned, her son was sitting on the edge of the bath wrapped in a towel.

'I feel a bit better now,' he said, fanning his face with his hand.

She shook her head. 'I'll ring for the doctor.'

'There's no need for a doctor. He can't help me. Nobody can help me.'

'You need sleep, Julian. You haven't been sleeping too well these last few nights,' she said, her bony finger pointing at him.

His face was screwed up, his eyes shut tight.

'What's the matter?' she asked, taking hold of his hand.

'I feel restless, more so than yesterday. I am frightened and utterly powerless. The weather is going to break soon, dear mother. The sky will open up and his anger will be released . . . The Axeman is coming.'

Sheridan switched the TV on and smoked a cigarette whilst waiting for the midday news. He wondered why Becky had not called to see him, and assumed she was waiting to hear the latest developments in the Ripper investigation. Try as he might, he could not ignore the doubt in the back of his mind.

The programme started. After the brief introductory music the newsreader said there had been an unusual development regarding the latest suspect. The scene switched from the studio to the crime correspondent who was standing outside the main entrance of Sedgeburn's police headquarters. The questioning of a 27-year-old Blackpool man had been postponed pending psychiatric evaluation. The reporter went on to say that forensic scientists had discovered vital new evidence at the suspect's home. The police declined to reveal the nature of the evidence and stressed that examination of the man's belongings was still in its early stages.

Sheridan switched the TV off. A knock on the door brought him face to face with Bert Davies. Davies managed to persuade his old friend to join him for a drink at the nearby pub. Sheridan had more time on his hands now that his investigation was over. He joined Davis for a friendly chat and a pint of beer. No whisky this time.

Frustration was eating away at Derek Oxley. He realised that the intense questioning of Nathan Walsh had adversely affected him. Walsh had become more and more incoherent as the pressure was increased.

Oxley was pushing for results, hoping for a conviction. He couldn't wait to face the reporters and camera crews to inform them that Walsh had been charged with the murders. He couldn't wait to phone George Naylor and say the words, 'It's all over. Walsh has been charged.' And what a relief it would be for an anxious and weary murder squad that had worked round the clock, hoping for the breakthrough to end one of Britain's biggest manhunts. What a relief for officers and staff who would, at last, be able to go home early to their wives and children.

Every member of the Serious Crime Unit believed it was only a matter of time before Operation Stamford could officially be terminated.

News reporters were expecting the news to break within the next day or two, as were the parents of the killer's victims.

Come what may Oxley was determined to nail Walsh for the murders - and that was his biggest mistake.

Gary Swan kept the dummy in his 'trophy room.' He had spent many hours in there, reliving his crimes.

He always thought of the other room as his 'torture room.' A few years ago he fitted a plug socket and furnished it with a table and chair. He bought a small TV and a video recorder so he could watch his videos without fear of disturbance. Not that anybody would have any cause to go down there.

It was always difficult watching them upstairs. Mother might have walked in and caught him at it, masturbating as he had done hundreds of times before. She would have been shocked had she seen even the mildest films in his collection. That wouldn't do at all. He couldn't risk her discovering the true nature of his personality, though she often suspected he harboured sadistic thoughts and feelings.

To him, Mother was merely a lodger. She hardly spent any time with her son. That suited him fine. He could live his life the way he wanted. She might as well have been living in an empty house, alone with her painful memories. The other lodgers didn't seem to like her very much. They kept themselves isolated. She was glad it worked out that way. No questions asked. No questions to answer.

Lately, Mother was troubled by her own questions. Gary was spending more time in the cellar. She was concerned because Annie had mentioned hearing screams in the night. She managed to convince herself that Annie had been dreaming.

It was an explanation that afforded her some comfort.

The metallic hammering sounds had bothered her, too. She came to the conclusion that he was carrying out some repairs. He was quite handy at doing jobs around the house.

At least she could sleep easy . . . . for the time being.

Swan had dragged Becky's limp body into the torture room. Fresh masking tape had been stuck over her mouth. In any case she was too weak to scream or speak.

He ran his eyes up and down her bruised and naked body. Her wrists were bound tightly with strong twine secured to a big nail which he had hammered into the mortar separating the greyish bricks.

The callous beating had sapped all her strength. She was using the last of her energy reserves to remain in a standing position, but her legs eventually gave way. She was totally at his mercy, unable to moan with discomfort and pain, unable to cry a single tear.

'Too bad you came here, Annie,' he said, pushing the video into the machine. 'Don't worry, I can't keep you for too long . . . Did you enjoy letting me sponge you down? Caring soul, aren't I? I was going to use boiling water. That would have been too much for you to take. We can't have you slipping into unconsciousness, can we?'

He chuckled to himself and pressed the play button. Thankfully, the picture was in black and white. The short film started rolling. 'I must have watched this a thousand times,' he said, wiping sweat from his shiny forehead. 'It was made in Hagen in the 1970s - an original snuff movie that's now impossible to obtain. You'd better watch it, Annie, or I'll get annoyed with you. I love it when she screams. She was a prostitute, taken off the streets and transported to a secluded spot in the countryside where they could enjoy ravishing her.'

The images were unbelievable - violence without reservation or remorse. Her body came apart, the blood spurting onto the depraved maniac whose disgusting blood lust could not be satiated. He went on slashing and stabbing her dead body. Becky closed her eyes, shutting out the final assault.

Swan ripped the TV plug from the socket. He was aroused and feeling all powerful. Becky watched him coming closer. He knelt down and sank his teeth into her thigh.

She had no strength left, could not fight back or do anything to repulse him.

His death-smile reveals red-tainted teeth . . . I am doing what a thousand men have done before.

As if that wasn't enough, he forced the cold chisel into her.

A fantasy was rekindled. He visualised Angela Ross and her white bulging breasts.

That girl would have been fantastic as one of Parlour's dolly-house girls . . . Suffer, you harlot . . . Suffer and be glad of it . . .

He kept the chisel in position and pressed his body against hers, images of extreme violence flashing through his mind. Her body, writhing in response to the internal shock, incensed him.

He was destroying her and feeding the hideous fantasies that were destroying him.

Becky was praying to die, praying to be released from the degradation and suffering imposed by his despicable, perverse desires. She turned her head slowly. Swan was delighted that she was still conscious. He sat down, unfastened the buttons on his shirt and dried his face with a towel. He stood up again and searched his pocket for the sharp object he had been planning to use on her.

'Sharper than a knife,' he said. 'Such fun to play with.'

He moved silently towards her, holding the razor blade between finger and thumb.

Sheridan must have rung Becky's mobile at least a dozen times since returning from the pub. There was no reply.

The afternoon drifted into evening, and his anger was negated by intense worry. He kept telling himself she was all right. He tried ringing her mother but nobody answered. Becky had probably gone out for the day with her mother and son, but he knew he was clutching at straws, making excuses for her.

9 p.m. He tried the number again. No answer. *Maybe I'm worrying too much,* he thought. *The police investigation is practically over. Walsh is bound to be charged in the next day or two.*

Sheridan read the paper until he dozed off. He awakened to the distant rumble of thunder. He got up and looked out of the window at an angry sky. The heatwave was finally over.

He fell into his chair. His concern over Becky's whereabouts was nagging him. He was longing to hear her voice. All he wanted was confirmation that she was safe and well.

He became restless, constantly looking out of the window, hoping that her car would pull up. Minutes seemed like hours. *What if the police had made a mistake? Suppose they had arrested the wrong man?* He considered the possibility that Becky might have decided to stay longer at the house on Bouverie Road. She was independent and headstrong. She was the kind of woman who would not ignore her own instinct.

The phone rang. Rivers' voice offered momentary relief. There had been an unexpected development in the investigation. Sheridan wanted to know the details.

'The killer stuffed tissues into Amy Tyler's mouth,' Rivers said. 'They were full of catarrh. Forensic had trouble extracting the cells for DNA analysis. It took them a few days longer to prepare the profile. The DNA taken from the catarrh isn't the same as Nathan Walsh's. Somebody else killed Amy Tyler . . . Sheridan, are you there? . . . Sheridan!'

Sheridan had cut him off. He tried Becky's mother again, breathing a sigh of relief when she answered; but his problems had only just begun. Her daughter hadn't returned home. She hadn't telephoned either. He told her he would be in touch as soon as possible. He punched Rivers' number into his mobile.

'What is it now, Sheridan?'

'You've got to listen to me. Becky is in great danger. She might even be dead.'

'You're still bothered about this Swan character,' he said calmly.

'I've got to get to his house as quickly as possible. *You* are coming with me.'

'I think you'd better tell me what's going on.'

'I haven't time to explain. Meet me outside my office on Chapel Street. Be there in five minutes. Do it Rivers. Just do it.'

FORTY-SEVEN

Sheridan was driving down Chapel Street, consumed with the dread of not knowing what to expect. When he arrived he parked on double yellows outside Darren's shop and got out. It was 10.45. He paced up and down the pavement, his stomach churning with a worried sickness. He threw glances towards the busy road, hoping that Rivers hadn't let him down. Time was against him, thoughts racing through his mind. *The journey to Sedgeburn will take another thirty minutes. Come on, Rivers. Come on.*

He looked up at the black sky. The thunder was louder than before. A downpour was imminent. That meant the journey would take longer. His heart sank. He checked his watch. Rivers arrived after a ten-minute wait. Sheridan got in. The car sped off before he had chance to close the door.

'Head for the motorway, quick as you can.'

Rivers stamped on the accelerator. 'Hope you know what you're doing,' he said angrily. 'This isn't the kind of thing I go in for.'

'Just keep driving. There's been no sign of Becky. God only knows what's happened to her.'

'You think she's at Swan's house, don't you?'

'I'm sure of it. I specifically told her that the police had found DNA which linked another man to the crimes.'

'If she wasn't held against her will, why didn't she leave straight away?'

'I'm not sure. If Gary Swan is a psychopath . . .'

Sheridan couldn't bring himself to finish the sentence. He allowed Rivers to concentrate on the road ahead. As soon as he hit the motorway he opened up the engine, powering the car to a life-threatening hundred and ten miles an hour.

Then the rain started, followed by flashes of forked lightning.

Rivers switched the wipers on and dropped the speed to a hundred.

The rainfall intensified in a sudden burst.

'I can't hold this speed for much longer,' Rivers said, his entire body stiff with the fear of losing control.

'Keep it up. We've to get there before it's too late,' Sheridan said, hoping against hope.

The rain ricocheted off the motorway like a hail of bullets. Rivers had no option but to slow down to a crawling fifty miles an hour. Sheridan took the opportunity to try and convince Rivers of their mission. He told him about the Susan Rawcliffe letter, details about Swan's sexual deviance and the real reason for Lewis's murder. Rivers was concentrating on the road ahead and, to Sheridan's surprise, he said, 'Okay. I'll go along with that. I believe you're on to something . . . I'm sorry I didn't have more faith in you.'

'I never thought I would hear you of all people say the word, "sorry." . . . Tell me one thing, Rivers: Did you *really* believe I'd killed my own daughter, and Carl Lewis?'

'It wasn't a question of belief. I was only doing my job . . . No hard feelings?'

'No hard feelings.'

'You gave me a good run for my money. The drug dealing really has ended you know.'

'You were scared, eh?'

'Yeah. I'm still a pervy bastard, though. I just can't keep away from that brothel at Wichonstall.'

'Why don't you get yourself a woman?'

'Enjoy the freedom too much, I suppose.'

Rivers increased the speed slightly. Fifteen minutes passed by, and the Sedgeburn signpost came into view.

'Made it,' Rivers said, raising a fist.

He took the slip road and circled the roundabout.

'Carry on, straight ahead. I'll tell you when to stop.'

They were travelling along Bouverie Road, but the weather made it difficult for Sheridan to locate the house. Eventually, he spotted some trees. They were close to Swan's house but missed the driveway.

'We must have passed it,' Sheridan said. 'Stop the car.' He got out for a clearer view. 'I can see it now. Follow me, Rivers.'

They dashed across the road, ran the fifty or so yards and scrambled up the driveway. The house was in darkness except for one lighted window on the top floor.

'Swan's car isn't here,' Sheridan remarked, out of breath.

Rivers reached the door first. He rang the ground-floor bell then pounded the door with both fists. A minute later the door was answered by a pale, haggard-looking woman dressed in a pink dressing gown and black slippers.

Rivers thrust his ID card in front of her face. 'I am Detective Constable Rivers.'

She moved back a few paces. Rivers pushed her out of the way and they stepped into the dimly lit hallway.

'Are you Gary Swan's mother?' Sheridan asked.

She nodded slowly.

'Where is he?' Rivers asked.

She kept silent. Rivers grabbed her shoulders and shook her.

'Now look here old woman, I'm not going to waste my time with you. Where is he?'

'He's asleep,' she blurted. 'I think he's asleep.'

The look on Rivers' face left her in no doubt as to his intention.

She shuffled along the passage and pointed to the bedroom door. He pushed it open, switched the light on.

'He's not there,' he said, turning towards her. 'Where is the girl?'

'She's returned home. That's all I can tell you,' she answered, clutching her gown with both hands. 'This was her room.' She pointed at the next one.

Sheridan looked inside. 'It's empty. Where has he taken her? Tell me!'

'I don't know what you mean.'

Rivers opened the door leading to the cellar. 'What's in here?'

'There's nothing down there,' she said nervously.

Sheridan went through the door. The light was on. He skipped down the stairs, Rivers following behind.

'There's nothing to see down there,' she bellowed.

Rivers cracked open the door to the first room they came to. The lights were on. Rivers met Sheridan's eyes and they looked in paralysing horror upon the grotesque mannequin, oblivious to the peels of thunder and the sound of mother wailing from the top of the stairs.

Sheridan recognised the earring. He touched the clump of hair that had been crudely stuck to the head. 'That's my daughter's earring,' he said, his voice cracking with emotion, 'and, if I'm not mistaken, this is Becky's hair.'

Rivers examined the footwear. 'Pemberton's shoes . . . You were dead right about Swan.'

He rushed off to investigate the second room. Sheridan took a few paces towards the newspaper display. He immediately recognised the pictures of

Elizabeth, Angela Ross, Elaine Pemberton, Amy Tyler and Carl Lewis. The picture of his daughter was the same 'school' photo that Irene had given to him when she had visited the office for the first time. It had been cut from a newspaper.

He wondered where he had taken Becky, and had lost all hope of getting her back alive.

He turned towards Swan's gallery of murderers and Becky's white shoulder bag, lying on the floor, caught his eye.

Rivers was standing in the doorway. 'There's nothing much in the other room apart from a TV and some porno videos. I reckon that's where he watched them.'

Sheridan bent down to pick up the bag.

'Don't touch it. His fingerprints might be on it,' Rivers said. 'What's that light that just flashed? There it goes again.'

Sheridan turned to the shelf in the corner. Becky's microcassette recorder was just visible between a couple of rusty paint tins.

'Is that a tape recorder?' Rivers asked, puzzled.

'Yes. Becky must have put it there, and she's left it in the auto-record mode. It will only record whenever someone speaks, or if there's a noise . . . She was here in this room.'

Rivers looked into his eyes, knowing what must have been going through his mind.

A tremendous crack of thunder sounded followed by a pitiful outburst of crying from Swan's mother. Rivers dashed upstairs and escorted her to the living room. He told her, in no uncertain terms, to stay there until further notice. He bounced down the stairs and told Sheridan he was going to call the SCU.

'Be quiet a minute.' Sheridan had the recorder pressed to his ear. 'It's Swan's voice. He's using rope to tie her. He's saying something about dragging her up through a cellar door.'

'There's a hatch at the end of the passage,' Rivers added.

Sheridan raised a hand, signalling him to be quiet again. He rewound the tape for a second and pressed the play button. 'I can just about hear him. He's saying, "The thunder is getting louder. What a night for it."'

'That recording has been made in the last half hour,' Rivers exclaimed.

'Right. And if he's talking to Becky . . .'

'She could still be alive.'

'He's talking to her again . . . "I'm taking you to a place where lightning never strikes twice . . ."'

'What does he mean?' Rivers asked.

'A place where lightning never strikes twice,' he repeated. He switched the cassette off and whispered the words over and over until Gary Swan's diabolical plan finally dawned on him.

'Lucy Beckett was buried in a shallow grave at a place called Plymbey,' Sheridan said, his voice flat and monotonous. 'He's going to murder Becky and bury her in the same place.'

'Come on,' Rivers screamed. 'There's still time left.'

Within minutes Rivers' car was speeding down Bouverie Road. Neither men knew how to get to Plymbey. He jumped the red lights and turned right. The car skidded into a pavement and came to a halt.

'What are you doing?' Sheridan asked.

Rivers got out and rushed into a nearby pub, returning after a few minutes. 'This is Withey Road. We go to the end of it, turn right, and keep going until we reach Plymbey.'

Rivers drove away at speed, failing to slow down as they approached a narrow tunnel-bridge. Luckily, nobody was approaching from the other side. When he came to the end of Withey Road he took a right turn and went into white-knuckle driving mode, occasionally skidding as he fought to negotiate the slippery bends. The street lights were becoming less frequent. After five minutes they were speeding through black country along the same route that Lucy Beckett had travelled some seven months earlier. The rain showed no sign of easing off. The humpback bridge failed to slow him down. Once again luck was on his side.

A few minutes later the Plymbey signpost suddenly appeared out of the darkness.

Sheridan spotted the trees bordering the woodland mass. A solitary street lamp marked the entrance to the narrow lane. Rivers missed the opening. He jammed the brakes on, reversed, and sped forward into the lane.

Swan's white Sierra appeared in the headlights. He pulled up a few yards behind it and switched the lights off. Sheridan got out and slipped on the mushy surface. Rivers was calling for backup. He opened the driver's door and yanked Swan's keys from the ignition. Sheridan was peering into the darkness, listening for any noises that might indicate where Swan had taken her. The heavy rain, battering the trees and foliage, was the only sound they heard.

They walked along the periphery of the wood, eyes and ears straining against the elements.

Sheridan noticed a faint light. 'Can you see it? It's a torch or something,' he said.

Rivers wiped his eyes with the sleeve of his coat. 'I see it.'

They scrambled through the foliage and into the wood, not knowing what horrors awaited them. It took only seconds to reach her. They froze as their eyes fell upon the dimly-lit scene, so shocking as to defy belief.

Their arrival interrupted Swan's ultimate fantasy. His fingers were locked around the axe, ready to be brought down onto Becky's lifeless body. Seconds later would have been too late.

She had been tied to a tree, as if in readiness for some revolting execution to take place. The rope, biting fiercely into her naked body, was the same rope used to hoist her through the hatch that led to the cellar. Swan, dressed only in his underpants, was overwhelmed with a crazed blood lust.

'Stay back,' he ordered, his voice deep and gravelly.

'Police,' Rivers cried. 'Put the axe down, or I'll shoot you. There's nothing to gain by killing her.'

'You haven't got a gun. You would have shot me by now.'

'I mean it, Swan. This is your last chance.'

'I am Frank Corbin - the Axeman.'

He let out a high pitched scream and swung the axe. Sheridan was too far away to save her, but the slippery axe fell from his hands and hit the gardening spade lying on the ground. An ungodly sound burst out of Swan's mouth. He picked up a long knife and disappeared into the surrounding darkness.

Becky was barely recognisable. Her breasts, bulging through the gaps in the rope, were bruised from Swan's ferocious biting.

'Get the ropes off,' Sheridan urged, 'and cover her with your coat.'

When the ropes finally came loose, her limp body slumped to the ground. Rivers cringed when he saw the myriad of razor cuts on her back. He covered her as best he could, grabbed Swan's torch and made his way towards the vehicles.

'Sheridan! Where are you?'

No reply came. No sign of him or Gary Swan.

Rivers could hear gasping and moaning coming from the direction of the cars. He ran as fast as he could, his legs weak from the shock of what he had witnessed. When he arrived at the vehicles he saw the two men struggling on the soggy ground. He switched his headlights on and moved forward for a closer look.

They were locked in battle, Sheridan twisting his arm until the knife fell free. Swan raised his shoulders off the ground. He spat blood into Sheridan's face and tried to push him off. But Sheridan was in control. He had the knife that had killed his daughter, and now the sharp blade was touching Swan's throat, ready to thrust, ready to end the life of a sick and tormented human being.

Rivers had been hesitating all the while, hoping that Swan would finally give in.

'Kill me,' he hissed, his red teeth clenched, his wet face distorted.

'Don't do it, Sheridan,' Rivers shouted. 'Don't do it, man! Think about the investigation. You can't end it like this.'

'What about my daughter? What about all those other girls this bastard has killed?'

'To hell with you Jim Sheridan,' Swan said. 'Do you think I care about your little daughter or about any of those pathetic harlots? They all had to die, and I enjoyed taking them, slicing them apart. I loved it. Don't you understand, you fool?'

'We've got him now. It's all over . . . Sheridan, please listen.'

'Back off. Go and see to Becky.'

'I don't think she's alive,' Rivers said, holding his head with both hands, overwhelmed by the blistering fever of the moment.

Swan smiled defiantly, his cold blue eyes blinking against the rain. 'I did it,' he said. 'I have done what a thousand men have done before . . . I am the greatest . . .'

The blade was poised for the kill. Swan let his arms fall to the ground, signalling his ultimate submission, his desire to die.

Revenge was Sheridan's prize.

Rivers cried, 'Don't do it' for the last time.

The knife sank deeper and deeper, silencing his last words. Sheridan turned his face away from the spurting crimson life force, luminous in the powerful light beam as if coming from a supernatural demon.

Seconds later, Gary Swan was dead.

FORTY-EIGHT

'George, you have a visitor,' Dorothy Naylor said.

She stepped to the side. Oxley walked into the conservatory to a warm welcome. He was almost tempted to give Naylor a big hug. They had missed seeing each other.

'I'll leave you two to have a long chat. George is bursting with excitement. Be prepared for a lot of questions.'

'No problem, Dorothy. It's my day off. The first one in months.'

'You certainly deserve it . . . I'm preparing some ham sandwiches, and there's plenty of red wine. Would you care to indulge?'

'Love to.'

Dorothy left them to it.

'Nice spot,' Oxley remarked, sitting in the wicker chair opposite his colleague.

'Nice and peaceful. A good place to relax . . . How are you, Derek?'

'Not so bad - all things considered.'

'I'm glad to hear it. I'm feeling a lot better now.'

'That's what I was hoping to hear.'

Oxley stared at the pile of newspapers on the wicker table.

'The papers are full of it,' Naylor said, sitting upright. 'Hardly a day goes by without some mention of the Ripper. I told Dorothy to buy all the dailies. I haven't had much contact with the crime unit, not since I went sick. I'm sorry it turned out the way it did.'

'In what respect?'

'It should have been you who caught him. I mean, how does a lousy PI manage to beat us to it?'

'I don't have all the details, and I'll tell you something George - I don't think I ever will.'

'That unconventional scoundrel, Rivers, steals the show,' Naylor said.

'My instinct tells me that Rivers knows more than he's prepared to tell.'

'Rivers is a waste of time.'

'The chief super doesn't think so. Rivers has gained a lot of respect. He might even be promoted.'

'You are joking, Derek.'

'Wish I was. I suppose he deserves some kind of reward. Let's face it, George, he could have alerted Sedgeburn HQ instead of his own unit. At least we got some of the credit for catching the Ripper.'

'He could have been caught months ago if that body had surfaced a bit sooner.'

'That's the way it goes.'

'The question is: Why was Lucy Beckett buried? None of the others were.'

'Because of her connection with his half-brother, Nathan Walsh. Do you recall what Dr Simmons said about the killer?'

'He said a lot of things,' Naylor replied with a look of disdain. 'My opinion on psychological profiling hasn't changed. Sorry, Derek, you haven't come here to listen to *my* gripes.'

'It's all right, George. I must admit, I was impressed by Simmons' mind-factor scale. He gave the murderer a mind-factor of seven. He reckoned the killer was fairly clever but would make a mistake sooner or later. Swan, in fact, made several mistakes. He would, for example, have stood a better chance of remaining undetected had he refrained from getting involved with Lucy Beckett. He knew she had terminated her relationship with Walsh, and he offered to get his music cassettes that she borrowed from him. It seems that Walsh was a bit infatuated with Lucy. Some of the recordings he made contained childish messages like, "I love you Lucy," and "Stay with me forever."'

'And a cassette was found at the crime scene in Plymbey. Walsh's voice was played on radio and TV.'

'That's right. The cassette could have been dropped during a struggle. We're not sure exactly what happened. Of course, Swan's plan was to murder her. He returned Walsh's belongings and told him that Lucy was planning to leave home; hence her disappearance.'

At that point Dorothy came into the conservatory with the chilled wine and sandwiches.

'She's been really good to me this last few months,' Naylor remarked when she had gone. 'Anyway, sandwiches can wait. Tell me more.'

'Swan and Walsh often exchanged porno magazines,' Oxley continued, eager to convey the relevant details. 'The search team found a particularly nasty magazine showing images of anal sadism. It also had a tiny smear of blood on the front page. Our press officer told the media that important new evidence had been found at the suspect's home. It turned out that the DNA in the smear matched Angela Ross's DNA profile.'

'I get the impression that Swan was hoping to frame Walsh for the murders.'

'It looks that way, but remember Swan was a serial killer. Even if Walsh was charged for the murders, Swan would have carried on killing. There's no way he could stop.'

'Surely, Walsh suspected he was doing the murders?'

'I can't be sure, George. Walsh was found to be suffering from a variety of neurological and psychiatric disorders. He is grossly lacking in self confidence. During the questioning it seemed as if he was out of touch with reality. He may have had doubts about Swan. I have to say, I found nothing to suggest he was covering for him.'

'What about the mother?'

'Denise Hewitt was twice married. Her first husband, George Swan, was a vicious, bad-tempered drunkard. His son was, no doubt, emotionally affected by the violence and abuse he witnessed. The marriage ended in divorce. Hewitt didn't have much luck with her second husband, Edward Walsh. They spent several happy years together and then he died of cancer.'

'Poor wretch. What did she have to say for herself?'

'Nothing. Denise Hewitt had a complete breakdown shortly after her son's activities came to light. I don't think she'll ever recover.'

Naylor poured two drinks. 'Come on, Derek,' he said, 'let's get some fresh air.'

They stepped into the spacious back garden and slowly walked along a gravel path.

'You haven't told me how Walsh became the main suspect,' Naylor said after some deep thought.

'It was due to a combination of factors, really. Purslow's post-mortem report, on Lucy Beckett, stated that she had a cut throat and stab wounds to the chest. Sedgeburn detectives found a connection between her and a man living in Blackpool.

'Walsh was easy to locate once the tape recording was made public. What strengthened the case against him was the fact the Swan borrowed his car,

311

and was using it at the time of the Amy Tyler murder. Maybe he was worried about his Sierra being spotted again. When Walsh was arrested I was eager to get a conviction.'

'As you would.'

'But it all went wrong when I was informed that the DNA found on the tissues in Amy Tyler's mouth didn't exactly match Walsh's DNA. At first, I thought there might be an accomplice. I questioned him about friends and relatives, and Swan came into the frame once again.'

Naylor asked the obvious question that Oxley was expecting.

'Why was Swan missed in the first place? His name was on the Sierra list, wasn't it?'

'It was, George. His car didn't entirely match the description as that given by a witness who saw his Sierra shortly after the Pemberton murder. By the time our lads spoke to him he had shaved his head and moustache. Swan was quite helpful, calm and in control. His mother gave him alibis for the nights when the murders occurred. Maybe she was scared. Who knows?'

'He was cunning enough to fool the murder squad.'

'Even down to the black wig he wore for the Tyler murder. Unfortunately, Sheridan got to him before we did. Full moon connection and all that . . .'

'I don't believe all this rubbish about the influence of the full moon. It's just a coincidence. He got lucky, that's all.'

'A fortuitous coincidence for Sheridan, maybe. He landed himself fifty grand - a gift from a local business man. Apparently, he used information obtained from a psychic who said the killer's name was Tony.'

'Absolute nonsense.'

Oxley stopped in his tracks. 'I'm not so sure about that. Our research into the family revealed his full name - Gary Anthony Swan.'

Oxley finished his wine. 'I must be on my way. Liz will be expecting me.'

'I'll stay here in the garden,' Naylor said, taking his empty glass. 'You take care now, Derek.'

Oxley started walking towards the house, happy that his boss was recovering from his breakdown. Before he reached the conservatory he said, 'We look forward to having you back. Be brave. Be good.'

Sheridan was strolling along South Shore Promenade on a crisp November morning. Even now, a few months after the Ripper investigation had ended, he was plagued by sleepless nights, and he couldn't stop recalling those final moments with the man who had taken his daughter's life and the lives of those other girls.

He leaned against the promenade wall and cast his gaze towards the horizon, his hair blowing in the biting breeze that whispered mournfully along an almost desolate sea front. He recalled the last time he had visited the beach when he hoped to quell what was left of a monumental hangover. His investigation into the murders had driven him into the alcoholic abyss. The investigation brought him out of it as well, but the same question was surfacing over and over: Was it really worth it?

Carl Lewis was dead. Sheridan blamed himself for giving up too easily; and why did he allow Becky to fool him into thinking she had left that house of horrors on Bouverie Road?

Thoughts.

Regrets.

Sheridan had been sucked into the life of a desperate psychopath who loved to inflict pain on defenceless vulnerable women - a man who thought nothing of taking a life in order to satisfy his dreadful, obscene urges.

Jim Sheridan deeply regretted his involvement in the hunt for the Seaside Ripper. It was a name he would never forget - and one he despised.

After several attempts he managed to light a cigarette. He strolled on, unaware of the patter of approaching footsteps. A little hand was tugging his coat. Sheridan turned and looked down at a little boy.

'You're the man who saved mummy's life,' he said, stepping back.

'Johnny?'

The smiling boy nodded and turned around.

Sheridan looked up and saw her coming towards him, her hair blowing in an easterly wind. The paleness of her skin, brought on by weeks of indoor recuperation, was so striking as to arouse feelings of deep sympathy.

Her mere presence testified to the fact that Rebecca Watts was a survivor - a woman who had overcome a trauma deep enough to consume any woman's confidence, perhaps strong enough to destroy any woman's desire to go on living.

Nobody would ever know the suffering she had been forced to endure.

He dropped his cigarette and opened his arms for her. They embraced each other - a long, silent and tearful embrace.

Johnny knew that they needed to be together for a while. He skipped back to his mum's car to play with the robot she had bought for him.

Becky wiped her eyes and managed a lovely smile. 'How are you, Sheridan, you old bloodhound?'

'Fine,' he replied, gently pinching her cheek.

'I called at the office. Darren said you might be somewhere round here.'

'You're supposed to be resting.'

'I've done nothing but lay around the house since I came out of hospital. I think I will die if I carry on resting much longer.'

'You are truly remarkable, Becky.'

Sheridan leaned against the wall and gazed at the choppy waters. Becky joined him.

'Thanks for the cheque, Sheridan. You didn't have to, you know.'

'You deserve it more than anyone in the world. Are the journalists still bothering you?'

'Not so much now. There's always somebody who wants the Big Story so they can write about the gory details. I don't want to live through all that again. I don't want to even think about it.'

'You don't have to. It's not worth it . . . Can I ask you something?'

'You can ask me anything.'

'How did you manage to conceal the recorder in that cellar?'

'It wasn't easy. He left me for a while, helpless and in pain. My wrists were tied too. Somehow, I managed to get it out of my bag and activate it. I used my teeth to place it on a shelf, hoping he wouldn't see it.'

'That recorder saved your life. Swan was planning to bury you in the same place as Lucy Beckett. The police knew about him, you know.'

'But you got to me first, Sheridan. If it hadn't been for your quick thinking I wouldn't be here.'

'Let's not forget Rivers' help, eh? He wasn't such a bad bloke, after all.'

There was a long pause.

'Why the axe?' she asked. 'He used a knife on the others.'

'Every time he killed someone he was copying the traits of convicted killers, like Bertram Haines. Jack the Ripper - the one they never caught - was his main driving force.'

'I thought something like that was going on in his mind when I saw those photos of murderers he kept in the cellar. Julian Francis had dreams and visions. I remembered your ex's transcript of her meeting with him when he said, "He is their disciple," and "I see different people." It all started to make sense, and I was to be his next victim.'

Their eyes met. Sheridan recognised the sullen look that spoke of an ordeal she would never forget.

'Even a man who is pure in heart . . .' he said.

'The full moon gave the clue,' she responded. 'Swan was under the influence of some mysterious demonic force. We'll never know exactly what it was.'

'Amy Tyler was murdered during daylight hours,' he reflected.

'During the *period* of a full moon. Swan's lover wrote about how his violence erupted on particular dates. Lucy Beckett went missing on January 21. That was during the night of a full moon.'

'I would never have spotted the connection. You did well, Becky, but you shouldn't have stayed at that house.'

'I had to find out. I just had to know whether it was him or not.'

'Well, it's all over now; and after all we've been through I'm considering quitting the enquiry business for good. What about you?'

'Too early to say. I don't think I want to stay in Blackpool. It's a big world out there.'

'You've thought about emigrating?'

'It's a possibility.'

Sheridan held both her hands. 'I sincerely hope you find love and happiness,' he said endearingly.

'Hope you do, too.'

'I'll love you and leave you.'

Becky wrapped her arms around him. They held each other tightly.

'Take care,' she whispered.

Sheridan turned and walked away. Becky called out his name.

'I want to know what happened during those last moments with Swan. The papers said there was a fierce struggle, that you killed him in self defence.'

'That's the story Rivers and I are sticking to.'

'Then, what really happened?'

'He tried to escape, fell into his own car and hurt himself. I had him pinned down. Rivers came to the rescue and said he thought you were dead.'

'So, you killed him?'

Sheridan looked down, then raised his head. 'He wanted to die, Becky. He realised he'd come to the end of his miserable existence. There was nothing more he could do. He succeeded. He became the serial killer he wanted to be.'

Sheridan nodded slowly, his eyes conveying the impression that there was another reason, far deeper, for his assault on Swan: a reason he would not care to admit to.

Becky understood.

She blew a final kiss.

Jim Sheridan waved goodbye.

Central Drive was busy with last-minute shoppers buzzing around, hoping to find that present to complete the shopping list.

Sheridan looked down from the office window and admired the blinking lights of the Christmas tree standing in the pub window. Some of the punters were wearing cheap red hats trimmed with white fur. The jukebox was playing Shakin' Stevens' 'Merry Christmas Everyone.'

It didn't seem five minutes since Sheridan last heard that song.

He sat down and opened the envelope Darren had brought up. Christmas cards usually arrived at his home. There were never more than a couple. This one had been personally delivered by 'an odd-looking, little man,' according to Darren.

It was a big expensive card with two handwritten lines: Do not reproach yourself. The world is a better place - JF

JF? . . . Must be Julian Francis.

He stood the card on the desk. The phone rang.

'Jim Sheridan speaking.'

'Am I disturbing you?' Irene Collinson asked.

'Not at all.'

'What are you doing tomorrow?'

'Eating turkey and watching TV on my own, as usual.'

'I'd like to make Christmas dinner for two. What do you say?'

'I can almost hear those sleigh bells ringing. What time?'

'Ten-thirty.'

'That's good enough for me.'

'Look forward to seeing you. Don't be late.'

Sheridan replaced the handset, leaned back and folded his arms.

A feeble knock sounded. The door opened. An old lady peered at him through round spectacles. Her hat, sitting lightly on her head, barely covered her tight-curled grey hair.

'Mr Sheridan?'

'That's me. Please, take a seat.'

She closed the door, removed her gloves, shuffled towards the desk and lowered herself into the well-worn client's chair.

'Jim Sheridan - the famous detective. Everyone says how clever you are. They say you are most gifted.'

'Oh, really?' he said, with a hint of modesty.

'I believe so. Can I engage your services?'

'Well, uh, I hate to disappoint you —'

'My name is Margaret Golding,' she continued, eager to tell her story. 'I have lived in this town all my life. The old resort has changed so much over the years.'

'Quite.'

'It's not the same you know,' she droned, shaking her head. 'Too rowdy nowadays.'

'As I was saying —'

'Three months ago I moved into a house on Cherry Lane. Have you heard of Cherry Lane?'

Sheridan opened his mouth to answer.

'Would you believe that the house is haunted?' she interrupted.

He closed his eyes in defeat, then opened them saying, 'Haunted by what?'

'By *who*, not *what* . . . I think my dear husband has come back.'

'Your husband?'

'He died three years ago.'

'You have seen him?'

'No, I have felt his presence; well, at least I think it's his presence. Do you understand? Perhaps the house is haunted by some other poor soul.'

'You think, but you're not sure, that the ghost of your husband is in your new home?'

'That's exactly what I want you to find out. There is more to tell . . .'

Sheridan stood up and sighed. 'Sorry, Mrs Golding. I have retired from investigative work. Anyway, ghost hunting is not my field.'

'Dear me, you should have said so.'

He helped her out of the chair. She shook his hand and wished him a happy Christmas. He walked her along the passage and watched her go down the stairs, step by step. When she reached halfway he called her back to his office.

Once again, she sat in the client's chair.

He waited until she got her breath back.

'The season of goodwill is upon us once again,' he said, smiling at her from across the desk.

'You have decided to help me, Mr Sheridan?'

'I'll make an exception,' he replied. 'Now then, tell me all about this ghost.'

About Peter Hodgson

Peter Hodgson is an energy analyst at a major industrial site in the north-west of England. His interests include True Crime, psychological profiling, science, philosophy and writing. His published works are Critical Murder (2009) and Jack the Ripper - Through the Mists of Time (2011), both published by Pneuma Springs. He has contributed a short story for Ripperologist magazine.

His interest in writing began at an early age after reading Conan Doyle's The Hound of the Baskervilles. Inspired by this story, he created his own fictional detective and wrote ten short stories set in the Victorian period. He has ideas for other novels which he hopes to complete in the fullness of time. Peter is married and lives in Blackpool. He is available for interviews most evenings.

Connect with Peter Hodgson

Via authors website or Facebook.

Book(s) by Peter Hodgson

Critical Murder, ISBN: 9781905809790

A dirty bomb explodes amidst an anti-war protest in North London. Tara Drake is a highly trained MI5 agent, called in to assist the investigation with the help of DI Dave Perry.

Tragic events unfold and Perry is forced into a confrontation against a formidable foe. His fight for survival is played out to its shattering climax.

Jack the Ripper - Through the Mists of Time, ISBN:9781907728259

Over a century ago a series of mutilation murders took place in a squalid district of Victorian London. Five women fell victim. The newspapers of the day gave him a chilling nickname - Jack the Ripper. From the long list of candidates the author reveals his prime suspect for the role of the world's most infamous serial killer.

Rippercide, ISBN:9781782283454

His perverted desire is to become the world's most infamous serial killer. He is a psychopath, emulating killers like Jack the Ripper. A popular seaside resort becomes his stalking ground. The terror intensifies as the bodies of young women are discovered mutilated. Piece by piece the clues emerge, but the nightmare has only just began.

Printed by BoD™in Norderstedt, Germany